Jo Goodman's best-selling novels of romance and adventure unite brave, beautiful women with their charismatic soul mates in breathtaking stories that delight readers everywhere Now, she brings her unparalleled style to the surprising and sensual conclusion of her beloved McClellan series—

FALSE PRETENSES . . .

Desperate to escape to America with her life—and that of the infant in her arms—Jessa Winter quickly weds a mortally wounded man, planning to flee England as his widow. She doesn't count on Noah McClellan's will to live—or his determination to make her deliver on *all* of their marriage vows. But baby Gideon and her own hidden secrets must be protected—even as Noah's passionate demands tempt her to trust him with everything: the truth, her life, and her heart. . . .

LEAD TO TRUE PASSIONS

Noah has every intention of getting his due from the cunning female who's played him for a fool. As they sail for America, he is torn between outrage and growing tenderness for this beautiful woman he now calls wife. Jessa's recklessness nearly cost him his life—yet he cannot fight the burgeoning desire to tease and tempt her into sharing more than just his name. . . .

Books by Jo Goodman

THE CAPTAIN'S LADY
CRYSTAL PASSION
SEASWEPT ABANDON
VELVET NIGHT
VIOLET FIRE
SCARLET LIES
TEMPTING TORMENT
MIDNIGHT PRINCESS
PASSION'S SWEET REVENGE
SWEET FIRE
WILD SWEET ECSTASY
ROGUE'S MISTRESS
FOREVER IN MY HEART
ALWAYS IN MY DREAMS
ONLY IN MY ARMS
MY STEADFAST HEART
MY RECKLESS HEART
WITH ALL MY HEART
MORE THAN YOU KNOW
MORE THAN YOU WISHED

Published by Zebra Books

TEMPTING TORMENT

JO GOODMAN

ZEBRA BOOKS
KENSINGTON PUBLISHING CORP.

http://www.zebrabooks.com

For Cathy and Amy and the men smart enough to marry them, my brothers Richard and John.

ZEBRA BOOKS are published by

Kensington Publishing Corp.
850 Third Avenue
New York, NY 10022

All Kensington titles, imprints and distributed lines are available at special quantity discounts for bulk purchases for sales promotion, premiums, fund-raising, educational or institutional use.

Special book excerpts or customized printings can also be created to fit specific needs. For details, write or phone the office of the Kensington Special Sales Manager: Kensington Publishing Corp., 850 Third Avenue, New York, NY 10022. Attn. Special Sales Department. Phone: 1-800-221-2647.

Zebra and the Z logo Reg. U.S. Pat. & TM Off.

First Printing: October 2001
10 9 8 7 6 5 4 3 2 1

Dear Reader,

When I began writing about the McClellan family in *Crystal Passion* I did not anticipate that they would be the subjects of several books. It was actually the mysterious Jericho Smith that made me want to revisit to the McClellans in *Seaswept Abandon*. Encouragement from readers and my own interest in the family (plus a strange desire to write about a character who gets seasick) prompted me to go back to them again a few years later to develop a story around Noah McClellan. *Tempting Torment* was that book. It is a pleasure to have it reprinted and to be able to introduce it to new readers.

Especially nice was Zebra's decision to reprint the hard-to-find short story "Tidewater Promise" and include it as a bonus with this book. "Tidewater Promise" was originally published as part of a Christmas collection and it focuses attention on a younger generation of McClellans while reconnecting with characters in the previous trilogy. I hope you will agree it was a nice way to wrap up the family's adventures.

As always, family matters are of particular interest to me as my work with children and families influences the kind of stories I want to tell. I hope you will take the time to write me in care of my publisher or e-mail me at *jdobrzan@weir.net* and let me know what you think. For more background information about my books (including that seasickness interest), visit *www.romancejournal.com/Goodman*.

Once again, thank you for your interest in my books.

All the best,

Jo Goodman

PROLOGUE

January 1787

Icy shards of rain hammered relentlessly against the leaded windows. Edward Penberthy stood facing the inner courtyard, legs slightly parted, his hands clasped behind his back. He rocked on the balls of his feet while he studied the dim yellow cast of candlelight from the nursery. The light was extinguished. Edward waited, his pale blue eyes shifting slowly as he imagined Jessica's silent retreat from the child's room to her own adjoining one. A moment later a lamp was lighted. He squinted, trying to make out Jessica's form as she passed back and forth in front of the window. The driving rain confounded his efforts, and his frustration showed as a faint tic along his narrow jawline. He almost thanked Jessica for at last turning back the lamp and putting an end to his vigil. Edward paused, then unfastened the ties that held back a pair of blood-red velvet drapes. They fell softly and soundlessly closed.

"You haven't answered my question, Edward."

The voice was at once petulant and demanding. Both

qualities grated equally on Edward's nerves. He turned
slowly, adjusting the lacy cuffs on both wrists, and
greeted his wife with a narrow smile. He was somewhat
startled to find her so beautiful. Her skin was like porcelain, unlined and unmarred by any blemish. The small
mole that set off the high curve of her cheekbone was
mere artifice, a heart-shaped beauty patch she applied
with delicate precision. Her thick black hair was coiled
smoothly at the back of her head. Not so much as a
wisp of it fell across her high forehead or curled around
her dainty ears. Quite simply, Barbara wouldn't have
allowed it. She abhorred not being in control. Familiarity, he thought, does indeed breed contempt. With his
eyes closed or his back turned, his vision of her was in
many ways clearer. He was not drawn to the dark emerald pools of her eyes or the allure of her shapely mouth.
He closed his eyes briefly, seeking patience, and in his
mind's eye he saw a harridan, perhaps a fishwife, a
harpy. How her eyes would spit at him if she suspected
the path of his thoughts! "I don't believe you posed a
question, Barbara. A proposal is what you called it."

"It still requires a reply," she said, refusing to be
ignored. Barbara Penberthy held her husband's hard-
edged gaze defiantly. Her eyes then wandered deliberately to the four thin scratches that scored his left cheek.
The scratches were nothing, she thought, but the wound
to his pride would be considerable. When she first saw
them she knew the time was right to approach Edward
again with her plan. He would want some sort of redress
now; his advances had never been refused. She wanted
to comment, then thought better of it. He might mistake
her interest as jealousy, suspect there was more to her
plan than simply ridding themselves of Adam. That
would not do. Not at all.

Edward sat sideways in the spindle-legged chair opposite his wife, throwing one of his legs over the chair's
arm. His position effectively removed the scratches from
her sight though he knew she was well aware of them.

He had offered no explanation for their sudden appearance, but Barbara was not a fool. She knew how he had come by them. He wondered if it amused her. "I thought the matter was settled," he said.

Barbara stopped fiddling with her emerald dinner ring and folded her hands in her lap. "I recall we did not so much settle the matter as table it. Honestly, Edward, your reticence ill becomes you. I will not believe that you have developed some special fondness for the boy. You've never made any secret of the fact that you cannot abide children."

"Adam is my cousin."

"Your third cousin. You barely knew his parents. Don't spout nonsense about blood being thicker. Kenyon and Claudia Penberthy had little use for you while they were alive. Now, they force you to take guardianship of their brat and deal with his estate and finances."

A faint smile flickered at the corner of Edward's lips. "I don't think they intended to die so young," he said dryly.

Barbara frowned at her husband's interruption. "That is neither here nor there. It remains that they *did* die. And quite without thinking things through. They made no provision at all for Adam's care. If their man of affairs hadn't located us, the responsibility would have fallen on a complete stranger appointed by the court."

"I fail to understand your dissatisfaction. What is it you resent?" He waved a hand negligently about the room, indicating the richness of their surroundings. A near priceless painting by Titian dominated the wall above the green-veined marble mantelpiece. The carpet beneath their feet had been imported from China at no little cost. The furniture had been designed by the finest craftsmen living during the reign of Queen Anne. "You have some objection, perhaps, to living in such luxury?"

"None of it is ours," she said, cutting to the heart of

the matter. "We have all the burden and none of the gain. When Adam comes of age everything will be in his control. I don't like it, Edward. It's unfair that we will be discarded without anything to show for our years of caring."

"You are creating problems where none exist. Adam is only six months old. Who is to say how he will deal with us when he reaches his majority? In the meantime, it is our duty to raise him as befits a Penberthy. Surely that does not inconvenience you. You have not visited the nursery above two times since we've been here. Adam has a wet nurse and a nanny. Eventually he will be sent away to school. It would seem to me that you will enjoy a great many benefits while shouldering very little of the responsibility."

"But if something were to happen to Adam . . ." she said slyly. "Things do happen to infants, you know," she added quickly when Edward's eyes narrowed darkly. "They are likely to get all manner of diseases."

"I'll pretend I didn't hear that, Barbara. You would be wise to keep such thoughts to yourself."

"I was only speaking of childhood diseases," she defended herself.

"You were opening a door to murder. Your implications are offensive."

Barbara cast caution aside. "It's because of *her,* isn't it? You are willing to put up with the boy because you desire her!"

Edward flicked a speck of lint on his satin breeches. "Would you care to be more specific? Precisely to whom do you refer?"

Barbara's chin shot up and her lips pursed with aggravation. "Do not pretend ignorance. You know very well I mean Jessica Winter. I do not delude myself into believing your frequent visits to the nursery have anything to do with Adam. You have been straining your breeches since you laid eyes on the girl."

"Don't be vulgar," he snapped.

"It is you who are vulgar! Your attempts to carry on an affair with her in this house, under my very nose, are pathetic! She is a servant, twenty years your junior, and the child's nanny!"

Edward leaned his head against the back of the chair and closed his eyes. He regretted that he had pushed Barbara's patience to the breaking point. She was going to be tiresome now, needling him about Jessica. "I understand from Mr. Leeds that Miss Winter was very well thought of by Kenyon and Claudia. The circumstances of her employment were most uncommon."

Barbara did not want to dwell on Jessica Winter's past. Kenyon's lawyer had explained all when he approached them to become Adam's guardians. Barbara refused to feel pity for the girl. "We don't owe her anything," she said repressively. "She can find employment elsewhere."

"It would be difficult for her. Her family was quality, after all. Many people would be uncomfortable having her in their home."

"Are my feelings of no importance? *I* am discomfited by having her in my home. If no one else will have her she can always go back to those friends of hers. They are a nuisance anyway, always coming around to the servants entrance. Cook has complained to me several times. She says they are common criminals. Smugglers and the like."

"Cook is probably correct. I do not consider it prudent to raise their ire by sending Miss Winter packing."

"Oh?" she said skeptically. "And how do you think they will react when Miss Winter tells them that her new employer is a lecher?"

Edward's lips pressed into a grim line. He turned his face toward his wife and raised a hand to his cheek. "I doubt Miss Winter will mention it at all. As you can see, she gave better than she got. It is over between us. I was mistaken in the matter."

Barbara's laughter was without humor. Her eyes

pinned Edward to his chair. "You're afraid of her! You're afraid of her friends! That's why you won't do anything about Adam. You don't want suspicion for his death falling on the girl."

"Stop it, Barbara," Edward said with deadly calm. "Let it be."

"I will not. I am not such a coward as you. You want the same things I want, you simply haven't the backbone to take them. Admit it, Edward! Admit that you want the boy out of your way! Every door will be opened to us. Think of it! Entrance to the most exclusive circles, not because we are the guardians of Adam's wealth, but because you are the Penberthy heir. It can all be yours."

Edward stood. "I can see there is nothing to be gained by trying to reason with you. You will do what you will do."

His cryptic words gave Barbara pause. "What are you saying?" she asked slowly.

"I am saying that you will do what you want regardless of my feelings on the matter. I suggest that you be very careful as to how you proceed unless you want to live out your days in Newgate. If you escape the hangman, that is."

He was giving his sanction! Barbara's heart thudded in her breast. She had been correct! No matter what his words to the contrary, he wanted Adam and the girl out of his life. "I'll be cautious," she said. "No one will ever know. You realize that once Adam is gone there will be no position for Miss Winter."

He nodded. "Her friends will find nothing strange in that . . . nor will she." Edward took a step toward his wife and searched her face for a long moment. There was no mistaking the hard resolve that tautened the pale skin across her cheekbones. "I never want to discuss this again, Barbara," he said at last. "Never." He left the room then, but not before he caught the smirk of complacency on Barbara's lips. Beyond the door his hands trembled and he thrust them into the deep pockets of his jacket. "God forgive me," he whispered into the emptiness of the hallway. "What have I done?"

CHAPTER ONE

March 1787

Noah McClellan lowered his hat over his eyes and settled back in his seat, pressing his broad shoulders against the stiff cushion. He longed to stretch his legs comfortably on the seat opposite him. As that would have put the heels of his muddy riding boots squarely in the lap of the vicar, he suppressed the urge. Everyone in the carriage had already identified him as a cloddish colonial, or more precisely, an ill-mannered *American*. They were wary of him; no one had deigned to speak to him in the half hour they had been on the post road to London. Not that he hadn't given them a right to be wary, he told himself. His behavior back at the inn had fulfilled every preconceived notion they had about Americans. He had been rude, even surly. Certainly he had chosen his words incautiously when speaking to the innkeeper, making extensive demands on the man's graciousness and patience.

A sheepish smile touched Noah's mouth and by clearing his throat and turning restlessly in his seat, he smothered a laugh at his own expense. His elbow accidentally dug into the ribs of the white-haired gentleman on his left. Noah surprised all seven of the other passengers by murmuring an apology before the gentleman could take exception.

"Will your animal be all right, do you think?"

It took Noah a moment before he realized he was the object of the softly framed question. He flicked back his hat with the tip of his forefinger and regarded the woman who had addressed him. Beneath her drab and dusty traveling cloak, the severe black lines of her gown proclaimed her mourning. A black satin ribbon and bow edged the unbecoming bonnet she wore. The bonnet itself was so stiff and confining it reminded Noah of blinders that a horse might sport. He wondered who she was mourning as his eyes drifted briefly to the sleeping babe she cradled in her thin arms. It was borne home to him that neither the vicar on her left nor the bored young lord on her right were accompanying her. She was quite alone, traveling without male protection, and Noah came to the unhappy conclusion that she was a widow. Her concern for his plight in light of her own circumstances touched him.

"I'm sure he will be," he said, raising his gold and green flecked eyes to hers. "A sprained foreleg," he added.

The corners of her mouth were touched by a smile. "So I heard," she said softly, dry amusement brightening her wide gray eyes. "The injury having occurred on these damnable English roads, I think you said."

Noah grinned, ignoring the swift censure the vicar directed at the young woman for having quoted Noah so accurately. The widow seemed equally unconcerned, though Noah was certain she had not missed the pointed throat clearing. There was, after all, a pale blush on her cheeks that had not been there before. "A comment I have every cause to regret," he told her. "You know very well how the innkeeper took exception and refused to sell or lease me a single animal from his stable.''

"I believe he doubted your riding skills.''

Noah's grin dissolved into a wry smile. She had put that very delicately. The innkeeper had been moved to denounce Noah's horsemanship, his nationality, and eventually his parentage. All in all, the exchange had developed into quite a row. It was saved from becoming a brawl by the arrival of the coach to London. Noah recognized there was nothing for it but to pay the innkeeper to stable his injured horse and make the remainder of his trip by coach. He had had to pay well for both privileges. The sum the proud and put-upon innkeeper demanded would have met the needs of a stable full of horses for a year. The driver of the coach, after a quick exchange with the innkeeper and an eye toward the main chance, charged Noah double for his place on the stage. There had even been some discussion about Noah riding on top with the baggage so as not to discomfit the other passengers. At that point Noah's gritty smile and lightly clenched fists came to his rescue and the driver thought better of his suggestion.

Noah leaned forward in his seat, surreptitiously taking measure of his fellow travelers. In addition to the vicar, the fiercely correct white-haired gentleman, the widow, and his lordship, the coach carried one of the king's soldiers, a dour looking farmer, and a portly tradesman. With the exception of the widow, none of them had shown the slightest inclination to warm toward him.

"Yes," said Noah, "I believe he did say something about not trusting me with his mule, least of all one of his good mounts." He chuckled. "It will be a good tale to tell my family," he explained when she looked at him oddly, surprised by his laughter.

"Oh?"

"I rode before I could walk." He paused. "We raise thoroughbreds."

Silent laughter made her shoulders shake and the

babe stirred in her arms. Her attention immediately turned from Noah as she bent her head over the child. The baby stretched awkwardly in the confining blankets and yawned in a disagreeable manner that boded ill for the other passengers. There was a collective sigh from everyone, but Noah, as the baby's face crinkled and a lusty cry emerged.

The bored young lord looked to the roof of the coach and beyond, seeking deliverance from the common rabble. He cursed the card game that had put him in his current financial straits so that he was forced to travel among them. Raising a perfumed handkerchief to his lips momentarily, he looked appraisingly at Noah. "Thoroughbreds, you say? Racing stock?"

"Mostly," Noah answered equably. "Although we don't limit ourselves. Draft horses are in demand, strong farming animals for the fields and pulling wagons."

In spite of himself, the delicate-featured young man was interested. He fancied himself quite knowledgeable about horseflesh. "Then you're here to examine new bloodlines," he said confidently. "Refresh your stock. You might want to visit Worthing's stables. His animals are prime."

Noah had no use for his lordship's condescending assumptions. "Actually," he drawled, "it has been my happy pleasure to deliver an Arabian stud *to* Lord Worthing. Now his animals are prime—or they soon will be."

"Indeed," the fair-haired lord said, flushing with embarrassment. He turned away from Noah and addressed the widow. "Madam, can you not quiet your child?" he asked impatiently.

The coach hit a rut in the road and tilted dangerously, compressing the passengers awkwardly, with their knees and elbows colliding. The baby's wail grew louder as he was squeezed protectively by his mother. The widow raised her eyes helplessly to his lordship. She lifted the child and patted its back soothingly. "I'm sorry, but there's little I . . ."

Noah leaned forward again and held out his hands. "Let me." His offer was greeted with horror by every passenger save the widow. She merely looked at him skeptically. "I assure you, ma'am, no matter what you may have heard, we don't eat children in Virginia." When she still hesitated, he added without a hint of humor, "Although they're considered something of a delicacy in Massachusetts."

Her laughing eyes belied the stern tone she adopted. "You're a terrible man, Mr. . . . ."

"McClellan."

"You're a terrible man, Mr. McClellan, but if you can calm my child I shall be in your debt." She lifted the baby toward him.

"As will we all," the dour-faced farmer murmured under his breath.

Noah took the child and laid him lengthwise along his lap so the baby was cradled by his thighs. Although he was concentrating on loosening the child's blankets, he was still seeing the widow's beautiful smile. Noah was glad no one could read his mind. He considered that he must be a rather reprehensible sort of character to have been so taken by that gentle curve of her mouth. Absolutely lacking in conscience, he thought, when one considered that she was in mourning and he had a fiancée waiting for him on the other side of the Atlantic. He felt like a young pup instead of a man of thirty-three years. Still, she had a smile that turned his heart over. "A name?" he asked.

The widow was momentarily disconcerted, even troubled. She opened her mouth to speak, but nothing came out.

Noah suppressed another grin, seeing that she had misunderstood him and thought he wanted to know her name. He must have seemed very forward to her.

"I mean the baby," he said politely, trying to decide if he was holding a boy or a girl.

There was a hint of relief in her winter gray eyes. "I call him Gideon."

"Ahh," he said wisely. "Gideon. Called upon by the Lord to free His people. Rather an avenger, was Gideon."

The widow gave a small start. "Yes, that's how I think of him. An avenger."

Noah caught something in her voice, something pained, something angry. He had an urge to look at her again, see the face more clearly beneath the horrible bonnet. He held himself back, feeling that his interest in her was unseemly. He was forcibly reminded he was not alone as the coach swayed alarmingly as it met another rut. "Well, he certainly has the lungs for it, hasn't he?" This comment brought no response from anyone save Gideon, who continued to exercise the organs in question. Noah looked at the vicar. "Trumpet blowing, I mean. I'm thinking of the correct Bible story, aren't I?"

The vicar's pursed mouth relaxed a little. "Yes, you're correct." His eyes were vague for a moment, then he quoted, " 'When I blow the trumpet, I and all who are with me, then blow the trumpets also on every side of all the camp, and shout, 'For the Lord and for Gideon.' " He glanced at the child. "Judges, chapter 7," he told the passengers solemnly. "Old Testament. And he does have the lungs for it."

Noah jiggled Gideon on his knees and tickled the baby's chin. Gideon continued to wail soulfully. Tears trickled from under the dark, spiky lashes of his tightly shut eyes. Noah wiped them away with one corner of the blanket. "Does anyone have any spirits?" he asked.

The vicar stiffened. "You're not intending to give the child spirits, are you?"

"I've got a flask." The offer came from the thick-shouldered tradesman who sat nearest the door. Until now he had been quiet, staring out the small coach window, wishing he were not rubbing elbows with quality. The young lord's perfume was stifling. Fop, he thought disgustedly. And no doubt his pockets were to let. Yet his lordship would stare down his aristocratic nose at the likes of himself and Mr. McClellan. The tradesman felt a sudden kinship with the American who had so neatly given the lord a set down—something he would not have had the nerve to do. He reached in the inner pocket of his greatcoat and retrieved a flask. "Here you are." He handed the flask to Noah, oblivious to the vicar's disapproving noises.

"I think Gideon's too young for spirits," the widow ventured uneasily.

The soldier was moved to say, "Never too young. Put a little hair on his chest." He sunk back in his seat at the vicar's cold reproof.

"I don't intend that he should drink the stuff," Noah said, stopping further comment. He poured a little of the whiskey on his fingertip and rubbed it on the baby's gums. Gideon was so surprised by this intrusion that he stopped crying almost immediately. His mouth closed greedily about Noah's finger and he blinked several times before he started sucking noisily. Noah withdrew his finger, applied a little more whiskey to it, and allowed Gideon to continue sucking. "He's cutting a tooth," Noah told Gideon's mother. "Two in fact. A few drops of spirits rubbed on the gums helps sometimes." He scooped Gideon into the crook of his left forearm, capped the flask, and put it in his vest pocket for future use. "Your young man has quite a ferocious grip." Noah felt the tips of his ears redden. She must know all about the fierce tugging of her son's mouth. He could imagine Gideon settling at her breast. With difficulty he banished the image and spoke quickly to cover his embarrassment. "How old is he?"

"Nearly nine months."

"He's a fine looking boy."

"Yes, he is. You're quite at ease with him. You have children of your own?"

"Oh, no," Noah said quickly. "I'm not married." He wondered why he didn't mention he was engaged, but he didn't, and the moment passed.

"Then you're a physician," she said.

"Don't be daft," his lordship interrupted rudely. "He says he raises horses."

"Actually it's something of a family enterprise," Noah told him, giving him a quelling glance. In his arm, Gideon burbled contentedly. "I'm a lawyer . . . a barrister, you would call it. I merely delivered Lord Worthing's stud as a favor to my brother Gareth and my father. They are chiefly responsible for the success we have with the animals. I was coming to England anyway, on other family business, so it seemed appropriate that I should handle everything." He gently dried the tracks of Gideon's tears and stroked the baby's cheek. Gideon kept his fascinated blue eyes on Noah's face. "In answer to your question," he said, addressing the widow. "I've had plenty of experience with children because I have a dozen nieces and nephews."

"How lovely for you," she said wistfully.

Noah nodded agreeably, equally fascinated by Gideon's unwavering gaze. "It is, rather. Heaven knows I spoil the lot of them."

"You must come from a large family yourself," the vicar said.

"Not so large. Only five of us. Salem—that's short for Jerusalem—is the oldest. Then Gareth. I'm next, then my sisters Rahab and Leah."

The vicar was pleased by the Biblical names. Perhaps there was something to recommend this young man after all. "And your Christian name?"

"Noah."

"Really," drawled his lordship in bored accents. "Must we be subjected to this? The trip is tedious enough."

"I'm interested," the widow protested quietly. She envied the American's easy friendliness. What would it be like, she wondered, to have no secrets? "Tell me about your nieces and nephews."

"Perhaps it is tedious," Noah admitted, looking at the other passengers.

"I'd like to hear," said the tradesman. It was the simplest method of needling the fop.

"Tell us," said the vicar, thinking that perhaps it wasn't true that the colonials were heathens.

"Don't mind hearing," commented the soldier as he polished a brass button on his uniform with the sleeve of his red coat.

"It's better than listening to 'im snore," the farmer concluded, pointing to the old gentleman situated between himself and Noah. That man was indeed snoring softly, his head resting back against the leather cushions. The Adam's apple in his neck bobbed as he swallowed.

"Yes, I suppose it is," Noah said gravely, his eyes dancing as Gideon chortled. "Well, Salem and Ashley have three children: Courtney, Trenton, and Travis. Gareth and Darlene have two: Elizabeth and Jordan. Leah and Troy are the parents of Edward, David, Michael, and Jacob. Scamps, all of them," he added fondly. "Rae and Jericho have three—all girls—Elyse, Katie, and Garland." He paused, clicking them off in his mind. "Yes, that's everyone. Of course, Ashley is increasing again. I suspect I may be an uncle for the thirteenth time before I return to Virginia. My business here is taking rather longer than I expected."

"What precisely is your business?" his lordship asked, eager to be off family matters.

"Didn't I say? No, I suppose I didn't. I am settling some estate matters for my sister-in-law as well as my brother-in-law."

"Your family has property here?" He failed to keep the surprise out of his voice, and everyone in the coach heard his patronizing tone again. They waited to see how Noah would respond to this second slight.

"Salem's wife is Ashley Lynne, the niece of the late duke of Linfield. More to the point, she is his sole heir. You may be familiar with the Linfield estate. That's where I was coming from when my mount came up lame." His lordship looked at Noah with new respect, not that Noah cared one whit. "I am headed for Stanhope. I understand this coach passes there on its way to London. Stanhope belongs to my brother-in-law."

"No, you're in the wrong of it there," corrected his lordship. "I know for a fact it's now the property of Lord Hunter-Smythe. He's been on the Continent a number of years now."

"Geoffrey Hunter-Smythe has never been to the Continent to my knowledge. He's lived in America most of his life, where he's quite content to be known as Jericho Smith. He's Rahab's husband."

"You're practically quality yourself, man," murmured the tradesman, much put out by this turn of events.

Noah laughed. "Hardly. I have as much interest in titles as Ashley and Jericho do, which is to say I have none at all. However, the estates must be maintained and there are problems inherent in being an absentee landlord, which is why I was elected to come here."

"How very . . . democratic," his lordship sneered.

"The decision was unanimous?" wondered the widow.

Noah shook his head. "No, there was one dissenting vote."

"Oh?"

"Mine," he said dryly.

"Somehow I think I suspected that. Here, I'll take Gideon now. He's all done in. Thank you. It's not easy traveling with a baby."

"Not easy traveling at all anymore," gritted the farmer, his florid face very stern looking. "Rather not have to make this trip at all. Brigands and highwaymen all along the post road nowadays."

Noah gave up his young charge reluctantly. He made a mental note to bring something very special back for Ashley's newest baby. "Surely that's an exaggeration," he said, trying to ease the worried look that had come over the young widow's face.

"Not much of one," the tradesman interjected. "A coach was robbed just north of here a fortnight ago."

"And they ain't been caught," offered the farmer gloomily.

"I'm sure the Lord will protect us this night," said the vicar.

The fop sighed loudly. "You trust the Lord. I'll look to this for help." He opened the front of his coat and pointed to the pistol outlined by the snug material of his satin vest.

The soldier patted the saber sheathed at his side. "And I, this."

"Oh, please," said the widow, hugging Gideon closer to her. "Do stop brandishing your weapons."

"Hardly brandishing it, ma'am," said the soldier. Still, he took his hand from his side and continued polishing his buttons.

His lordship closed his jacket. "One has to be prepared for any eventuality."

"I don't hold with carrying weapons," said the vicar.

The tradesman nodded. "It's just as simple to hide one's money."

"Aye," said the farmer. He eyed the chain of gold which dangled from the fop's jacket pocket. "And your valuables. No sense in calling attention to one's wealth."

The widow interjected again. "Please, you make it sound as if we are certain to be waylaid. There is no cause to believe such a thing." She patted Gideon on his bottom. "In any event, the safest place for your valuables is in a child's blankets. No highwayman I've heard about has ever thought to search in such a place."

Noah laughed at the suggestion. He could well imagine how the widow would take on an entire band of robbers in order to protect her child. "I believe you're in the right of it there, ma'am."

"Yes, I believe you are," said his lordship thoughtfully. He tugged on his gold chain and pulled out a timepiece, turning it over in his hand. "Would you keep this for me? Just until we arrive safely in London?"

Noah's eyes widened. He hadn't realized how quickly the thread of hysteria would bind the passengers. The fop was quite serious in his request.

The widow hesitated. "It was only a jest, my lord," she said softly, eyeing the finely crafted watch as if it would bite her.

"Please," his lordship insisted, "and these rings also. You may have spoken in jest but rarely has a suggestion been more accurate. Highwaymen have their own code. At least that's what I'm given to understand. My valuables would be quite safe with you."

Her brows drew together as she thought it over. "Very well, but I think you are making too much of this talk." She took the watch and gingerly placed it beneath Gideon's blankets. "Not all of your rings, my lord. You must keep something of value lest the villains think you've hidden your goods elsewhere." Her smile mocked the fop's concern, but he seemed oblivious to it.

The vicar cleared his throat. "I have a money purse I should like to arrive in London the same time I do. Would you?" He reached in his pocket and brought out a leather change purse and held it in the flat of his palm.

"I don't think . . ."

"I would be very grateful," the vicar pressed his concern.

"Well, perhaps you should keep a few coins in the purse." The widow made a fold in Gideon's blanket. "Drop the others in here."

The vicar did so without hesitation. "Thank you. I feel much better."

The widow shook her head as if she couldn't understand what had overtaken the man. " 'Tis frankly absurd," she said, "but would anyone else feel more the thing if Gideon kept the riches?"

"If you wouldn't mind," said the farmer. He bent forward and took off one of his sturdy walking shoes, withdrawing a money purse similar to the vicar's though much lighter in weight. He extracted a few coins, placed them back in his shoe, and gave the widow his drawstring bag. "The purse was deuced uncomfortable anyway," he said sourly.

Shrugging, the tradesman lifted his hat, took his purse from where it rested on his bald pate, and held it out. His lordship passed it to the widow. A moment later the soldier slipped off his money belt and gave it over. Since the old gentleman was still sleeping, oblivious to these new arrangements, everyone looked expectantly at Noah. He held up his hands, palms out. "I'm afraid the coachman took what the innkeeper didn't. I assure you I've been robbed already."

The widow laughed appreciatively. "It's just as well. I don't think Gideon could hold another farthing."

Noah found himself liking the sound of the widow's laughter. He wished he could think of something amusing to say. How his family would gloat if they ever became privy to his interest in the widow! None of the McClellans really approved of his fiancée. Not that they would come right out and say so. Their approach was more subtle, or at least they considered it to be. "She's certainly lovely," they would say. "A trifle distant, don't you think?" Or, "She's very proper, Noah. Does she ever smile?" It was merely their way of pointing out that Hilary Bowen could be rather chilling when she set her mind to it. Noah was of the opinion that Hilary was slightly intimidated by his large, gregarious family. He spent much of his courtship shielding her from them. His family, true to form, spent much of their time poking fun at him.

Though he never defended his choice to his family,

he told himself that Hilary Bowen was precisely the sort of wife he required. It did not occur to him that perhaps he told himself this too often. Hilary's background was unexceptional. Her father and grandfather were bankers, heading a prestigious firm in Philadelphia, where he had met Hilary. Her only sibling, a brother, had been killed at Yorktown before the surrender of Lord Cornwallis. Hilary was the consummate patriot, even after these five years since the end of the war. She rejected all things British, disdained them to the point of near obsession. Or so his family pointed out. Except for the fact that Hilary was less than cordial with his British in-laws, Noah was unperturbed by it. He considered it made Hilary all the more desirable as a partner, especially since he had been chosen to work on drafting revisions for the Articles of Confederation. As his career in government began to take hold, Noah realized Hilary Bowen would be an asset, not a liability. "Aren't you being a trifle too intellectual about wanting to marry Hilary?" asked his mother shortly after meeting her. Charity McClellan had blushed then, but continued gravely. "What about passion? What about love?"

"I love Hilary, Mama," Noah had said. He had not mentioned passion and his mother hadn't persisted. Noah appreciated his mother's delicacy in not pressing the issue. He wouldn't have liked to tell her that he was intimately acquainted with Hilary's passion. He couldn't count on his mother's discretion and soon everyone would be nudging him in the ribs and casting sidelong glances at Hilary's waistline.

Noah became uncomfortably aware that he was staring at the widow's bent head, wondering what color hair was hidden by her bonnet. He looked around, saw that the other passengers had lapsed into their own individual thoughts now that they felt secure, and reluctantly tore his eyes away from the widow and her child. Dammit, he thought testily, if Hilary had accompanied him he wouldn't be entertaining these musings about the widow. It was easier to blame Hilary than to examine the reasons for his roving eye.

If Hilary had not been so stubborn, they would have been married already, enjoying a wedding trip to England. But England was the last place she wanted to go and Noah had respected her wishes. Neither did she want to marry and have her husband leave almost immediately. Since his business trip to England had been arranged for months, there was no putting it off. In point of fact, he had put it off a number of times, hoping someone in his family would go in his stead. They knew how he hated even the thought of a sea voyage. For a while it looked as if Salem and Ashley would go, then Ashley announced she was pregnant and did not want her child born in England. Jericho and Rae had no desire to visit Stanhope or Linfield again. Noah could not hold that against them since their only contact there had been both dangerous and deadly. No one else in the family knew the intricacies of the law well enough to handle the affairs of both estates. It was left to Noah and he finally surrendered. He was not unaware that his family had an ulterior motive for sending him to England. Their eagerness to have him away from Hilary was a near palpable thing. Obviously they did not know him very well if they thought distance and a few months absence were going to make a difference in his feelings for Hilary. He was not a McClellan for nothing. He bore the same stubborn streak and unbreakable will as the rest of them.

Noah came out of his reverie, feeling the widow's eyes on him. She looked away immediately, embarrassed at being caught in a bold stare. Noah reflected that the curiosity he felt about her was returned, though she would have denied it, as would he. What did she see when she looked at him? he wondered.

Noah was not unaware that some women found him attractive, but perhaps that was not the reason the widow stared at him so. He had never wanted for female companionship, and until his commitment to Hilary Bowen he had been quite happy not to bind himself too closely to one. All around, it was an amicable arrangement. But Noah did not fool himself into believing all women were drawn to his face. He could think of any number who showed no interest in him, probably thought he was quite ordinary looking. Certainly there was nothing special about his dark chestnut hair unless one remarked, as his mother did, that it was uncommonly thick and as lustrous as a girl's. His eyes, well, he had two of them. More than that he couldn't say. They were neither green nor gray nor gold. Somewhat to his disgust, they were a mixture of all of that with a few flecks of sable brown thrown in for good measure. That both his sisters had been moved to say they envied him his thick dark lashes, Noah didn't care to think about. He had the McClellan jaw, with its firm and implacable thrust, and he had also inherited the McClellan height, which was to say he stood nearly a head again taller than most of his contemporaries. Perhaps the widow found his height disconcerting or perhaps she was wishing he had the refined features of the young lord at her side. Noah knew there was nothing delicate about him if one discounted his damnable lashes. His nose was straight, strong, even bold. His mouth was not softened by the McClellan dimples. The high cast of his cheekbones could make him appear formidable, which was all right in the courtroom but not necessarily a good thing when he wanted to make a young lady's acquaintance.

Dash it all! What did he care what the widow thought? No doubt she was comparing him to her husband and found him lacking on all counts. Even if she wasn't, nothing could come of it any . . .

The thunderous report of a pistol brought Noah up straight and effectively shattered every thought he had about the widow except those concerning her well-being. Another shot was fired, the stage slowed dramatically as the coachman reined in his team of four horses. There was shouting beyond the confines of the coach, but little of it could be heard as the shouting within the carriage was almost deafening.

"Told you the roads weren't safe," the farmer said grimly to no one in particular. "Ain't this just the way of things."

"Blast and damn!" said the old gentleman, coming awake at last. "What's toward?"

The soldier and the tradesman were peering out their windows, each shouting at the coachman to outrun the bandits. Gideon had awakened and added his screams to the others. In his corner the vicar had taken up prayer and the fop was cursing the fates loudly. Noah alone had nothing to say. He extended his hand across the narrow aisle and placed it on the widow's arms. She was trying to console her son and was close to tears herself.

"Everything is going to be fine," Noah told her. "Just fine. No one is going to harm either you or your son."

The widow shook her head fretfully, tilting her chin in the direction of the soldier and the fop. "But they mean to use their weapons."

Noah understood her concern immediately. Any sort of resistance on their part could put the child in grave danger. He told the men to put their weapons beneath the seat just as the call came from outside to stand and deliver. "Just do it," he whispered urgently. "Your money is safe enough. Don't do anything to provoke them. You might lose a few shillings, but what's that compared to coming away with your skin?"

The young lord still hesitated, watching the soldier hide his sword. He stared down his finely arched nose at Noah, nostrils flaring slightly. "How simply you state the alternatives when you have no valuables to speak of. I, on the other hand, still retain some priceless rings on my person. And I have a reputation as something of a marksman. There is no reason to suppose I shall miss my target."

Noah was done arguing with his lordship, though no one suspected the end of his patience had been reached. The bare-knuckle facer he delivered to the young man's delicate jaw put a period to their conversation. The fop slumped in his seat, his chin resting on his chest. Noah relieved him of the pistol and hid it under the leather cushion just as the coach door was thrown open.

"Everyone out!" The order was issued gruffly and showed a singular lack of regard for its victims. So much for gentleman robbers, Noah thought grimly. A flaming torch was brandished in front of the open doorway, lighting the exit. "Come on! Out with ye!" It was then the thief noticed the condition of his lordship. "Here now, wot's this? This good fellow faint at the thought of having his pockets picked?" He laughed gleefully at the idea. "Hurry now. Ain't got all night."

The passengers alighted from the coach and faced the highwaymen. Noah counted only two men on horseback in addition to the man who stood by the coach door. Torchlight flickered across the travelers but never rested for more than a moment upon the thieves. Noah had to credit them with knowing their business. They had stopped the coach on a particularly deserted section of the post road where the forest abutted both sides. Although the night was clear, very little moonshine penetrated the overhanging boughs, thus wreathing the robbers in darkness. Their identity was safe even if they hadn't sported low-slung hats and black kerchiefs across the lower portion of their faces. Noah felt the presence of the widow at his side and he edged closer, determined to protect her.

The highwayman nudged the passengers into a semicircle several paces away from the coach. The driver was encouraged to come down from his perch, which he did with surprising quickness, in spite of the limp he had recently acquired.

"He's been hurt!" whispered the widow.

Noah nodded, following the driver's halting progress to the group. In all likelihood the man's leg had stopped a pistol ball when the first shots were fired. He heard the driver swearing eloquently under his breath. "I think there is little cause to worry. It's his pride that's been injured more than his leg."

"No talkin'!" called one of the men on horseback. "Not unless yer asked to speak." He dismounted hastily and made his way to the semicircle of travelers. Doffing his cap in a gesture filled with contempt, he turned it over and presented it to the passengers. "Yer donation to the poor is strongly suggested and greatly appreciated."

"I'll get the bloke in the carriage," offered the other thief. "I saw a ring or two that took my fancy." He planted the butt of his torch in the ground, illuminating a small area which encompassed the passengers, then swaggered toward the coach.

Had it not been for the widow, Noah realized he would have taken the opening given to him. He could have easily wrested the pistol away from the highwayman in front of him. That man was more interested in what was being dropped into his hat than in protecting his pistol.

None of the passengers spoke as they parted with the few coins they had kept on them. The rogue was thorough in his search, patting down their pockets, making them remove their shoes, and checking their hands for jewelry. Silently they all gave thanks for the widow and her baby. The highwayman passed over her after dumping the contents of her reticule on the ground and sifting through it with the toe of his boot.

"Can't you stop that squawling?" the highwayman demanded irritably of the widow. He searched Noah's pockets, found nothing, then relieved him of his hat because he fancied it, and went on to the soldier.

"Do you want me to take Gideon?" Noah asked lowly.

The widow shifted the baby in her arms. "No." Her voice was nearly inaudible. "I'll manage." She stroked Gideon's back but her movements were agitated and the baby merely cried harder.

"No talking, I told yer!" yelled the man on horseback, steadying his restless mount as well as the ones on either side of him.

Noah realized that Gideon's incessant crying was playing havoc with everyone's nerves. Without thinking of anything but quieting the infant, Noah reached inside his jacket to pull out the flask of whiskey. He had his hand over the flask when he felt the barrel of a pistol in his side. Startled, he jerked away, prepared to reveal he was not attempting to bring out a weapon. The flask glimmered briefly in the torchlight and in the next moment there was another flash of light, the deafening report of a pistol, and the acrid smell of gunpowder. The sequence of events was clearly defined in Noah's mind. He blocked out the pain in his side, the force that threw him backward, and his ignominious fall to the ground.

"Oh, dear God!" cried the widow. Her pained voice shattered the silence that had followed the shot. Even Gideon had been startled into quiet. She dropped to her knees beside Noah. "You've shot him!" She lifted her face, framed by the black bonnet, and stared accusingly at the thief who had fired his weapon. "Damn you! He wanted nothing more than to comfort my baby! He never meant to harm you!" She carefully laid Gideon on the ground and slipped her hand inside Noah's jacket. Her fingers were immediately wet and slick with his blood. With her other hand she felt for a pulse at Noah's neck. It was faint, but definitely there. "Give me your scarf!" she demanded imperiously of the thief who had fired at Noah. "I need to stem this flow of blood."

Above his kerchief the highwayman's eyes widened. He jerked his pistol at the semicircle of frightened passengers causing them to huddle together. No one stepped forward to help the widow. "Not bloody likely with them lookin' on!"

The man on horseback moved forward, herding the passengers toward the coach. "In with ye!" The horses shuffled close, kicking up a light spray of dust. The widow was intimidated, but she did pick up Gideon and hold him closely. Her jaw was set stubbornly. "He's not fit to travel," she told the robbers. "We must get help."

All three highwaymen laughed at that. "You can stay 'ere with 'im if you've a mind to," said the one who had taken the fop's last valuables. "In fact, jest to be safe, you'd better stay 'ere. With us. That'll give these gents pause about fetchin' the authorities. Eh?" He picked up the torch and waved it threateningly in front of the driver's face. "You understand? Anyone comes after us we'll 'ave to 'urt the laidy."

"That's unconscionable," protested the old gentleman.

"She must come with us," said the tradesman trying to subdue the frantic note in his voice. He stared pointedly at Gideon's blankets which held the sum total of the passenger's wealth. "You can't mean to abduct her and the child."

The man who had shot Noah already had one hand firmly at the back of the widow's slim neck and was pulling her to her feet. The gruff order was repeated. "In the coach with ye."

"Release her," demanded the soldier, taking a menacing step forward and reaching for his absent saber.

The highwayman grinned beneath his kerchief as the soldier's hand came away empty. "Be advised to seek the safety of yer coach," he said tightly. "An' quickly."

The driver ascended to the box awkwardly and picked up his whip. "You'll go to 'ell fer this."

"That's a certainty."

The widow lost her footing and fell against the highwayman. His obscene remark drew her stiffly upright and her voice was unsteady. "What about Mr. McClellan? He will die without help."

"Ain't our affair."

"Then I'm staying," said the vicar as the tradesman stumbled into the coach. "He has a right to clergy."

A pistol was leveled at the vicar's chest. "Yer goin' with the others! The guvnor 'ere lost 'is rights."

The vicar backed toward the coach, his face pale. His eyes were not resting on Noah now, but on the baby cuddled in the widow's arms. "I can't go. I must stay! That man's soul . . ." His voice drifted off as he read the intent in the robber's eyes. "But my money . . ."

"Eh? Wot's that?"

The vicar swallowed hard. "Nothing," he said nervously, climbing into the carriage. "Nothing at all."

One by one the travelers were made to enter the coach. "At least let us take the child," the farmer said.

The widow shook her head, plainly horrified by the suggestion and the greed which she suspected prompted it. "No. Gideon stays with me." Her voice broke as she turned her attention once again to Noah. "Really, they've said they won't hurt me as long as you don't bring the authorities."

"Ye 'eard 'er! It's a good lot we are. Leave 'er off in the woods, we will. She'll find 'er way back." The coach door was slammed shut and the driver was given the signal to take his leave. The faces of the vicar and the tradesman were pressed against the window as the carriage jerked forward then took to the road with ever increasing speed.

The passengers looked at one another uneasily and finally elected to stare at their laps. The young lord remained slumped in his seat, oblivious to what had taken place. No one mentioned their money now.

"Do you think she'll be safe?" ventured the old gentleman. "Can't like it above half that she's back there with those brigands. Would have liked to help. Thing of it is, I didn't know what to do."

The farmer snorted and mumbled something under his breath.

"What was that?" asked the older man.

"I said, she's got our money."

The vicar cleared his throat uncomfortably. "It's a shame about that American fellow. I doubt there is anything a physician can do for him. We'll bring one back, of course. We must, no matter what those rogues said, it's our duty. But . . ."

Everyone agreed that a physician must be found. No one admitted aloud that it was a mere excuse to return to the place of the crime and get their money. Each man thought it likely that the widow would not be found alive. With varying degrees of horror they imagined her raped and murdered. And on the heels of that thought they wondered about the child. Would the baby be left unharmed? Their valuables intact? This last thought brought a flash of guilt and it was resolutely extinguished. No, the infant would not be harmed. That sort of heinous crime did not happen often, for it quite naturally commanded the attention of every citizen, from lord to commoner, and brought down the wrath of crown and constable alike.

Still, it was not unheard of. None of the travelers had to search their memories long. It hadn't been many months ago that young Adam Penberthy had been abducted from the Penberthy estate, from his own nursery. Not much above a week later, the infant lord was found dead in the woods adjoining the property. The child had been left in the wild and died of exposure to the elements.

The thought chilled them and hardened their resolve to bring help and see that the highwaymen were brought to the crown's swift justice.

Two hours later, when they returned to the site of the robbery with a physician and a small force of the King's troops, they were not so certain justice would be swift. Other than a splash of blood on the ground where

Noah McClellan had lain, there was no sign that anything untoward had taken place. The highwaymen had made their escape, taking the widow, her child, and, it seemed, the American as well.

CHAPTER TWO

Jessa touched the tip of her forefinger to Noah's temple, smoothing away a dark, damp lock of hair. His beautiful eyes remained closed to her and though he stirred, he did not wake. His small movement was enough to make Jessa pull back her hand sharply. Dipping a cloth into the basin on the bedside table, Jessa soaked it and twisted out the excess water, then washed Noah's face with the same gentleness she would have used with Gideon. Beads of perspiration were wiped from his forehead and upper lip, only to reappear a moment later as his fever continued to rage.

Jessa dropped the cloth in the basin and checked the bandage at Noah's right side. At least the bleeding had stopped. This bandage, the fourth she had applied since coming to the cottage, was only stained pink with his blood. It occurred to her that perhaps he simply didn't have much blood left, that he had lost too much already. The thought so frightened her that she refused to give it credence and resolutely smothered it, keeping herself busy by applying the damp cloth to his face still another time.

As Jessa bent over Noah, a strand of her pale hair fell over one shoulder and caressed his cheek. She watched him turn his face to the side and unconsciously wrinkle his nose as he tried to remove himself from her unintentional tickling.

"Oh bother!" she said under her breath. She straightened quickly and impatiently braided her waist-length hair until it fell in a single line down her back. Satisfied that she could keep it out of his way, she bathed his face and neck again and again, pausing only when she heard Gideon alternately babbling and crying in the other room. Occasionally Noah turned restlessly and murmured something, but Jessa, though she leaned forward and listened carefully, could make out nothing. "I won't let you die," she told him, repeating aloud the litany that she had been saying to herself. "I won't let you die."

Hours later, her own strength severely tested, Jessa took her leave of Noah. Shutting the door quietly behind her, she leaned against it, eyes closed, and marshaled what remained of her resolve.

"Ye look like death itself."

Jessa merely accepted the observation, ignoring the strident tone in which it was delivered because she knew that genuine concern had prompted Mary to speak. With some effort Jessa pushed away from the door and walked to the rough-hewn table where Mary sat nursing Gideon. The baby was suckling noisily at Mary's breast, oblivious to anything but his own needs. "Shall I make you a cup of tea?"

"Make me a cuppa tea?" Mary's upper lip curled in derision and her dark brown eyes widened. She smoothed back a tendril of her flyaway red hair. "You're daft, child. Sit down." She pushed out the chair opposite her with the toe of her shoe. "Sit! As soon as Adam 'ere is done wi' 'is dinner, I'll fix the tea. You 'aven't been off yer feet since the boys brought you and the guvnor back. And them! Closed mouth as I've ever seen.

Wouldn't tell me a word of what 'appened. Me own 'usband didn't 'ave a word for me. Drops a kiss on me cheek and Adam in me arms and sez he'll be seein' me when 'e can. The lout.''

"Don't call him that," Jessa corrected tiredly, rubbing her eyes. The candle in front of her seemed to waver precariously. She reached out to steady it only to realize it was she who was wavering. Gripping the sides of her ladder-back chair, Jessa held herself rigid.

"Davey? I'll call 'im a lout if the shoe fits."

"No. I meant the baby. His name is Gideon. You mustn't forget. Especially now that we have Mr. McClellan in the next room."

"Oh." Mary stroked Gideon's cheek. "McClellan. That the name of the guvnor?"

"Yes. Noah McClellan. He's an American."

Mary was much struck by that information. "Imagine that. Don't seem right somehow, what wi' 'im gettin' mixed up in this business. Davey seemed mighty sorry it 'appened. 'Course I don't know precisely *what* 'appened. Thought everything was planned to a hair's breadth of perfection." She looked at Jessa expectantly, her round face as smooth and guileless as the baby's at her breast, yet there was no denying the shrewd, knowing look in her eyes.

Jessa's tenuous threadlike hold on her emotions snapped. Tears welled in her eyes as she relived every part of the robbery gone wrong. She slumped forward, laid her head in the cradle of her forearms, and sobbed quietly.

Mary was instantly contrite for having pressed Jessa for information. " 'Ere now. What's this? It weren't yer fault. I'm sure of that as I'm sure of anything." When this did nothing to relieve Jessa's misery Mary sighed empathetically. "Oh, go on. 'Ave a good cry. Then ye tell me everything. We'll sort it out. I'll 'ave Davey's guts for garters if 'e's done this to ye."

Jessa raised her head and wiped her eyes with the

hem of her black gown, giving Mary a rare watery smile. "No one's done anything to me. Oh, Mary, everything went wrong! And I'm afraid he's going to die! We'll be murderers then! I can't live with that."

Mary reached across the table and patted Jessa's hand firmly. "Hush. Yer speakin' nonsense now. There's no cause to talk about livin' or dyin'. Not for you, not for the guvnor. He'll be right an' tight in no time. Mark me if he ain't. Ye did good by 'im. Better than Dr. Gardener could 'ave done. I swear ye did! And ye sewed 'im up as pretty as a cross-stitched rose. I never saw the like before."

"But he's feverish, Mary, and he's never come around. It's been hours. I don't know what else to do for him." She held up her hands in a gesture of defeat. "Mayhap I shouldn't have stitched the wound. He's so weak. I think the ball did even more damage than I first thought."

Gideon's head had fallen away from Mary's breast and the baby was sleeping comfortably in the crook of her soft arms. "Here, ye take this sweet one. He's done in." She righted her bodice after Jessa took the baby. "I'll make us both a cuppa tea." With characteristic purpose Mary set about her task, crossing the small room to the stone hearth and taking down the kettle. Her movements were deft and economic as she poured the water and steeped the tea. "There's a bit of rabbit stew 'ere if you want some."

"No. Nothing for me. The tea will be fine." Jessa pressed her cheek against Gideon's forehead. "I couldn't eat anything." She looked up when she heard Mary's disagreeing clucking. "You shouldn't mother me. I'm one and twenty, Mary. Hardly a babe."

"And I've only got four years on ye, pet, but it seems to me it must be four score. Ye don't take care of yerself at all. Look at ye! Thin as a willow, no color in yer cheeks, and yer eyes as puffy as clouds. You'll not do the little one a bit o' good if ye keep on this way. Gideon needs ye, Jessa. Yer the only one what can 'elp 'im. You've got to think about that.''

"It seems that it's all I can think about," Jessa said wearily. She laid Gideon in the cradle Mary had placed near the window seat. "You'll have to sleep in here, little man. Our bedchamber is occupied." Deciding that Gideon did not seem put out in the least, Jessa drew the yellowed window curtains closed and returned to the table, taking the mug of tea Mary placed in front of her.

"I'll sleep on the window seat tonight," said Mary. "Ye take my bed in the loft."

Jessa shook her head. "No, I'll want to look in on Mr. McClellan from time to time. It's better if you stay in the loft. Now that Gideon's sleeping through the night you won't have to be up and down the ladder."

"I can see to the guvnor. Ye need to rest."

Jessa set her mug down hard. "No. I need to assure myself, Mary. He's my responsibility. He was shot because he was trying to help Gideon and me. I owe him."

Mary blinked in surprise at Jessa's adamant tone. "Very well," she said quietly. "I'll take the loft. I won't sleep much anyway, not with Davey out there. I never sleep good with 'im away."

"I don't think he'll be gone more than a few weeks. Just until the authorities call a halt to their search. You know how it is. Sometimes they quit after a few days."

"But no one's ever been 'urt before. Leastways not so that everyone would think he's dead."

"I couldn't leave Mr. McClellan there. He *would* have died. We had to try to save him."

"I understand. Ye did the right thing. Mayhap ye should tell me the whole of it. What 'appened on the road tonight?"

Jessa brushed back a wayward strand of hair with the back of her hand. Her clear gray eyes closed briefly and when she spoke it was in a dull, pained voice that she hardly recognized as her own. "Davey took me to Topping just as we planned. I walked to the inn with Gideon and purchased the fares for the stage to London. Everyone was very solicitous and I began to realize that Hank was right, that being a widow with a child was going to be very helpful."

Mary nodded wisely. "Davey's brother knows these things. 'E wouldn't take us down the wrong path."

"Yes, well, everything seemed to be fine. No one on the coach was talkative but they were kind. I can tell you I wasn't feeling very good about what was going to happen."

"That's just like ye," Mary said sympathetically. "We knew it would be 'ard on ye."

Jessa ignored the comment, intent on getting through her explanation quickly. "The stage made several stops, including one at Hemmings, near the Linfield estate. That's where Mr. McClellan came on. He'd had a terrible row with the innkeeper about his horse and he was desperate to get out of Hemmings and go to Stanhope. I felt so sorry for him. No one said a word. I think they were afraid. He was really the most congenial sort of person, Mary. Gideon was being so fussy and Mr. McClellan quieted him. He even showed me how to apply a bit of spirits to Gideon's gums. It helps with teething, you know."

Mary's mouth pursed but she remained quiet. How like Jessa to befriend a Yankee. It was not to be borne!

"If it hadn't been for Mr. McClellan I don't know how I would have broached the subject of the other robberies. I knew time was getting short and that I had to find a way to encourage the passengers to trust their valuables to Gideon's care, yet I couldn't think of any way to say it. Nothing we practiced seemed right."

"Yer just not very good at deceit, and that's just as well," Mary said soothingly. "No reason you should whip yerself for not takin' to it."

Jessa supposed that was a compliment of sorts. Her

smile was rueful. "Somehow Mr. McClellan had every-one talking and it just came up naturally. And not a moment too soon. Hank, Davey, and Will stopped the coach not long afterward. Mr. McClellan even delivered a facer to Lord Gilmore because his lordship was intent on fighting."

"Gilmore is a pup. Too 'igh in the instep if you ask me."

"He's also a crack shot. He could have hurt Davey or the others."

"Aye. I suppose I 'ave to thank the guvnor for that."

"I don't know that he'll be pleased when he discovers the truth." Jessa sighed and sipped her tea, warming her hands around the steaming mug. "We all left the coach just as Davey ordered. He was completely ill-man-nered."

Mary caught back a laugh. "Highwaymen ain't noted for politeness, no matter what others think. It's a dirty business and you've always known it." She held Jessa's troubled gaze and said more gently, "But go on, what 'appened then?"

"Will gathered up the few valuables the passengers still had on them while Davey took some rings from Lord Gilmore. Davey was on his way to the coach roof to check the baggage when Will made some churlish comment about Gideon crying. I know he was trying to be mean, for effect, you know, but Mr. McClellan didn't know that. He reached in his vest for the flask of spirits and Will panicked."

"Will didn't know Mr. McClellan wasn't carrying a primed piece."

"I know that. No one feels worse about the shooting than Will. The entire reason I joined this escapade was to prevent violence. None of us wanted that."

Mary shook her head sadly. "Poor Will. No wonder 'e looked so sickly. Davey and 'Ank will be givin' 'im a proper set down once they're settled in 'iding."

"He deserves it," Jessa said without sympathy. "After

the shooting Hank took charge, forcing the passengers back in the coach and making the driver take to the road.''

"They didn't suspect ye were part of it, did they?''

"I don't think so. They wanted Gideon of course, though whether it was his safety or their money they were worried about I don't know. They might have put up more of a protest if Mr. McClellan hadn't already been shot. They really had no choice but to leave me behind. I doubt they suspect I would have been made to stay with the highwaymen no matter what happened. They couldn't know that Gideon keeping their valuables was all part of the plan.''

"Then we only 'ave to keep the truth from Mr. McClellan. I don't know if it was a good idea to bring 'im 'ere after all.''

Jessa looked at her friend in bewilderment. "What else could I do, Mary? Traveling by coach to town would surely have killed him. Your cottage was much closer. Will built a litter and Hank and Davey covered the traces. I think we're safe here.''

"For a time. The search will widen come first light. Someone's bound to be around on the morrow askin' questions.''

"And you'll take care of that. They won't search the cottage. They have no cause.''

"Aye, I'll take care of the King's men when they come, but you'll 'ave to see that the babe and Mr. McClellan are kept quiet. And no good will come of it if they see you. Yer not fancy free yerself.''

Jessa nodded, setting down her mug. "No, I'm not, am I?'' Rotating her head gently she tried to take some of the stiffness out of her neck. "I'm so tired of it all, Mary. I don't know where to turn. If it weren't for you and Davey, Gideon and I would have no one.'' She bit her lip, stifling a sob, and turned her head so Mary wouldn't see her tears again. "I don't know what's wrong with me. I'm not usually so self-pitying.''

Mary stood and circled the table. Her hands were large and sturdy, but infinitely tender as they closed about Jessa's thin shoulders. "Don't make yerself sick with worry. You've come this far. Adam—I mean Gideon—is safe. He wouldn't be if it weren't for ye, Jessa. Never forget that."

Jessa's shoulders sagged and relaxed under the pressure of Mary's kneading hands. "How can you be so calm? And so good to me? The sacrifices that you've made, Mary, they were enormous."

Mary's hands stopped their soothing motion briefly. "There was nothing that could be done for my baby. 'E was never 'ealthy, not like Gideon. I'm thankful for the time I 'ad with young Davey. From the moment I saw my boy I knew I'd be sayin' farewell to 'im before the first year of 'is life was over. There's nothin' in the world what can replace my son, and I wish I 'ad more time wi' 'im, but I don't regret that 'is death 'elped ye and Gideon."

Jessa stared at the faint blue network of veins on the back of her pale hands and her thoughts traveled three months back in time. In her mind's eye she could see Mary and Davey laying the body of their infant son on a bed of fallen pine boughs. Mary was stoic about her loss. It was Davey who wept, Davey whose harsh sobs were captured in the bitter cold air. Gideon was uncharacteristically quiet during the brief ceremony, and it was Jessa who knelt and covered the dead infant to protect it from animals. When the body was found everyone assumed the child had died of exposure just as everyone assumed the infant was Adam Penberthy. It had been Lady Barbara, who had never seen her nephew above twice, who had identified the tiny body. Jessa felt ill every time she thought of the Penberthys mistaking young Davey for Adam. Surely that proved how little they cared for the child.

Mary gave Jessa a reproving shake and began to unfasten the back of Jessa's mourning gown. "Lady Barbara wouldn't 'ave rested until she found you or Adam. She can afford to be generous now that she thinks it's Adam restin' in the Penberthy vault. My son 'ad a fine burial, Jessa. 'E's at peace. And so should ye be.''

"You said it yourself. I'm not fancy free."

"Not yet. But soon. Soon as we can get you and Gideon out of England. Things have slowed some. No one's lookin' so 'ard for ye now." She finished unfastening Jessa's dress. "There now. Put on yer shift and get some sleep. The sun will be up before ye know it and the guvnor will 'ave us busy." Mary yawned and stretched, arching her back. "I've a mind to get a bit of sleep myself." She winked at Jessa as she rounded the table on her way to the loft. "I've got to be fresh for the King's men."

Jessa wished she had some of Mary's easy confidence. Mary's husband and brothers-in-law were in hiding. The cottage had been turned into an infirmary for a wounded man, a nursery for a baby, and a refuge for a woman still hunted by the law. Yet Mary shrugged it off as if it were all meant to be. Jessa couldn't think of it that way. It seemed to her that life should not be so cruel, that she was somehow responsible for everything that had happened and that at each crossroads she kept making the wrong decision.

Mary would have scoffed at this idea. Jessa would not permit herself the luxury. She slipped into her sleeping shift and blew out the candles on the table. A log dropped in the hearth and the sparks of heat and light cast an eerie shadow across the room. Jessa huddled on the window seat, resting her head on her forearm. One hand hung over the side, close to where Gideon lay, and she drew comfort from his nearness. "I think we're survivors, Gideon," she said softly. "I think we must be. There's no turning back, no way to undo all that's been done. Even if we live to regret it, at least we will live."

Jessa closed her eyes and in moments she was asleep. A loud thud brought her instantly awake. Attuned as she was to every conceivable noise that Gideon could make, Jessa's first thought was for the baby. Stretching out her arm, she felt for him in the darkness. He was still in the cradle, sleeping soundly with his legs curled under him and his butt in the air. Jessa sat up and tried to orient herself. The sound was not repeated and she realized it could not have come from the door. Soldiers would not have stopped with one knock. Careful not to trip over the cradle, Jessa lighted a candle at the hearth and padded barefoot to the bedroom.

Noah McClellan was lying on the floor in a tangled heap of sheets and blankets. The nightstand had been knocked over and the heavy basin lay very near his head. The puddle of water was being quickly soaked up by the sheets.

Jessa righted the stand and set her candle on it. Moving the basin to one side, she ran her hand gingerly through the thick cap of Noah's hair. It appeared he had narrowly missed being struck by the basin. Jessa breathed more easily. She worked quickly, tossing the blankets aside to keep them dry. She untangled the sheets from around Noah, then used them to mop the water.

"You really belong in bed, Mr. McClellan," she said softly. "it's too cold for you here on the floor." Her comment brought no response. "But I don't suppose you're of a mind to be cooperative." Jessa pulled away the bandage and could have cried again when she saw her handiwork had been torn apart. Tears were useless. Beating her clenched fists against the floor proved just as futile but it made her feel better. Anger at her own helplessness lent her strength. Hooking her arms under Noah's shoulders, Jessa pulled him high enough so that she could drag him toward the bed. Unfortunately she did not judge her position correctly and when he collapsed on the bed it was with her under him. Her shift tore at the shoulder as she twisted away, baring her breast. The sensation of her skin pressed intimately against Noah's taut back froze her into immobility.

"I should die of embarrassment if it would not prove so awkward," she told herself and the man who could not hear her. Heaving herself upright, Jessa untangled her legs and pulled Noah completely onto the bed. She just managed to miss being trapped by his arm as he rolled on his side. "Oh, no," she said, pushing him onto his back. "I've got to dress that wound again. And I think you need a poultice." Jessa slid off the edge of the bed and went into the other room to get more water and a fresh bandage, and to make the milk and oil poultice. When she retuned Noah was lying very still in the center of the narrow bed. Jessa's breath caught in her throat and she held it until she saw the faint rise and fall of Noah's chest. Hurrying to his side she placed the basin on the floor and began cleaning his wound.

"Beautiful."

Jessa's hand jerked away from Noah's skin and she blinked hard. What a thing for him to say! Not a particularly vain person, Jessa had an urge to look over her shoulder to see whom he was addressing. Instead she followed the path of Noah's gaze and was mortified to discover he was staring at her uncovered breast. "Oh! How dare you!" She quickly righted her shift, tying a knot in the shoulder to keep it in place. Jessa huffed, prepared to make further comment, then realized it would have been a waste of her breath. Noah's eyes were closed and he appeared to be sleeping again. She stared at him hard, testing the depth of his sleep. When he didn't move or even flutter his lashes, Jessa released the breath she was holding.

Jessa continued her ministrations with deft assurance, but only a small part of her mind remained on the task. Noah's statement had left her more shaken than she was prepared to admit, even to herself. There had been so few occasions in her life when men had told her she was beautiful that Jessa was suspicious of the lavish compliment. It seemed the men who said it had certain expectations, as if she were supposed to be so flattered by the observation that she should willingly fling caution and propriety aside and fall into their arms. That had certainly been the case with Edward Penberthy.

She laughed at her own musings. "I doubt it was your intent, Mr. McClellan. You're as weak as a babe, more helpless than Gideon." She wagged a slender finger at his unconscious form. "Still, should you be getting any ideas I recommend you take the time to visit upon Lord Penberthy. The thin white scars on his face may give you pause."

Having said her piece, Jessa applied the poultice to Noah's wound and turned him on his side so she could wrap the clean bandage around his waist. Her fingers brushed against his warm skin, and as she leaned forward her soft breath whispered across his shoulder. She worked efficiently, fighting the feelings of awareness she had for her patient. Those feelings, she had discovered, were prone to make her fingers clumsy. Had he been conscious they would have tied her tongue in knots.

It was difficult not to be aware of Noah McClellan. For Jessa, that awareness had begun at the inn in Hemmings. He was the sort of man women noticed, Jessa thought, remembering how the innkeeper's wife and the two serving girls had regarded him with bold eyes and teasing smiles. Yet in fairness to Noah, he had done nothing to encourage their attention. He had simply walked into the inn. Jessa felt herself blushing. Oh, how this man had walked! His easy gait, the self-assured stance, had drawn her eyes also. He didn't swagger; he didn't have to. There was a certain confidence in his long stride that was both masculine and graceful.

Jessa pressed her hands to her warm cheeks. She remembered lowering her eyes so he wouldn't suspect she had been staring as he walked toward her table. A moment later he was past her, speaking with the innkeeper, and she would have had to turn completely around to look at him. Even if she had not been cast in the role of a grieving widow, Jessa would not have turned around. She envied the serving girls, neither of whom had the least reservation about doing just that. Surreptitiously she watched their antics, the sly winks they exchanged, and by doing so, she saw Noah McClellan through their eyes.

They shared a giggle as they stared unashamedly at his back, taking in his wide shoulders and the taut length of his legs. Fluttering their lashes, they preened, waiting for Noah to turn around so they could feast on something besides the expensive cut of his clothes. Jessa had hidden a smile against Gideon's forehead. She doubted either of the girls was paying the slightest attention to the conversation between Noah and the innkeeper.

Noah's voice had caught Jessa's interest immediately. The hint of a drawl was lilting and melodious and fell pleasantly on her ears. It was a voice for lullabies, she had whispered to Gideon. Or at least it had been until Noah became angry with the innkeeper. There was no trace of the gentle cadence of his speech once he raised his voice. It was harsh, clipped, and angry, boding ill for anyone in earshot.

Jessa shied away from that memory, not daring to think what it would be like to have that fearsome voice directed at her. She remembered instead how Noah's kindness on the coach had captured her admiration. "I think when you left the inn I was the envy of those serving girls," she told him. Jessa covered Noah with two blankets, tucking them under the feather tick. "They'd have expired where they stood if they'd seen as much of you as I have this evening." She knelt on the floor by the bed and rested her head against the tick. "You're an exceedingly handsome man, Noah McClellan." Then she prayed for his life to be spared.

* * *

Mary pushed open the door to the bedroom with her hip and carried in a wooden tray of tea and buttered bread. Setting the tray on the nightstand, she nudged Jessa's shoulder with her hand. " 'Ere now, it's time you let me take a turn at this." She clucked her tongue in gentle disapproval. " 'Ave you been 'ere all night?"

Jessa raised her head and immediately put her hand to her stiff neck. Her wide gray eyes fluttered open. "What? Oh, it's you."

"And who'd you think it be? Come on, up with ye. Ye could 'ave slept in the rocker. Leastways it wouldn't 'ave been so uncomfortable."

Jessa allowed Mary to help her into the ancient rocker a few feet from the bed. The runners had been mended so often that the chair wobbled sideways when it was rocked. "It didn't seem so bad last night. I don't even remember falling asleep." She barely was able to raise her hand in time to stifle a yawn. "What time is it?"

"Gone eight."

"Eight!" Jessa sat upright. She would have bolted from the chair if Mary hadn't blocked her path.

"Stay where ye are, Miss Jessa. Yer in my 'ouse now and I'm sayin' 'ow we go on from 'ere." She merely flashed a fulsome smile when Jessa glared at her. "That's better. Ye lean back and give it a rest. I've made some tea for ye and the guvnor." Mary passed a mug to Jessa then bent over Noah, checking his forehead with the back of her hand. " 'E's not so feverish as he was last eve. But not ready to take any of my tea. I see that well enough." Drawing the blankets down Noah's chest, she checked the bandage. "You've added a poultice. When did ye do that?"

"Sometime last night. Perhaps it was early this morning. I don't know." Jessa sipped on her tea and grimaced slightly. Mary had been heavy-handed with the milk and sugar. "He fell out of bed and rent the stitches. I thought a poultice would be better than sewing him up again."

Mary glanced over her shoulder. "Ye put 'im in bed by yerself?" she asked in amazement.

"Well, yes," she admitted, uneasy under Mary's hard stare. "It wasn't so difficult."

Mary snorted. "I don't believe ye. 'E's a big one. Ye should 'ave called me."

"Don't be cross, Mary. It's done now." Jessa closed her eyes. "I couldn't leave him on the floor. It was too cold."

Mary was not relenting. "So ye spent the night there yerself. Now that's usin' yer sense." She opened the trunk at the foot of the bed and took out a woolen blanket. Brooking no nonsense, she tucked it around Jessa. "All we need is for ye to fall ill. That would truly 'elp the babe."

Jessa realized she was achingly tired. She hadn't given Gideon a thought until now. "I haven't heard Gideon at all this morning." Usually his slightest cry captured her attention. "He's not sick, is he?"

"That one's doin' fine. Just fine. Sarah came by early and took 'im with 'er."

Jessa's eyes flew open. "But why?"

Mary's hand settled over her ample hips. "Because she's got three of 'er own and she can 'ide the boy among them. It was 'Ank's idea."

"Hank never mentioned it to me."

"It's what 'e told Sarah to do come first light. She's was just doin' what 'er 'usband wanted. It's safer for Gideon."

Jesse hadn't thought Hank would stop at his own cottage before going into hiding, but it made sense. Sarah would have been frantic with worry if he hadn't returned, however briefly, last night. "Was Sarah very upset about what happened?"

"No, she takes it in stride, same as I do. We knew the sort of men we were marryin'. Went into it with our eyes open."

"Davey and his brothers were only smugglers when

you married," Jessa reminded her. "It wasn't precisely an accepted occupation, I'll grant you, but most everyone turns their head to it. Some people even say it's justified."

Mary shrugged. "On water or on 'orseback, it's still thievin', and don't ye forget it."

Jessa was surprised to hear Mary say so. "I know, but they wouldn't have taken to the road if it weren't for me."

"If it weren't fer Gideon," Mary corrected. "And they're not complaining, so why should ye? Besides, if people knew why they were needin' the money they'd say it was in a good cause."

Jessa doubted that but she held her tongue and smiled at Mary. "Gideon and I are blessed to have friends like you."

Mary began straightening the room hurriedly, uncomfortable with Jessa's heartfelt sentiment. "Why don't you make a fresh poultice and . . ." She stopped because Jessa had come up behind her and laid a hand on her arm.

"I mean it, Mary. Gideon and I are blessed." Jessa kissed Mary on the cheek then fled the room, dragging the blanket after her.

Mary picked up Noah's soiled and bloodstained clothes, which had been relegated to a pile in one corner, and carried them out with the damp sheets and used bandages. Her heart went out to Jessa. She couldn't think of anyone who had been less blessed this past year than Jessica Winter.

Jessa was fiddling with the fire in the hearth when Mary returned to the outer room. "I think we should leave the door open," she said. "There's a chill in there. Perhaps this fire will help. I should have thought of it last night." She put aside the poker and picked up her clothes as well as Gideon's cradle. "I suppose I should put these things away."

"It would be best," Mary agreed, dropping the dirty

laundry in the wooden washtub. "Put the mourning gown in the trunk. We don't want the soldiers seeing anything that could connect you with the robbery. 'Ide the cradle on the far side of the bed, under a blanket."

Jessa frowned, wondering why she had to hide the things that were going into the other room. "But you agreed the soldiers wouldn't search the cottage."

"It's just a precaution. Don't fret." She smiled with more confidence than she really felt. "I told ye I'd take care of the men. If they come at all," she added.

But Jessa knew they would come and she also knew that she had placed Mary and her family in terrible danger by bringing Noah McClellan to the cottage. It would take only one small piece of evidence to damn them all. She shut the lid on the trunk and her eyes fell on Noah. Hardly a small piece of evidence, she considered wryly. The bed could hardly contain his length.

Jessa rushed out of the room, uneasy with her thoughts. She did not like being so aware of this man.

Mary looked up from the stew she was stirring as Jessa came back in. "What's 'appened to ye?"

"Nothing," she said quickly, too quickly.

Mary's eyes narrowed thoughtfully. "Are you going to make that poultice?"

"What? Oh, yes. I'll make it. Now."

"And do ye think ye might be gettin' dressed today?"

Jessa looked down at herself. Her comical expression of dismay brought a chuckle to Mary's lips. "After I make the poultice," she said, looking defiantly at Mary.

Mary watched Jessa silently and knowingly. "The guvnor's a fine lookin' man," she said as Jessa stood on tiptoe to reach the shelf where the linseed oil was kept.

Startled, Jessa nearly knocked the jar over. She caught it as it tipped forward and pressed it against her chest. "You may be right," she said airily, avoiding Mary's shrewd stare. She placed the jar on the table and ladled a cup of warm cow's milk into a bowl. Adding the oil, she stirred vigorously. She didn't look up as Mary handed her the healing herbs. "He's very tall," she said casually. "My head doesn't reach his shoulder."

"That's true enough, but since I've only seen 'im laid out, it wasn't what I noticed about 'im."

"Oh?" She added the herbs, stirred, and poured the mixture into a small kettle which she hung on a hook in the hearth.

Mary was not fooled by Jessa's pretense of unconcern. "Mr. McClellan 'as a beautiful mouth," she said.

"Mary!"

"There's no 'arm in lookin'. Leastways that's what Davey tells me every time I catch 'im sneakin' a glance at Margaret Wilson. I don't mean nothin' by it."

"I should hope not," Jessa said, stirring more briskly now. She didn't dare look at Mary.

Over Jessa's bent head Mary grinned. "And 'e's got such long lashes. Wouldn't I just love to 'ave such a pair." She fluttered her red-tipped lashes coyly. "I wondered about 'is eyes, though. Blue, I think."

"They're green."

"Green's very nice."

"Well, they're not precisely green," Jessa said, annoyed with this conversation. "They have flecks of gray and gold and a bit of brown."

"Hazel then."

"Yes, hazel. Completely unremarkable."

"Oh, yes. Completely unremarkable. I'm surprised ye took any notice," she prompted.

Jessa sighed, pulling the thickened poultice mixture out of the hearth. "You're making too much of it, Mary. I could hardly help but notice the man's eyes. He was sitting on the opposite seat on the coach. We talked and he made himself helpful with Gideon. I know how many brothers and sisters he has, where he's from, and where he was going. I even know how many nieces and nephews he has and I could probably name half of them. It's hardly worth noting that I remember the color of his eyes."

"Certainly," Mary pretended to agree. "Now, take my Davey for instance. You've known 'im almost as long as I 'ave. 'E was a proper groom in your papa's stables."

"When he wasn't joining the local band of smugglers."

Mary waved that aside. "Tell me the color of 'is eyes."

Jessa paused in spreading out the cheesecloth on the table. Her fingers flitted over the edges as she smoothed them. "They're brown." Mary's hearty laughter washed over her and she knew she had guessed wrong. "Well, they're dark," she said, defending herself hastily.

"They're blue," Mary said. "And as soft and light as 'eather."

Jessa spooned out the contents of the kettle and wrapped the cloth around it. "I'll take this into him now." She fled Mary's company as hastily as she had earlier fled Noah's. Against her own advice she closed the door in order to block out Mary's satisfied laughter.

Jessa was briskly efficient in the face of Mary's pointed observations. She was less than gentle as she tugged at the old poultice and replaced it with the fresh one. It was Noah's soft moan that stilled her hand and reminded her that he was not at fault for all her wayward, wicked thoughts. She bathed his face and supported his head, trying to get him to take some of the lukewarm tea Mary had brought in earlier. He was having none of it. "Stubborn man," she said, righting his blankets. "I don't know . . ."

Jessa stopped, every sense alert to the new danger. Through the cottage walls she could hear the pounding of horses and the orders a commander delivered to his men. She dropped Noah's head back on the thin pillow and sat on the edge of the bed, waiting for the soldiers to announce their presence at the door. She wished there was a window in the tiny bedchamber where she could look out. Almost as soon as she wished it, she changed her mind, thankful for the dark protection of the four walls. She turned back the lamp until its light flickered, then was extinguished. Jessa folded her hands in her lap and waited.

Mary had heard the soldiers also. She composed herself, taking a deep breath and patting down her flyaway hair, and opened the door to them. "Lor', it's a cold day to be out on yer 'orse," she said, wrapping her arms around her middle. "Lost yer way? The post road's through those woods, about five miles as the crow flies."

The commander of the small troop of five dismounted and gave his reins to one of his men. "I'm Sergeant White," he introduced himself as he approached Mary. He was a large man, broad at the shoulders and equally so at the waist. He held himself very stiffly, seemingly unaffected by the biting wind. "We're here on the King's business, Miss—"

"Shaw. I'm Mary Shaw." She didn't correct his assumption that she was single. It was better that he should think so though Mary thought her charm would be lost on him. In dealing with this man she realized she had better use her wits. He seemed too duty bound to have his head turned by a fluttery smile. "Ow can I 'elp ye, sergeant?"

"I've orders to make a thorough search of the area. There was a robbery on the post road last night."

Mary's eyes were as wide as sovereigns as she feigned shock. "That's terrible!"

"Bloody awful it was, Miss Shaw, if you'll pardon my blunt manner. A man was shot and a woman and a child taken hostage."

Mary leaned back against the door and hugged herself more tightly. " 'Tis a terrible thing, all right. But why 'ave ye come 'ere?"

"Orders," he said tersely. "Beggin' your pardon, I have to search the house and grounds. We've been combin' the woods since daybreak." He turned from her and ordered his men to begin with the grounds, including the woodshed and the ramshackle stable. "I'll look in the house myself."

This time Mary's shock was not feigned. "Ye 'ave no right," she said stoutly, stiffening her shoulders. "This ain't proper! What is it ye expect to find?"

The sergeant was impatient, eager to be out of the cold for a little while and almost as eager to be done with this fool's errand. He was somewhat familiar with the locals and the clannish nature of the population. If any one of them had anything to do with stopping the coach he'd wager a month's pay no one would speak of it. "I don't expect to find anything," he said truthfully, "but I'm ordered to have a look anyway. Now, if you'll step aside, I'll be about my business then I'll be on my way."

Mary was backed into the cottage. As soon as the sergeant passed her she shut the door. "I don't understand what yer lookin' for," she said again, raising her voice a notch so that Jessa would hear her. "My mistress won't be pleased about yer intrudin' on 'er."

The sergeant paused in his survey of the room and sidled over to the hearth where the stew was simmering. He breathed the aroma deeply and warmed his hands over the kettle. "Your mistress?" he inquired. "I thought you were alone."

"I never said I was, did I? And ye didn't ask it of me."

He turned away from the fire and glanced about the cottage again. Everything was neatly ordered and painstakingly cleaned, yet it wasn't the home of someone who kept a servant. The dishes set above the rough stone chimneypiece were chipped and mismatched. The curtains in the window were frayed at the edges and permanently yellowed from the smoke that escaped the hearth. The table was scarred and the chairs each bore signs of mending. "Your mistress lives here?" he asked, skeptical.

Mary drew herself up and tapped one foot impatiently on the floor. "Of course she don't. I keep the place for

'er so she can use it upon occasion.'' She cast a significant glance at the closed door and lowered her voice.
''If ye get my meanin'.''

The sergeant frowned and rubbed his forehead with
his thumb and forefinger. So it was a trysting cottage.
That did not bode well for him. ''Who *is* your mistress?''

''I'm not likely to tell ye that, am I? She'd toss me
out on me ear. This is a secret place for 'er. I don't
want 'er name on the lips of gossips.''

He studied the door for a moment. ''She's not alone
now I take it.''

''That's not for me to say,'' Mary said, not giving an
inch. She watched the sergeant squirm uncomfortably
and bit back a smile. She could well imagine what was
going on in his mind and she enjoyed his struggle. He
was trying to decide whether to believe her. She kept
her face carefully blank as he turned toward her and
studied her features, searching for some sign that she
was lying.

''I think I'll search the loft,'' he said finally.

''Fine. Yer welcome to it. Mind the ladder. It's not
used to bearin' much weight.'' The sergeant muttered
something under his breath that Mary could not catch.
She was not of mind to ask him to repeat it. She turned
away and stirred the stew. He was back down the ladder
in a few moments.

''I've decided to have a look in the other room,'' he
said.

Mary shrugged. ''That's up to you. Can't say I didn't
warn ye. Work, though, it be 'ard to come by.''

''I can't be concerned with your employment.''

''I was thinkin' of yers,'' she said frankly. ''My mistress,
she's one to be reckoned with.''

Sergeant White hesitated again. What if Mary Shaw
were lying and there was no mistress? Could she be
hiding the very highwaymen he sought? Worse, what if
she were telling the truth and he confronted a lady of
quality conducting her illicit affair? It would explain

why the lady in question had not come out at the first sign of trouble. If there was a lady at all. "I have to see for myself," he said.

In the folds of her heavy skirt Mary's hands clenched. "As ye will," was all she said. Then she held her breath.

One of the sergeant's hands closed over the door handle. The other hovered over the pistol tucked in the waistband of his white woolen breeches. He braced himself for either eventuality and twisted the handle.

Sergeant White's hand fell away from his pistol as he confronted the scene in the bedchamber. In his mind he cursed the orders that had brought him here, then he cursed himself for not believing Mary Shaw. He attempted to retreat but it was as if his feet had taken root. Behind him he heard Mary approach and still he couldn't move.

In the dim light which filtered in from the outer room Sergeant White could make out the intimately coupled bodies. For a few moments the man and woman on the bed were oblivious to his intrusion. The man lay on his back beneath the woman. His eyes were closed. His skin was drawn tightly over the bones of his face. Perspiration glistened on his chest and the taut indrawn plane of his stomach. Above him the woman rocked, straddling his loins. Her head was thrown back, revealing the slender white stem of her neck. Her naked breasts, larger it seemed than her reed-thin body could support, quivered deliciously as she thrust herself over her lover. The curling ends of her long hair brushed the man's thighs.

Mary peeked around the sergeant's shoulder and gasped softly at the sight of Jessa and Noah McClellan apparently in the last moments of a deep passion. She was so shocked she nearly giggled. Instead she pressed her hand to her mouth and nudged the sergeant.

Jessa's head turned slowly, shaded in part by the long fall of her hair. The haughty, slightly vicious expression she wore was turned fully on the sergeant. She didn't have to say anything. Sergeant White backed out of the room so quickly that Mary narrowly missed being caught underfoot. The door shuddered as it was yanked shut.

Arms akimbo, Mary confronted the sergeant. "I warned ye. Never say I didn't. If ye ever breathe a word . . . a word, mind ye . . . she'll 'ave yer guts."

Sergeant White nodded slowly, still dazed by what he had witnessed. He hoped his coat hid the rock-hard bulge in his breeches. He shifted his weight from one foot to the other. "I'll take my leave, Miss Shaw. I'd be grateful if you didn't mention my name to her."

"Only if it don't mean losin' my position."

"Yes, well, I understand that . . . only . . ." His voice trailed off and he glanced at the closed door, his face pale. "If you could just make her understand I was following orders."

Mary was thoroughly enjoying the sergeant's squirming. "We'll see," she said noncommittally.

"Mary! Mary, come in here at once!"

Mary jerked her chin toward the door. "Ye'd better go. She's got 'er back up now. No sense in offendin' quality any more than ye already done." Mary tamped back her smile, realizing she could have saved her breath. As soon as he heard Jessa's demanding call the sergeant moved toward the door. He was outside before Mary finished speaking.

"Mary!"

"He's gone, Miss Jess," Mary called back, hurrying toward the bedroom. "They're all leaving. There's no need for that tone now." Mary pushed the door open. "Did ye 'ear? I said they're goin'."

Jessa had slipped back into her shift. She was standing beside the bed, leaning over Noah, as Mary swept into the room. She looked up, her eyes anguished. "Oh, Mary, I think I've hurt him."

Mary touched Noah's forehead with the back of her hand. "Aye, 'e's burnin' up. But it's nothin' you did to 'im. It's the fever. Davey 'as a bit o' liquor around 'ere.

We'll give the guvnor 'ere an alcohol bath. That should cool 'im some."

Jessa bit her lip. "But his breathing is so shallow."

" 'E's probably not used to be ridden like a stallion," Mary said bluntly.

Jessa's pale cheeks colored deeply. "But I didn't . . . not really . . . I wouldn't know how."

One of Mary's brows arched skeptically. "That isn't 'ow it looked to me and the sergeant." She turned away. "I'll get the alcohol."

Resting her hip on the edge of the bed, Jessa brushed back a damp lock of hair from Noah's temple. His face was unnaturally flushed and his breathing was harsh. "He's going to die, isn't he?" she asked when Mary returned.

"I can't say," said Mary. She sat on the opposite side of the bed, the shallow basin filled with alcohol in her lap. Wringing out a cloth, she folded it and gave it to Jessa. "Do 'is face and neck. I'll bathe 'is chest." The women worked in purposeful silence for a few minutes, intent on their task. "You've nothin' to be ashamed of," Mary said at last, sparing a knowing glance at Jessa's taut features. "Ye did exactly what needed to be done. Ye certainly convinced the sergeant."

Jessa's hand stilled. "I still don't believe I did it, Mary," she said quietly. "I could hear everything you were saying to Sergeant White. I knew what you were implying." Her smile was rueful. "I wanted to strangle you. If you had been near I think I might have."

"What was I supposed to tell 'im?" she asked defensively. " 'E wasn't about to be charmed, thickheaded oaf that 'e was. Anyway, my tale almost stopped 'im from comin' in 'ere." She snapped her fingers. " 'E came that close to turnin' away. And ye should 'ave seen 'im fly out of 'ere! That wasn't 'is tail tucked between 'is legs, I can tell you!" She chuckled at her own ribald humor. "That man didn't know which way to turn after 'e saw you and Mr. McClellan 'ere."

"Don't remind me. I don't want to think about it."

"I was shocked meself," Mary persisted. "I never expected ye to give such a performance."

"Mary! Please!"

"Ow'd ye know to do such a thing?"

Jessa brushed Noah's upper lip with a less than gentle stroke. "I've seen things," she said a shade defiantly.

" 'Ave you now?"

Jessa sighed, knowing Mary wouldn't let it rest until she heard the whole of it. "When I was twelve I saw the dairy maid and one of the grooms coupling that way in the stable. And no, it wasn't your Davey. And yes, I stayed hidden and watched. I know it was wicked, but I was ... well, I was fascinated. I thought they were hurting one another at first, then later I realized they were enjoying it."

"Aye, there's pain and pleasure in the doin'."

"I wouldn't know about that," Jessa said primly. "I was only acting."

"Did ye get a rise out of the guvnor?" asked Mary baldly.

Jessa nearly brought the damp cloth to her own hot face. "No!" It wasn't precisely true. She remembered the tightening of Noah's loins as she straddled him, the imprint of his manhood against her inner thigh. The thin cloth of his cotton drawers was not much of a barrier. "No," she repeated. "He wasn't naked, you know."

"There's no need to fly off into the boughs. I told ye, ye did nothin' to be ashamed of. The soldiers won't be back and that's what we set out to accomplish. Sergeant White saw both you and Mr. McClellan, in the flesh as it were, and 'e's none the wiser. I'd say it all worked out for the best."

Jessa wasn't as certain but she said nothing. Mary would make light of her fears. "What about Mr. McClellan? What are we going to do for him?"

"We're doin' all we can now, Miss Jessa. And I've

been givin' it some thought. If the guvnor takes another turn for the worse there's but one thing you can do. It would solve a great many problems.''

"What's that?"

"Marry 'im.''

CHAPTER THREE

Noah knew that he was dying. Or rather he suspected it. To his way of thinking there could only be one reason the priest was bending over him. Noah tried to cut through the heavy fog that enveloped him and tell the priest he had no intention of dying. His jaw worked from side to side but he could not form the words. His eyes would not stay open. The words spoken over him were slurred and disagreeably guttural and he could not make them out. The priest smelled strongly of spirits.

Another voice spoke, soft and lilting. Noah was struck by an odd sense of familiarity and he strained for recognition. It would not come and he felt himself being drawn against his will into an ever-widening darkness. He struggled to be released from it and was denied.

Some part of him sensed the priest bending still closer, murmuring something that remained incomprehensible. I won't die, Noah told himself. I don't want to die. He forced his mouth to shape the words. "I do—" It came out on a single puff of air and Noah was satisfied that he was understood. He slipped into unconsciousness.

"There," interrupted Mary, smiling widely with satis-faction. "You 'eard 'im. I told you 'e wanted to marry 'er. We all 'eard 'im." She nudged her sister-in-law.

"I 'eard 'im," Sarah said quickly, taking Mary's cue. In her arms Gideon gurgled pleasantly. The dimples on either side of his cupid's mouth deepened.

The priest straightened slowly, gripping one bedpost to right himself. His kind eyes were slightly glazed and the expression on his florid face was vague and bewil-dered. There was a momentary struggle for dignity but the effects of Mary's corn liquor proved to be more powerful. He glanced at Jessa, who was standing at the other side of the bed holding Noah's hand in hers. She did not meet his eyes but he was not sure if she was avoiding him or if he could not focus. "Very well," he sighed, closing his prayer book. "Then I pronounce you man and wife." He shook his head, trying to clear it. "Most irregular," he slurred.

Mary slipped her arm beneath the priest's elbow, sup-porting him and at the same time ushering him out of the room. "It's legal though, ain't it?"

The priest looked affronted. "Quite legal. The license was signed and it will be duly recorded in the church. Still, most irregular."

"That's neither 'ere nor there." She helped the priest with his greatcoat and retrieved his knobby walking stick from the hook by the door. "Sarah will take you home in 'er wagon." Mary took Gideon from Sarah's arms and gave her sister-in-law a quick kiss on the cheek. "Thank ye, Sarah," she whispered. "Ye've been a great 'elp."

Sarah looked doubtful. She threw her cloak over her thin shoulders and wrapped a scarf around the lower half of her face. Her large brown eyes spoke eloquently to Mary, clearly saying what she thought of the mad scheme. "I'll take 'im to the church and make sure 'e marks the weddin'. Doubt 'e'll remember 'alf of it on the morrow." She sniffed. "Probably just as well."

Mary stood in the doorway, sheltering Gideon against the cold air, and waved them off. "What do ye think o' that, Master Gideon? 'Ave there ever been such goings on?" Gideon laughed as she stepped back in the cottage and tickled his chin. "Aye, there's no need to say it. I'm a quick-witted one. There's no denyin' it. Come on, let's see yer mama. She's no doubt wonderin' if she's done right by ye."

Jessa was sitting in the rocker which she had placed directly at Noah's side. She eagerly took Gideon from Mary's arms. The child squirmed playfully against her, tugging at the heavy braid that fell over her shoulder. He tried to stuff it in his mouth. "Oh, Mary, what have we done?"

"We found a way to get ye and the babe out of England," she said practically. "Ye know very well it was for Gideon."

"But the price, Mary? What of the price?" Jessa said. Gideon cried out as he was squeezed too tightly. Jessa relaxed her hold at once and absently removed her hair from his mouth. "If Mr. McClellan lives he will never forgive me," she said lowly. "If he dies, I shall never forgive myself."

Noah turned his cheek toward the coolness of the damp cloth. On his forehead he felt the whisper trail of three fingers brushing back a lock of hair. One corner of his mouth lifted in the beginnings of a sweet smile. The weights that seemed to press his eyelids in place were lifted. Noah opened his eyes slowly and focused on the shadowy face above him.

Her beautifully shaped mouth was slightly parted. Noah could see the tip of her pink tongue run across her teeth as she concentrated on her task. He was suddenly aware that *he* was the object of her concern. Noah thought he liked that very much. His eyes fastened on the coronet braid of her hair and the question he had asked himself on the coach was finally answered. It was the color of corn silk. Silken threads of yellow and white gold framed her face. It seemed so perfect for her that Noah wondered why he hadn't thought of it. His glance dropped to her darker brows, the fan of still darker lashes, and he understood how he had been misled to think she might be a brunette or even a redhead. Now he realized it wouldn't have suited her. Her hair was as soft and fine as a baby's. His fingers curled into the feather tick and he controlled the urge to touch her. It would startle her. She was so intense that she hadn't even noticed he was watching her. It was just as well. Noah thought that if she turned those pale gray eyes on him he could easily be lost in the misty void that had surrounded him for days.

Jessa pulled carefully at the bandage at Noah's side and replaced the poultice. She no longer had any faith in its efficacy but she didn't know what else to do. That he had survived these last seventy-two long hours seemed something of a miracle. Mary insisted it was the marriage ceremony that had brought him around. He had been close to death before that. Jessa agreed there was probably some truth in Mary's statement. Secretly she thought Noah was making his slow recovery just for the opportunity to do murder.

"You have gentle hands."

Those gentle hands fell away from Noah so quickly they might have been scalded by his words. Jessa started to stand up but Noah caught her wrist. Demonstrating more strength than she would have credited him with he held her fast. She sat down again.

"You've been taking care of me?" he asked. Lack of use had given his voice a husky timbre.

She nodded, avoiding his eyes. "I should get Mary." Jessa tried to pull away again but Noah wouldn't let her go.

"Who's Mary?"

"She's my friend. She's been helping me." With her

free hand Jessa flicked a tendril of hair behind her ear. "You really shouldn't be doing so much talking," she said uneasily. Or holding me, she thought just as uneasily. "I think it would be better if you rested."

"That's all I've been doing," Noah objected. "How long have I been here?"

"A little more than six days." Her eyes dropped to his. His expression was thoughtful, not alarmed. "You don't seem surprised."

"Actually, I thought it had been a little longer. I remember a few things that marked the time."

"Remember?" She swallowed a gasp and schooled her features, trying not to look as panicked as she felt. "What do you remember?"

Noah wasn't going to share his erotic fantasies with her. They were embarrassingly detailed and not for repetition. At least not in the company of the woman who had figured so prominently in them. "Just people coming and going. I suppose it must have been you and Mary. Oh, and the priest."

"You remember him?" Her heart fluttered erratically against her breastbone.

He nodded. "It was kind of you to bring him to see to my soul, though it showed an astonishing lack of confidence in my recuperative powers." His eyes glinted with laughter.

Jessa had never felt less like laughing. Her smile was wan. She couldn't think of anything to say short of telling him the truth and she didn't think he was ready to hear that. She certainly wasn't ready to tell him.

"How did I get here?" he asked. "And where precisely am I?"

When Jessa tugged at her arm this time Noah released it. She stood, picking up the basin and held it in front of her like a shield. "Do you remember being shot?"

Noah's hand drifted across the blanket and touched his injured side. "Vividly." He turned slightly so he could face her. Pain tightened the full line of his mouth.

He suffered it in order to see her better. He saw the protest forming in her eyes and made a brusque motion with his hand, waving it aside before it was said. "Tell me what happened after I was shot."

Still holding the basin, Jessa sank into the rocker. Droplets of water splashed out of the bowl and fell on her hands. She didn't notice. She could only think that the web of lies was ready to be spun. "The highwayman ordered everyone back into the coach. Everyone but you and me and Gideon. They didn't think you could survive and I . . . I didn't want to leave you."

"They let you stay with me? I'm surprised."

"They threatened to . . . to hurt me and Gideon if the others returned too quickly with help. I think they meant to take me with them. After the coach left I bargained with the highwaymen. I told them that I would pay them handsomely to bring us here. I'm not certain why they believed me, but they did."

Noah regarded Jessa solemnly. "It's because you have the face of an angel."

Jessa nearly choked. She had never felt less angelic. Oh, Lord. This was going to be difficult. "The men brought us to Mary's cottage—we're not far from the post road now—and I gave them the valuables that were in Gideon's blanket."

"So they got everything that belonged to the others after all."

"Yes." She hesitated. "Do you think that was wrong of me? To give them what wasn't mine? I didn't have anything of my own."

"I'm hardly the person to judge, am I? What you did saved my life." His expression was gravely sincere. "I thank you for that."

Jessa was uncomfortable with Noah's gratitude. "You were trying to help me when you were shot. There was a debt."

"Well, it's more than been repaid." He would have said more but his body was reminding him there were more urgent matters to attend. Noah cleared his throat and looked past Jessa's shoulder. "I was wondering . . . that is, I need . . . is there a chamber pot?"

Jessa's face flamed. "Oh! Of course." She took the chamber pot out of the cupboard in the base of the nightstand. "I'll leave you alone."

Noah laughed, then grimaced in pain. "Yes. I think that would be best. I'll be able to manage." By the time he swung his legs over the side of the bed Jessa was gone from the room.

Gideon squirmed in Mary's arms as soon as he saw Jessa. "Ma. Ma. Ma."

Jessa's heart swelled and in that moment every lie she had told Noah, and would tell Noah, was justified in her mind. "Did I hear him correctly?" she asked. "Did he actually call me Mama?"

Mary laughed happily and decided it was not a good idea to tell Jessa that Gideon had been calling most everything mama this afternoon. "Would you like to feed 'im?" she asked. "I've mashed a bit of cereal."

"Yes, I'll take him." She sat down and pulled Gideon onto her lap. "Mr. McClellan is awake."

Mary nearly dropped the bowl she was setting on the table. She caught it before it slipped off the edge. "Why didn't ye say so?"

"I just did." Jessa ruffled Gideon's dark hair. "No, don't go in there, Mary!"

"Why ever not?"

"Mr. McClellan is . . . ah . . . he's occupied."

"Oh." Mary turned away from the bedchamber door, picked up her mending, and sat down heavily. "Ow long ago did 'e wake?"

"Not long." She wiped Gideon's mouth and chin with one corner of her apron. He was showing a strong tendency to like porridge only when he was wearing it. Not intimidated, Jessa waved another spoonful in front of him. When he laughed she plopped it in his mouth. "He asked a number of questions."

Mary fiddled with threading a needle. "Well, are ye goin' to tell me? What 'appened?"

"Sssh. Lower your voice. Do you want him to hear?"

"What 'appened?"

"He asked the expected: where was he and how did he get there. I told him the story we outlined."

"Good. A little truth. A little of the other."

"The other is called lying, Mary. And nothing good is going to come of it."

Mary simply let Jessa's warning roll off her back. She laid a patch on one knee of her husband's breeches and basted it in place. "Do you think you should check on 'im again?" she asked after a time.

It was not something Jessa wanted to do. She was not prepared to be engaged in further conversation with Noah McClellan. Using Gideon as an excuse, Jessa suggested that Mary be the one to peek in the other room.

Mary was only too happy to oblige. She was visibly disappointed when she found that Noah, far from being talkative, had fallen asleep. She carried out the chamber pot, ignoring Jessa's quiet laughter, and emptied the contents at the privy. When she returned to the cottage, Jessa was at the hearth, Gideon balanced carefully on one hip, stirring a kettle filled with chunks of ham and sweet beans. Mary put the chamber pot in Noah's room then returned to her mending. "That pot can be yer chore from now on," Mary said. "Seems to me I left yer family's service so I wouldn't 'ave to do the like anymore."

Jessa grinned. "You never emptied a pot during your length of service. And don't try to say otherwise. Mama used to despair that you were not meant to be a servant."

"Lady Anne was in the right of it there. She was as 'appy to see me go as I was to be gone."

"I missed you," Jessa said truthfully. "Mama may have despaired of our friendship, but I would have been lost without it."

Pleasure at Jessa's words caused the tips of Mary's

ears to redden. She bent her head quickly and applied herself to affixing the knee patch.

Smiling, Jessa took the kettle from the hearth and spooned a bowl of ham and beans for herself and Mary. Gideon was placed on the floor on a blanket and Jessa sat down to her meal, feeling as if the routine of past weeks was finally going to be resumed. Caring for Noah had meant that more household responsibilities had fallen on Mary, and Jessa was determined to right the balance of chores. Throughout the meal she and Mary talked quietly of inconsequential matters, and for the first time since the robbery their conversation was not focused on Noah McClellan.

"I think this scamp belongs in here."

Jessa and Mary both gave a start of surprise at the intruding voice. Noah was leaning casually in the open doorway to his room. He was wearing his breeches but no stockings or boots. His dropped-shoulder shirt was open at the throat and only partially tucked in at the waist. It was obvious that Gideon had interrupted him while dressing. What impressed Mary and eased Jessa's mind was the fact that he did not seem at all bothered by the interruption. His masculinity was not challenged by the squirming infant in his arms. Mary thought Noah McClellan looked supremely male. Jessa preferred not to think.

"I'll take him," Jessa said, crossing the room to Noah. She held out her hands. "You shouldn't have creeped in there," she scolded Gideon. "I'm sorry, Mr. McClellan. Mary and I didn't even know he had left the room. Oh, that doesn't sound very good, does it? I usually keep a better eye on him, but . . ."

"It's all right." Noah smiled. "He's just testing his freedom. Rather like I'm doing." He looked over the top of Jessa's head and made a short bow to Mary, then he walked to the table and introduced himself. His steps were slow and halting, marked by some pain, but he chose not to dwell on that.

Mary's mouth gaped and she stammered her name.

"I'm very pleased to meet you, Mary Shaw. I've been told you are a friend to my rescuer. I'm grateful for your care."

Jessa rolled her eyes as Mary bounded out of her chair and bid Noah sit down. She had never seen her friend simper, yet that was precisely the response Noah was exacting from Mary. "Really, Mr. McClellan," Jessa said firmly. "Do you think it's wise for you to be out of bed?"

"Very wise," he said.

"But your wound," she protested.

"I'm on the mend." He turned his attention to Mary. "Might I have something to eat?"

Mary's hands fluttered. "Of course ye can!" she said quickly. "I'll serve it right up. Oh, what ye must think of our manners." She hurried to the hearth. "Get 'im a pair of Davey's stockings, Miss Jessa. 'Is feet must be cold."

Ignoring Noah's protest, Jessa set Gideon back on his blanket and climbed the ladder to the loft. She found a pair of heavy stockings in Mary's small clothes chest and brought them down to Noah. She looked at him doubtfully. "Can you put them on?"

Because she was so patently skeptical, Noah had an urge to prove he wasn't an invalid. He took the stockings and rolled them over his feet and up his legs. Bending over made his head swim and brought a grimace of pain to his lips, but he was determined not to let her know. When he straightened, his smile was in place though a trifle wan. "Nothing to it," he said cheekily.

Jessa's look remained doubtful but she withheld comment. Mary set a bowl in front of him and a large chunk of fresh-baked bread. Noah thanked her politely and began to eat.

"Please," he said. "Sit down. I didn't mean to interrupt your meal. Hmm, my compliments. This is delicious."

Mary snorted delicately as she picked up her spoon.

"Anythin' would taste good to ye now. Ye 'aven't sipped more than 'erb tea since ye been 'ere."

Noah broke off a bit of bread and dipped it in his ham and beans. "No, I mean it. This is very . . ." He stopped and tilted his head in Gideon's direction. "There he goes again."

Sighing theatrically, Jessa scooped Gideon in her arms as he tried to creep past her.

"Ma. Ma. Ma," he said, flinging his arms wide and struggling for release. Jessa held him fast, ignored his crying, and continued to eat her own meal.

"Who is Davey?" Noah wondered aloud, watching Jessa's easy handling of her young son. It occurred to him that perhaps he was wearing her dead husband's stockings. It made him slightly uncomfortable. Beneath the table he wiggled his toes.

"Davey's me 'usband," Mary said. " 'E's in Lunnen now, lookin' for work."

Jesse was amazed at the ease with which Mary could lie. She studiously avoided Mary's eyes and concentrated on her food.

"I see," said Noah. "Then you women are alone."

" 'Ardly," Mary scoffed. "I've got family scattered all over. There's always someone to lend a 'and if me and Miss Jessa need one."

"That's good. Still, it couldn't have been easy for you to care for me. I appreciate the sacrifice you've made."

"It was hardly a sacrifice," Jessa put in. "I was returning a kindness."

"I was wondering why you didn't pay a visit to either Linfield or Stanhope. I believe I mentioned them both when we were traveling together. Someone from either of those places would have come to take me off your hands."

Jessa swallowed hard. There was nothing addled about Noah McClellan's wits. "Frankly, I didn't give it a thought. You shouldn't have been moved again anyway."

Mary pushed away from the table. "I think I'll take myself off to Sarah's for a while. Gideon can come with me. Sarah's children like to play with 'im."

Jessa felt as if she was being abandoned to the slaughter. "Mayhap I'll go with you." She made to get up but Mary pressed her back and whisked Gideon from her arms.

"No. Ye stay 'ere and explain the 'ole of it to Mr. McClellan."

"Noah," he interrupted. "Please call me Noah. And what is there to explain?"

Mary ignored most of what he said. "Ye explain it all to Noah, Miss Jessa. 'E'll understand. Mark me if 'e don't. I'd just be in the way 'ere while ye work it out among yerselves."

Noah looked from Mary to Jessa, plainly bewildered. "Explain what?" he asked again.

This time both women ignored him. Jessa's shoulders slumped and she stared at her hands in her lap. Mary busied herself bundling Gideon. Jessa had hoped the explanation could wait. Mary thought there was no time like the present.

Too quickly, as far as Jessa was concerned, Mary was ready to leave. "How could you do this to me, Mary?" she whispered frantically as she opened the door for them. "Your brain turned to mush the moment he looked at you!"

"Nonsense. Ye tell 'im everything. Just the way we planned it. I tell ye, 'e'll not mind. I see the way 'e looks at ye."

"How he looks at me?" Jessa stammered, stepping outside. "What do you mean?"

"Yer the one with maggots in your 'ead. 'E's interested in ye, I tell ye. 'Is eyes just gobble ye up."

"Mary!"

"Go back inside. 'E's bound to wonder what yer doin' out 'ere in the cold." Mary gave Jessa a small shove. "Go on wi' ye! Now! I tell ye, there's nothin' to worry about." She turned and began walking briskly in the direction of Sarah's cottage.

"Mary . . ." Jessa whispered her name forlornly. When her friend didn't turn around, Jessa backed into the cottage and right into Noah McClellan's hard chest. "Oh, I'm sorry," she said, twisting around quickly. Her eyes were on the same level as his open collar. Jessa blinked hard. "Did I hurt you?"

"No." Noah's arms lifted on either side of Jessa. Behind her, he pushed the door shut, effectively trapping her. His eyes bore into hers darkly but with a hint of laughter. In truth, he found all the furtive whispering and telling glances more amusing than mysterious. "I'd like to have that explanation now."

Jessa was not amused. She quickly ducked under his arms, escaped him, and began clearing the table.

"Jessa."

Not looking at him, Jessa said, "I haven't given you leave to call me by my Christian name."

"It's the only name I know," he said reasonably. "And that much I had to learn from Mary."

"Mary talks too much."

Noah went to the window seat and sat down, stretching his legs along the length of the bench. He plucked Gideon's blanket off the floor, folded it, and put it behind his back. "She did rather leave you in the lurch, didn't she? But what could you possibly have to tell me that's so terrible?"

Jessa itched to wipe the smug look off his face. She restrained herself. Smug he might be, but it was better than the look that would surely follow once he knew about the marriage. Jessa placed the bowls in a bucket of water to be scrubbed later and sat down at the table. She felt more comfortable with the barrier and half the length of the room between them.

"I hardly know what to tell you first," she said. "You've already asked why neither of us paid a visit to Stanhope or Linfield."

"And your explanation did not ring quite true."

Wonderful! He already suspected she was a liar. "Well, it was true as far as it went," she began. "But there is another, more important reason why I didn't inform anyone in either of those places where you were." Jessa plucked at a piece of lint on the bodice of her drab brown dress. "You see, when you met me in the coach I was running away." Her wide gray eyes lifted, imploring him. "I couldn't tell anyone where you were or I should be found myself."

Noah sat up a little straighter. "Running? From whom?"

"My husband's family," she said quietly. "Or rather, my dead husband's family. Robert passed away a few days before Christmas." Tears glistened in her eyes. Surely, Jessa thought, she would burn in hell for this. "It was the influenza. There was nothing the doctors could do for him. It was very sudden." She drew in a breath. "We lived with his parents at Grant Hall since the time we were married. Robert was an only son and the heir. Now Gideon is the heir and his grandparents want him."

Noah was at a loss as to how to comfort her. "Surely that's not a bad thing. My own parents dote on their grandchildren."

"I expect your parents don't make it known they want nothing to do with the mother of those children."

"Of course not," he said, beginning to understand. "Is that what's been made known to you?"

Jessa nodded, sniffing inelegantly. She pulled out a scrap of linen that had been bunched under the cuff of her sleeve and wiped her nose. Composing herself to show Noah that she was not without backbone, she went on. "The duke and duchess of Grantham don't want me at the hall and they've spoken rather plainly about it. They objected to my marriage to Robert and have made no secret of their desire to have me gone since his death."

"But why should they object?"

"Being an American, I doubt that you'd understand."

"I might."

Jessa pretended to look doubtful, hoping she had captured his full attention, then pressed on. "I brought nothing into the marriage. I was the paid companion to Lady Howard when Robert met me in London during the Season. It's not an accepted thing, you see, to take a position like that when one's parents are—were— quality. My father was a baron. It is not nearly so grand as being a duke but it allowed my parents entry to almost anywhere they chose. They loved parties and dancing and entertaining. I do not mean to suggest that my parents were dissolute or without any cares. They simply enjoyed life enormously and they did not look to the future—mine, or their own."

"They were in debt," Noah supplied, forming a picture in his mind of how events had proceeded.

Jessa nodded. "It could have gone on for years that way. It's not so unusual. Papa would pay a little here, a little there, and everyone was satisfied. He could charm anyone. Our estate brought in a satisfactory income and there was no cause for worry. I certainly had no idea anything was amiss."

"And then?"

"And then there was the fire." Tears clogged in Jessa's throat and she swallowed with difficulty. Her face was taut, her skin pale. "It happened two years ago, in the dead of winter. Mama and Papa were killed. The house and the stables were destroyed. Will, that's Davey Shaw's younger brother, carried me out of the house. I had fallen on the stairs, trying to get away. By the time I regained consciousness there was only a smoldering shell." Jessa's fingers toyed with the handkerchief, twisting and pulling. "I'm sorry. You're probably wondering why I'm going on. Really, I had no intention of telling you all of this. It's just that you asked why Robert's parents objected to the marriage and that's the whole of it. Everything of value was lost in the fire. The estate was parceled off to pay the creditors, and still some of them went away with empty pockets."

Noah swung his legs off the bench and leaned forward, placing his elbows on his knees. "I take it there were no relatives."

"None. That's why I took the position as a paid companion. I was fortunate to get that. Not many people are willing to have someone like me under their roof. It makes them very uncomfortable."

"I think it probably reminds them how tenuous their own fortunes and positions are."

Jessa stuffed the handkerchief back in her sleeve and folded her hands on the tabletop. "Then you can understand how Robert's parents felt. Not only had my parents been foolish enough to lose everything and to make no provision for me, but I had actually been *employed.*"

"They must have made things uncomfortable for you."

Jessa continued haltingly. "It was ... difficult. Oh, Robert tried to ease the strain. We had our own wing at Grant Hall, but I never felt as if I truly belonged there. I thought they would be more accepting once they found out about the baby. If anything, things became worse. Lord and Lady Grantham had so many plans for my child—all of which excluded me. Robert told me not to worry, but even he got caught up in their planning."

Noah found he was glad to hear it. He had been very much afraid that Robert Grantham had been a saint. Almost instantly he felt guilty for the path his thoughts were taking. He had no right to wonder what Jessa's feelings toward her husband were. Closing his eyes briefly he tried to picture his fiancée's face. The image was vague and elusive. When he looked at Jessa again his eyes were dark and brooding.

Jessa wondered at the expression in Noah's eyes. She

had no idea what had caused it to be there. "From the moment Gideon was born, Robert's parents hovered over him. I felt like a . . . a brood mare whose usefulness was over," she finished with startling frankness. Mary had suggested those words. "Then, when Gideon was only a few months old, Robert became ill. After Robert's death I was shut out of my son's life. If I visited the nursery I was accused of being overbearing. If I played with my son I was made to feel that he was becoming dependent on me. Nothing I did was the right thing."

"So you decided to leave."

She nodded. "Mary was the only one I could think of who would take me in and not give me away. Before she and Davey married they had both been employed by my parents."

"So you were coming here the night of the robbery."

"Yes. But not for the first time. I've lived here for a few months. Gideon and I were coming from Hemmings. I took him to a physician there. We weren't at the inn very long ourselves before you came in."

Noah crossed his legs at the ankle and regarded Jessa considerately. "You have no need to worry that I'll speak to anyone of this. I can understand why you felt you must share this with me, else I may have given you away without meaning to, but surely there was no reason to be so apprehensive about it." He smiled engagingly. "Have I given you the impression that I am an ogre?"

"Not at all," Jessa said truthfully, then she remembered the row with the innkeeper and amended her statement. "Well, you were rather fearsome at the inn."

He laughed, forgetting his wound. His hand went immediately to his side and he pressed the bandage and poultice. "I'm hardly likely to behave that way to you," he said.

"You don't know everything," Jessa told him, staring at her tightly folded hands.

"Oh? And what more could there possibly be?" he asked cheerfully.

His open face and kind eyes were nearly Jessa's undo-ing. She quailed at the thought of telling him the rest. Chewing on her lower lip, she continued. "The Gran-thams are searching for Gideon and me. If they find us, they'll take Gideon away and have me locked up."

"But surely—"

"No! You don't know how they are. They would have me committed to an asylum. I would never see my son again. And they can do it, Mr. McClellan. I know you think they can't. I can see it in your eyes, but you're wrong. They'll find a way. The duke and duchess are powerful and I have no means to fight them. Why do you think I left Grant Hall? They were talking about sending me away even then! I made plans to leave as soon as I discovered what they wanted to do." Jessa's fingers clenched and unclenched. "That's why I have to leave England, Mr. McClellan. Gideon and I aren't safe here. But there's not enough money for our pas-sage. Mary and Davey have been so good to me but there's no money even to borrow from them. Mary told you that Davey's in London looking for work, but she didn't tell you why. He went there to earn money to help me."

Noah held up his hands and cut Jessa off. His eyes were compassionate. He would have gone to her, put his hand on her shoulder, offered her comfort, but he didn't think he had the right. "Wait, Jessa. There's no need for you to worry about the money any longer. I'll gladly supply the funds you and Gideon require. Is that what this has all been in aid of? Have you been afraid to ask me for the money? I understand how hard it would be for you to do so, but it's a small enough request in the circumstances. You saved my life."

She wished he would stop saying that. It only made her feel worse. Agitated, Jessa stood and braced her arms on the table. She spoke crisply, wanting to finish with this at last. "I appreciate your offer, Mr. McClellan. I knew you had a generous spirit. What I didn't know was if you would live long enough to show it to me. That's why I couldn't take a chance. I needed your protection and I thought you were going to die." Jessa watched Noah become increasingly bewildered. His dark brows knit together. She took a deep breath and finished in a rush. "The priest that you remember being here wasn't brought to the cottage to hear your dying confession. He came to marry us. He did marry us," she finished on a thread of sound. She sat down slowly and waited for the explosion. It was so long in coming that Jessa began to think he was going to make her repeat herself.

Shards of gold and green glinted in Noah's eyes. He held Jessa immobile on the strength of his glance. "You're not spinning a Banbury Tale, are you?" he asked coldly in the manner of a man who already knew the answer.

"N-no."

"That priest actually married us?"

"Yes."

"Have you any idea what you've done?" he demanded.

"I told you, I thought you were dying. I wouldn't have done it otherwise." She raised her chin defiantly. "You don't think I *wanted* to marry you, do you? Well, do you?"

Noah blinked hard. My God, this wisp of woman was trying to put him on the defensive. He could span her waist with his hands and snap her in two. One part of his mind, the part that wasn't thinking clearly, he told himself, admired her spirit. "Madam, I don't *care* what you wanted or didn't want to do. The fact is you did it." He shook his head. "No," he muttered to himself. "No part of me is thinking clearly." Noah held her glance again. "I want proof. Do you have any?"

Jessa nodded. "I have the license. And there is a record of it in the church."

"Let me see the license," he said tiredly.

Jessa scrambled off her chair and retrieved the paper from her Bible in the trunk. She was slightly breathless as she handed it to him. "I assure you it's legal."

Noah merely grunted and Jessa backed across the room. "What sort of priest would perform this ceremony?"

"A very drunk one."

Noah cursed, recalling the strong smell of spirits. He stared at the license. "This isn't my signature."

"Well, I'm sure it doesn't look like your signature, but you signed it with your own hand."

"With someone's help, I'll wager."

"Yes, but the priest witnessed it."

"It doesn't matter. By your own admission he was three sheets to the wind, and I sure as hell didn't know what I was doing!"

"But you said your vows. You did!" she insisted when his mouth curled to one side in absolute disbelief.

If it were possible for a voice to smirk, Noah's did. "I vowed to stay by your side in sickness and in health, for richer, for poorer?"

"No, of course not. You were too ill to say all that."

"Then, pray, what did I say?"

"You said, 'I do.' We all heard you. Mary, Sarah, the priest. Even Gideon heard you."

"Gideon is hardly a reliable witness."

Jessa slumped in her chair again. "I know. It was a stupid thing to say."

"No matter. I'm rapidly revising my opinion of you. It fits neatly with this entire stupid affair." He tossed the license on the window bench and missed the stricken look in Jessa's eyes. "Tell me, what were your intentions if I had died?"

"I thought that was obvious. I was going to present myself at either Stanhope or Linfield as your widow. I would have told the people there that it was your last wish that I marry you, that you wanted me to go to America and this was your way of providing for me. I would have given some version of the truth to provide cause and produce the priest if necessary. I'm certain I could have found someone to believe me.''

"Oh, I'm sure that would have been the least of your problems," he said with absolute conviction. "Someone would have put you and Gideon on the first packet to America.''

"That's what I would have hoped for.''

"My God! Your incredible gall is not to be believed!''

"You asked me what I would have done and I told you!'' Her pale eyes frosted like a winter mist. "It's rather a moot point, isn't it?''

Noah strove for calm. The ache in his side was nothing compared to the steady pounding in his head. "Then let us discuss what happens now that I'm alive. That is hardly a moot point. You must have considered that I might recover.''

Jessa shook her head. "I didn't. Not really. I didn't want you to die,'' she added quickly, lest he misunderstand.

Noah sighed. Supporting his head in his hands, he massaged his temples. It was a superior headache. "No, if you had wanted me to die you could have accomplished it easily enough,'' he admitted.

That eased Jessa's mind a little. At least he understood she hadn't tried to murder him. "It's not as if it has to be a real marriage, Mr. McClellan. It would—''

"Don't you think that under the circumstances you could call me Noah?''

"Noah then,'' she hastened to agree, not wanting to fight with him over something as inconsequential as a form of address. "As I was saying, it need only be a marriage of convenience.''

"It's decidedly inconvenient.''

"But there's no reason why it should be. I only need your protection as long as we're in England. We can have the marriage annulled in America.''

"We can have the marriage annulled here," he said tersely.

"Oh, no! Please, you don't understand how difficult it would be. That sort of thing can never be dealt with quietly. The Granthams would learn of it."

"I'm beginning to think you belong in an asylum," he said cruelly.

Jessa gasped. "That was a terrible thing to say!"

"I'm hardly of a mind to be pleasant," he ground out. "Do you think it will be so easy to obtain an annulment in America? How do I explain this to my family? Better yet, *Mrs. McClellan*," he sneered, drawing out each syllable. "How do I explain you to my fiancée?"

Jessa's head snapped up. "Your fiancée? But you said on the coach . . . or rather you didn't say . . ." Her voice died as Noah's eyes narrowed.

"I think I said too much on that coach. Or not enough. Were you eyeing me even then as prospective material for your marriage?"

"Of course not! Such a thing never entered my mind!"

But something like it had crossed Noah's, and he didn't like himself for it. Or for remembering it now. If he were honest with himself he knew that some of the anger he directed at Jessa was meant to atone for his own wandering thoughts. "So what do I tell Hilary?" he asked harshly.

Jessa's head bowed. She had never thought of a fiancée. Why hadn't he said something? It seemed he had talked of every other thing. "I don't know," she said miserably. "I wouldn't have done this thing if I had known about her."

"Your scruples are of little comfort now."

"I'm sorry."

"And your apology even less so."

"I don't know what else to say."

Noah leaned back against the window and stared

down the length of his body to his stockinged toes. "Amazingly enough, neither do I."

They both raised their eyes in the same moment and stared at one another for a long time. Jessa looked away first.

Noah stood. He rocked slightly on the balls of his feet. "I am going to retire for the evening. If you have need of anything in the other room, I suggest you get it now. Frankly, I'd rather not see you again tonight. I'm still debating whether or not I should turn you over my knee."

"You wouldn't!"

Noah walked to the table and placed his hands on Jessa's upper arms. Without the slightest effort he drew her to her feet. Sitting or standing, he still towered over her. He patiently waited until she raised her eyes to his. When she did he spoke with soft, gritty intent. "If you have even the slightest bit of gray matter resting between your ears, you will not speak so foolishly or provokingly in the future. As you have pointed out, I am your husband. I can do anything I want with you . . . or to you. Anything."

Jessa stumbled backward as he released her and turned on his heel. The shudder that went through her was matched by the shudder of the door as Noah slammed it closed between them.

Well, she thought dazedly, I'm still alive. Jessa hugged herself, briskly rubbing her arms to rid the sudden chill that swept her. She should have been terrified of him, yet she realized she wasn't. Awed, certainly, but not frightened. Noah McClellan could be vastly intimidating, but Jessa doubted he was violent. She could not believe he would intentionally set out to harm her or assert any of his husbandly rights. Still, she reflected, it was easier to believe that once he was gone from the room. When he stood above her, pinning her with his sharp and angry eyes it seemed he was capable of anything.

Jessa decided that neither reflection nor idleness were helpful in her present situation. She became a veritable whirlwind of activity in order to put her conversation with Noah completely out of her mind. She washed dishes, dusted, swept the floor, drew fresh water for the animals stabled behind the cottage, and finished what was left of Mary's mending.

A gust of wind circled the room as Mary and Gideon entered the cottage. Mary stamped her muddy clogs in the doorway and gave Gideon to Jessa who had rushed up to meet them. "What 'appened?" Mary asked in a husky whisper, hanging her cloak by the door. "Where's Noah?"

Jessa pointed to the other room. "He's resting." She unwrapped Gideon, took him to the hearth, and rubbed his small chubby body to keep him warm. Gideon laughed delightedly. Jessa kissed his forehead.

"Restin', is it?" Mary said skeptically. "More like 'e's sulkin'."

Jessa turned sharply from the fireplace. "And if he is, can you really blame him? Try to imagine how he must feel, Mary!" She walked briskly to the window bench, snapped open Gideon's thick blanket and laid the blanket and the baby on the floor. "Noah didn't choose me for a wife, nor Gideon for a son! You can hardly expect him to rejoice!"

Mary's brown eyes widened. "My, my, my," she said softly, taken aback by Jessa's fierceness. "I take it some 'eated words were exchanged 'ere. Funny," she mused, "I thought 'e would take to it better."

"Well, he didn't," Jessa said stiffly. "He was as outraged as he had every right to be. He has a fiancée, Mary! Do you have any idea how I felt when he told me that? If the cottage had collapsed on my head I would have been grateful."

Mary's fiery eyebrows drew together in consternation. " 'E's betrothed? Oh, dear. That's not very good, is it?" She put a kettle on for tea and set two mugs on the table. "It would 'ave been nice if we 'ad known that tidbit. What's he goin' to say to 'er?"

"I have no idea and neither does he."

"Did ye tell 'im the 'ole thing was my idea?" Mary's furtive glance at the closed door was rife with trepidation.

Jessa let her friend squirm for a moment. "No. I was tempted, but what did it matter? I went along with you. If I hadn't agreed, we wouldn't be discussing this now." She knelt on the edge of Gideon's blanket and pulled the wandering infant back on to it. Jessa lifted the window seat and found two blocks Davey had made for his own son. Pulling them out, she dropped them in front of Gideon. He clutched one, brought it to his mouth, then threw it at Jessa. She laughed and tossed it back. Gideon rolled on his side as his arms flung wide to catch the block.

There were tears in Mary's eyes as she watched the play between Jessa and Gideon. She keenly felt the loss of her own child in that moment.

"Mary! Mary, what's wrong?"

Mary blinked back tears and gave Jessa a watery smile. "Just missing my boy," she said.

Jessa jumped to her feet and put her arms around Mary. She held her friend close, offering no words of comfort because she had none to offer. It was Mary who broke the embrace, stepping back and drying her eyes with the heel of her hand.

"Don't mind me," she said apologetically. "I've been weepy lately."

If she had been, Jessa thought, she had been successful in hiding it. A suspicion formed in Jessa's mind. "Mary? Are you pregnant?"

"I—I think so." She saw Jessa's stern look. "Yes, I'm pregnant."

"But that's wonderful! Why didn't you say anything?"

"I didn't want ye to worry for me. And I know ye would. It's in yer nature. Ye 'ave enough to think about."

"Oh, Mary," Jessa said sadly. "You worry too much about me. I'll muddle through somehow. I always do. Does Davey know?"

"No."

"But why haven't you told . . . Never mind. I know why. He wouldn't have gone if you had told him."

Mary poured boiling water into the teapot. "Aye, 'e wouldn't 'ave gone with 'is brothers and stopped the coach if 'e 'ad known. But what of it? We needed the money."

"*I* needed the money."

Mary shrugged. "It's all the same. You and Gideon are family."

Jessa knew the uselessness of arguing with Mary, especially on this subject. They drank their tea in silence while Gideon banged his blocks together. His enthusiasm for this new game brought a smile to both women. Afterward, Jessa readied him for bed and let him whimper in his cradle until he fell asleep. Mary washed out the cups and teapot and went to the loft. When she was gone, Jessa knew a terrible sense of loneliness.

Jessa stripped to her shift and laid huddled on the window seat covered with blankets. Whether she slept for hours or minutes, she didn't know, but when the noise woke her she stayed very still and waited. Intuitively she knew who had caused it. Her eyes slowly adjusted to the darkness, and she saw Noah pass in front of the dimly lit hearth. He was dressed except for his riding boots, which he carried in one hand. Jessa realized he must have dropped one and that's what had woken her. Through lowered lashes she watched him cross to the door and open it gingerly. Jessa had too much pride to stop him. She wanted to tell him he could have made all the noise he wished and it wouldn't matter to her. She wouldn't hold him back or even beg him to stay.

Then nothing she could have said would have made any difference. He was gone.

Jessa buried her face in the crook of her arm and cried.

"Dammit, Drew!" Noah cried out. "Have a care, will you? That bandage was sticking to my skin! Look, it's bleeding again!"

Drew Goodfellow snorted derisively as he tossed the bloodstained linen away and folded a fresh bandage for Noah's wound. His arthritic hands made his movements awkward, but he had patience and persistence and those qualities stood him fast. "I've a mind to send ye back to the widow," he said quellingly. "Let 'er take care of ye. There's nothing in me arrangement with yer brother-in-law that says I 'ave to play nursemaid. I look after things 'ere at Stanhope for Rae and Jericho and I ain't 'ad no complaints yet."

Noah's head fell back on his pillow and he closed his eyes briefly, rubbing the lids with his thumb and forefinger. He had abused the estate manager's kindness sorely in recent days but there was no one else he could turn to or trust. "Sorry."

"What?"

The corners of Noah's mouth lifted in a reluctant, halfhearted smile. "You heard me perfectly well, you sly fox. There's nothing wrong with your ears." The grin faded as he opened his eyes and stared at the ceiling. Jessa's face was there. The pale gray eyes haunted him and he hated her for it. Her image robbed him of sleep at night and peace of mind during the day. The more he tried to banish her from his thoughts the more her ethereal presence overwhelmed him. "What she did to me was unconscionable," he rapped out.

Drew's forehead became more deeply creased as he listened. He didn't have to ask what Noah was talking about. He had heard the whole of it nearly a week ago when Noah arrived at Stanhope in the middle of the night. Since then at odd moments, Noah continued the conversation he had begun, picking up on the last thought he had uttered aloud. Drew wisely understood that Noah was not looking for answers from him so he kept his counsel accordingly. It seemed to Drew that part of learning to talk was learning when *not* to. He made some encouraging murmurs under his breath and concentrated on applying the new bandage.

"The hell of it is, Drew, she's got no one to help her."

"Hmmm."

"But why me? I made a decision to protect her on that coach, but surely that was just simple human decency. Look how she repays me! God, what a coil! I need to have my mind clear. I'm supposed to be thinking about the upcoming convention in Philadelphia. That's what I have waiting for me when I return. A chance to shape a government! The last thing I need is this woman and her child dogging my footsteps and forever damaging my political career!"

"That's understandable," Drew said agreeably.

Noah sighed. "You know, if she were alone in this I'd not be having these second thoughts. There'd be no question but that I'd leave her here. Who would know? I wouldn't have to tell my family, or God forbid, Hilary. I could go on with my life and pretend this never happened."

"You could do that," Drew said noncommittally.

"If only it were so easy," Noah contradicted himself. "What about Gideon? How can I forget about him? I pity him, Drew. What kind of life will he know with *that* woman for a mother?" Noah paused as Jessa's face shimmered out of focus for a moment. It grated on his nerves that he had no difficulty calling it back. "The thing is, she loves her son," he said, his voice dropping to a mere whisper. "Whatever else there is to be said about that deceitful little wretch, it's clear she cares about him."

"There's that."

"Yes, but it doesn't give her the right to make a ruin of my life!" Noah massaged his forehead, trying to ease the pressure that was building behind his eyes. "Did I tell you she has the face of an angel?" He didn't wait for Drew to respond. "She does. It's hard to credit that anyone who looks so innocent could be so cunning. I'll never be able to turn my back on her, Drew." He pulled the covers up to his chest when Drew finished dressing the wound. "She'd stab me as soon as look at me."

"Aye, ye'd 'ave to be cautious."

"No," he said firmly, changing his mind again. "No, I don't. Because I don't have to take her with me. I don't have to take her son."

"No, you don't."

"And even if I did," Noah went on, switching course once more. "I wouldn't have to live with them when we arrived in America. I can have the marriage annulled there. She suggested that herself. I could settle her with a little money just so she wouldn't be a recurring nightmare in my life and then I could wash my hands of her."

"Wash 'em clean," Drew agreed moving away from the bed. He turned his head so Noah couldn't see the smile that was playing at the edges of his mouth.

Noah held up his hands and slowly turned them, studying them from all angles. Finally he intertwined his fingers and slipped the cradle of his hands behind his head. The tension in his temples eased slightly. "There's no reason I can't take her and the boy to America. Where would be the harm?"

"Where indeed?"

"And there's no reason I shouldn't enjoy myself on the voyage."

Drew frowned and his fingers stiffened on the wad of bandages he held. "Oh?"

"Certainly." Noah's half-grin was smug. "I might pity her, Drew, for the circumstances that led her to me, but that's not going to sustain my generosity for six tedious weeks on the Atlantic. If I'm going to wash my hands of her anyway, there's no reason to keep them entirely to myself, is there?''

CHAPTER FOUR

April, 1787

"Oh, Gideon! Look! It's a flower." Jessa hunkered down and tilted Gideon forward so he could view the tiny yellow bud closely. "This is the first flower of spring. See? Isn't it pretty?"

Gideon babbled appreciatively and tried to swipe at the flower.

Jessa pulled him back. "No! You mustn't pick it. No one else can enjoy it then. If the sun stays out it will spread its petals." His arms flew wide. "Yes, just like that. Do you think you're a flower, young man? Is that what you want to be? It will never do, of course."

Gideon lost interest in the flower and wrapped his fingers around Jessa's thick braid. He pulled on it so hard that Jessa's head was forced down. She unwound his fingers and trapped them beneath her hand.

"You're not very kind," she said with mock severity. "Come on, let's go inside. We've seen the horse and the cow and the chickens. The hens didn't like you much, did they? That's because you laugh at them."

Jessa stepped inside the cottage. Mary was ladling soup into three bowls. "Look! Mary has our supper ready. Isn't that lucky? See? It's a good thing we came in."

Mary rolled her eyes. "Do ye 'ave any idea 'ow silly ye sound always chatterin' away at 'im?"

Jessa was not in the least offended. "Nonsense. Gideon enjoys these conversations." She fit a bib around Gideon's chest and sat down with him on her lap. "It finally feels like spring is truly coming, Mary. Gideon and I found a flower at the corner of the cottage."

"So I 'eard."

Jessa laughed as she spooned soup into Gideon's yawning mouth. His expression reminded her of an unfledged bird. "We did rather make a fuss over it. But it's the first that he's ever seen. I thought the occasion demanded a little fuss."

Mary set her spoon down hard. " 'Ow can ye be so cheerful?" she demanded. "I promised meself I wouldn't bring it up again, but then I was never one to keep me mouth shut. It's been nearly three weeks, Miss Jessa! Are ye really not goin' to go after 'im?"

"I've already told you I'm not," Jessa said calmly. "He's probably on his way to America by now." She blew on another spoonful of the mushroom soup and slipped it to Gideon. "I think it's safe to assume that he's done nothing to give me up to the authorities. That was the only thing we had to concern ourselves with. Let it rest, Mary. I have."

"Hmmpf." Mary began eating, though she was so angry she couldn't have said what she was tasting.

"Davey left here early this morning," Jessa said, changing the subject. "Where did he go?" Mary's husband had returned one week after Noah's departure. The search for the highwaymen had cooled considerably, and Hank, Will, and Davey decided amongst themselves that it was safe to come home.

" 'E went to 'elp Will mend 'is wagon. The axle's broken."

"That was nice of him."

Mary said nothing.

Jessa sighed. "How long are you going to be angry about my decision? Because if it's longer than two more minutes, I'm taking Gideon and we're going to Sarah's for the day."

"Jessa." Mary's eyes and voice pleaded.

"It's *done*, Mary. He doesn't want us!"

Startled by Jessa's sharpness, Gideon slapped at the table and upset his bowl. The soup made a puddle on the table and dribbled to the floor.

"Damn!" Jessa swore. She pulled off Gideon's bib and began to mop up the mess, checking the baby's dimpled hands at the same time to make certain he wasn't scalded. When she realized he wasn't hurt she gave her frustration full expression. "Damn, damn, damn!"

"Dam!" Gideon mimicked loudly. "Dam! Dam!"

The tension between Mary and Jessa vanished as they exchanged surprised looks. They didn't know who started laughing first or who was the first to cry. But they laughed and cried and laughed again, and Gideon waved his arms gaily and repeated his wonderful new word.

It was the knocking at the front door that sobered them.

"You get it, Jess," Mary said, wiping her eyes. "I'll clean up this mess."

Jessa peeked out the window before she went to the door. There was an open carriage at the end of the walk and no driver. The horse had been tethered to the blistered fence. She recognized neither the carriage nor the bay mare. Uneasiness held her motionless for a moment. She needed to be reminded by Mary to see to the door.

The stooped-shouldered man on the other side of the door bore no resemblance to Noah McClellan. His inquiring eyes were deeply crinkled at the corners. The lines in his face were mute witness to his advancing years. The hands that rested on his walking stick were gnarled grotesquely by arthritis. "Ye be Mrs. McClellan?" he asked without preamble. His eyes fell to the baby in Jessa's arms. "Course ye must be. The face of an angel, that's what he said. And this be Gideon." He reached in his pocket and brought out a small, brightly colored cloth ball, which he placed in the baby's dimpled hands. Gideon clutched it and tried to jam it in his mouth. "Knew he'd like it. Just the thing for a babe his age." He raised his eyes to Jessa who was staring open-mouthed at him. "May I come in?" he asked. When Jessa didn't move, he added. "M'Name's Drew Goodfellow. I come from Stanhope."

Jessa's heart thumped madly as she stepped aside. "Please. Come in."

Drew Goodfellow leaned heavily on his cane as he entered the cottage.

"May I take your cloak?"

He shook his head, glancing around the cottage. "Thank ye, but no. I'm most always cold these days. Rheumatism, don't ye know." He stared at Mary who had not recovered her manners and stared right back. "Ye be Davey Shaw's wife?"

"Y-yes," she stammered.

He nodded. "Davey did good by himself, then. You're a fine lookin' woman."

Mary blinked, not knowing whether to be flattered or wary. "Do ye know Davey?"

"Knew his father better. Smuggled a bit in my day."

That piece of information decided Mary. She blushed becomingly and smoothed her fiery hair. "Please, won't ye 'ave a seat." She pulled a chair close to the fire. "We were 'aving a bit o' soup. Would ye like some?"

Drew took the seat but declined the soup. "I don't dare be long." He turned his attention to Jessa. "Mr. McClellan says I was to fetch you right away."

"Fetch me!" Jessa gasped indignantly.

Mary clapped her hands and practically danced across the room to Jessa's side. "Oh, this is wonderful! Do ye 'ear, Miss Jessa. 'E's sent for ye! The guvnor's sent for ye!"

"But . . ."

Mary placed her hands on Jessa's shoulders and gave her a firm shake. "Don't ye dare be thinkin' twice about this! If 'e wants ye, ye should go and be thankful for it!"

"But . . ."

Drew interrupted. "Mary's right, Mrs. McClellan. The *Clarion* leaves London in a few hours."

"In a few hours!" Jessa protested. "But I can't leave that quickly!"

"And why ever not?" Mary demanded. "It's not as if ye have a wealth of things to pack."

Jessa turned to Drew. "Would you mind, Mr. Goodfellow, if I discussed a few things with Mary in private?" Without waiting for an answer she marched into the bedchamber. As soon as the door was closed she rounded on her friend. "Mary! You're not thinking! How am I to feed Gideon on the voyage?"

"He's almost weaned," Mary said practically.

"But he still needs milk! How am I to get that in the middle of an ocean?"

"I'm sure Noah's thought of that. 'E wouldn't have agreed to take ye if 'e 'adn't made provisions for Gideon. Now, are ye goin' or not?"

"I don't want to leave you, Mary."

Mary set her jaw stubbornly. "That's a damn fool thing to say. Are ye thinkin' of the child at all? What kind of life is there for 'im 'ere? 'E's quality, just like yer quality. It's no use pretendin' you belong 'ere with Davey and me. We know it, even if ye don't. This life suits me and Davey just fine, but it ain't for ye. There's rivers what run through our lives, Lady Jessa. D'ye 'ear me? I can call ye that now. Ye be Lady Jessa and ye be knowin' that river can't be bridged no matter 'ow much we may wish it otherwise. It's a lady you are and the young one's a proper lord. That may not be important where ye be goin', but it's everything 'ere!''

During Mary's speech Jessa had been steadily backed toward the bed. Now the back of her knees bumped into it and she sat down heavily. "All right," she said at last. "We'll go."

Mary blinked back tears and the urge to hug her friend and told Jessa to wait with Drew. "I'll pack yer things. It won't take but a minute."

Jessa was pacing the floor with Gideon when Mary dragged out the trunk. Drew hobbled over to help her with it.

"I can manage," said Mary. "It's not very heavy."

"I'm not helpless," Drew said. He picked up the trunk's other strap. "Just go easy and we'll not have a problem."

"It seems we can't leave quickly enough," Jessa told Gideon once they were alone. She laid him on the window seat and wrapped him in his blanket, then got her traveling cloak and drew it across her shoulders. The black mourning gown she was wearing was as serviceable as anything she owned. In any case, she thought dully, it would have to do because the only other dresses she had had already been loaded in the carriage. She scooped Gideon from the bench and left the cottage without a second glance, afraid she wouldn't leave at all if she dwelled on it. "I need my bonnet, Mary. Is it in the trunk?"

"That black one?"

"It's the only one I have," Jessa reminded her.

"But it's such a beautiful day. Why don't ye—"

"Please, get it for me."

Mary looked at Jessa's pale face and quivering lower lip. She knew what it was costing Jessa to remain poised. She opened the trunk and took out the bonnet. " 'Ere it is. Not even crushed."

Drew turned in his seat and glanced at the stiff bonnet. "It would take a hammer to crush that thing."

Jessa smiled weakly and set Gideon on one of the plush carriage seats while she fastened the bonnet, then she sat beside him. Grasping Mary's hand, she squeezed it. "Say good-bye to Davey for me. You'll thank everyone, won't you?" she asked earnestly. "Please tell them how much I appreciate everything they've done."

Mary hugged Jessa tightly. "Of course I will. Ye'll write sometimes, won't you?"

Jessa's laugh was tense. "You don't know how to read, Mary."

"That doesn't matter. I'll find someone to read it for me. Davey knows a little."

"Then I'll write."

Mary released her. "Good." She picked up Gideon and kissed both his downy cheeks. "You do right by yer mama, young man," she told him with feigned sternness. "There's no one what loves ye better than she." She gave him to Jessa then jumped out of the carriage. Her face was streaked with tears. Jessa and Gideon were both a blur. "Go on with ye!"

Drew applied his whip to the horse and the carriage jolted forward.

"I'll want to know all about the baby!" Jessa called.

Mary couldn't speak. She nodded jerkily and raised her hand, waving them off. She kept waving even after the carriage disappeared around the bend in the lane.

To keep her mind off her impending meeting with Noah, Jessa talked to Gideon. She pointed out hickories, oaks, and pines all along the road. Occasionally there was a thatched cottage in a clearing, and Jessa made up stories for him about the people who lived there. When Gideon napped, put to sleep by the gentle swaying of the carriage and by Jessa's lilting voice, she counted sheep and cows to amuse herself and to keep her thoughts from wandering to Noah. The sun shone warmly on the back of her hands. Jessa lifted her head and let the redolent spring air bathe her face.

"Why are we stopping here?" she asked when Drew Goodfellow directed the carriage to the Rose and Crown Inn. "We're still ten miles from London."

He turned his head and looked down at her. "Aye. We be that."

Jessa continued to stare at him expectantly, waiting for an explanation. When she saw his eyes dart to the door of the inn she followed the direction of his gaze and watched Noah McClellan stride across the yard toward them. He moved exactly as she remembered— gracefully, confidently. He was wearing fawn breeches, which closely contoured the length of his legs. His dark blue jacket was unbuttoned. It parted as he walked to reveal the white linen shirt and fawn vest he wore beneath it. In one hand he carried a basket. His manner was unhurried, his posture relaxed. He was smiling. "I thought he would be waiting at the ship," Jessa whispered frantically, trying to catch Drew's eye.

"Well, ye can see that he ain't," Drew pointed out the obvious. He tipped his hat to Noah. "Good afternoon, Noah. How's our time?"

"You've done very well indeed, Drew. We should make it to the ship with thirty or more minutes to spare. Where are Mary and Davey?"

"Davey wasn't there when I arrived. Mary made the decision to stay."

This was all news to Jessa. She didn't know Mary had been asked to go. As if sensing her confusion, Drew turned to her. "I gave her Noah's invitation when we loaded your trunk. She said you'd understand that she belonged right where she was."

Jessa nodded faintly. "Yes, I understand."

"All right, Drew," said Noah. "I only wanted them to have a choice." The smile he had for his driver vanished the moment he turned his eyes on Jessa. His narrow stare took in her bonnet, the drab traveling cloak, and the mourning gown. Neither did he miss the pale gray eyes, the bone china face that was tautly composed, or the willow-thin figure that was perilously close to being gaunt. He jumped in the carriage, dropped the large wicker basket on the floor, and seated himself opposite Jessa, his back to Drew. "You can go," he told the driver. His eyes never wavered from Jessa as the carriage rolled forward smoothly. When he spoke his voice was grim and his chin jutted belligerently. "Did you wear that to spite me?"

"What?" she asked, bewildered.

"That bonnet. That dress. Your damn widow's weeds, for God's sake! If you wanted to start this arrangement off on the right foot you've made a bad beginning."

"Mr. McClellan, I—"

"Noah," he fairly growled.

Jessa sat back sharply under his cold glare. "Noah," she began again in what she hoped was a reasonable tone, "I was scarce given time to think let alone consider what I might wear. I assure you I didn't choose these clothes purposely to offend you. I was wearing this dress when Mr. Goodfellow announced himself at the door."

Far from being placated, Noah's scowl became even deeper. "Once we're on the ship you'll get rid of it. It's not the sort of thing a bride wears."

Jessa acquiesced softly. "You should know, however, I haven't many gowns at my disposal. I don't think the others will please you overmuch."

"Anything's better than what you're wearing now." He leaned forward. "Let me have that bonnet."

"But it's the only one I have."

"It's abominable. Take it off."

"You could try saying please," she said coolly. When he continued to glare at her darkly she relented. "Very well. But if I had known you could be so boorish, I wouldn't have . . ."

"Wouldn't have what?" Noah laughed humorlessly.

"Wouldn't have married me? Madam, you don't know how often I've wished I had shown you this side of me earlier!"

Seething, Jessa yanked at the ribbons of her bonnet and slapped it down on his lap. "There! Give it to the horse for all I care!"

"The horse wouldn't have it," Noah said scathingly. He tossed the bonnet over the side of the carriage and it disappeared beyond a hedgerow.

Jessa watched it go out of the corner of her eye. "My face will burn," she ventured quietly.

"Your face is too pale." Noah leaned back against the seat and stretched his legs. They nudged the basket. He took off his cocked hat and laid it beside him, raising his face to the sun as Jessa had done earlier. He closed his eyes.

Jessa fumed. He was behaving like a beast! An absolute beast! He hadn't addressed one kind word in her direction. Jessa turned her head to one side and rested her cheek against the downy cap of Gideon's dark hair. She adjusted his blanket so it covered more of his head. Why hadn't she thought to put on his bonnet? Because she had been rushed, she remembered angrily. Herded as if she were livestock. And Mary! How could Mary encourage her to go to this terrible man? And then let her go alone!

Jessa glanced down at her gown. Had he really thought she wore it to spite him? Of course he did. He thought she was rubbing his nose in the circumstances of their marriage. He thought she was still in love with her dead husband! Jessa had an urge to laugh but the tangle of lies she had told bound her tongue and silenced her voice.

Why should it matter to Noah if she was in love with the fictional Robert Grantham? Noah didn't love her, nor she him. He knew that love had nothing to do with the reason she married him. It certainly had nothing to do with Noah's decision to have her with him now.

Jessa stole a glance at her husband, the only husband she ever had or was likely to have. His eyes were still closed. His beautiful lashes fanned spiky shadows against his high cheekbones. His jaw was relaxed, his finely shaped lips slightly parted. He didn't have to worry about the sun burning his face, she thought, a shade enviously. Noah's complexion had a natural bronze cast to it. It went farther than his face, she remembered. His chest. His arms. The hollow of his buttocks. Stop it, Jessa! Stop it! She knew if Noah had opened his eyes then he would have seen her face was a veritable riot of color. Jessa gritted her teeth and stared at Drew's back. Not only were her thoughts wicked, they were unwise. There was no place in this marriage for attraction, even if it were solely one-sided.

Jessa touched the back of her head and pulled her braid forward. Gideon's sticky fingers and wet mouth had made a mess of it. She wished she had taken the time to repair it. She hadn't considered that Noah might want her to look like a bride. She hadn't known his pride would be stung by her less than fastidious appearance. Jessa sighed, tossing the braid back. There was nothing she could do about it now, but she promised herself that she would take more care in the future. Noah was concerned about the way they looked to others, and Jessa told herself she should be happy that he wanted to keep up appearances. She hoped it meant that in the company of others he would treat her with a modicum of civility.

"What are you thinking, Jessa?" Without having seemed to, Noah had been watching Jessa carefully. He regretted the harsh words he had spoken to her even as they were pouring from his mouth. Still, he was too stubborn to change course in midstream. It seemed proper that he establish his authority at the outset. If Jessa suspected how easily he could be manipulated Noah doubted he would have any peace. He had already given her more than enough proof. She was with him now, wasn't she?

Not only was Jessa startled that Noah spoke to her, she was surprised he'd done so in a tone that gave no hint of his previous anger or sarcasm. He sounded as if he were genuinely interested. Jessa glanced away shyly. There were some of her thoughts to which he would never be privy. "I was wondering why you asked me to come with you. When you left the cottage that night I thought never to see you again."

Noah grunted softly. His voice was cool. "I changed my mind."

That much was obvious. But why had he changed it? Jessa was too uncertain of his temperament to pursue it. "It was kind of you to ask Mary and Davey to join us," she ventured softly.

He shrugged carelessly.

"Well . . . I just want you to know . . . if you should think better of your decision to take Gideon and me with you, I'll understand. I mean, there's still time for you to change your mind again."

"Before we get to the ship, you mean?"

"Yes."

Noah sat up and stared hard at Jessa. "Madam, if I choose to change my mind in the middle of the Atlantic it won't be too late. I can rid myself of you there as easily as I can in London."

"Oh!" Jessa's mouth opened in astonishment. "But where . . . that is, what would I do?"

"Swim," he said succinctly. He ignored the wash of tears that glistened in her eyes and instead reached for the basket on the floor between them. Noah helped himself to a chicken leg and offered Jessa one also.

She shook her head, blinking back tears. I will not cry in front of this odious man, she told herself. I will not! "I'm not hungry," she said when he put back the leg intended for her and dangled an apple by its stem.

Noah palmed the apple and dropped it back in the

basket. "Very well," he said, raising the chicken leg to his mouth. "But you really should eat. You look as if a strong wind could carry you away."

"Then I'm surprised you haven't ordered one to do so," she said sweetly.

Noah chuckled, then bit into his food with particular relish. Secretly he applauded her show of spirit. It would be a singularly dull voyage if she never gave as good as she got.

Jessa admitted that she simply did not understand him. One moment he was delivering a sharp set down, in the next he was giving the appearance of enjoying her company enormously. It would be a singularly uneasy voyage if she never figured him out.

Noah watched the play of emotions across Jessa's face: bewilderment, confusion, uncertainty. They were there, clearly displayed in the lift of her dark brows, the gentle pursing of her finely cut mouth, the darkening of her large gray eyes. Noah's eyes slid over her clear and delicate profile as she turned her head aside. Tendrils of corn silk hair brushed coyly past her ear. He would have liked to curl one around his finger just to test its softness. He had never tried to deny that he found Jessa an astonishingly lovely woman. Even if she appeared to be unaware and unaffected, Noah was not. He would have been a fool not to take measure of the attraction he felt toward her. Noah knew he was vulnerable, but there was a certain strength in knowing one's own weaknesses. He would have to deal with Jessa from a position of strength. He could accept nothing less.

Gideon woke just as they reached the outskirts of London. He was cranky, wet and hungry. Noah had Drew stop along the road while Jessa changed Gideon's diaper. Jessa silently thanked Mary for her foresight in laying Gideon's things on top so she didn't have to burrow through the trunk to get what she needed. She was apologetic about her son's crying, but Noah brushed her concerns aside. When Drew whipped the horse forward again Noah took Gideon onto his own lap.

"Your arms must be tired," he said.

They were, but she didn't think he would have cared. Gideon was only partially satisfied by his dry condition. He didn't need words to let everyone know he was hungry. Noah burrowed one hand in the basket and brought out a silver flask. He slid off the cap with his thumb while he bobbled Gideon on his knees.

"Oh, no!" Jessa cried out, alarmed as Noah tilted the flask to Gideon's rosebud mouth. "He can't drink spirits!" Gideon grasped the flask awkwardly in his dimpled fingers as Noah urged it toward his mouth. A droplet of milk splattered on Gideon's chin. "Oh," she said again, much relieved.

"Indeed," Noah said dryly.

"You could have told me what was in there."

"What? And deprive myself of the opportunity to see you take up cudgels for your son?" In his arms Gideon sipped contentedly from the flask which Noah kept tilted at low angle. "I didn't think you'd want to nurse him on the open road so I came prepared." His eyes dropped casually to her breasts.

Jessa drew her cloak closed. "I never nursed Gideon."

Noah's lip curled. "Why not?"

Jessa realized he thought her reasons for not nursing Gideon were rooted in vanity. "Because Lady Grantham would not let me," she invented. "She said it was common. Gideon had a wet nurse."

"I see. But you left Grant Hall when Gideon was quite young. How could you—"

Jessa felt heat creeping into her cheeks. "I couldn't feed him myself by then, if that's what you mean." Really, this conversation was beyond everything decent. "Mary nursed him. Her own baby died shortly after I arrived at the cottage."

"I'm sorry," he said solemnly. "It must have been very hard for both of you."

"Yes, it was." Jessa's fingers fidgeted in her lap. "Mary was weaning Gideon."

Noah nodded. "Well, since Mary isn't with us I suspect Gideon has had his last suckle," he said practically. "He does very well from the flask. Ooops! I spoke too soon." He wiped Gideon's chin with the handkerchief Jessa quickly thrust in his direction. "I think you've had enough. Better now?" He capped the flask, dropped it in the basket, and raised Gideon on his shoulder to burp him.

Jessa simply stared at him, dumbfounded.

Noah grinned at her expression. "I told you, one cannot have a dozen nieces and nephews without learning something of import from it. As to this problem with his milk supply, which I think you were trying to get around to delicately, it's already been handled. The *Clarion* is carrying some livestock in addition to her regular cargo."

"That must have cost you dearly."

"Are you trying to discover if I'm wealthy? Well, I'm not. Certainly not by your late husband's standards."

"I didn't mean—"

"My family owns the *Clarion,*" he said tersely. "She's made several trips between Virginia and London since I've been here. Once I concluded my business at Stanhope I had only to wait for her return." Gideon belched loudly and Noah set the child on his lap. "So you see, the only price I've paid for your passage is my freedom. And, yes, that has cost me dearly."

Jessa gritted her teeth in silence. There was simply no talking to the man! She heaped a dozen curses upon his head and plotted his death by fire, flood, and pestilence. All of which were a quicker end than he deserved.

Seemingly oblivious to her plans for his demise, Noah was taking great delight in pointing out the sights to Gideon. Drew had had to slow the carriage as the traffic on the London streets became clogged with horses, wagons, curricles, and vendors. People shouted, selling their wares. Somewhere a driver yelled for a passerby to get out of his way. A gang of poorly clothed urchins chased one another down the street, laughing shrilly and dodging traffic with heart-stopping agility. Fashionably dressed matrons with their giddy daughters in tow glided in and out of shops in search of tasteful gowns, jaunty hats, and colorful ribbons and feathers. Men gathered outside a coffee shop to continue an argument that had not been settled inside. A dowager berated her servant for stepping on the hem of her gown. Above the din a church bell tolled the hour.

Gideon was less fascinated by what was going on around him than he was by Noah's face and his rich baritone voice. His wide blue eyes rarely wavered from Noah's.

Drew Goodfellow was the first to see the closed carriage bearing down on them. He cursed loudly seeing the other driver did not have control of the matched set of bays. People were scattering, pressing themselves against buildings to avoid being crushed by the dangerously swift carriage. Drew tightened the reins on his animal and urged the mare over to make room for the other vehicle. He thought he had avoided a collision when the matched team veered suddenly and came perilously close to brushing his carriage. The other vehicle tipped and rode several feet on two wheels. Before it righted its rear wheel caught the edge of Drew's carriage.

Although they were all jostled Jessa felt most of the impact. She screamed as she was thrown sideways, narrowly missing being pitched from the carriage altogether. She felt Noah's arm circle her waist and then she was being pulled roughly onto the seat beside him. The grip she had on his jacket was bloodless. She buried her face in his shoulder.

"Are you all right?" he asked tightly. "Jessa? Are you hurt?"

She shook her head, but didn't lift it. People were

beginning to gather round the carriage. She didn't want to look at them.

"We're all of one piece, Drew," he told his man. "No, stay where you are. I'll have words with the other driver myself. You disperse the crowd." Noah extricated himself from Jessa's hold and gave her Gideon. The baby was squalling loudly, but other than being frightened, he was fine.

Jessa huddled in one corner of the carriage and hugged Gideon to her breast as Noah jumped out. She watched him stride purposefully toward the other vehicle, which had finally halted its reckless course some seventy-five feet down the street. The driver had bounded down from his perch and was opening the door to his passengers. "Oh, no! No!" Jessa shook her head in disbelief as her eyes fastened on the carriage's crest. It was the Penberthy carriage! "Noah!" she called urgently. "Noah, please come back here!"

Noah stopped and turned. "Drew will help you," he called back.

"Noah! Please. I need you! Now!"

Caught by the very real fear in her voice, Noah broke off in a run toward her. The crowd, which Drew had not been successful in moving, parted swiftly as Noah returned. "What is it?" he demanded roughly, taking in her china-white face and trembling lips.

"Please," she whispered. "I want to leave." She glanced over his shoulder as Lady Barbara Penberthy alighted from the carriage. Edward was directly behind her. Jessa took Noah's hand, squeezed it, and raised her eyes beseechingly. "We must go! That carriage—"

She didn't have to say anything more. Noah reacted swiftly. Jessa's safety was his responsibility now. He tapped Drew on the back and sat down beside Jessa. One arm circled her protectively. "Drew! We're off!"

"Aye!" came the reply. He raised his whip and people moved aside. The carriage rocked and shot ahead.

"Hurry!" Jessa said. Her eyes were tightly squeezed shut now. "Oh, please hurry!"

Noah spared a glance for the man and woman standing beside their broken carriage. They were both staring open-mouthed in Jessa's direction. The man started to run toward them, but something his wife must have said halted him in his tracks. He thrust his hands into the deep pockets of his jacket, shoulders slumping, and turned around.

Jessa did not open her eyes until the carriage rounded a corner. "Did they see me?" she asked.

"I'm afraid so," Noah said. "Was it the Granthams?"

"What?" Jessa could not think clearly. She almost forgot all the lies she had told.

"Were they your late husband's parents?"

"Oh. No. No, they are friends of the Granthams. Lord and Lady Penberthy." Why had she told him that? She could have given any names at all and he wouldn't have known the difference. What if he had heard or read about Adam Penberthy's abduction? Would he begin to suspect the truth? She shuddered violently, suddenly cold. Gideon whimpered softly in her arms. "Do you think they will follow?"

"No. Their carriage has a broken wheel. Lord Penberthy made a stab at running after us."

Jessa hated to hear Lord Edward's name on Noah's lips. She didn't think Noah ever forgot anything. "He did?"

"Yes, but the lady called him back. He obeyed like a whipped dog." *Much the way I did when you called me,* he thought a shade resentfully.

Edward Penberthy was no one's whipped dog, not even Lady Barbara's. Jessa could have told this to Noah but she wanted to avoid any more discussion of the Penberthys. "Will we be at the ship soon?"

"In a few minutes. We're almost at the wharves now. I'll send Drew on his way as soon as we've unloaded your trunk and you're safely on board. No one will be able to trace us."

"Thank you." Her breathing steadied. She lifted her face and smiled faintly. "You have been—"

Noah lowered his head and captured Jessa's mouth with his own. The kiss was light. A mere tasting. Passionless because Noah willed it to be so. When he pulled away he saw a measure of color had returned to her face. Her lips were moist where she had quickly run her tongue over them. His eyes assessed her critically and somewhat coolly. He decided his kisses became her and wondered if that were necessarily a good thing. He would have to give it some thought.

Drew pulled the carriage up beside the *Clarion*, unaware of what had just occurred between his passengers. Someone from the ship called to him and he returned the greeting. Noah slipped his arm from around Jessa, patted Gideon on the head, and leaped down from the carriage.

Dumbly, Jessa took the hand he offered and alighted onto the wharf. Why had he kissed her? He was going to make her insane, turning hot and cold the way he did. It was a fiendishly clever plot, Jessa decided. By the time they reached America he could have her committed to whatever passed for an asylum there. She smiled to herself. At the end of six weeks in the company of Noah McClellan, she would probably offer to go willingly. She stood quietly off to one side while Noah thanked his driver.

Noah took Drew Goodfellow's gnarled hand in his. "Jericho said you were someone I could trust. Thank you for listening to all my arguments these past weeks."

Drew glanced at Jessa and the babe. "It's a good thing yer doing, taking them, that is. Things are bound to work out."

"Things are temporary, Drew," Noah reminded him. "I've never pretended that I'm a saint." He squeezed

Drew's hand very gently. "You'll be keeping in contact with Jericho, won't you? About the estate?"

"Aye. I'll let him know if there's anything amiss, just as I always have. If today's little uproar causes any problems I'll let ye know about that, too."

"Thank you." Noah released Drew's hand and called to someone on the ship to unload Jessa's trunk and take the basket. He waited until that was accomplished before going to Jessa's side. Hooking an arm through hers, he waved Drew off then escorted his wife and child up the gangboard of the *Clarion*.

The *Clarion* was a three-masted schooner, sleekly lined from bowsprit to stern. She was built for relatively light loads and speed. Her cargo holds had been filled at one time or another with spars and tallow, silk and tobacco. She had hauled rum from Jamaica, tea from India, and guns and men for a rebellious nation. The *Clarion* waited proudly in the harbor now, her gleaming white sails only slightly puffed in the spring breeze.

Jessa stepped onto the gently swaying deck and turned happily to Noah. "Gideon will love this. It's like a huge rocking chair!"

Noah paled a little and the smile that touched his lips was humorless. "Ay, yes . . . just like a rocking chair. Come, I'll introduce you to the captain and show you to our quarters."

Jessa followed him to the mizzenmast, where a small, wiry man was bent backward at the waist looking up into the yardarms. His hair was iron gray, queued at the nape of his neck, and tied with a black grosgrain ribbon. He put a hand to his forehead to shade his eyes from the sun and shouted an order to the man above.

"Aye, you're a clumsy one!" he yelled, shaking his head. "No, t'other way around. Take the rope to starboard! That's it. Let her drop. Have ye ever sailed before?" He sensed Noah's presence and straightened, rolling his eyes heavenward and extending his hand at the same time. "New man. Name's Booker. I'll have to speak to Porter. I don't know where he finds these men." He dropped Noah's hand and made a spritely bow to Jessa.

"Jessa, I'd like you to meet Captain Jackson Riddle. He's in command this trip. Jack, this is my wife and our son Gideon."

"Mr. Riddle," Jessa said pleasantly, nearly glowing because Noah had said *my* wife and *our* son. "I'm very happy to meet you."

"A pure pleasure for me it is, Mrs. McClellan. And what a fine looking boy." He rocked on his heels, hands at his back, and his bright green eyes shifted to Noah. "Your brother is going to be sorry he didn't come himself this time, what with you waiting here with your bride and son and all."

"I'm sure Jerusalem is just as happy to be with Ashley," he said.

"Has she had her baby then?" Jessa asked.

Noah was surprised Jessa remembered. She must have engraved his every word spoken on that damnable coach in her mind.

"I'm sure she has," the captain answered politely. "Salem was dogging her every step when we set sail. He never gets used to it, that one doesn't." He bathed in Jessa's bright laughter. "Well, if there's anything I can be doing for you, ma'am, just let me know. It's been gratifying to meet the woman that snatched our Mr. Noah from Miss Hilary Bowen. Won't her nose be tweaked proper."

"You've said quite enough, Jack," Noah bit out. "We'll take our leave." He took Jessa's elbow in a less than gentle grip and hustled her to the entrance to the lower decks. "I'll have him abandoned on an iceberg," Noah muttered under his breath. "I'll damn well have him keelhauled. I'll—"

"I'm sorry, Noah," Jessa interrupted softly.

"You should be," he agreed tersely as they descended the narrow steps to the companionway. "If it weren't for you, I'd—" He came up short when Jessa stumbled on the stairs. "Dammit, let me have Gideon before you break his neck as well as your own."

Jessa passed the baby to him. "No, you wouldn't want me to do that, would you? It might deprive you of the pleasure of doing it yourself."

Noah scowled. "Keep that sassy tongue in check, Mrs. McClellan, or I may take my pleasure right now." He brushed past her, cradling Gideon in his arms, and went to the end of the companionway. The door to the cabin was slightly ajar. He pushed it open with his shoulder and stepped inside.

Jessa followed hesitantly. When she entered the cabin she could only stare open-mouthed in astonishment. She had never expected anything like it. Never! She felt Noah's eyes on her, watching her critically. Did he expect her to find fault with these accommodations? "It's lovely, Noah. Really, it's quite grand."

"Salem bought the *Clarion* after the war with an eye toward his comfort," he explained. "He did not want to give up sailing, but neither did he want to leave Ashley and the children behind every time he left. He had this section of the ship gutted and rebuilt to suit his needs."

If one discounted the cottage loft, the cabin was bigger than Mary's home. There was a large sitting area sectioned off by an oriental rug. Two comfortably worn lounging chairs had been bolted to the floor. A black lacquered table sat between them. An oval dining table sat off to one side. A candelabra had been affixed permanently to its center. A huge mahogany wardrobe stood against the wall on Jessa's right. Beside it was a small cupboard for the chamber pot. A large porcelain bowl and pitcher sat on its polished surface. Above it hung a mirror and an open shelf filled with linens for washing and drying. There was a small version of a Franklin stove in the corner for the cold Atlantic crossings. Behind Jessa, on either side of the door were shelves filled with books, maps, and manuals. In front of her was a large bowed window made up of two dozen smaller panes of glass. All along the bottom of the window was a storage bench, its top cushioned by thick red upholstery. Jessa turned to her left. There were two doors along the wall. Each of them was closed. Jessa didn't really care what was beyond them. It was what was centered between them that held her attention.

The bed was enormous.

Jessa felt a prickly sensation all along the nape of her neck. She turned to see if Noah was watching her. He was. Her eyes slipped back to the bed. She tried to be casual about inspecting it. After all, it wasn't as if she would be sleeping there with him. The window seat was more than sufficient for her needs, many times longer and wider than the one she had used in Mary's cottage. So what did it matter about the bed?

Its design was simple, ingenious really. She had never seen anything like it. It jutted out into the room at a right angle to the wall. There was no head or foot board, nor were there any tall corner posts. The bed rested on a platform of sorts that housed four long drawers, two to a side, one on top of the other. A thick down comforter served in place of a counterpane. Three pillows, covered with lace shams, lay at the head. A brightly colored quilt was folded neatly at the foot of the bed.

"Come, I'll show you Gideon's room." Noah's voice was husky. He had been staring at the bed, too. "Through here." He opened the door nearest Jessa just to the left of the bed. He stepped aside and let her in, then followed. The room was tiny, L-shaped, but more than sufficient for Gideon's needs. Two small bunks filled the short part of the room. A crib was braced against the long wall. Beneath it were more drawers and beside it, a changing table.

"It's perfect!" Jessa exclaimed. "Your brother's thought of everything!"

"Yes, well, Salem is rather thorough. And Ashley had

a hand in it." He pointed to Gideon. "Will he cry if I put him in the crib?"

"Probably, but it's all right. He missed his morning nap and only slept a little while in the carriage. Look, he can hardly keep his eyes open now."

Noah leaned over the crib and gently laid Gideon in it. He loosened the baby's blanket, adjusted his tiny shift, and wiped a bubble from Gideon's parted lips. The baby didn't make a sound.

Jessa and Noah backed out of the room quietly. As soon as Noah closed the door Gideon let out a piercing wail. Noah started to go back inside. Jessa stopped him, placing her hand on the sleeve of his jacket. "No, just leave him. He'll be fine."

Noah was skeptical. He was used to being the doting bachelor uncle, not the father—even temporarily. The roles were decidedly different. "All right," he said. "There's one more room to show you."

Jessa followed as Noah skirted the bed and went to the door on the other side. This room was also L-shaped. Its purpose was purely functional. There were two large wooden tubs on the floor. A copper kettle hung from a hook by the door. Several pails were stacked in one corner. "This is where Ashley washes everyone's clothing and where you can have a bath. Fresh water is strictly for drinking. Bathing and washing has to be done with salt water. It dries the skin and will probably irritate Gideon. It bothered Ashley's youngest children."

"I'm sure it will be fine," Jessa said, just thankful for a place to wash and hang Gideon's diapers. She didn't have many for him. She suspected she would be spending a great deal of time in this room. "How do I get the water?"

"Someone will bring it to you. I'll talk to Jack about it."

"I could get it myself. I'm used to hauling water. I don't mind."

"I do," he said tightly. He turned on his heel and

retreated to the main cabin. "I'm going on deck to find what they've done with your trunk. I'll send someone down with it. When it comes, do something about that gown. Whenever I'm gone I want you to keep the cabin door locked." He drew the bolt back and forth to make certain it worked properly. "I know most of the men on board, but not all of them. You're the only woman they'll be seeing for at least six weeks. There is no sense in tempting fate."

Jessa took a few tentative steps forward. The ship was rocking more noticeably now. They were already moving down the river. She could feel the deck coming up to meet her feet.

"Yes? What is it?" he asked brusquely.

"May I go on deck with you?" she asked. "Just to say farewell? I know you don't want to be seen with me in this dress, but I'd—"

"The dress has nothing to do with it. I brought you on board in it, didn't I? You can say your farewells over there," he said, pointing to the window. He shut the door and was gone.

Jessa stared blankly at the closed door, bewildered by Noah's shifting moods. She threw the bolt with a vengeance. "It would serve him right if I locked him out." The window seat turned out to be quite comfortable. Jessa sat with her legs curled under her and one forearm resting against the glass. She was glad for the knock at the door when it came. She hadn't expected to feel so ineffably sad watching London slip away from her.

The boy who dragged in the trunk was just a few months shy of his thirteenth birthday. He tore off his cap and held it in both hands in front of him, waiting for Jessa's orders. His yellow hair was cropped short so that it could not be pulled back at his nape. Strands of it fell in his eyes. He was thin and scrappy and Jessa's heart was tugged by his shy, darting look. She directed him to put the trunk at the foot of the bed and had to suppress the urge to assist him. He looked too proud to think kindly of any offer she might make.

"Thank you very much," she said gravely.

He ducked his head and shifted his weight from one ill-shod foot to the other. "If'n that's all, ma'am . . . I'd best be goin'." He started to bob past her.

"Wait." Jessa put her hand on his shoulder. "What's your name?"

The boy bit his lip and eased himself from under Jessa's hand. "I'm called Cam," he said diffidently. "I've got to be goin', ma'am. The cap'n wouldn't like it much if I was here too long. Mr. McClellan neither."

Jessa sighed. She should have known that Noah had something to do with the boy's skittishness. "Very well. Thank you."

Cam jammed his knit cap on his head and bolted out the door. He hesitated in the companionway until he heard Jessa lock herself in, then he raced topside, his heart near to bursting. Lord, but she was a pretty one! No wonder Mr. McClellan told the men to keep their distance.

Noah's hand curled around the scruff of Cam's neck as the boy raced past him. "Whoa! Did you take down the trunk?"

"Yes, sir!"

"And she locked the door after you were gone?"

"Yes, sir! I didn't have to remind her, sir!"

Noah nodded and released the boy's neck. "Do you know much about taking care of babies, Cam?"

"Babies?" He wrinkled his nose, thought better of it, and stared up at Noah stoically. "Yes, sir. I have four brothers and three sisters, all younger than me. I figure I know about babies."

"Good. You can help my wife on occasion with Gideon."

Cam's shoulders sagged. "But, sir, I come to sea to get away from the little ones."

Noah laughed, though the sound was strained. "Oh,

Cam, you might as well learn now there's no escaping one's destiny." The boy looked at him oddly. "Never mind, go on with you. Find something to do before Jack puts you in the sails." When Cam was gone Noah went to the starboard taffrail and leaned against it heavily. He kept his eyes on the horizon.

"Thought I'd find you up here," Captain Riddle said. He leaned against the taffrail also, but his back was to it. His arms were crossed against his chest. He watched his crew as he spoke to Noah. "Couldn't stay below, could you?"

Noah shook his head. "No. Not this early in the voyage."

"You're a piece of work all right."

Noah merely grunted. His stomach roiled.

"How's Mrs. McClellan taking it?"

"She seems fine. In her words, 'It's like a huge rocking chair.'"

"Aye. It is that. The sea cradles her ships like they were newborn babies. Rocking . . . and rolling . . . and rocking."

Noah turned his head toward the captain and scowled. "Have your fun, Jack. Just remember I'll have my revenge when you least—"

Jackson Riddle bolted away from the taffrail just as Noah leaned over the side and proceeded to lose what remained of his breakfast and all of his midday meal. "Aye, you're a piece of work," he chuckled. "Christened after a man who stayed afloat through the worst storm mankind's known, and you can't help but turn green watching the tide come in." He walked away, humming under his breath. "Should have kept your eyes on the horizon."

CHAPTER FIVE

"You should have asked who I was," Noah said brusquely when Jessa opened the door to him. He handed her the wicker basket he had had on the carriage and without another word went straight to the bed and lay down. He cradled the back of his head in his hands and stared at the ceiling. His face had lost a little of its color. His lips were pale.

Jessa gripped the basket's handle tightly, holding it in front of her. "Are you feeling quite the thing?" she asked cautiously, unsure of his mood.

Noah felt as if a mule had kicked him repeatedly in the gut. "Quite the thing," he gritted.

"It's just that you've been gone so long. . . . I was worried that something had happened."

Something had happened all right. He had made a fool of himself in front of the crew. It didn't matter that those who knew him had seen it all before. It had long been a standing joke that his Christian name and his temperament for the sea were not matched. Usually he accepted the irony more gracefully. But that was before Jessa. He found nothing amusing about making an idiot of himself in front of this woman. "I'm fine," he repeated, making an effort to smile. "I wanted to come earlier but I was . . . occupied."

Jessa sat the basket on the table. "Would you like something to eat? There's plenty of chicken and beef. Oh, good. There's milk left. Gideon will be howling soon for his dinner. I'll mash a bit of this meat for him."

"Jessa."

"What?"

"Just leave everything. Cam will be here with dinner for you and Gideon."

"But this food, we shouldn't waste it."

"Save the fruit. Give the rest to Cam."

"Oh, you think it's spoiled already. Hmmm, I think you're right. The beef has turned a bit green at the edge. And the chicken is sickly gray. It was—"

Noah bounded off the bed, threw back the bolt, and was out the door before Jessa could finish her sentence. Behind him he could hear Jessa's soft laughter. Damn her! She had known very well what was wrong with him. She had gone on and on about the food just to needle him.

When he returned to the cabin an hour later Jessa was clearing dishes from the table and placing them on the tray Cam held out to her. Gideon was sitting on the oriental rug, clutching the cloth ball Drew made for him. He dropped the ball and slapped his hands against the carpet when he saw Noah.

"Feeling better?" Jessa asked. When Noah merely glared at her she turned her sweet smile on the boy. "That's all, Cam. You can take the tray away now. Thank you for bringing the water, too. Oh, and when the cook can spare you, bring a pot of tea and some crackers for Mr. McClellan."

Cam bobbed his head and left the cabin quickly. Lord! But if Mr. McClellan ever looked at him the way he did his wife, he'd expire on the spot!

"I've turned down the bed for you," she said. "Cam

says you usually sleep through the first day or so on board.''

"Cam talks too much.''

"And you say too little. The next time I ask you if you are feeling quite the thing you should tell the truth. At first I thought it was your wound that was bothering you.''

Noah sat down on the edge of the bed and removed his shoes. He took off his jacket and vest and tossed them on Jessa's trunk. "My wound's healed.''

"But I didn't know that.''

"Well, you know it now. And a lot of other things besides.'' He lay back on the bed.

"Is there anything I can do for you?''

"No.'' He closed his eyes and rubbed his temples with the tips of his fingers.

Jessa scooped Gideon off the floor then went to stand by Noah's side. "I could do that for you,'' she said quietly. "Mama had megrims. I used to rub her temples. She said I had a soothing touch.''

Noah glanced up at her. Her eyes were enormous, very gray and very earnest. He remembered her gentle hands. "All right. I think I'd like that.''

Jessa skirted the bed and crawled on from the other side. She put Gideon at the center. He immediately pulled himself toward Noah and slapped at his thigh. The ball was of no interest to him anymore. Jessa started to move him away but Noah caught her wrist. "No. Let him be. I don't mind.'' Then he tugged on her hand and drew it to his face.

Jessa folded her legs to one side and spread her skirt so that it lay all around her. Noah shifted to rest his head in her lap. His eyes closed as soon as her fingers sifted through the thick cap of chestnut hair and touched his scalp.

"You changed your gown,'' he said softly, a hint of tiredness in his voice. "I'm glad.'' The dove-gray gown she wore now still reminded him of mourning but it also matched her eyes. For that reason alone he could tolerate it. He also noticed she had combed her hair and replaited it. It fell over her shoulder. The tip nudged the underside of her breast.

"Your orders were rather clear on the point of my gown."

"Orders? Was I as demanding as all that?"

What was this? Remorse? "You were a veritable tyrant." She kept an eye on Gideon. He had laid his tiny fist in the center of Noah's palm and was preparing to play with Noah's wiggling fingers.

"As bad as that?"

"Yes."

"Hmmm. That feels good. What did you do with the black thing?"

"I gave it to Cam for the rag barrel. I thought it would save you the trouble of throwing it overboard."

"Good."

Jessa's fingertips made light circles on his temples. "Noah, why didn't you come to the cottage yourself today?"

"I didn't want to force your decision one way or the other."

"Were you surprised to see me when we got to the inn?"

"Not half as surprised as you were to see me. I take it you thought I would be waiting for you at the ship." He grimaced slightly as Gideon bit the pad of his thumb. "Hey! What are you doing to me?"

"Gideon! Stop that!" She extricated the infant from Noah's hand and moved him away. Gideon promptly crawled back, cleared the obstacle of one of Noah's legs, and squeezed himself between Noah's calves. He put one thumb in his mouth and closed his eyes, sucking contentedly. "I should put him in his crib," Jessa apologized.

"No. He's comfortable. I'm comfortable." He reached for her hand and drew it back to his forehead.

It was all very well for both of them, but Jessa was feeling distinctly uncomfortable. Noah was not her mother and touching him evoked decidedly different feelings. Her fingers threaded through his hair, curled around his ears, and stroked the strong column of his neck. She searched for something to say. "I was surprised to hear from you at all," she said finally. "I thought you had already gone to America."

"I still had business to finish at Stanhope. If you're wondering why it took so long for me to call on you . . ."

"No. That is, I don't care . . . really, it's all right."

". . . it's because I only came to my final decision this morning," he finished bluntly. "When you didn't hound me at Stanhope I realized you were giving me a choice, either that or you thought better of all your scheming."

He couldn't make what he thought of her much plainer than that, she thought dismally. "When you left the cottage I thought you had already made your choice," she said quietly.

"So did I."

Jessa wondered what had changed his mind, but she didn't ask and Noah didn't offer. She continued to knead his shoulders, his head, his temples. Her fingers sifted lightly through his hair even after he fell asleep. When Cam entered the cabin carrying a tray with tea and crackers Jessa raised a finger to her lips, smiled gently, and pointed to both her sleeping men.

Cam set the tray down, backed out of the room on tiptoe, and closed the door quietly. For the first time since he left home at age eleven, Cam longed for his mother's arms.

When she was certain Noah was sleeping deeply, Jessa eased herself from beneath him. She picked up Gideon and placed him in his crib. He woke briefly while Jessa changed his diaper but the steady swaying of the ship lulled him to sleep again, just as she had known it would. There were extra blankets in one of the drawers beneath the bed. Jessa made a place for herself on the window seat. Her dress was folded neatly over the back of one of the chairs. She was hesitant to place it in the wardrobe next to Noah's things. He didn't need any more reminders that she was a fixture in his life—at least for the present. Slipping out of her shoes and stockings, she padded to the bed and arranged the comforter over Noah. She marveled that he could look so innocent when he was sleeping. It made her bold. She whispered her thanks, touching his cheek gently.

Afraid lightning would strike her, she quickly blew out the hurricane lamps and laid down on the window seat. Her toes curled under the blankets and when she finally fell asleep she was still smiling.

Noah was not in the cabin when she woke. The bed was made and the tray of tea and crackers was gone. In its place were two place settings, one of which had already been used. He must be feeling better, she thought sleepily, if he could eat this morning. She burrowed her face in the pillow beneath her without wondering how it got there and stifled a yawn with the back of her hand. Stretching, Jessa turned on her back. One long look out the window warned her she had slept longer than was her wont.

Gideon was not in his crib. Jessa breathed a little easier. At least he hadn't been neglected; Noah would have the babe with him. Jessa went back into the other room. As she passed the table she saw that in addition to the two place settings there was also a bowl half filled with porridge and a cup with a little milk left in it. She smiled wistfully, wishing she could have seen Noah feeding Gideon. What Gideon lacked in manners he more than made up in enthusiasm for his food.

Jessa washed her face, combed out her braid, then plaited it again. Yesterday she had discovered Mary hadn't packed any of her pins. There was nothing for it but to tie the end with her ribbon and let it fall down her back.

She was standing in the middle of the room, barefoot and in her cotton shift, looking around for her gown, when Noah came in the cabin. Jessa didn't know which way to turn first. She backed toward the window seat to get a blanket to cover herself.

"What you have on is modest enough," Noah said. The eyes that slid over her were casual in their regard, but not without a certain amount of interest. Behind him he pushed the door shut and bolted it.

"Just the same, I'd like to dress."

"I don't think so." Noah wanted to keep her slightly off balance. For what he had to discuss it was necessary.

"What?! You can't stop me!"

"Do you know where your gown is?"

"I'll get another," she said defiantly and started toward the trunk.

"I've taken your clothes out of there." He saw her glance dart to the wardrobe. "And if you make one move in that direction I'll just haul you back. Since last night proved you have an aversion to being with me, I assume you'd rather not have me touch you."

Bewildered, Jessa backed away from the wardrobe. Her hands fluttered uneasily to her side. What on earth was he talking about? His eyes were glinting dangerously and his mouth had thinned so that it seemed a mere slash across his face. That he was fiercely angry, she didn't doubt. But why? Because she had slept on the window seat? Surely that's what they agreed to. Hadn't they? "I don't understand," she began. "What—"

"Sit down." He pointed to one of the dining chairs.

Jessa's chin came up and she stamped her foot. "I will *not!* Where is my son, Mr. McClellan? What have you done with Gideon?"

Noah advanced on her.

Jessa held her place.

Noah was impressed that she didn't bolt.

Jessa was too frightened to move.

Noah picked her up at the waist and tossed her over

his shoulder. Before she could react he had kicked out a chair and was dropping her into it. Hard. He shoved the chair back to its place so that Jessa's middle was pressed against the table's edge. "Now stay there!"

Jessa stared at her hands which she had placed on the table to brace herself. Beneath the table she could feel her legs quivering. She dug her toes into the carpet. "I've always despised men who use force as a substitute for reason," she said softly, with great dignity.

"And I've always despised liars," he shot back. Noah gave her chair an angry shake because he didn't have his hands around her neck and he wanted to shake something. He let go of the chair abruptly and cursed under his breath. He hardly recognized himself. In his family he had always been considered the sensible one, levelheaded. Until now Noah had accepted that view, believing himself to be rational, logical, and even-tempered. He doubted Jessa would describe him that way. Damn, but he couldn't even think of himself in that light any longer. He could barely think. Period.

Noah pulled out the chair on Jessa's left and sat down. When he spoke his voice was even, threaded with a measure of calm. "Gideon is with Cam. He is being entertained in the captain's cabin. No harm will come to him. Cam is completely responsible and he knows where we are if the babe needs anything."

Jessa nodded faintly. Perhaps if Noah had told her Gideon was creeping up the mainmast she might have objected. Given his present mood, she wasn't even certain of that. She continued to stare at her hands, afraid to look in any direction but down.

"There are a few issues that must be resolved between us," Noah began. "And I didn't want to be distracted by the babe."

"Issues?" she ventured timidly.

Noah reached in his vest pocket. "This being the first issue." He opened his palm at an angle. Lord Gilmore's gold timepiece slid out of his hand and skidded along the polished surface of the table. "Do you recognize it?" When Jessa didn't reply immediately, he prompted, "I found a number of other valuables in your trunk. Rings. Coins. Shall I get them now? Perhaps it's just the timepiece you don't remember?" He started to get up but Jessa's voice brought him back.

"It belonged to Lord Gilmore," she said lowly.

"Ahh, another mystery unraveled. I didn't know the young fop's name. Now let's see if you can solve another puzzle. I seem to remember you told me that you had given all the spoils to the highwaymen. How is it they ended up in a leather purse in your trunk?"

"Mary must have put the purse there." In that moment Jessa could have cheerfully wrung her friend's neck. She knew Mary's intent had been to help, to give Jessa something of value so that when Noah left her in America she would not be penniless. "I didn't know about it."

Noah thought that over. It was probably true as far as it went. Jessa seemed to be very good at telling the truth—up to a certain point. "Yes, well it doesn't explain how it came to be in Mary's possession, does it? What about the highwaymen?"

"Obviously I lied about giving it to them," she said sharply. "That's what you wanted to hear, isn't it?"

"Don't try to put me on the defensive," he said. "What I want to hear is the truth."

"That *is* the truth. I lied."

He lifted her chin and pointed her face toward him. "The entire truth," he said meaningfully. "If you did not give the highwaymen the booty, how did you persuade them to take me to Mary's cottage? And please don't tell me you merely begged prettily and they relented. My brains aren't completely addled. There's much more to it than that." He released her chin and watched her eyes drop away from his.

Jessa formulated a half dozen lies in her mind and none of them served.

"I'm waiting, Jessa. You were part of the robbery, weren't you?"

She nodded.

Noah released a long sigh. "And Mary?"

"She wasn't part of it, not directly. Davey and his brothers were the highwaymen."

"I see. So Davey hadn't gone to London looking for work. No wonder Mary didn't choose to accept my invitation. A bit of conscience must have struck her. Though we can't say the same for you, can we?" He didn't wait for an answer. The question was purely rhetorical. "Was it Davey who shot me?"

"No. His youngest brother. Will." She raised troubled eyes to him. "It was only the second time they took him to the road."

"That explains it then," he said with a trace of sarcasm. "An attack of nerves."

Jessa said nothing. It had been stupid to try to defend Will.

"And you, Jessa? How many times have you played the grieving widow and mother for them, suggesting with just the right touch of pathos that the passengers should get rid of their weapons, suggesting with just the proper touch of innocence that their valuables would be safer with your son?"

Only the once. I swear it!" she said when Noah's mouth curved derisively. "Just the once. I did it to prevent violence! Hank thought my presence would have a calming effect on the passengers."

"It worked for awhile."

"Believe me, the last thing any of us wanted was for someone to be hurt! We're not murderers!"

"The coach driver was shot."

"That was an accident! Davey was as shocked as I that he actually hit something. He was never meant to be the high toby. He's a smuggler by trade."

"Oh, yes," he sneered. "Now *there's* an acceptable calling."

Jessa ignored that. "And Will, well, I've already explained about Will. But we didn't abandon you!" she added hastily. "You would have bled to death if we hadn't taken you to the cottage!"

"I wouldn't have been shot if you and your friends hadn't been on the road that night," he reminded her pointedly.

Jessa's eyes pleaded with him to understand. "But you know why we were there. I needed money. Davey, Hank, and Will were only trying to help me secure passage to America."

"Your reasons make you no less a criminal."

Criminal. There, it was out. He had said it. Jessa went cold all over. Only her palms were sweating. "What are you going to do?"

"Do? What do you think I should do?"

There wasn't enough money in the world to make Jessa answer that question. She was not such a fool that she would sentence herself.

Noah regarded her thoughtfully. She was truly frightened, completely defeated. What did she think he was going to do? Turn the ship around and give her over to the authorities? Given the trepidation with which she was looking at him, apparently that was precisely what she thought. Noah would have liked to let her worry a little while longer, but there were other, and in his mind, more salient issues before them, and he would not hold this matter over her head now. Neither would he forget it. She was making it easier for him to go on as he planned. When the time came, washing his hands of her would not be so very difficult.

"I'm not going to do anything, Jessa," he said softly, a shade too softly. "I wish you would have told me the truth at the outset, but that is neither here nor there. I can't even say if it would have made a difference in my decision to take you home with me, so there is no use refining the point. We're here. We're together. And, for the length of this voyage at least, we're married."

Jessa was still reeling at the shock of his generosity when she heard his last words. The hopeful light that had flickered briefly in her eyes was extinguished. "W-what do you mean?" she stammered.

Noah fiddled with Lord Gilmore's timepiece, flicking it with his forefinger so that it spun and wobbled. "As long as we're on this ship I mean this marriage to be a real one, Jessa," he said finally, catching her gaze and holding it.

"You should have warned me ... said something before you allowed me to board. You forced me to make a choice without telling me everything."

"We're even then. You did the same to me."

"Yes, but this is ... this is different," she finished lamely. "We ... we agreed it was a marriage of convenience."

"No, that's what you called it. I didn't agree at all. And you are forgetting that convenience doesn't necessarily preclude ... friendship."

Friendship? He was talking about friendship! Jessa almost leaped from her chair and threw her arms around him. "Yes," she said eagerly. "I should like it if we were friends."

"Or mutual respect," Noah went on, watching her carefully as he expanded on his theme. He was going to enjoy her discomfort immensely. "Or loyalty ... honesty ... attraction ... passion."

"P-passion?"

Noah nodded, his eyes narrowing slightly as she stumbled over the word. Was she still so in love with her dead husband that she could not imagine feeling anything for another man? Or did she find him so repulsive that she could not imagine feeling anything for him in particular?

"Do you mean for us to share a bed?"

"At the very least I mean for us to do that. I don't expect you to sleep on the window seat again, Jessa.

Ever. Neither do I expect you to spread your thighs for me at my whim."

Jessa gasped at his crudity. "Don't speak—"

"What I do expect," Noah continued, pushing his chair back and standing, "is that you will lower your guard enough so that we might come to know one another. I am not insensible to the fact that you have recently lost your husband. I can appreciate that you may feel you are betraying his memory. But I hope you are not insensible to the fact that you are, however briefly, married to a flesh and blood man. I have certain expectations regarding our arrangement. You would do well to honor them. To twist a trite phrase: you have made our bed and now we will lie in it—together!"

Jessa felt her disadvantage keenly. Noah was on his feet, towering over her, while she sat attached to her chair like a barnacle. She couldn't say where she found the courage, it was simply, suddenly, there. Pushing back her chair with a force that rippled the rug, Jessa stood. It was not enough. Even standing her body was shadowed by his. She stepped back, out of his shadow and glared at him. Her spine and shoulders were stiff. He was going to learn right now that she would not tolerate his tongue lashings. She had had enough of his arrogant assumptions.

Noah didn't appear at all perturbed by the feral look in her eyes. He hadn't even noticed it. His eyes had dropped to the twin peaks of Jessa's breasts. The thin cotton shift was less modest than Noah had earlier believed. He felt very, very lucky.

"Would you please look at me?" Jessa asked indignantly.

Noah's smile was wicked. "I believe I am."

Agitated, she stamped her foot. Her breasts bobbed slightly beneath the shift. She saw his eyes widen and his wicked smile deepen. Jessa folded her arms across her chest and glared at him.

Noah sighed. He lifted his eyes and tried to look

grave. He was only partially successful. His smirk showed he was clearly unrepentant. "You have my full attention."

It was the smirk that was her undoing. She was so angry that mere words could not express her thoughts. "Oooooh!" She laid her hands squarely against his chest and shoved him backward. Before Noah recovered Jessa spun on her heel and stormed over to the window seat. She wrapped herself in a blanket then turned her back on him. A tear pricked her closed eyelids. And another. Another. She furtively wiped them away. When Noah came up behind her and rested his hands on her arms with the lightest of touches, Jessa found she was simply too weary and heartsick to pull away.

Sensing her small surrender, Noah's arms crossed in front of her and gently urged her off balance until her weight rested against him. His arms and thighs cradled her. His chin rested against the top of her head and he felt the silkiness of her pale, corn silk hair for the first time. "Do you know," he said lowly, "I've always despised women who use force as a substitute for reason." He sensed, rather than saw, her watery smile. "You nearly knocked me off my feet back there."

"You deserved it," she said dully.

"Hmm. I rather think I did."

"You were making light of me."

"I'm afraid I was."

"You want everything your own way."

That was truer than Noah was prepared to admit. "What do you want, Jessa?" he asked instead.

"I want to sleep on the window seat."

"No."

"I want you to sleep on the window seat."

"No."

"Then I want you to promise not to touch me!"

"No!"

"You can't really want to share a bed with me," she

argued weakly. "You already know I'm a criminal and a liar. Those are hardly mere peccadillos."

"Hardly," he agreed. He didn't require reminding.

"I can't be a wife to you, Noah . . . I can't be intimate."

Since she was already enfolded in his arms, since he was already coming to know the sweet curves of her body, her statement didn't carry much weight with Noah. He was willing to exercise caution and a little patience. "We'll see. It's only for the length of the voyage, remember," he said, making certain she understood the terms clearly. "If it—"

"No!" She pulled away and turned on him. "No, I mean it, Noah. I can't be what you want me to be. Not now! Not ever!" Oh, God! What if he forced her? How was she going to explain having a son *and* being a virgin? Hysterical laughter nearly bubbled to her throat, and she covered her mouth with her hand. She felt as if she were going to be sick.

"Jessa," he said calmly, watching her carefully. "You seem to have some peculiar ideas that you're in a position to dictate terms to me. Nothing could be further from the truth. I can be reasonable to a certain point. You would do well not to push me too hard or too long. I doubt you will enjoy the consequences. Am I understood?"

Jessa's mouth gaped. She considered all the things she wanted to say and finally swallowed them all. In the end she nodded slowly.

Noah smiled briefly, satisfied. "Good. Now, why don't you dress and I'll bring Gideon back. Cam has probably had his fill of the imp by now." At the door he paused and delivered his parting shot. "And while I'm demonstrating that I can be reasonable and give you some time, I still intend that we should share a bed. The window seat is out of the question."

Jessa glared at the closed door. "Coward!" she called heatedly. She glanced at the bed, color rising in her face. At least its dimensions were enormous. There was a gift in that. She probably wouldn't even notice that he was in there with her. "Liar," she whispered. "You would notice him if a half mile were stretched between you."

The wardrobe was divided into two large sections. Jessa opened the left door and found Noah's clothes. She lightly passed her hand across the garments. There was no faulting his taste in clothes, she thought miserably. No wonder he had despised her bonnet. His jackets were satin and velvet, braided with gold or silver trim on the wide, turned back cuffs. There were matching vests, some brocaded, others stylish in their simplicity. His shirts were folded neatly on the bottom shelf. They were soft to the touch. Jessa shut the door quickly.

The other side of the wardrobe held her gowns—and someone else's. Jessa's heart sank as she stared at the beautiful clothes. The colors caught her eye: hunter green, pale rose, violet, sky blue, ivory. The fabrics were linen, taffeta, velvet, satin, and silk. Soft cotton chemises with lace trim at the neck and sleeves hung from some hooks at the back of the cupboard. Ruffled pantalettes and stockings shared one shelf. Kid slippers, silk brocade shoes, and dainty black leather half boots filled the floor of the wardrobe.

She found her own scuffed and well-worn shoes buried in the pile. Her stockings were easy to pick out because they bore signs of mending. The dove-gray dress seemed colorless next to the others. Jessa pulled it out.

She had just managed to slip into her shoes when Noah returned with Gideon. Cam was behind them, carrying a tray with her breakfast on it.

"You didn't bolt the door," Noah said in the way of a greeting.

Jessa ignored him and held out her hands to Gideon. The little boy shook his head and continued to clutch Noah's shirt. Jessa felt as if she had been kicked in her midsection. She turned away quickly to hide her distress.

Noah directed Cam to put down Jessa's food and take

away what remained from his own morning meal with Gideon. When the boy was gone Noah spoke gently. "I'm merely a novelty, Jessa. He's just an infant. He didn't mean anything by it. Is this the first time he's ever refused to go to you?"

Jessa nodded. She sat at the table and smoothed a linen napkin over her lap. Her smile was a trifle too bright to be sincere. "I suppose I should be grateful to be able to eat my meal in peace."

Noah accepted her words at face value, though he knew she was bitterly hurt. He felt an unwelcome tug of pity for her. What sort of life did she think she could make for herself and the child in the United States once the marriage was legally ended? Did she expect to go back to the highway to support herself and her son? Noah rolled his eyes at the thought. Heaven help us all if she does! He set Gideon on the rug, hunkered down, and rolled the cloth ball past the boy. Gideon watched it go past, then bounced backward on his bottom to get it. The sight of his chubby legs pushing against the rug for purchase made Noah laugh and brought a genuine smile to Jessa's lips.

Noah reached in his vest pocket. "Cam whittled these for Gideon." He held up five wooden beads strung together on a thin strip of leather. "Can he have them?"

"Is the string secure? Gideon would as soon eat those beads as play with them."

Noah chuckled, testing the strength of the leather. "I've noticed just the opposite is true at mealtime." The rawhide held against his best efforts, but just to be certain he tied another knot. He glanced at Jessa, and when she nodded he dangled the beaded necklace in front of Gideon. The infant slapped at it and Noah pulled it back, teasing. The play continued and Gideon's cherub face turned red with frustration because he could never quite grasp the beads.

"Dam! Dam! Dam!" he cried, kicking his heels and

giving every appearance that he knew precisely what he was saying.

Jessa was mortified.

Noah was astonished and not a little upset. "I'll speak to Cam about his language in front of the babe," he said apologetically. "I never thought—"

"Cam's not to blame," Jessa said hurriedly. She nudged her scrambled eggs with her fork, moving them around her plate. "I'm afraid he learned that from me."

Brows raised slightly, Noah regarded Jessa with new interest. "You actually cursed?" he said, pretending to be appalled.

Jessa knew he was laughing at her. "Very well," she said lightly, "now you know yet another of my faults." Gideon was wailing soulfully for his toy.

"I'll be certain to make a record of it," he said dryly, making her wonder if he were serious. "Here, Gideon. I'm giving you these beads because they were Cam's gift to you and not because you're pitching a fit." Noah dropped the beads, Gideon blabbered in delight, and Jessa merely shook her head, amused by Noah's reasoning.

"You don't think he understands that, do you?"

Noah shrugged. "Not a word. Still, I was teasing him first. We'll sort it out later when he pitches his next fit." He stood, shaking out his legs, and took a seat at the table. "Is your breakfast satisfactory?"

"Yes." She swallowed a mouthful of eggs. "I appreciate you caring for Gideon this morning. He can be quite a handful. I don't usually sleep so late. I hadn't realized I was so tired."

"I doubt you slept very well. It couldn't have been comfortable on the seat," he said pointedly.

Were they back to that again? Jessa buttered a muffin to occupy her attention then set it on her plate because she realized she wasn't hungry any longer.

"You don't eat enough," he noted, eyeing the discarded muffin.

"I manage."

"Eat!"

"Mr. McClellan! If that is the tone you adopted with Gideon I'm surprised he ate at all!"

"If you call me Mr. McClellan again I'll adopt another tone entirely!"

Behind them Gideon had stopped amusing himself, fascinated by the adult voices.

They became aware of their interested audience simultaneously. Jessa's voice dropped to a harsh whisper. "You are insufferable! Your fiancée cannot have been thinking when she said yes! She should thank m—"

Noah stood so abruptly that his chair tipped over. He ignored it as well as Gideon's consequential howling. "And your *husband*," he gritted, "must have been thankful for the end when it came!" He stormed out of the cabin. "And lock the damn door!"

Jessa sank back into her chair and tossed her napkin on the table. "Oh, Gideon, do be quiet!" she snapped. The infant was startled into silence and Jessa was instantly remorseful. She righted the chair then sat on the floor beside him. The string of beads found their way into her hands and she sifted them through her fingers like a rosary. "I don't know how we go on from here," she said softly. "I really don't."

Noah stayed away from the cabin all day. Cam was in and out, bringing food, removing dishes, hauling water. Jessa enjoyed his company even though each visit was brief. She washed things for Gideon, read a little from a book that looked interesting and was not, and when she spied a hole in the elbow of Cam's blue and white striped shirt she held him still long enough to repair it. Mostly she was bored, and because she was bored, she worried.

By the time Noah returned her nerves were as taut as the sails overhead. She didn't look up from her book as he entered and braced herself for some comment about the door not being locked again. When it didn't come she worried even more.

"Gideon already in bed?" he asked. He sat on the edge of the bed and kicked off his shoes.

Just like that, she thought, astonished. Like they had never said horrible things to one another. She nodded in answer to his question.

"Will he wake if I go see him?"

"Probably not. I put him down a while ago."

Noah padded softly to the baby's room and opened the door a crack. Gideon had pushed off his blanket and his nightshirt was bunched about his thickly padded bottom. Noah righted the shirt and blanket and touched the back of his finger to Gideon's downy cheek. He stayed that way, staring at the baby for a long time before he went to join Jessa.

He sat down on the opposite lounging chair and stretched his legs, crossing them at the ankles. "Have you found something good to read?"

Jessa shut the book and laid it on the lacquered table. "No, it's very dry."

Noah picked up the book and read the embossed letters on the leather spine. *"A Treatise on the Industry of Pilgrims to the New Worlde."* He set the book aside. "It does sound rather dry," he said pleasantly.

"Please, stop this," Jessa pleaded. "I shall go mad if you just go on and on as if everything were right between us!"

Noah frowned a little, uncertain if he had heard correctly. "Pardon?"

"Please, Mr. McClel—," she caught herself, "Noah, I mean. See, I will say it any way you please, from the top of the mainmast if you insist. Noah! More loudly if you wish it. *NOAH!*"

"Jessa! What maggot have you got in your head now?"

"Maggot?" she laughed shrilly. "A little Noah maggot. It has wormed its way inside my head so that I can call no thought my own! How dare you come in here

and smile and be pleasant and act for all the world
like—''

Noah cut her off. ''Are you taking me to task because
I'm *not* arguing with you?'' he asked incredulously.

Well . . . since he put it that way. Jessa knew she was
behaving like a recalcitrant child. Gideon had better
manners and more sense than she. ''I'm sorry,'' she
apologized softly. ''For everything. The things I said
today . . . earlier . . . they were unforgiveable. You have
been so kind to Gideon . . . so patient with him. I had
no—''

''But not to you,'' Noah said with a trace of self-
loathing. ''I haven't been kind or patient with you, have
I? No, you don't need to answer. I know the truth well
enough.''

''It doesn't matter about me,'' she said earnestly. ''I
tricked you, lied to you, you nearly died because of me.
Your feelings are understandable.''

It occurred to him to tell her that she didn't know
anything about his feelings. Instead he said, ''If I were
you, I would not look for opportunities to remind me
of your perfidy.''

Jessa blinked, struck by his cool tones. ''I shall
endeavor not to be a constant thorn in your side,'' she
said gravely.

Noah wasn't certain he liked the sound of that. ''The
thorn,'' he said quietly and without a hint of his previous
coolness, ''is the price one pays for having captured the
rose.''

Startled by his pretty words, Jessa stared at him. ''A
rose?'' Was that squeak her voice? ''Me?''

''Hmm-mm. A delicate white rose.'' His eyes slid over
her face and the petal smooth skin of her cheeks became
tinged with pink. ''Now you've gone and confounded
my description,'' he chuckled. He left his chair and sat
on the rug at Jessa's feet. She was forced to move her
legs to one side so he could lean against the seat of the
chair. Noah waited to see if she would know what he

wanted, waited to see if he had to direct her hands to his shoulders and neck. He didn't. There was only a moment's hesitation on Jessa's part, then he felt her fingers slide across the nape of his neck. He bent his head forward. "Why didn't you wear one of your other gowns today?"

"I have but three gowns," she said. "I did warn you that my wardrobe was sadly limited." When she had fled the Penberthys she had only taken her most serviceable dresses, all of which were from the period she had spent in mourning for her parents. They were terribly somber when compared to the others in the wardrobe, but they had suited the anonymity she sought at Mary's cottage.

"But what of the others? Weren't they to your liking?"

Jessa's hands fell still briefly. "The others? But . . . but I thought they were a gift for your . . ."

"For Hilary? You can say her name, Jessa. We can't tiptoe around one another for the next six weeks. No, the gowns aren't for Hilary. For one thing, Hilary is four inches or more taller than you and rather . . ." He trailed off, searching for the right word.

"Statuesque?" Jessa supplied. Unconsciously her fingers tightened on Noah's shoulders.

"Hmm-mm." It was true, Noah thought, that Hilary was more, well, more filled out than Jessa, but he had not forgotten how Jessa had felt against him this morning or how her thin cotton shift had laid against her breasts. That vision caused Noah a bit of discomfort and he changed his position slightly.

"And the second thing?"

"What?"

"You said there was a first thing," she reminded him practically. "Usually that is followed by a second thing."

"Oh. And the second thing is that I am not in the habit of buying clothing for my fiancée. It's not the done thing." Even to his own ears he sounded self-righteous and priggish.

"Then why—"

"Even on this ship there are appearances to maintain. I find it odd to remind you you're my wife when it was clearly you who initiated the event."

Actually it had been Mary, but Jessa was wise enough not to split hairs. "The gowns are lovely. I admit I admired them earlier."

"Did you try any on?"

"Oh, no! I never thought they were meant for me!" That they were intended for her confused Jessa greatly. Noah had spoken of making his decision to take her with him as if it had been made at the last possible moment, yet the gowns seemed to suggest otherwise. They could not have been fashioned in a few hours time. He must have wrestled with his conscience for weeks and changed his mind any number of times. Jessa cautioned herself not to make too much of the gowns. Their presence signified no permanency. He was not letting her forget that he intended to let her make her own way once they were in America.

"Well, they are," Noah said a trifle gruffly. "Did you find Gideon's things?"

Jessa had chanced upon several drawers filled with shirts, nightgowns, diapers, bonnets, and socks, but she had never considered they were meant for Gideon. "Do you mean the clothing beneath the crib?"

"Of course I mean the clothing beneath the crib. Don't tell me you thought it was for Hilary as well?"

With great daring Jessa gave the back of Noah's head a little shove with the heel of her hand. "Don't be stupid," she said indignantly. "I thought it was meant for Ashley's children."

"Oh."

"Oh, indeed. I'm not in the habit of making free with what doesn't belong to me, you know."

That statement brought Noah's head around. One brow was lifted for ironic effect and his green-gold eyes regarded her skeptically. "I can think of a few fellow travelers who would take exception to what you've said. Lord Gilmore, for one."

"I should have known you would bring that up," Jessa said, angry with herself for giving him the opening. "But I *did* say I wasn't in the habit of doing it."

Noah's slightly cynical expression lost its edge of humor as he studied her almost dispassionately. He turned around again and leaned his head against Jessa's thigh. "Wear the rose gown tomorrow." He paused and thought about honey catching more flies than vinegar. "Please."

Jessa wondered at the effort that *please* cost him. "All right." Quite without thinking her fingers brushed his temple and traced the outer edge of his ear.

A shiver shimmied down Noah's spine. Did she think she could hold him at arm's length by teasing him like that? She obviously didn't know what she wanted. Well, he did, and if it meant setting her a little off balance tonight he could do it for the sake of future gains. Noah let a long comfortable silence yawn between them before he finally said, "I m going to bed, Jessa. Are you joining me now?"

It was a foregone conclusion that she would share his bed. They both knew it. Jessa was very well aware that Noah held every advantage in a contest of wills. But Jessa was a strategist. If she were to ultimately win the war she decided there were moments when she would have to give some ground. She also knew Noah would be suspicious if she surrendered too easily to any of his dictates. Therefore, in response to his question, Jessa said, "Not right now. I'd like to write a letter to Mary first."

Noah did not like her delaying tactic but he accepted it. As he readied for bed Jessa sat at the table and began her letter to Mary. She hardly knew what she wrote; her mind was too filled with Noah. He circled the cabin once, blowing out the lamps until the only light came from her table. Out of the corner of her eye she watched him shed his shirt, stockings, and breeches. He threw back the covers on the bed and crawled in wearing only his linen drawers. Where is his nightshirt? she wondered. She was not even aware that she had penned the question to Mary until she reread the letter. Embarrassed by her wandering thoughts, she scratched it out.

Jessa worked on her letter for some fifteen minutes after Noah had retired. She thought he might badger her into finishing quickly, but each time she glanced in his direction his eyes were closed and he gave every indication that his intention was to sleep. It gave her the confidence she needed to prepare for bed.

Jessa removed her gown and put it in the wardrobe along with her shoes and stockings. She washed her face then extinguished the last lamp before she stripped off her undergarments and slipped into her nightshift. Easing back the comforter, Jessa slid into the bed and lay on her back at the very edge of the feather tick.

"You're going to fall out," Noah said sleepily. He burrowed a little deeper into the covers and plumped his pillow.

Jessa was so surprised to hear his voice that she nearly did fall. "I'm fine," she said stiffly. Her body was as rigid as a corpse.

Noah's short laugh was husky. "Jessa, there's plenty of room in this bed. There's no need for you to hug the very edge."

"When I could be hugging you, you mean."

"I'm shocked at the way your mind works. The thought had not occurred to me." When lightning didn't strike him for that lie Noah turned on his stomach and closed his eyes. "Good night, Jessa. Pleasant dreams."

Jessa could hardly believe her ears. He was going to sleep! While she had never truly believed he would force himself on her, she had thought he would make her lie beside him, perhaps take her in his arms, perhaps . . . Enough! she admonished herself. Jessa had no patience

with her own confusion. Angry with herself, she turned
on her side away from Noah, closed her eyes, and gritted
her teeth. Pleasant dreams, she thought. Hah! No
chance of that.

But Jessa had no conscious control of her dreams,
and the one from which she eventually woke had been
decidedly pleasant. Reality fell far short. The thick bed
of clover in which she had been lying was nothing more
than the plump mattress. The warm band of sunlight
that had caressed her turned hip was Noah's arm thrown
possessively across her. The butterfly wings that had
tickled her cheek were Noah's fingers making a light
trail across her skin.

Jessa's eyes opened wide.

"Before you throw a tantrum," Noah said softly, "you
should know that I did not initiate this." He was
propped on one elbow and his eyes were grave. He
continued to stroke her cheek. The night was very clear.
Starshine cast a pale blue light in the cabin and across
Jessa's face. He had been watching her for a very long
time. He knew the fine contours, every angle, every
plane, of her face. His left leg was caught between both
of hers. Perhaps when she realized she was holding him
and not the other way around she would believe what
he said. "You curled around me like a kitten, Jessa."

"Oh," she said in a small voice. "Did you . . . did we
. . . that is, did—"

"No."

"Oh."

"Did you really think I would take you while you
slept?"

She shook her head. His eyes seemed more gold now.
Cat's eyes. They held her prisoner more surely than the
arm about her waist. She could only stare at him.

"I want you," he said, "but I am not so selfish as to
take you like that."

"You . . . you said we should come to know one
another before . . . before we—"

"I did say that, didn't I?" Noah's head dipped slightly. "There are many ways to know a person," he cajoled, bent on manipulating her to his own ends. There could be no better time than now to show her how he intended that they should go on. In the space of a heartbeat his mouth captured hers. The kiss was gentle, taming. He did not press his advantage even when Jessa offered no resistance, no struggle. His lips touched the corner of her mouth, her cheek, her jaw. He raised his head and looked down at her. "That wasn't so terrible, was it?"

"N-no."

"You're my wife, Jessa," he said deeply. "I would be well within my rights to take you whether you say to me yea or nay. You know that's true."

She nodded. Panic darkened her eyes and she lowered her lashes, too proud to let him know she was afraid of him.

Noah cupped her chin and raised her face. "Look at me." When she did, he went on. "But that's not what I want now." He almost believed it himself. "Let's talk of learning, not taking. There has to be a beginning. This is ours. I want to hold you. I want to know your touch and you to know mine." Noah's green-gold eyes held hers. "Nothing against your will," he added, confident that his will would eventually win hers over. His thumb passed along the lower edge of her lip. "What say you to that?"

Jessa felt her common sense dissolving beneath Noah's liquid, lullaby tones. Her mouth parted. She touched the tip of her tongue to his thumb.

CHAPTER SIX

Noah's soft groan was born of desire and it surprised him that he could feel such a deep wanting for the beautiful jade who shared his bed. The sound was caught by Jessa's mouth, trapped by her lips, as his mouth covered hers. His tongue traced the line of her lips, parted them at the center, and when she drew in a tiny startled breath he pressed deeper. Her mouth was sweet, her response shy. That surprised him also. She had not been so shy in her sleep. His tongue stroked, teased, tasted, and he sensed her following his lead.

The arm that lay across Jessa's waist lifted slightly. Noah's palm slid onto the curve of her hip and rested there without moving, waiting to see how she would respond. His mouth lifted, hovered, then recaptured hers. He felt the smooth line of her calf rub against the length of his leg. He held himself still.

Jessa liked the kissing very much but she was wary. The only comparison she had to Noah's kiss was the one Edward Penberthy had leveled on her mouth as he pressed her against the nursery room door. She had been forced to suffer that kiss. Scoring his cheek with her nails had kept her from suffering another. In spite of her fear she never considered clawing Noah. In one small part of her mind she knew that what she was doing was dangerous, yet what were her choices? If she pretended to give a little of herself now, then perhaps the promise inherent in her actions would hold him at bay. Only what she was doing did not feel very much like pretending. Her insides were uncurling. It was the most confusing experience of her life.

Gently, so gently, Noah nudged Jessa's hip until she turned fully on her back. Now his leg that had been caught between hers covered them. Noah's weight rested against her lightly; his thigh pressed hers.

"You can touch me, Jessa," he said. He found himself wondering how different he might be from her late husband. Was she comparing his kisses? That bothered Noah. Since he had awakened with Jessa in his arms he had never once thought of Hilary. There was more than a hint of anger in the next kiss he pressed on Jessa's mouth. He wanted to banish Hilary and Robert Grantham. It was done the moment Jessa accepted his kiss as she had all the others, eagerly and passionately.

Jessa's arms curved around Noah's shoulders. Her hands cupped the back of his head, fingers threading in his hair. She was distantly aware that she had begun to feel safe in his arms. Hadn't he said he only wanted to touch? Jessa wanted to be relieved of responsibility for what was happening. She chose to take Noah at his word. Because he had promised that he would not force passion's final intimacy on her, Jessa discovered she very much wanted to know everything that came before it.

Her hands slipped to Noah's chest. She traced the breadth of his shoulders, felt the warmth of his flesh beneath her palms. His arms were taut and smoothly muscled. Beneath her questing fingers his male nipples hardened and she felt a peculiar tension pass from him into her.

Noah's hand curved to the underside of Jessa's breast.

It filled his palm and he ached to strip away her shift and bring the tip to his mouth. Her breasts were full and high, firm and faintly swollen with the force of her desire. His thumb rubbed against her nipple. Her shift added an abrasiveness that was not unpleasant. She moaned softly as the tip became pebble hard beneath his touch.

Noah's head bent as Jessa's lips parted. He teased her, nuzzling her ear, nipping the sensitive cord of her neck. His mouth touched her temple, her eyelids. When their lips finally met it was a hard, bruising kiss of barely checked desire that brought their bodies flush to one another. The contact sent a frisson of heat through both of them.

Swallowing a sob, Jessa pulled back first, appalled by what Noah was making her feel. He had spoken of learning, but it was clear if she did not stop him he would have the taking of her as well. She pushed at his shoulders, frightened that her response to him had been so abandoned. She no longer felt safe. "No," she said, trying to wriggle away from the bold outline of his body. "This is wrong."

Noah sucked in his breath and let Jessa go. Damn her for a tease! She had been eager enough moments ago. What had gone wrong?

"Noah?" Worried by his silence, Jessa touched his shoulder.

He shrugged her off sharply and lay on his back. His breathing was harsh. When he had it under control he said, "I take it you don't intend to finish what we've begun."

How could he even think she would? Jessa had a sudden picture of herself in Noah's arms, giving him every encouragement once he began touching her. She was able to answer her own question.

"Jessa?"

"No . . . I can't."

Noah struggled to get the rest of himself under control. He thought of how he was betraying Hilary with this woman. It helped him cool his heels. "All right," he gritted. It was only a matter of time before Jessa relented. At least she was aware of him now as a man, not as some medieval protector complete with shield and white charger. And Hilary . . . well, Hilary was never going to know about this indiscretion. Noah found it incredibly easy to blame Jessa for bringing him to this pass.

"Are you angry?" she asked timidly. Her skin tingled. She was shamed by the tightening between her thighs. She had a vision of rubbing herself against him to relieve the ache. Jessa pressed her legs together instead and reflected on how wicked her thoughts had become since she met Noah McClellan. How could he make her body respond so eagerly when she wasn't even sure she liked him? How could she have turned to him in the darkness of her dreams? She flushed hot and cold when she realized how little willpower she had exercised, how quickly he had coaxed the responses he wanted from her.

"No, not angry." Anger didn't begin to describe what he was feeling. Beneath the comforter his hand sought and found hers. He stroked the underside of her wrist, softly at first, then without warning squeezed it hard enough to make Jessa wince. "You would do well to think before you begin to tease a man so."

"Tease?" she asked, bewildered. "But I—"

"Have you forgotten that you were the one who turned to me?" He didn't expect an answer and Jessa didn't give him one. After a moment he said, "I think we should both get some sleep."

Jessa pulled her hand free and began to scoot away. How dare he blame her? He was the one who made promises that he had no intention of keeping.

"Where are you going?"

"In the circumstances," she said stiffly, "don't you think it would be better if I slept on the window seat?"

"What circumstances?" he snapped.

His tone made her cautious. "I just thought ... I mean ..."

Lightning quick, Noah slid a proprietal arm around Jessa's waist and dragged her back. Turning on his side, he cradled her against the length of him. "If I want to suffer," he grated in her ear, "then you'll damn well let me suffer."

"You're insane." And she meant it. There was no possibility that she would ever understand him. Not in six weeks. Not in six lifetimes. Thank God it would not come to that.

Noah left her no choice but to remain at his side. Because he made her, Jessa fit herself against him and did not pull away from the heat and hardness she could feel pressed to her buttocks.

They were both a long time getting to sleep.

"You become that gown," Noah said.

Jessa turned quickly, unaware until he spoke that he had entered the cabin. "I'm sorry about the door, Noah, truly I am. Cam just left a moment ago and I have not had time to bolt it."

Noah crossed the room to where Jessa stood by the porcelain basin. He took her hands and lifted them outward then surveyed her in the gown again. "I have given you a very pretty compliment, madam. Can't you think of anything to say besides the door wants bolting?"

Jessa looked up at him shyly. He was a constant source of surprise to her. Upon waking this morning she hadn't known what to expect. Yet Noah had dropped a kiss on her forehead, bounded out of bed, and talked to her of this and that the entire time he dressed to go on deck. He had made her laugh. He had almost made her forget that she had clung to him most of the night. Almost. "Thank you, Noah. I'm happy you like the gown."

"I like the gown on you." He held her eyes a moment, then his gaze dropped to the square-cut bodice. "I didn't describe the measurements quite accurately, did I?" The fabric was stretched tautly across Jessa's breasts. Neither were her breasts completely contained by the neckline. Their sweet curves were visible for anyone to ogle. Noah cleared his throat. "Don't you have a fichu . . . a shawl . . . something?" he finished inadequately.

Embarrassed, Jessa crossed her arms in front of her. It had an effect opposite to the one she wished, raising her breasts still higher above the neckline. Luckily Gideon chose that moment to crawl from beneath one of the lounging chairs to demand Jessa's attention. Unfortunately, when she scooped him off the floor and held him against her, his dimpled fist dived directly between her breasts. "Gideon!" she cried in outraged accents.

Noah nearly choked on his laughter, raising his hands innocently as Jessa looked to him for help. "I swear I did not teach him that!"

"Fool!" she said, though she was hard pressed not to laugh herself. She tried to remove Gideon's fist and part of his chubby forearm, but he was squirming and kicking and she needed both hands to steady him. "Would you please take him?"

Noah pulled Gideon away, held him up high, and gave him a wriggle. "Oh, Gideon, how I envied you!"

"Noah! That's a horrible thing to say to him."

Noah was unapologetic. "He didn't understand a word. And, anyway, I did envy him."

Jessa turned away, hiding her smile. She righted her bodice as much as she was able. "Just so you know," she said over her shoulder. "I am letting out the seams in all the gowns."

"All of them?" Noah sat down in a chair and bounced Gideon on his knee. The baby wobbled and teetered and never stopped giggling. "They all fit the way this rose one does?"

"Yes. I am not so skinny and ill-fed as you think."

One eyebrow arched wickedly. "Only with one, er, *two* exceptions," he said dryly.

"You are incorrigible."

Noah gave his full attention to Gideon. "D'you hear that? I believe I am making progress. Yesterday I was insufferable. Today I am merely incorrigible."

Jessa threw up her hands in surrender. Ignoring Noah's laugh she went to the table and served herself from the large platter Cam had brought earlier. "Did you eat breakfast?"

Noah nodded. "Gideon?"

"I fed him before I dared put on this gown."

"Then your food's probably cold by now. Do you ever get a warm meal?"

"Occasionally," she said, marveling at his mood. It was as if last night had never happened.

"Well, eat up. I came to take you and Gideon topside for some fresh air. Come on, Gideon, we'll see if we can find something in the wardrobe to make your mother look matronly. Or at least respectable."

"There are always my dresses," she reminded him.

"I said respectable, not dowdy." After a few minutes searching in which he found nothing, he pulled out her traveling cloak. "This will have to do. I never gave a thought that you would require a pelisse."

"Noah, you've been more than generous. My cloak will be fine." Since she arrived in it it hardly seemed to matter that she was seen in it again. "It is a perfectly respectable garment," she told him. "And you did say that's what you were striving for."

"She has me there," he told Gideon.

The hours they spent on deck were charmed in Jessa's eyes. They strolled the deck several times at a leisurely pace, taking turns holding Gideon. He wanted to crawl free and that, of course, was impossible. For all that Noah hated sailing, he was quite knowledgeable about how it was done. Or at least it seemed so to Jessa. He could have been telling her a series of lies and she wouldn't have known the difference—or cared. Like Gideon, she was content to simply listen to Noah's soft drawl, his lullaby voice.

Noah introduced her to various members of the crew with whom he was better acquainted. They were polite to Jessa, made a fuss over Gideon, and no one mentioned Hilary Bowen or questioned the circumstances of Noah's marriage. It seemed a good omen.

The sun was shining. The breeze was stiff. Nettles of salt spray stung Jessa's face when she stood at the taffrail. She leaned forward and raised her face to it, smiling. "Isn't it delicious, Noah? You can taste the air!" But when she glanced over her shoulder to see if Noah had heard he was turning away and she saw the dark, brooding look was back in his eyes. His deepest thoughts were closed to her and her own position was too precarious to permit prying. He could merely lift an eyebrow and remind her that she had no one to blame for her situation but herself.

Worse, she could not begin to understand what it was he still wanted from her. If he continued to desire her she would have never suspected it by the way he acted toward her that night or each of the fourteen successive nights. Although he held her in his arms, fitting her body to the contours of his own, there was never any hint that he was interested in a repetition of the first night they shared a bed. He never kissed her. Except to keep her close to his side he rarely touched her. His compliments were even less frequent.

Jessa could have been relieved. She was a better worrier, so she practiced that.

Her routine was established around Gideon's schedule, and Jessa welcomed the stable pattern of her day. Noah spent a large part of each day in the captain's cabin. He read his law books there where he wouldn't be constantly interrupted by Gideon. He pored over letters he had received while in England from other members of the delegation who would gather in Philadelphia sometime in May. He studied the soon-to-be-revised Articles of Confederation, made notes, drafted plans, outlined and altered his ideas again and again. When he wasn't closeted away he was with Jessa and Gideon.

Jessa loved to watch him with Gideon. Sometimes she joined in their play, often she sat back and observed the special relationship Noah had established with the infant. Gideon, who wasn't used to any male attention, regarded Noah with something of a proprietal air. But Jessa also looked forward to those few occasions when Gideon was napping and Noah would unexpectedly walk into the cabin—she had never acquired the habit of bolting it—and spend time with her alone. It didn't matter if they talked or if they simply shared a quiet meal together, Jessa sensed in those moments slender threads of hope that he would not completely abandon her. She would never beg him to keep her, of course—not even for Gideon would she do that. But if he were to change his mind? Would it be so terrible to remain married to Noah McClellan?

"What are you thinking?" asked Noah. Jessa was lying on her back beside him in bed. Her beautiful pale hair was unplaited for once. Rivulets of molten gold and silver framed her face and fell over her shoulder. She was absently twisting one of the strands around her finger, a faint, thoughtful frown at the corners of her mouth. Noah turned on his side, bunched a pillow under his head, and stared at her clear, delicate profile. She never failed to look lovely to him and in some ways he resented it. There seemed to be a constant tightening in his loins and now was no exception. He drew his knees a little toward his chest.

Jessa tilted her head toward him. "Hmm?"

"I asked what you were thinking. You've been uncharacteristically quiet most of the day."

"Meaning I'm usually a chatterbox, I suppose."

"Hardly," he said truthfully. In the little over two

weeks they had spent almost exclusively in each other's presence, Noah had discovered that Jessa was singularly reticent to discuss anything about herself. On the other hand, she was an excellent listener. Noah found himself discussing his law practice, his future work on the Articles, and his family with equal ease. She drew him out with seemingly no effort, and though it was clear she didn't understand a third of what he said about the problems of drafting a new guideline for the government, she made it possible for him to hear his thoughts aloud. "And you're shifting the subject," he said. "What's wrong?"

"I've been thinking about what you've said of your work," she told him. "You'll be going to Philadelphia, won't you?"

"Soon after I arrive at the landing. I'll be living there until the delegation designs something with a little teeth in it. Afterward, I will have to divide my time between my law practice in Richmond and politics in Philadelphia. I thought you knew that"

"I suppose I did. I just didn't really think on it before. Somehow I thought you would be living with your family longer."

"My home is in Richmond, Jessa. I don't live at the landing year-round any more. I haven't since after the war. If you were to meet my family, you'd understand why."

"How can that be? They sound wonderful," she protested, hiding her hurt. She supposed she couldn't blame him for not wanting to introduce her to his family, but did he have to throw out the fact so carelessly?

"They are. And we're very close. It's just that there's so *many* of them. It can be overwhelming when the McClellans gather for the holidays or summer picnics on the James. Leah and Troy and their brood have to travel from New York, but everyone else either lives at the landing or very near. Gareth and his family have a home in Williamsburg, but they are always in and out because Gareth and my father raise the horses. Salem and Ashley and their three, no *four*, children are there when Salem is between trade runs. Rae and Jericho manage the plantation, so the landing is permanently their home. My mother and father love all the noise and confusion. I like it as well—but in smaller doses. In my place you'd feel the same. After a few days at the landing, you'd be happy to leave for Philadelphia."

Jessa doubted it. An only child, she had longed for brothers and sisters. Everything he told her sounded appealing rather than the opposite. She would have enjoyed the noise and confusion. In her own home she had tiptoed and whispered through her childhood because her mother had a megrim or her father had a hangover. "If you did bring me to the landing as your wife how would you explain me to your family?" she asked. "Gideon and I would be something of a shock to them."

"Thinking about changing the terms of our marriage, Jessa?"

"No," she said quickly. "I was just curious."

"As long as that's all it is. I'm not prepared to take on any more responsibility than I already have where you are concerned."

"I understand."

"Good. The truth is that my parents would probably accept whatever I chose to say, even the truth. Stranger things than this have happened in my family."

"Oh?"

Noah shook his head. "Some other time." His eyes had focused on her mouth. It was still slightly parted in the shape of her last word. "I've another matter on my mind." He bent his head and kissed her.

Jessa surprised them both by accepting him willingly. Caught off guard, she gave herself up to the pressure, the taste, the feel of his mouth on hers. All concern for caution dissolved; clear thought was swept away by the swift rush of desire. Her body echoed the bent of her mind.

Jessa's arms circled Noah's back, bringing him closer. She made her own demands now. It had been borne home to her more surely than ever before that she had no place in his future. But she had the present and she could make what she wanted of it. Her responses to him were defiant in nature. Every time he touched her it became clearer that love did not matter in the grand scheme of things. She could answer his kisses without loving him and he had to know it. Love could only hurt her and it had no place in what was between them. Even if she was just learning that, it was clear Noah had known it from the beginning.

Jessa's fingers curled in his hair and held him against her. Her tongue teased his upper lip and she captured his hungry groan as the kiss deepened and their tongues battled.

Noah kicked at the comforter, pushing it away because it had wedged itself between them. He wanted to feel her flush to his body. His hands drew her closer while his mouth left hers and traced the column of her slender neck. He kissed the hollow of her throat, nuzzled the curve of her shoulder. One leg insinuated itself between hers; his knee nudged the hem of her shift upward. Noah's mouth trailed along the lacey neckline of her nightgown. One hand slipped from her back and cupped the underside of her breast, gently lifting the point to his mouth.

Jessa's back arched as his lips closed over her nipple. His tongue made a damp circle on the cotton shift. His teeth caught the material and the pearl tip of her nipple and tugged, demanding her uninhibited response and getting it. Jessa felt the rush of heat all the way to her toes. Her legs pressed against him and her hands fell from his head and clutched his shoulders as his attention was claimed by her other breast. Just when Jessa thought she could not tolerate the hot urgings of his mouth any longer, Noah released her. His breathing was soft and quick. She placed a hand on his chest, palm flush to his heated skin, and she could feel the racing beat of his heart.

His darkened eyes searched her face. For a long time neither of them moved nor spoke. Jessa wondered if he could hear the thunderous beating of her own heart. Finally, "Jessa?"

She didn't understand that he was asking a question. There was little inflection in the husky way he said her name. What she did know was that she didn't want to talk. She wanted his mouth again. She wanted his hands on her, touching her, caressing her, making her feel as if she were desired if only for these few moments. Jessa was shielded from her selfishness by her own innocence; she wasn't thinking of Noah's needs or of the fact that his wants might be different from her own. She didn't realize when she brought his mouth to hers and kissed him with the fullness of her own defiant passion that he would take it as the answer he had been waiting for. Jessa wasn't aware that he would want to touch and caress her more deeply, that he would want to be inside her.

Jessa's mouth trailed over Noah's face. Her lips brushed the hollow of his cheeks, the hard line of his jaw. She felt the strength and heat of him against her hip but she was unafraid.

Noah's knee pushed her shift higher. His hands joined the effort and his palms and fingers grazed the length of her legs. He stroked the inside of her thigh. The heel of his hand pressed against the soft thatch of hair on her mound. His fingers caressed. She was damp and warm, ready for him. He unbuttoned the front fall of his linen drawers.

At first Jessa shied from the intimacy of Noah's touch but then the heat was blossoming inside her and he had become so tender, almost reverent, that she forgot what he was doing to her and gave herself up to it.

Her breath came even more rapidly. Her head moved restlessly on the pillow. Soft, mewling cries parted her lips, then Noah was kneeling between her thighs, stroking her breasts, caressing the taut plane of her abdomen, and only when she felt the pressure of his manhood against her parted thighs did Jessa have the cobwebs lifted from her mind.

She didn't ask herself how either of them had allowed things to go so far. There wasn't time. She said the one word that she hoped would turn Noah from her, the one word that would attack his pride and keep her secret safe. She closed her eyes and said, "Robert."

The name hung in the air between them.

Noah recoiled as if struck. He couldn't get away from her quickly enough. The skin of his face took on a gray cast while his eyes narrowed with fierce, cold anger.

Jessa had pushed her nightgown down her legs. Now it even covered her curled toes as she leaned one shoulder against the wall at the head of the bed. Her breathing was uneven and her hands trembled. "I'm sorry, Noah," she apologized. But her remorse was less for what she had said than it was for deceiving him. If he despised her it was no more than she despised herself. "I didn't mean to—"

"Don't say another word," he gritted. Turning away, he buttoned his drawers and climbed out of bed. "You've reached the end point of my tolerance. I suppose I should have expected it from you. Sometimes you're so obvious it's laughable. Did you think I'd take you home to the landing in exchange for your favors? That's what you had in mind, wasn't it? A commitment from me?" He didn't give Jessa the opportunity to confirm or deny it. "You certainly miscalculated there! You have to keep your lovers straight!" He found his breeches exactly where he had dropped them on the floor. With an angry sweep of his hand he picked them up and jammed his legs into them. They were uncomfortably tighter in the crotch than they had been when he took them off.

"Noah? Where are you going?"

"On deck!" he spat. "I'm leaving you to your ghost. Frankly, Jessa, there's not room for three of us in that bed."

Jessa watched him go, helpless to call him back. "Unless you were thinking of Hilary Bowen," she said softly to the closed door, "there were always only two of us sharing this bed." Pressing her knees to her chest, Jessa laid her head against them and stared painfully dry-eyed at the milk-white moon.

When Noah returned to the cabin Jessa had once more taken up a bed on the window seat. He stood over her sleeping figure a long time before deciding what to do. Finally he picked her up, sliding an arm under her knees and her shoulders, and carried her to their bed. He laid her on the feather tick and then he climbed in. This time, however, it was he who turned his back on her and slept on the very edge of the mattress.

The strain that existed between them from that point on was a near tangible thing. Noah spent most of his waking hours in the captain's cabin or on deck. Jessa felt like a prisoner but she enjoyed Noah's company even less. She had even taken to bolting the door so he could not walk in unannounced. Gideon was often fractious when they were together, sensing the tension between them. Because Noah seemed to genuinely enjoy Gideon's company, Jessa made certain she was occupied elsewhere while he played with the infant.

Cam was a frequent visitor to the cabin and he became Jessa's lifeline. Hardly more than a child himself, he was still often the only person who shared a conversation with her throughout the day. Even during afternoon strolls on deck the crew was reluctant to engage her attention. Jessa had no way of knowing this was because Noah had discouraged them from becoming too friendly with her. He had never felt any need to give the same advice to Cam. He might have done so if he had remembered how painful first loves could be.

"Where's your shadow today, boy?" Captain Riddle asked when he came upon Cam without Jessa. Even though the boy's hands were busy whittling a pipe, Jack could see Cam's thoughts were elsewhere. Cam's task didn't require the deep concentration he appeared to be giving it now.

Startled by the interruption, Cam's head jerked up and connected with the signal box he was leaning against. Rubbing the back of his head, a sheepish grin stole across his face. Cam squinted as he raised his eyes to the captain. "My shadow, sir?" He started to get to his feet but Jackson waved him back down and further surprised Cam by hunkering down beside him.

"Mrs. McClellan. Like salt and sea air the two of you are. Don't you usually escort her on deck about this time?"

Cam shifted uncomfortably. "She's not feeling quite the thing, sir."

"Oh? Not the same problem that afflicts Noah, I hope."

Since the sea was unusually calm today and the wind was mild, Cam didn't think seasickness was the problem. But he had a pretty good idea what was. He had glimpsed Jessa's puffy eyes and tear-stained face before she quickly turned away and told him she wouldn't be joining him this afternoon. He had also seen Noah McClellan looking very grim not twenty minutes before that. "No, Captain. It's not seasickness."

"That's good." He didn't say anything else, letting a silence build while he continued to look at the boy expectantly.

"I wouldn't treat her so shabbily if she was my wife," Cam finally blurted out.

Jackson Riddle blinked in surprise. He couldn't recall ever hearing Cam speak so vehemently. Somewhat to his regret he realized he had opened a veritable Pandora's box. He hadn't expected that Cam's thoughtful brooding was related to Jessa McClellan. "It's not really any concern of yours, Cam. What's between a man and his wife, well, it's just between them, you understand?" He cleared his throat. "Try not to take any notice of it. No such thing as smooth sailin' in a marriage." Too late he realized he had actually confirmed Cam's opinion that trouble existed between Noah and Jessa. Hell, how could he help it? All the crew knew something was amiss.

"Can't help but notice it," Cam said stubbornly. "She tried to hide it, but some days she's just so sad that you can't miss it."

"We can't make it our affair. There's a sayin', boy, and you're seein' the truth of it now: marry in haste, repent at leisure."

Cam grimaced. He had no appreciation for Captain Riddle's truisms. "The point is that if Mr. McClellan don't have a care he's going to lose her."

Jack gave a short, hearty laugh. "You'll take her away, will you?"

"I might," he said firmly, thrusting out his chin for good measure.

"Don't you let Noah hear you say that. A man has his pride."

Cam knew he was being ribbed. The captain didn't believe for a moment that he was a threat to Noah McClellan's pride. His own pride injured, Cam held back from telling Riddle that there were other men on the *Clarion* who had similar thoughts about Noah's indifference to his wife. Only a few days ago he had heard Ross Booker tell Henry Alder that maybe Mrs. McClellan was missing a real man in her bed now that Noah was prowling the deck at night. Henry had put his fist squarely in Ross's gut and Cam never heard Ross say anything about Mrs. McClellan again, but he did notice that Booker's eyes followed Jessa whenever she was on deck. "If Mr. Noah wants to keep what he has, then he should have a care. That's all I'm sayin'."

"That almost sounds like a threat, Cam," Jack said, a pointed note of caution in his voice.

Cam swallowed hard and looked away. He knew he had gone too far. "I'd never do anything to hurt Miss Jessa," he said. He could have told Jack that he never left her cabin without waiting in the companionway to make certain she locked the door. Someone had to look out for her what with Ross Booker thinking she was ripe for picking. "Never hurt Mr. Noah either. I like them both separate. It's just that together . . . I don't know . . . it confuses me."

"They are a little like oil and water, aren't they?" Jack acknowledged thoughtfully.

Cam nodded energetically. His hair, almost white in the bright sunlight, fell over his forehead. He raked it back with his fingers.

"Of course," the captain continued, "I don't know that you'd mix any better. Now, Noah's niece, there's a girl for you." He bit back a smile as Cam's cheeks reddened.

"Courtney's all right, I suppose." Cam's eyes dropped away and he busied his fingers with whittling.

Jackson stood, giving Cam's shoulder a small squeeze as he did so. "She's more than all right. I'd say she's sweet on you *and* she's not married." The captain walked away whistling under his breath. He hoped he'd given Cam someone to replace Jessa McClellan in his affections.

"I need some milk for Gideon's porridge, Cam," Jessa said. "He won't eat it this dry. He likes a nice paste he can smear everywhere." She laughed when she saw the boy sigh. He had been so good to her and Gideon that she felt horrible having to send him on another errand. They were only ten days away from the Virginia shore and no doubt Cam would be glad to bid them farewell. "Here." She plopped Gideon into Cam's thin arms. "I'll get the milk and you stay with Gideon."

"Oh, no, Mrs. McClellan." He tried to give Gideon back but Jessa backed away. "You can't go into the hold! Mr. Noah wouldn't like it!"

"Mr. Noah won't know about it, not if you don't tell him. Really, Cam, do you think I can't do it? I know where the livestock is stabled and I know how to milk a cow." She picked up Gideon's cup. "I'll be back in a few minutes."

Jessa hurried down the companionway, taking the ladders to the lower decks and finally to the main hold where one cow, Noah's thoroughbred, and two dozen chickens made their home. She wrinkled her nose at the odor of the confined animals, placed Gideon's cup on top of one of the stall ledges, and set a milking stool and pail by the cow. "I only need a cup, Elizabeth. That sounds more dignified than Bessie, don't you think?" She patted the cow on the flanks and sat on the stool. "Hmm, it looks as if you've been neglected this morning. You're fair to bursting with milk."

"That'd be my job, ma'am."

Jessa was so startled by the intrusion that she nearly fell off her stool. She had a vague recollection of the man who stood before her. She had seen him occasionally on deck, but neither Noah nor Cam had introduced her. "I'm getting some milk for my little boy," she explained unnecessarily.

Ross Booker could hardly believe his luck. He hadn't been this close to a woman in ten months. Newgate prison had been his home for most of that time. When he was released he headed straight for the wharves intending to find a sailor's whore. Instead he signed on with the *Clarion* and decided whoring could wait until he reached America. On the voyage he had changed his mind. Not that he would have done anything about it, he told himself. The things he said to Henry Alder were just talk. But he had never counted on Jessa McClellan presenting herself in the hold. Alone. He had an urge to press his hand against the bulge in his pants.

"I'll do that for you, Mrs. McClellan." He blocked her path so that when Jessa left the stool she was forced farther into the interior of the stall.

"Th-thank you." Jessa knew almost instantly she didn't like him. His face was handsome in a hard, irregular sort of fashion, but his eyes were cold. Even when he smiled, perhaps especially then, his eyes were cold. She waited, trying not to show her impatience or her fear as he milked the cow. She didn't like the way his hands closed over the cow's teats or the suggestive way he looked at her as he rhythmically tugged the cow's udder. "I only need a cup," she said.

Ross shrugged. His eyes wandered to Jessa's breasts. "It'll only be a minute, ma'am. I might as well finish what I've started."

Jessa wanted to adjust the ruffle of her chemise above the neckline of her bodice. She had let out the seams in all the gowns and she knew there was nothing the least revealing about her lilac dress, yet she felt as if this man could see more than was shown. At her sides her hand clenched in the folds of material and she refrained from lifting them and calling attention to herself. "I'll get my cup," she said. She wanted to go past him and get to the open end of the stall.

Ross pushed the stool out farther and blocked her way. "Almost done, ma'am."

Jessa was forced to wait. To get past him now she would have to touch him. She didn't want to do that.

Ross stood, picking up the pail. He lifted it in front of him and tilted it to show Jessa the contents. "Sweet, sweet milk," he said, staring at her face. "Why, your skin's the same color." He raised one hand and touched her face. "Just as smooth."

Jessa turned her cheek and slapped his hand away. "Don't do that!"

Ross's face flushed. He grasped her chin. "There's no call to be pushin' at me. I ain't done a thing."

"Please let me pass. I promise I won't say anything to my husband."

"There's nothing to tell him. Nothing's 'appened." He stepped closer, lowering the bucket. One hand still held Jessa's chin. "Now, if I were to kiss you, *then* something would 'appen." Without warning he pressed Jessa into the corner and ground his mouth against hers.

Jessa almost gagged as his tongue intruded on her mouth, seeking entry. Mutinously she kept her lips closed. Her hands came around his back and she yanked hard on his hair. He growled in pain and lifted his head. Before he knew what she was about Jessa lifted the pail of milk by its rim and tipped the contents over the front of his breeches. It startled him long enough that she was able to squeeze past him. Jessa had just managed to clear the stall when she felt Ross's hands on her waist. She screamed and tried to twist away, clawing at his hands. Her momentum pulled them both to the floor. Jessa was vaguely aware of the chickens cackling wildly in their pen. Noah's horse was tossing its head and snorting restlessly in the stall. Her fear had become theirs. She pushed at Ross's shoulders and tried to squirm away. His hard groin was thrust against her thigh.

"It will take more than a little milk to cool what ails me," he gritted, rubbing lewdly against her. He grabbed both her flailing arms by the wrists and slammed them to the deck.

"Noah will kill you!"

Ross laughed. "Everyone knows yer 'usband don't bother wi' ye."

The voice that interrupted was hard with menace. "Then everyone's wrong." Noah bent and clutched Ross's collar in his fist. He hauled the man to his feet, shoving him against a stall gate. "Are you hurt, Jessa?"

Jessa was on her knees now, breathing hard. She saw Cam standing in the doorway. Embarrassed by what he had seen, he was looking everywhere but at her. "N-no. I'm not hurt."

Noah's grip on Ross's throat didn't relax. "Then go with Cam back to the cabin and stay with your son, madam. Where you belong!"

"Noah?" She said his name timidly, afraid of what he was going to do. "Are you—"

"Go Jessa! Now!"

Jessa ran the entire way to her cabin, Cam close on her heels.

"Gideon's in his crib, Mrs. McClellan," Cam explained as he followed her into the cabin.

She nodded, keeping her back to him. Jessa didn't want him to see her tear-streaked face. "You can go. And Cam?"

"Yes, ma'am?"

"Thank you. You were right to get Noah." When he was gone Jessa stripped out of her soiled gown. She had never wanted a bath as badly as she did then but hauling the water would take too much time and Gideon was crying, demanding her attention in the other room. Jessa let him cry while she scrubbed at the basin. Her face and arms were pink by the time she was finished, but she had erased Ross's touch and the path of tears across her cheeks.

"You'll have to eat dry, lumpy porridge," she told Gideon when she brought him to the table and sat him on her lap. Tears pricked her eyes again and she blinked them back. "Mama doesn't have your milk."

"No! No!" Gideon turned his face away when Jessa brought the spoon to his mouth.

At another time Jessa would have made a fuss over the new word. Not now, and not that particular word. "Please, Gideon. Eat something . . . for me, darling . . . will you do that?" She pressed the spoon to his lips.

In answer Gideon screwed up his face and tightened his lips stubbornly.

"Oh, please, don't do this. I need you to be a good

boy right now . . . eat your porridge." When his mouth opened to object again Jessa slipped the spoon in. "There! That's not so terrible, is it?"

Gideon spit the porridge out. It dribbled down his chin and onto his shirt. When Jessa tossed the spoon down and gave him an angry little shake he began to cry.

After a moment she joined him.

That's how Noah found them—both sobbing, neither able to provide comfort to the other. He quickly took control, lifting Gideon from Jessa's arms and bouncing him lightly in the crook of his elbow. He wiped off Gideon's mouth and chin then took him into the other room and changed his shirt and diaper.

Jessa was washing her face at the basin when he returned with a much quieted child in his arms. She gave Noah a watery, tremulous smile as he came to stand beside her then ducked her head quickly and went to the window seat to sit down. Drawing her knees to her chest, Jessa wrapped her arms around her legs. The shift covered her like a tent and hid her shaking legs.

Noah took the quilt from the foot of the bed and with Gideon still in his arm, awkwardly wrapped it around her. Jessa provided no assistance. If this were a real marriage his arms would be around her, Noah thought. But he couldn't bring himself to touch her, afraid of her reaction as well as his own. "Were you hurt after all?" he asked.

Jessa shook her head and stared straight ahead. "No, not the way you mean . . . a few bruises . . . nothing . . . you came in time."

The promises Noah made to himself in regard to being sensitive to Jessa's fragile state were forgotten. His fear, his inadequacy to comfort her, the terrible consequences of his neglect and Jessa's rejection were all immutably tangled within him and knew but one expression for release: sudden, blinding anger. "Damn you, Jessa! Were you thinking at all when you left this cabin? Have you no regard for my wishes? No regard for your safety? Did you want to be raped?" Gideon whimpered and Noah realized he was holding the infant too tightly. He set Gideon on the rug, found the cloth ball, and returned to Jessa only marginally cooled. Her face was ashen now except for twin splashes of color on her high cheekbones. She looked as if she had been struck by the back of his hand, and turning her head, had been struck again. "Have you nothing to say? No? Then let me tell you what happens now. You will get dressed and I will bring Cam to watch Gideon. Then you and I will join everyone assembled on deck and we will observe Ross Booker's punishment at the main-mast."

Jessa's head came up. The color in her cheeks had disappeared and her pale gray eyes betrayed her revulsion. "No!"

"I'm afraid you don't have a choice," he said tersely. "You will be there if I have to carry you!"

"Why must you torture me also?" she cried out. "I don't want to see a man's back laid open! Did you think I would?" Jessa's hands balled into bloodless fists. "And don't look at me that way! I know you're thinking that if I really did nothing to encourage him, then I would enjoy seeing him flayed. Well, I'm telling you now, I did *not* encourage that man and I still do not want to observe his punishment!"

"Ross has already told the captain a different story. He says you flirted with him, teased him, exchanged a few kisses, and when he wanted more you changed your mind. You must admit it had a certain ring of familiarity when I heard it. Did you mistake him for Robert as well?"

Jessa gasped. "You're disgusting! Believe anything you like, Noah! You will anyway! Place all the blame and responsibility for what happened on my shoulders! I can bear it there,"—she pointed to her shoulders, then pressed her forefinger against her temple—"but

I'll never accept it here! My body is my own, Noah, and I have a right to say who uses it and in what fashion! I repeat, I did *not* encourage that man! What he attempted was vile, a violation of my person! And yes, I want him punished! But I do not want to witness it! Every man up there will be thinking as you do. If I will not accept your censure do you really think I will accept theirs?''

Noah was struck by her vehemence. He had never seen her so passionately angry or heard her speak with such conviction. Her speech was not delivered with the halting spontaneity of someone who had just conceived of these ideas. It was clear she had given the matter much thought over a long period of time. Noah was very much afraid this was not the first time someone had tried to force their attentions on her, himself excluded. He drew in a deep breath and released it slowly. "I never said I believed Ross Booker," he said carefully, calmly. "I merely said that his explanation sounded familiar."

"Tell me," she challenged, "if you did believe him, if I had flirted and teased, would you still want him punished?"

Noah was a long time in answering. He had never considered the question of rape from a viewpoint like Jessa's. The commonly held opinion was that the woman either brought it on herself or she didn't. And the burden of proof remained with her. If the attack were without provocation, then the outcome was clear. But doubt regarding her motives and actions would cloud the picture.

"Yes," he said finally. "I would still want him punished."

Jessa was skeptical of his answer and it showed in her eyes and the slightly derisive lift of her mouth. "Why? Because I'm your wife and therefore an attack on me is an attack on you? Is it the affront to your pride, your honor, that must be dealt with?"

"No," he said gravely. "It's because what you said before is true. You should have rights regarding your own person." He caught her pointed, accusing stare and continued chillingly. "Don't push me, Jessa. There is a difference between me and Ross Booker. When you married me you gave me certain rights. That you're refusing to honor them makes you the criminal, not me. I'm willing to admit that leaving this cabin unescorted was not an invitation on your part, nor is leaving the door unlocked. But don't make the mistake of confusing my actions with Booker's, your dead husband's, or anyone else's." Almost as an afterthought he added, "I regret asking you if you wanted to be raped. That remark was beneath contempt."

"I'm glad you realize it," she said, only somewhat mollified.

"But leaving here without protection showed a shocking lack of caution, Jessa," he went on, determined to make his own point. "I did not issue the order that you remain here behind a bolted door on a whim. I recognized danger and I acted accordingly. You did not. That is not to say you deserved what was done to you. I am only saying that you disregarded responsibility for your own safety."

Jessa's fingers twisted the end of her braid. She nodded slowly, eyes downcast, accepting the truth of what he said.

Noah studied her a moment, knowing what he was about to say would erase the submissive expression from her face. "I want you to get dressed now. You'll still have to accompany me on deck."

The winter gray eyes she raised to him were desolate, despairing. "Please, I beg of you, don't make me go!"

Noah held fast, though it was painful to look at her. "You must go, Jessa. It's expected that you witness the punishment. To stay below would be admitting guilt in the eyes of the others."

"But I'm not guilty!"

"I know," he said lowly. "I would spare you this if I could, but it's not in my hands. Jack Riddle is the captain, and his word is law on this ship, not mine. There can be only one man on board who is in command. Jack is that man. He is punishing Ross Booker as he sees fit. He didn't believe Booker's tale anymore than I did. Even before Henry Adler and Cam stepped forward to tell what they knew, Jack had decided the punishment. He has also decided that you should be there." Noah went to the wardrobe and took out Jessa's dove gray dress. A somber, sober color was what the occasion called for. He laid it over the back of a chair. "Wear this, Jessa. I'm going to . . ." A tentative knocking at the door interrupted Noah. "I suppose I don't have to get Cam after all. The men must already be assembled. You'll have to dress quickly." He went to the door and talked to Cam quietly on the threshold, glancing over his shoulder from time to time to make certain Jessa was dressing. When she was finished he let Cam into the room and pointed to Gideon under the dining table. The infant was alternately gnawing on his ball and the table leg. Cam immediately got down on his knees and crawled in after him. In other circumstances Noah would have laughed, smiled at the very least. Instead he held out his hand to Jessa. When she took it he escorted her from the cabin with a graveness of expression that could have led one to believe he was going to his own punishment.

The men were lined single file on either side of the mainmast where Ross Booker had been secured by his wrists. His shirt lay at his feet and his broad, naked back glistened with the sweat of fear. He sensed his accusers had come on deck by the sudden stillness of the men around him. Ross tried to twist his head to see them but his bonds made it impossible. He strained against the ropes and cursed viciously under his breath.

Rob Durham was the one who would be wielding the water-soaked cords of the cat, and he poked Booker in the ribs with the whip handle. "You'll hold your tongue," he whispered harshly. "Cap'n Jack would just as lief have you strung up in the yardarms."

Noah saw Booker's struggle against the mast and he glanced down at Jessa. Her entire body was rigid with tension but her face was composed. He realized then that she was not really looking at Booker or the crew or even at the captain. She could see them all yet she saw none of them. Her eyes held only the vaguest awareness of her surroundings. She was shielding herself from everyone, everything.

Noah led Jessa to their place beside Captain Riddle. He nodded shortly to Jack to indicate they were ready and pressed Jessa's arm to his side.

Riddle raised his hand and motioned to Rob Durham to begin the flogging. "Twenty lashes! Count 'em out!"

Three strokes were called before Ross Booker cried out. His back was scored with thin red lines of beaded blood. At ten he was screaming. The cuts were laid open; salty sweat mixed in the wounds. Fifteen. Sixteen. He was moaning softly and slumped against the mast. His fingers curled and uncurled weakly above his bonds. Droplets of blood stained the waistband of his breeches. Nineteen. Twenty. He was cut down, nearly unconscious.

But not nearly enough. As Noah and Jessa turned to go he beheld Jessa's blank stare. The murderous intent in his own eyes was enough to spear the shield she had carefully erected. When he saw he had captured her attention he raised his fist and railed, "I'll see you in 'ell for this, bitch!"

Noah would have picked up the whip himself but Jack was already directing two men to fasten Booker to the mast again and Rob Durham was prepared to do the deed.

"Twenty more will still his tongue!" Jack ordered.

Jessa never heard the command. As soon as Noah's

grip on her arm relaxed she had slipped to the deck in dead faint.

Three men left the line to help Noah and he waved them all away. He bent on one knee and lifted Jessa in his arms, carrying her toward their cabin before Rob had counted out his first stroke.

"Open the door for me, Cam!" he called.

Cam scrambled to his feet. He was carrying Gideon on his shoulders. "Yoww! Gideon, you're pullin' my hair!" He opened the door and stepped back. "Oh, Lord! What's happened to Mrs. McClellan? Is she dead?"

"She's fainted." Noah strode over to the bed and laid Jessa on it. "Would you please take the child off your head and fetch a cloth and the basin? And put fresh water in it!"

Cam hunkered down, untangled Gideon's sticky fingers from his hair, and put him on the floor. "D'you mean fresh salt water or fresh fresh water, sir?" he asked hurriedly. "Coz if you mean fresh fresh water then I'll have to be goin' out to get it. Your drinking barrel's empty." He shifted his weight from one foot to the other, anxious to please and prepared to run in any direction once he knew what Noah wanted.

"Fresh fresh water," Noah gritted, hardly believing the ridiculousness of this conversation. "And be quick!" God, but it seemed to him that a woman should be able to faint and then be cared for with a little more dignity than was given to this occasion. Cam danced around as if he were about to wet himself and Gideon was slobbering all over a chair leg.

Sighing, Noah sat down on the edge of the bed and took Jessa's hand in his. His other hand brushed back a tendril of hair from her forehead. Her lashes fluttered. He traced the line of her brows with his fingertips. "Jessa?"

"I'm all right," she said tonelessly. She squeezed his

hand lightly. "I did not give a very good account of myself, did I?"

"You were braver than any of us had a right to expect. The punishment was brutal and . . . and Booker's threat was ugly." His green-gold eyes regarded her solemnly. "I'd say you gave a very good account of yourself."

"What will happen to him?"

He realized she didn't know about the additional flogging Jack Riddle had ordered and he decided not to mention it. "He'll be locked away for the remainder of the voyage. You have nothing to fear from him. Now or later. Jack won't let him leave the ship once we're in Virginia. When the *Clarion* sails again, Ross Booker will be on it. He'll be set ashore in London or somewhere equally distant."

She nodded. "Thank God. I would have worried . . . he was so angry . . . I think he meant what he said."

Noah placed his forefinger across her lips. "Shh. Don't think about it. No one's going to hurt you, least of all Ross Booker." His finger slid away and his mouth replaced it, whispering a healing, tender kiss across her lips. It didn't mean anything he told himself. She just looked so damn vulnerable that he couldn't help himself. He owed her a little kindness, he supposed. After failing to protect her he could afford to be magnanimous.

Noah would have given her another kiss but behind him he heard a throat clearing and realized Cam was back in the room. He turned to the boy, who was nervously holding a pail of water in front of him. At least he wasn't dancing, Noah thought, a glimmer of a smile coming to his lips. "Empty the pail into the barrel, Cam. Do you want some water, Jessa? Yes? Cam, just bring a cup of the fresh fresh over here and endeavor not to spill any, please."

"Noah, don't tease him!" Jessa whispered. "He's only a boy. And what's fresh fresh?"

He didn't answer her. "Thank you, Cam," Noah said

soberly when the boy returned. He took the cup, and as Jessa propped herself up on her elbows he offered it to her, holding it to her mouth and tipping it gently. "And Cam?"

"Yes, sir?"

"I'd be obliged if you'd crawl under the table again and pull Gideon out. You didn't teach him to nibble on the furniture, did you?"

"Yes, sir . . . I mean, no, sir . . . I didn't teach him that." He hunkered down and pulled Gideon out, screeching a little when Gideon tugged on his hair. "What should I do with him, Mr. Noah?"

"Well, don't put him on your head again. That nearly turned my hair white." Noah took the cup away and quickly set it on the floor as Jessa sputtered. "There's no cause to choke," he said tapping her back. "Gideon wasn't really on Cam's head. Just his shoulders. And he had a firm grip. Not Cam. Gideon. Cam most likely would have dropped him on his head. Not on Cam's head. Gideon's. That is, Gideon would have fallen on his own head. Not Cam's."

Jessa sat up a little straighter and found that her smile did not take as much effort as she would have thought. She appreciated Noah's attempts to coax that smile even though she suspected his motives. "I think I understand," she said gently, patting Noah's hand as if he were seriously addled and she was patronizing him. "Bring Gideon here, Cam. You can put him on the bed beside me." Cam did so and Gideon sat on the comforter, leaning back against Jessa with his head resting just under the curve of her breasts. She stroked his hair with her fingertips, making little curls. "Have you eaten anything at all today, baby? Hmm? Have you? Is that why you nibble on the furniture? That's what your papa says you do." She shot a guilty glance in Noah's direction. "I'm sorry. I shouldn't have said that."

"It's all right," he said without inflection. "He's too young to understand." He turned away then rather than let Jessa see that he was more than a little moved by the thought of being Gideon's father.

Their exchange thoroughly confused Cam. He thought it best to pretend he hadn't heard it. "Gideon ate some of that porridge for me," he said. "He didn't like it much, but I sort of insisted."

"Thank you, Cam."

"Yes, thank you," Noah repeated, recovering himself. "Jessa, if you don't mind I'd like to go on deck with Cam. There are some matters I want to discuss with Jack."

"I don't mind." She didn't. She was content that he had even thought to ask her. "I think Gideon and I will both take a nap."

"You're certain?"

"Mmm. Go ahead. I'll be fine. I *am* fine." Jessa gave him a shove to start him toward the door.

"All right. I'm going," he said, raising his hands in surrender. He picked the cup off the floor and set it on the table, then he followed Cam into the companionway. Before he was five feet from the door he heard the grating noise of the bolt being thrown. As much as he was grateful to hear that sound he also deeply regretted it was necessary.

Jessa laid back down beside Gideon. They fell asleep almost immediately and neither of them heard the commotion of Ross Booker being hauled to the lower decks. They were blissfully unaware of the strangled curses he heaped upon Jessa's head.

Gideon woke first and amused himself by playing with Jessa's braid until she was roused out of sleep by the constant, less than gentle tugging. Cam returned shortly after that with their midday meal and fresh milk for Gideon.

"Is Mr. McClellan still with the captain?" she asked while Cam set everything out for them.

Cam's eyes skittered guiltily. "Yes, ma'am. He and Cap'n Riddle are still . . . well, they're together, Mrs.

McClellan.'' Cam carefully refrained from revealing that they were drinking. That's what they were doing, at least Mr. Noah was. Putting the grog away like it was all water. Two drinks to Cap'n Riddle's one. Cam didn't know if Jessa would care, but he was sure he wasn't going to be the one to tell her.

Hours later when he returned with dinner, Jessa raised the question again and Cam gave her the same evasive answer. He regretted it when the captain tagged him soon after to assist him in getting Noah back to the cabin. Cam could just imagine how they would be received. He had seen his own mother take a broom to his father when that worthy had returned to the house with one sheet to the wind . . . and Mr. Noah, well, Mr. Noah had at least three sheets aflutterin' in the breeze!

CHAPTER SEVEN

"You're foxed!" It was all Jessa could think to say when she opened the door and confronted the unsteady trio in the companionway. Captain Riddle and Cam were both faltering as they tried to support Noah between them. Noah stood so much taller than either of them that his arms were wrapped around their necks and rested heavily on their shoulders. He looked as if he had somehow grown a head under each armpit.

Noah glanced at Jessa's face. He still had enough sensibilities to look sheepish and the smile he gave her was endearingly crooked. "Indeed I am. Good evenin', wife." He attempted a small bow and nearly brought his companions to the floor in the process.

Jessa could not help herself. She burst out laughing. She motioned to the captain and Cam. "Please! You'd better bring him in! Can you get him to the bed?" She stepped away from the door as the three of them tried to enter. Cam managed to squeeze through the threshold under Noah's arm without sustaining any injury. The captain, however, winced when his shoulder was slammed against the door jamb as Noah lurched for-

ward. At this stage it was difficult for Jessa to tell who was
carrying whom. She bit back more laughter, doubting
Captain Riddle would appreciate her amusement at his
expense, and ran over to the bed and pulled back the
covers. "Just drop him here," she said.

"M'wife wants t' get me in bed," Noah told his companions, wiggling his eyebrows in an absurd parody of
wickedness. Then gravely, "But she don't want me when
I'm there."

The tips of Jack's ears reddened. "Don't mind him,
Mrs. McClellan," he said as Jessa raised her hands to
her burning cheeks. "He doesn't mean anything by it.
I had him almost sobered once this afternoon, then,
well, you can see he didn't have much use for that state.
This ain't a common thing with him, ma'am. Fact is, this
is the first time I've seen him foxed without a brother on
each arm." Simultaneously they gave Noah a hard shove
and he tumbled onto the bed.

Noah groaned softly and rolled on his back, covering
his eyes with his forearm. The entire cabin was tilting
alarmingly. "Can't you find calmer waters, Jack?"

Captain Riddle rolled his eyes. "It's not the sea that's
giving you a spin," he said unsympathetically. He turned
to Jessa. "I have to be goin', ma'am, but if you want,
Cam will stay and give you a hand."

Since Cam was already edging toward the door, clearly
wanting to make his escape, Jessa declined the help.
"I'm sure I can take care of my husband, Captain Riddle.
My father was inclined to drink more than was good
for him. This is not entirely a new situation for me."

"Very well," he said a trifle uncertainly, glancing at
Noah. "I think he's goin' to sleep it off, though he's
bound to have a sore head come morning. If he gives
you any trouble, you come straight to me. You're a little
bit of a thing to be tanglin' with this bear."

"I'll be fine," Jessa assured him. "Thank you for
bringing him back. I suspected something like this was

in the offing when Cam couldn't quite answer my questions earlier."

Cam ducked his head. "Thought you'd be angry, ma'am."

"It's difficult to be angry at such a sorry sight as the three of you teetering in the doorway," she said. "And you, Captain, look as if you could use a little help getting to your own cabin as well. I don't think Noah was drinking alone."

"Aye, we tipped a few together," he admitted, failing in his attempt to square his shoulders and stand perfectly straight. "Didn't seem fittin' that he should drink by himself."

Jessa's smile was wry. "I'm certain."

Cam slung one thin arm about Jack's waist and let the captain lean on him. "We'll take our leave now. G'night, Mrs. McClellan."

"I'll see you in the morning, Cam." Jessa bolted the door after them then turned her attention to Noah. "You, sir, are indeed a sight to behold," she sighed.

Noah lifted his forearm a fraction. "I am?"

"I thought you were sleeping."

"S'whish I were," he slurred, lowering his arm again. "Another pint would do me fine." He kicked clumsily at his shoes, trying to remove them. "Deuced uncomfortable."

"Another pint would do you in," she said tartly, walking toward the bed. She sat down on the edge near his feet. "Here, let me help. You have all the coordination of a newborn calf."

"Please, madam, your compliments will turn my head."

Jessa grinned, shaking her head. "Fool." She slipped off his shoes, dropped them on the floor, then loosened his breeches at the knees and rolled down his stockings.

"Are you undressing me?"

Jessa's hands stilled. "I won't if you don't want me to, but I doubt you'll sleep well in your clothes."

"Oh, Jessa," he laughed shortly, "I want. I *want.*"

Rather than being offended or even frightened by what it was that Noah really wanted, Jessa found herself smiling. He was no more threatening to her in his inebriated state than Cam ever was. In fact, he seemed as young and helpless as the veriest schoolboy. She pinched his calf lightly. "Behave yourself or I shan't be held accountable for my actions."

"Yes, ma'am," he said solemnly. He lay very still while Jessa divested him of his stockings and breeches. Because he wanted to be contrary, he wasn't much assistance when it came time for Jessa to help him out of his jacket, vest, and shirt.

The jacket and vest came off by turning Noah back and forth on the bed until she managed to work the garments down his shoulders and arms. The shirt was another matter. It had to come off over his head. Frustrated when her best efforts came to nothing, Jessa straddled his waist and tried easing the shirt upward.

"Put your arms over your head," she said.

Grinning, Noah dutifully held his arms straight up in the air.

"Not like that!" Jessa took his wrists and pushed his arms to the bed so they laid above his head. She was leaning over him, her breasts only inches above his face.

Through the fan of his thick lashes Noah had a pleasant view of what Jessa's rounded bodice could not quite contain in her present position. "Hmmm. Juss like m'dream. Mebbe even nicer."

Jessa jerked up so quickly that Noah groaned as her weight settled more forcefully on his taut belly. "Wh-what did you say?" she asked, adjusting the neckline of her gown with a sharp tug.

Noah blinked up at her, his eyes a little vague as she seemed to sway above him. "M'dream," he repeated. "When I was sick . . . I dreamed that you and I . . . that we . . . juss like this. Made love. S'beautiful."

"Oh, my God!" Jessa scrambled off Noah and sat on

the far side of the bed, her heart racing. He remembered! She wanted to bury herself under the covers and never face him again. Unfortunately, Noah was at this moment tangled in his own shirt and struggling to get it off. One arm was free but the material was hopelessly caught over his head and his other arm. He looked so ridiculous that Jessa gave in and helped him. What did it matter if he remembered what had happened at the cottage? It was only a dream as far as he was concerned. There was no reason he should ever learn it was more fact than fantasy.

"Thank you," he said in solemn tones when he was at last freed. "S'very kind of you t'help."

When Jessa climbed off the bed she gave him a tiny mocking curtsey and began gathering his clothes.

"Juss leave 'em," he said, pointing to the pile in her arms. "You don't have to pick up after me."

"All right." She dropped his things on the floor, happy to oblige his mood. "I think it's best if you get some sleep," she said, turning away. "The devil will take his due on the morrow." After peeking in on Gideon, Jessa sat down at the window seat and picked up the mending she had been doing earlier.

"Come to bed, Jessa." Noah was laying on his side, hugging a pillow to his chest. He was staring at her with a little-boy-lost expression. "Please. Can't sleep when you're not here."

"But I'm not tired," she protested.

"Then we'll talk."

"If you will pardon me for saying so, you are not at your most eloquent."

"Then we'll do something else."

"That's rather what I want to avoid."

Noah sighed dramatically. "You wound me." He clutched the pillow tighter as if it would stem the flow from his bleeding heart. "Juss thought we could cuddle."

Jessa bent her head over her work. "That's the drink

talking. You haven't wanted to touch me in weeks."
Thank God, she almost added.

"Not the drink," Noah protested. He shook his head
to emphasize his point but the movement caused the
room to start spinning. Closing his eyes only made everything worse. His moan was muffled by the pillow.

Hardening her heart to him, Jessa continued to work
on her stitches and didn't encourage conversation by
glancing in his direction. It wasn't until she heard the
gentle, slightly labored sound of his even breathing that
she put aside the mending, dressed for bed, and turned
back the lamps. When she slipped beneath the covers
she discovered the bed was not so enormous as she had
supposed, not when Noah had managed to cast himself
in the middle with his long legs and arms sprawled in
every direction. She pushed at one of his arms and
nudged his leg aside gingerly, making room for herself.

"You want t' cuddle after all?" he asked huskily.

Surprised, Jessa bolted upright. "Aren't you asleep
yet?" she demanded.

"Juss nappin' . . . waitin' for you. Anyway, how'm I to
sleep when you're crawlin' all over me?"

"I was not crawling! You, sir, have commanded both
sides of the middle!"

He laughed. "What?"

"Kindly move."

"Oh." Noah obliged by turning on his side. He was
still squarely in the middle of the feather tick but his
arms and legs were pulled in. He patted the empty space
beside him. "You can sleep right here." In case she had
other ideas or further objections, Noah grasped Jessa's
wrist and gave her a tug. Off balance, she fell on her
side and faced him.

"There was really no need for that," she said stiffly,
trying to release her wrist. Noah relaxed his fingers and
Jessa eased away.

"See?" he asked in the manner of a man who had
already made his point obvious.

Jessa remained confused. "See what?"

"Soon as I let you go, you go. Don't you like me at all, Jessa?"

"You're talking nonsense, Noah. In fact, you're quite bosky." And frisky, she thought to herself. Noah's hand had wandered to her hip and he was slowly rubbing his palm up and down the length of her thigh. She slapped him away playfully, not wishing to rouse his anger.

"S'cruel t' me." His hand went to his heart in a theatrical gesture. "S'very cruel."

Jessa was not proof against his silliness. She laughed and poked him in the chest. When he managed to trap her hand beneath his she didn't yank it back, but left it there, feeling the warmth of his flesh against her palm, the beat of his heart filling her hand. "You're foxed, Noah McClellan, absolutely foxed."

"Hmmm," he said agreeably, a smile touching the corner of his mouth. "You said that before. Lovely feeling though."

"It certainly appears that way."

Noah's thumb stroked the soft, delicate underside of Jessa's wrist. "This is a lovely feeling, too." His tone became more serious and his gaze rested on Jessa's upturned face. "You never answered m'question. Don't you like me at all?"

"It was a ridiculous question."

"Not so ridic ... ridi ... silly." He waited for a response and when none came he prompted, "Well?"

"Most often I like you well enough."

"Oh." He decided he could be satisfied with that. What had liking to do with what he wanted from her? He had said as much to Jack after a few pints of grog had loosened his tongue. Jack's censorious silence had been excuse enough to drink more. "That's good." He was thoughtful a moment. "Did I ever tell you you have beautiful breasts?"

"Noah!" She withdrew her hand only to have him pin both her legs beneath one of his.

"It's true," he insisted, leaning into her. One arm rested in the curve of her waist.

"This conversation is absurd. I believe I already pointed out that you are not at your most eloquent. Would you please let me up?" She pushed at his shoulder and couldn't budge him. "Noah, please! I don't think you know what you're do—" Jessa stopped in the middle of her thought. Was it true? she wondered. Come morning, would he remember?

From her own experience she knew her father had sometimes forgotten events when he was deep in his cups. Once, while secretly watching her parents entertain fifty or more guests in the ballroom, Jessa had dislocated her shoulder when she tumbled from her secret perch on the stairs. Her father had ridden for the physician himself, helped the man set her shoulder, and stayed at Jessa's side the rest of the night. The following morning he didn't know why he had awakened in her room and couldn't recall riding for the doctor or setting her shoulder. When he discovered, seemingly for the first time, what she had done he had given her a thorough dressing down for her willfulness and unladylike behavior, showing none of the compassion and sympathy he had demonstrated the night before.

Could it be the same with Noah? And even if he remembered, was he in any state now to know precisely what he had done? Would he realize if he made love to her now that she was a virgin? Jessa felt his hand at her breast. This time she didn't move it away. His stroking was clumsy, lacking the finesse and erotic deftness he would have given her had he been completely in control of his actions. Hah! He probably even thought he *was* acting with gentleness and charm!

Jessa made her decision. She would suffer his caresses this night and let him have his way. He would be none the wiser and she would be rid of the only evidence which could damn her. In keeping with this excellent plan Jessa wound her arms about Noah's shoulders and pulled him closer. As his mouth settled over hers she was moved to change one opinion. Perhaps she wouldn't be suffering after all.

She thought his mouth would be sour. It wasn't. There was the lingering taste of rum and something else. Peppermint? Her lips pressed a smile against his. Had Noah thought he could conceal his drinking by sucking on a peppermint stick? It was probably Cam's idea. The boy had a stash of them somewhere, had even offered them to Gideon on occasion. She was glad he had offered one to Noah. The kiss was sweet.

Noah's mouth captured Jessa's sigh of pleasure. His tongue teased her sensitive upper lip and she moved a little restlessly beneath him. Her fingernails marked the flesh of his back with tiny crescents. Noah's thumb passed back and forth across her nipple. Beneath the thin fabric of her shift he could feel her arousal.

"You like that, don't you?" he asked on a thread of sound.

Jessa was surprised, he noticed, and a trifle embarrassed as well. Burying her face in his shoulder, she nodded. Noah's soft laughter tickled the nape of her neck a moment before his mouth touched her there. She felt his hands move to her hair and begin to unwind her braid with astonishingly deft fingers. Vaguely aware that his movements were no longer groping or lacking in persuasive tenderness, Jessa felt a frisson of fear that he was not as drunk as he seemed. Just as she would have pulled away, wary now, Noah's fingers became hopelessly tangled in her hair.

Jessa laughed softly at his puzzled, helpless look and eased her hair out of his grasp, drawing it over her shoulder. "That's why I keep it braided," she said. "It has a will of its own."

Noah's eyes fastened on the fine spill of her hair. In the moonshine it was a pale wash of color, gold and silver strands blending evenly and framing her face in radiant light. Noah felt the impact of her ethereal, outer-worldly beauty with all the force of a blow to his middle. For a moment it was even difficult to breathe. More carefully now he touched the soft curling ends with his fingertips. The back of his fingers brushed her breast.

There was a reverent quality to Noah's hesitant caress which struck Jessa deeply. She took his hand and held it still for a moment, then raising it to her lips she kissed the backs of his fingers. When the tip of her tongue touched the pad of Noah's thumb she heard his sharp intake of breath and felt desire shiver through him. She was not aware that she was smiling a siren's beckoning smile or that her eyes issued a sorceress's invitation. But when Noah's mouth covered hers she knew he had done precisely the thing she had been wanting.

At first the pressure of his lips was light, teasing, just hinting at the passion he felt. It was when Jessa taunted him in kind, flicking her tongue along his upper lip then retreating coyly, that Noah deepened the kiss and eased the steady pull of desperate longing.

Jessa's arms circled him. Her fingers threaded in his thick hair then drifted lower, brushing his nape, his shoulders, tracing the taut length of his spine. And lower still, insinuating themselves beneath the waistband of his drawers and the warm flesh of his buttocks. She touched him as she had longed to, released from her shyness by the knowledge that he couldn't possibly know how much she ached at this moment. She drew patterns on his back, felt the bunching of his arms beneath her palms and tightening in his legs. She loved the smell of him, the lingering scent of rum and peppermint and the musky, male fragrance that was peculiarly Noah's own. Her hands drifted again to his waist and her fingers slipped below his drawers, teasing him with the lightest of touches.

Growling deep in his throat, Noah broke the kiss, raising his head a fraction. His hands lifted to frame her face and he captured her darkening eyes with his own. "Who'm I, Jessa?" he demanded.

She was surprised by the question but didn't hesitate answering. "Noah," she whispered, holding his gaze. His face was beautiful, stamped with desire he made no attempt to hide. His eyelids looked heavy but not sleepy. His mouth was parted but not slack. His lips were moist from her kisses and she wanted to touch her tongue to them again. She touched her own instead. "You're Noah. You're my husband . . . and I want you." Her hands slid from his back and paused on either side of his waist. She looked at him uncertainly, then sensing that he would not help or encourage her, Jessa made the decision entirely on her own. Slipping her hands between their bodies, she unfastened the front fall of his drawers.

Noah sat up, stilling her hands when she tried to push the material down his narrow hips. "Couldn't stand it if you were teasin' me, Jessa. Are you?"

She shook her head. "No. I'm not teasing." A measure of fear returned because Noah, except for the slight slur in his speech, seemed remarkably clearheaded. Again her wariness was pushed to the back of her mind when Noah's efforts to rid himself of his drawers proved awkward and clumsy. His sheepish expression tugged at her heart. Jessa sat up and helped him sort out the tangle he had managed to create around his ankles. She let him toss the drawers over the side of the bed and laughed at the smug, victorious look he shot them as they landed on the floor. Her laughter died when he turned to her and his expression was no longer smug, but serious . . . and alert, watchful.

"Now you," he said.

"Me?"

"Hmmm. Your shift."

Jessa's mouth was dry. Even when she had been helping him strip she had studiously avoided looking at Noah's shadowed thighs. But her gaze had dropped the

moment he pointed out it was her turn to undress and
she could not seem to pull it away. While Noah seemed
completely at ease, even indifferent to the proud, jutting
state of his manhood, Jessa couldn't begin to pretend
nonchalance. She wasn't sure she could swallow,
breathe or blink. She knew she was staring stupidly and
that if she didn't stop Noah was going to know she had
never seen an aroused man before. Still, Jessa couldn't
turn her head. The simple mechanics of the intimate
act they were going to share completely overwhelmed
her. Her body couldn't accommodate . . . *that!*

Noah broke the spell by drawing one corner of the
sheet across his hips. Leaning forward, he touched Jessa's chin with his forefinger and raised her face. "I'll
take that look as a compliment," he said, smiling crookedly. "I'd like t'be able t'return it. Take off your shift,
Jessa. I want to see you."

Jessa sat up on her knees and grasped the hem of
her gown in fingers that trembled. She eased it up her
thighs slowly, not because she wished to be provocative,
but because her shyness had returned. Noah's hands
closed over hers and helped her raise the gown. The
ruffled hem drifted past her naked thighs, her buttocks,
the taut plane of her abdomen. The material tickled
the tips of her breasts, her shoulders, then it was being
pulled over her head, and as her silky hair fell back into
place she was in Noah's arms and the things his mouth
was doing to hers curled her insides.

The delicious tension didn't ease as Noah pressed
her against the bed and partially covered her with his
body. Nor was there any lessening when he murmured
husky endearments against her ear and touched the tip
of her lobe with his tongue. "You're beautiful, Jessa. I
don't think you know . . . sweet, so sweet." He kissed
her eyelids, the soft pulse at her temples. His mouth
followed the curve of her cheek. He nibbled at the
column of her throat. Her breasts filled his palms and
then his mouth claimed one. He laved the swollen bud

with his tongue and suckled her gently. When her tiny gasp of pleasure reached his ears he gave attention to her other breast until he drew a like response.

Jessa felt as if tiny flames were licking at her skin. Her fingers curled around Noah's shoulders and her leg rubbed restlessly against the length of his. When his hand stroked the inside of her thigh and touched her intimately, Jessa didn't shy from the caress. Instead she flowered beneath the gentle manipulation of his finger. Even her pulse thrummed to the rhythm he created. Her legs parted without his prompting, directed by the new urgency she felt within her. She was no longer afraid at the idea of taking him inside her. It was where she wanted him to be.

"Please, Noah," she whispered. "Now. Please love me."

Noah hesitated a moment, wanting to stroke her a little longer, caress her until her insides were as knotted as his, but then she begged him again and he was lost. He slid between her parted legs, cupping her buttocks in his palms. "Help me, Jessa."

Coaxed by some instinct wiser than her fogged senses, Jessa guided Noah into her, lifting her hips slightly. She was the one, unconcerned by the consequences, who thrust upward and forced his entry. Swallowing a cry of pain, Jessa's hands dropped to the mattress and her fingers clutched the sheet beneath her.

Noah leaned forward, supporting his weight on his elbows. His mouth hovered near Jessa's. "Did I hurt you?" he asked, searching her face. He held himself perfectly still, allowing her to get used to the feel of him, though it took every last vestige of control to do so.

Jessa felt him warm and hard, throbbing inside her now, and the pain she had experienced gradually became no more than a sweet ache. It was all right, she thought. Everything was going to be fine. "No, you didn't hurt me."

God, she sheathed him so tightly! How couldn't he have hurt her? "You're so tight . . . small." His hips moved slightly in response to the picture his words were evoking in his mind. "And . . . God, so sweet." It was agony for him to remain still. "Are you sure?"

"Hmmm. I'm sure. It's . . . it's been a long time." All my life, she added silently. "Robert and I didn't . . . you know, when he found out I was pregnant, we didn't . . . and when I was ready again . . . after Gideon's birth . . . Robert was ill." She looked at him anxiously, wondering if she had gone too far by mentioning Robert's name. "I'm sorry, I shouldn't have brought up his—"

"Ssshh." He touched her lips gently. "It's all right. I'm glad you told me. I'll be careful." And he began to move inside her.

Jessa could have cried then. She could have accepted roughness and pawing more easily than his tenderness. One would have assuaged her guilt, the other merely added to it.

She didn't want to feel the return of the coiling tension, but Noah wouldn't have it otherwise. He was far more patient than she expected, and in her own mind, more patient than she deserved. Noah's hands caressed her slowly; his mouth played with hers. His loins applied a steady pressure, building a flame at the center of her. Jessa's palms stroked his back, dipped lower and slid across his buttocks. Her knees nudged his legs and her heels pushed against the mattress for purchase. Her throat arched and his lips felt the vibration of her excited cries before they were given sound.

Nothing that was happening to her seemed real. She was a stranger to the sensations Noah was exacting from her. It was as if he held the key to a door she had never known existed. Sparks of color flickered behind her closed eyes as sparks of heat skittered across her skin. Tension snapped and rushed through her with a force that left her breathless. And then she smiled because in the sweet aftermath warm, languid pleasure bathed her limbs.

"Look at me, Jessa," Noah urged. His own body tightened, straining for release, and still he held back because he wanted to see her eyes, wanted to be certain that she knew it was his seed that she would accept, not Robert's.

Jessa's lashes fluttered then she opened her eyes. Their pale gray color was only evident at the outer edge of the iris. The centers of her eyes were wide, fathomless, black and bright as polished onyx. "Noah," she whispered.

"Oh, God, Jessa," he groaned, raising himself slightly. "Thank you for that." His thrusts were shallow now and quicker, and if she had screamed Robert's name at him Noah knew he wouldn't have been able to stop. But it was his name she said as she clutched his arms. It was his name that echoed in his ears as his back arched and his eyes closed and his body shuddered above her.

Neither of them moved immediately. Jessa's tapered nails whispered across the back of Noah's neck, stroking his skin lightly. Her eyes were closed, hiding a sheen of tears. She didn't know if she were happy or sad or some confusing emotion between the two. When Noah drew away she knew a profound sense of loneliness. He covered them both with the sheet and the comforter, but to Jessa it was a poor substitute for the warmth of his body. Even the arm he slipped about her waist as he turned on his side did not seem sufficient. She wished he would say something. Or was he expecting her to say something? Did one talk at all after sharing what they had just shared?

Apparently not, Jessa decided as she spared a glance at Noah's face. His head was resting on his outstretched arm and it would have been clear to even the meanest intelligence that he was sound asleep. He had gotten what he wanted. Oddly enough, she thought, so had she.

Jessa turned on her side, facing him and touched his cheek softly with the back of her hand. "Come morning," she whispered, "it will be all right if you don't remember a thing. I have memories enough for both of us." Jessa's hand slipped to his neck and she closed her eyes, waiting for sleep to claim her also.

Noah woke at first light and remembering yesterday's events was the least of his problems. He recalled everything with a clarity that only added to the pounding in his head. Had he really just rolled off her and fallen asleep like some green youth sated with his first woman? Yes, he had done exactly that. Noah sat up, swinging his legs over the side of the bed, and held his aching head in his hands. God! He must have made her feel like a whore! Hell, he had treated tavern wenches better than he had treated this woman.

And he had taken her too soon. He knew that as well. She hadn't been ready for him and he had known it even if she didn't. He should have realized there would be some pain for her after so long an abstinence. And she was small . . . and tight . . . and . . . sweet, so sweet. Noah groaned aloud. He had told her that, too. He had never spoken to another woman like that, no matter how much drink or passion had loosed his tongue. It didn't set well with him that he had lost control. Making love shouldn't have been so special with her. He was only exacting the price for his protection. She was only—finally—paying the piper. Why should anything he said or did with her bother him?

Noah stood, slipped on his drawers, and walked over to the washbasin. He poured clear, cold water into the bowl and splashed his face with it. After he rinsed his mouth of the sour taste of grog, sleep, and the odd taste of peppermint, he shaved. The face that stared back at him in the mirror was less haggard than he expected it to be. One night of drink and debauching hardly showed, he mocked himself. The hammering in his head, however, was another matter entirely. Noah put down his razor and wiped the last traces of soap from his chin. When he heard Gideon moving about in the other room he was relieved to have something to do other than torture himself with more questions and recriminations.

Noah changed the infant, found the cloth ball and the string of beads, and carried Gideon and his toys into the main room. "Don't wake your mother," he whispered. "Cam will be here with your breakfast before you realize how hungry you are."

"His mother's already awake," Jessa said sleepily. She patted the space beside her. "Bring him over here. We'll wait out Cam together."

Noah approached the bed and saw Jessa's shift lying at the foot of it. Beneath the covers she was naked, and he remembered everything about her slender form. The lithe line of her surprisingly long legs. The curve of her bottom. Her delicate waist. The lush fullness of her breasts. Everything. He swallowed hard. "I think it would be a good idea if you put something on, Jessa. Else Cam might get an eyeful." Or I may be reduced to a blithering idiot, he added silently, and I won't thank you for it.

Jessa was becoming used to the feeling of shame accompanied by the desire to burrow under the covers. Until this moment she had quite forgotten the state of her undress and the reasons for it. Apparently he had not. Noah was watching her carefully, thoughtfully. He might be cooing in Gideon's ear and bouncing the baby in his arms, but his green-gold eyes were on her. Waiting. And she hadn't the slightest idea what he was expecting.

Thoroughly unnerved, Jessa groped at the foot of the bed for her shift while trying to keep the comforter discreetly situated in front of her. She clutched it in her fingers and gave in to her fondest wish. Dragging the thick blanket over her head in a desperate flourish, she buried herself and the shift beneath it.

Gideon laughed because Noah laughed. Noah laughed because the sight of Jessa trying to put on her shift underneath the comforter was something to behold. There could have been three people under there for all the activity that was going on. She stretched, kicked, and cursed, and the comforter billowed, tangled, and fluttered. When she finally peeked out over the edge Noah wasn't even alarmed by the glaring look she sent him. He knew her well enough to know it was feigned, exaggerated at the very least. He also knew from watching her moments before she went into hiding that she didn't regret having slept with him. Her clear gray eyes told him that. Noah believed the remainder of the journey to Virginia would not be without its rewards.

He plopped Gideon beside Jessa and sat cross-legged at the foot of the bed. "You weren't this shy last night," he pointed out with an amused half-grin. "Reticent, perhaps, but not timid."

"That was . . . different," she said lamely.

"Oh?"

Jessa sat up and straightened the modest neckline of her gown. "Gideon wasn't here then," she said primly.

Noah choked back more laughter. "You can do better than that."

She glanced at Gideon and saw that he was supremely uninterested in the conversation. He was amusing himself with his beads and kicking at the comforter. "And it was dark last night."

Noah's eyes glinted with humor. "It usually is. Dark, that is. At night."

"You know what I mean."

"I don't think I do. If you mean that I couldn't see you last night, then you're mistaken. I saw you very well." His eyes darkened as they traveled over her suggestively. "You were wearing moonlight and starshine. The only thing I don't know is the color of your nipples." He paused a beat. "Pink?"

Jessa picked up Gideon's ball and threw it at Noah's head. He ducked and it sailed right over him. Not that it would have had much effect, she thought dismally. Dropping a blacksmith's anvil directly on his skull from a height of ten feet might, just might, have the desired consequence.

"What are you plotting?" he asked.

She blinked, startled by his perception. "How did you know?"

Noah shrugged. "I just do. You have a very expressive face, you know. I'm afraid it doesn't do you much good to dissemble. Your eyes and your mouth give you away every time."

Jessa could have told him a few truths that would have erased his smug look. Noah didn't know as much as he thought he did. "They do?" she asked sweetly.

"Hmm-mm. A moment ago you were contemplating murder. Now you're thinking there are things about you I don't know."

She wasn't quick enough to hide her surprise. "Aren't there?" she asked uneasily.

"I'm sure there are." Noah leaned forward on his hands, careful not to disrupt Gideon's play, and stole a kiss from Jessa's parted lips. "The color of your nipples for one." He lifted his head and held her gaze. "Have a care with your secrets, Jessa," he warned. "Don't use them to taunt me. I can be quite ruthless in searching them out if I choose."

Jessa paled but said nothing.

Noah sat back and ruffled the edge of the comforter to get Gideon's attention. The infant giggled and made a grab at it. But when he spoke it was to Jessa. "I've been thinking about what happened last night."

"You have?" she asked. She wished he wouldn't talk about it.

"I didn't give a very good account of myself. I had

too much to drink, forced my attentions when I promised not to, and then passed out."

"You didn't force me," she said, wondering where he was leading. "I never said no."

Noah shook his head. "As I recall, you did. Several times."

His memory certainly hadn't been impaired, Jessa thought anxiously. Still, he had no cause to reproach himself, at least not on this matter, and as yet, she had no reason to fear he believed anything but what she told him last night. "You were rather more persistent than usual," she teased, striving for lightness.

Noah wasn't having any of it. "I hurt you. That was never part of what I wanted."

"N-no. You didn't." What would he think if he knew he had helped her get rid of the one bit of evidence that could have destroyed her future as well as Gideon's? He had actually freed her to belong to another man, a man who might love her and one she could love in return. She would never have to fear that it would be discovered that Gideon wasn't her child. "And anyway, it . . . it was my fault if you did. I . . . I was too eager." She lowered her eyes, embarrassed.

About to tell her that he had found her eagerness exciting, Noah swallowed the words whole. His gaze fastened on the part of the bed revealed as Gideon pushed the comforter aside. The sheet beneath was stained with blood. He threw back the blanket and saw several smaller stains. "Oh, dear Lord, Jessa. Why didn't you say anything?"

Jessa's attention was drawn to the sheet and she felt herself near fainting with the enormity of her deception. She hadn't given any thought at all to the fact that she might bleed. It was odd, she thought miserably. There were women who would have been proud to show their husbands the proof of their virginity. Some women were even reduced to trickery to give the evidence. And here she was, the morning after her true wedding night, having to find some reason that would explain it away.

There were three things she could tell him. One was the truth and it would not serve. Second was to fall back on the explanation he was so ready to believe: that he had rent her while forcing his entry. Jessa shied away from telling him that. For reasons she could not entirely fathom she didn't want to make Noah feel guilty.

So it was the third explanation that came tumbling out of her mouth. "It's my monthly courses, Noah . . . I didn't realize. Oh, God!" She raised her hands to her warm cheeks. "I'm sorry. Is it possible to expire from embarrassment?" she asked woefully. Neither her expression nor the tone were entirely feigned.

Noah quickly threw the comforter back into place and put Gideon on top so he couldn't push it aside again. "I didn't mean to embarrass you," he said. "I thought I had done . . . I don't know, *something.*" He raised his hands helplessly, vaguely embarrassed himself. "Is there something I can get you? I don't know much about—"

"Oh, please, don't go on." She peeped at Noah from between her fingers. There was ruddy color in his own cheeks! Jessa had to restrain the urge to laugh. "If I could just have some privacy," she told him gently. "Perhaps you could find Cam and ask him about our breakfast."

Noah was off the bed and gathering his clothes before Jessa finished her sentence.

"It's not leprosy, you know," Jessa said, biting back a smile as Noah hopped on one foot and jammed his other leg into his breeches. "I don't even have to be quarantined."

"I know that," he said, changing his stance and repeating the procedure. He fastened his breeches at the waist, shooting a sideways glance at Jessa. "Are you making light of me?"

"A little. I didn't mean for you to rush out of here."

She picked up Gideon and put him on her lap, ruffling his hair with her fingertips.

"I'm not rushing," he denied, pulling on his shirt. "You wanted some privacy, didn't you?" He slipped on his shoes without putting on his stockings, but just to make certain she didn't think he was in such a hurry to leave, Noah leaned over the bed and gave Jessa a very thorough, very leisurely kiss. He only broke away because Gideon knocked him in the chin with a dimpled fist. Noah chuckled, brushed her lips again, and dropped a kiss on Gideon's downy cap of hair. "Just wait, young man, until you want to kiss a beautiful woman. You won't want any interference, either."

He was at the door when Jessa found her voice. "Noah?"

"Hmm?" he turned, opening the door behind him.

"Your shirt is on backward."

"Oh." His grin was sheepish. So much for not rushing.

"And inside out."

Noah made his escape quickly and as he stood in the companionway righting his clothes he heard Jessa's happy laughter, then Gideon's musical giggles. He didn't even try to suppress the smile that came so easily to his lips.

Noah bumped into Cam on the narrow stairs leading to the upper deck. He grasped the boy by the shoulders and steadied him. "There. That's better. Mornin', Cam."

"G'mornin', Mr. Noah." He eased himself out of Noah's grasp, offered a quick smile, then resumed his rush down the companionway.

"Hold up!"

Cam skittered to a halt and turned. "Yes, sir?"

"Where are you going in such a hurry?"

"Have to tell the cap'n that Ross Booker's been put aboard the *Sargus.*"

"Wait a minute," Noah said, approaching the boy.

"Do you mean the prisoner's been transferred? When did this happen?"

"Just a little while ago. It was Captain Riddle's orders, sir, just as soon as Mr. Macy told him about sighting the other ship. 'Ask them if they'll transport our prisoner,' says the cap'n. And Mr. Macy signaled the *Sargus* and they said they would and then Booker was rowed over to them and now he's gone. On his way back to England, he is. Only the cap'n don't know it's been done coz he's nursin' a sore head in his quarters." Cam paused for breath and darted a glance at Noah. "You don't look near as bad as the cap'n, if you don't mind me sayin' so."

Realizing his headache was indeed gone, Noah grinned. "No, I don't mind you saying so, but don't tell Captain Riddle. I'm sure the only thing easing his suffering is the thought that I'm suffering more."

Cam smiled brightly. "Those are almost his exact words."

Noah chuckled. "Well, when you've given him the message, will you take care of breakfast for my wife and son? Gideon's good humor this morning can't be pressed much longer."

"What about you, sir? Your breakfast, I mean."

"I'll eat something with the crew." He started to turn away, then stopped. "Oh, and Cam? Mrs. McClellan will be needing water for washing Gideon's things. Get someone to help you with it though; don't do it all yourself. And some water for bathing, too. That's fresh salt water, Cam," he added when Cam looked as if he were about to ask. "On both counts." He watched Cam bob a quick assent then hurry off. Noah realized he was going to miss the boy once they anchored at the landing. If he were taking Jessa and Gideon to Philadelphia he'd have asked Cam to join them. Noah put a brake on that thought almost as soon as he heard himself say it. God! What was he thinking? Jessa and Gideon in Philadelphia? It was absurd!

Once Noah got to the upper deck he went straight to the taffrail and joined several of the crew who were also in need of answering nature's early morning call. He ignored their gentle ribbing when they accused him of being too shy to relieve himself in front of his wife. Their humor was ribald and bawdy but directed at him, not Jessa, and Noah let them have their fun. Nothing, he thought, was going to interfere with his good spirits this morning. Yet a moment later, when he glanced down at himself as he was righting the front fall of his drawers and saw the flecks of blood on his member, he found out how wrong he could be.

Slightly dazed by his discovery, Noah fastened the front of his breeches and walked away from the taffrail. He sat down slowly on a coil of rope directly below the mizzenmast. His knees were hunched to his chest and his back pressed firmly against the mast for support. Staring straight ahead, without seeing anything but the image of Jessa's face, Noah tried to make sense of this new evidence.

He no longer believed the blood on his own person was the result of Jessa's monthly courses. It seemed highly unlikely that her flow had begun when he penetrated her. And she would have had some suspicion that her time was near, wouldn't she? Yet she hadn't prepared for it. She hadn't worn anything beneath her shift, and Noah had lived with her long enough to know some of her intimate habits. Jessa was nothing if not fastidious about her personal care. Ticking back the days on his fingers, Noah tried to remember the last time he was vaguely aware that she was having her monthly flow. He only had to go back two weeks for his answer. Not nearly long enough for Jessa's explanation to ring true.

Noah pressed one hand to his forehead, massaging the ache that had returned with a vengeance. Above him the sails snapped with all the vicious noise of a thunderclap. The sun disappeared behind a cloud and a cold gray shadow fell over Noah, suiting his mood perfectly.

So why had Jessa lied? he wondered. Why hadn't she told him that he had hurt her very badly indeed? Unless . . . unless that wasn't the truth either. But that would mean . . . no, the idea was patently absurd. Noah massaged his temple harder as if he could rub out the last thought. But it would not be erased so easily and Noah found himself dwelling on it, arguing both sides of the question.

She had been a virgin.

No, fool, she was married.

She *says* she was married.

But she has a child.

She *says* Gideon is her child.

Of course he's her son. You can see how much she loves him.

There's no denying she loves him, but *is* he her son?

Yes. Yes. Gideon's her child.

Then she wasn't a virgin.

"Dammit, she *was* a virgin!"

Several nearby crew members stopped working and glanced in Noah's direction. "Beggin' your pardon, Mr. McClellan," one of them said, "but none of us ever made a comment one way or t'other."

Noah scowled at the man. "I wasn't talking to you. I was thinking aloud."

"Aye, that you were. No good ever comes of it." He ducked his head and bent over his mop when Noah continued to glare at him.

Shaken that he had actually spoken his thoughts out loud, Noah gritted his teeth to keep it from happening again. Now where had he been? Oh, yes. Shouting that she was a virgin. There was a Banbury tale, he grimaced, yet the longer he considered it, the more he believed it was true. He thought about Jessa's insistence that the marriage be one of convenience, her desire not to have it consummated. The cunning bitch. She wasn't mourning a dead husband, she was guarding herself.

So why did she allow me to make love to her last night?

Because she thought you were so stinking drunk you'd never be the wiser.

And Noah knew that was the truth, too. There had been that incredible look of astonishment on her face when she had seen him fully aroused. Groaning softly, he remembered her tightness, the resistance, all of which she swept away by thrusting into him. This morning she blushed beautifully and shyly told him she had been eager. With his new insight, Noah realized she had been desperate, not eager. If it hadn't been for the blood and Jessa's quickly constructed lie, which had more holes than a sieve, he might have never stumbled upon the truth.

Not that he understood how everything fit together, he acknowledged grimly. Yet there was a point on which the lines of truth and falsehood seemed to converge: Gideon.

Who is he?

Ask Jessa.

I can't. Well, I *could*, but she won't tell me. She doesn't trust me.

Not yet. That could change.

She doesn't know how to tell the truth. She wants her damn secrets.

You'll have to win her confidence.

Why would I want to do that? I want to strangle her.

Choices, choices, mocked the inner voice.

Beginning to fear for his sanity, Noah stopped the dialogue going on in his head. He could go back to the cabin and confront Jessa with the truth—and Noah *knew* he had some part of the truth now—but what would it serve? Everything she had done, every lie she had told, had but one purpose: to keep Gideon at her side. But why? Who was the child to her? It seemed certain to

Noah that the infant was no kin. She could have easily explained he was a brother or a cousin, yet she had maintained her deception as a grieving widow even after Noah had learned of her role in the post road robbery. It was very important to her that he believe she was Gideon's mother.

Oh, God! What if her tale about the asylum were based on some fact? Was she mad? Did she think Gideon was in fact her son? Had she stolen him?

Something about that last thought niggled at the back of Noah's mind, but he could not bring it to the forefront or make any sense of it. Neither could he believe that Jessa was mad. Whatever she was doing, Noah was forced to conclude that she was in some way trying to protect Gideon.

Protect. It was an odd word to use, he thought. Why should the child need Jessa's protection?

Noah realized he still had far many more questions than answers, but a few things were clearer than others. Jessa was not insane. Discounting her role in the robbery, neither was she a criminal. She was not capable of doing anything with real criminal intent. But that didn't mean what she was doing was entirely within the law. Noah would stake his reputation on the fact that she was involved in something far more serious—and potentially dangerous—than she had ever let on. That being the case, how was he supposed to wash his hands of her? He could not avoid the painful truth that he was an accessory to whatever it was she was doing. After all, he had brought her here. Damn her for the lying jade that she was! She had forced him into this untenable position. In order to protect himself, his name, and his career, he would have to honor the marriage longer than he wanted. It was the only course left open to him. Divorce or an annulment meant that she could testify against him. If she were caught at whatever clever game she was playing, Noah had no doubt that she would be vindictive enough to revenge herself on him.

His decision made, Noah pushed away from the mizzenmast and stood up. If gaining her trust was the only way he could learn the whole of the truth from her lips then he would do it. But to hedge his bets he would write to Drew Goodfellow immediately and ask him to find out what he could. Mary Shaw could prove to be a valuable source of information. Noah realized that a reply would be months in coming; the letter couldn't even be sent until he reached Virginia and put it on a packet bound for England. Still, he would feel better having composed it. Perhaps it would put his own thoughts in order and help him decide how best to deal with Jessa. She was using him, relying on the protection of his name for herself and for Gideon, and Noah took strong, violent exception to that. He was neither so generous nor forgiving to have decided she shouldn't suffer for her deceit.

She had also carried her lies into their bed. She had purposely called him Robert to keep her secret—and her virginity—intact. Of all the things she had said or done, that trifling lie still stung the most.

He might have to gain her trust in order to find out what she'd done, but he'd be damned if she'd close this new trap about him without feeling the bite of it herself.

CHAPTER EIGHT

Noah didn't return to his cabin until Cam told him the table was laid for dinner. He didn't think he could trust himself to deal with Jessa before then. As he had written the letter to Drew, he alternated between wanting to flay Jessa alive and simply wanting her. It bothered him more than a little that he could still be attracted to her when she had done nothing but use him for her personal fool since their first meeting. Attraction was a paltry word to describe what it was he felt. Intrigue. Desire. Hunger. All morning and afternoon those emotions had warred with his sense of pride, making him bitter, resentful, and fiercely angry by turns. He had managed at last to quell the powerful and unsatisfying emotions because he could not face Jessa if he didn't. The thought of facing her now that he was privy to secrets she had no idea she had revealed brought Noah a curious sort of pleasure that he was not about to deny.

Noah had to cool his heels in the companionway until Jessa answered his knock at the door. As she stepped aside to let him enter his first thought was that she had no right to look so beautiful. She was wearing a deep blue satin gown that did remarkable things for her eyes, lending their normally pale gray color a luminous sapphire hue. Her fine silky hair was secured by a dark ribbon at her nape, but a delicate fringe of gold and silver brushed her forehead and temples and curled at her ears. Her hair was a splendid gilt frame; her face, an inspired portrait.

Noah's eyes drifted to the soft and tremulous lips that parted in a sweet smile of greeting. God help him, but he wanted to kiss that mouth.

So he did.

His lips lingered over hers, sipping, tasting. He kissed the corners of her mouth, ran his tongue along the sensitive underside of Jessa's upper lip. Her tiny gasp was an invitation. Noah's tongue slipped inside her mouth and began a deliciously languid battle with hers. As the kiss deepened the rhythm of his stroking changed, becoming sensual, measured thrusts that were meant to remind Jess of a joining more intimate than their mouths. He felt the rise of heat in her body, then his own.

Noah straightened, curving his hands around Jessa's waist and lifting her slightly. She stood tiptoed, her weight supported by the hard length of Noah's body. Her fingers curled in the material of his shirt, clutching it for purchase so she wouldn't have to break the kiss.

As soon as Noah felt the fullness of Jessa's abandoned response he began to draw back, lifting his head so that his mouth hovered above hers, then brushing his lips across hers, sipping once more, tasting the sweet nectar of her moist lips. He set her down gently and felt her fingers slowly open in the folds of his shirt. Her eyes were as wide and wary as a startled fawn's, but they shimmered with the pale colors of a spring rain. For a moment her palms lay flat against his chest, then she seemed to remember herself and her hands fluttered uneasily to her sides just as Noah's dropped away from her waist.

Jessa looked away, uncomfortable beneath Noah's steady, narrow regard. His expression was reserved, shuttered, giving nothing of his thoughts away. "Your . . . our dinner is getting cold," she said, glancing at the table.

Noah was angry—and aroused—and angry because he was aroused. He did not want to want her. He wanted to enjoy her, use her, command her trust and then command her body as payment for his protection, but he did not want to desire her. When Noah answered he managed to keep both anger and arousal out of his voice. "I'll join you in a moment. I want to wash first." He brushed past her and went to the basin. "Where's Gideon?" he asked, dipping his hands into the cool water and splashing his face.

"Under the table."

Noah looked past his reflection in the mirror and saw the infant was gnawing on a chair leg. Gideon, at least, could make him smile and mean it. "It looks as if he's starting dinner without us."

"Oh, Gideon!" Jessa said, dismayed. She got down on her hands and knees and pulled the infant out, scolding him all the while. "He's absolutely ruined the furniture, Noah. I had no idea four tiny teeth could do so much damage!"

Noah forced a small laugh because he thought it was expected and joined her at the table. He held out a chair for her, then seated himself. "Don't worry about it. I doubt all those marks are Gideon's. Don't forget that Salem's children have occupied this cabin before." He lifted the cover on their main course and groaned. "Rice and animals again."

"What?"

"Rice and animals," he said, pointing to the platter. "That's what we called this meal during the war. Sometimes we only had rice. But occasionally, if we were fortunate, there'd be bits of meat in it." He smiled crookedly. "Except no one really knew, or wanted to know, what kind of meat. So . . . rice and animals."

Jessa made a face. "I think I've lost my appetite," she said, leaning forward to inspect the tiny pieces of meat mixed with the brown rice.

Noah spooned a large serving onto her plate anyway. "It's salt pork, Jessa," he said.

"You're certain?"

"Absolutely."

"All right, but you've given me more than I can eat."

"Eat what you can," he said, letting his eyes slowly drift over her face, her shoulders, then her breasts. "I'm very aware that you're neither underfed nor undernourished."

Color tinged Jessa's cheeks. She averted her head and began feeding Gideon his milky rice soup while Noah filled first her wineglass then his own. Gideon smacked his lips, carried on a cheerful, incomprehensible monologue, and kept trying to grab the spoon as Jessa fed him.

"Do you know," Noah said thoughtfully, casually, "he really doesn't resemble you. Does he take after his father?"

Jessa nearly dropped the spoon. Gideon sputtered when she missed his mouth and she quickly wiped his chin, composing herself. Where had that question come from? And why hadn't she thought to prepare for it? "Hmm-mmm. He has his father's features," she said, thinking of Kenyon Penberthy. "Dark hair and blue eyes. And the eyebrows. See how they're slightly winged? Those are his father's brows. Devilish, don't you think?"

Noah made no comment on Jessa's faltering, though he had observed it. He accepted her answer at face value. "Indeed. Though Gideon's more of an imp than a devil." He leaned across the table and tapped the infant's chin with his forefinger. "Aren't you?" Gideon laughed gaily and his head bobbed up and down as if in agreement. "And your husband," Noah asked, "was he something of a devil?"

Wishing that Noah would be done with this subject, Jessa concentrated on keeping her voice even. Thinking of Kenyon again, she replied, "No, not really. He was very even tempered." Not like you, she added to herself. "He was conscious of his position and its responsibilities."

"I see," he said in a flat tone. "How old was he when he died?"

Jessa began feeding Gideon again. "Twenty-seven." She frantically searched for a way to turn the conversation and realized he had given her a lead. "How old are you?"

Noah laughed shortly. "Odd, isn't it? We really know so little about one another. I'm thirty-three—no, thirty-four. I had a birthday recently."

"How recently?"

"Since we've been on board," he told her. "April sixteenth."

"But you didn't say a word!"

He shrugged. The matter was of complete indifference to him. Before he was privy to Jessa's latest intrigue he might have been flattered by her interest. Now he saw it for what it was: another example of her cunning. She only pretended interest. It was all part of the trap. "Does it bother you that I'm so much older than your husband was?"

Jessa blinked, startled by his question. "I never thought about it. I'm not so very young myself. I'll be twenty-two in August."

"So old," he mocked. He pointed to her plate. "Eat something, Jessa."

She set down Gideon's spoon and picked up her fork. "Yes, Papa," she said dryly.

"Very amusing." He pushed away his empty plate and slid Gideon's bowl in front of him. "Here, let me finish feeding Gideon." He took the boy off her lap without waiting for her reply. "He's getting heavy," he said, bouncing Gideon on his knee. "You shouldn't carry him around on your hip anymore. You'll set your back out of place."

Since he spoke as if he knew what he was talking about, Jessa acquiesced. She was touched that he noticed things like that and cared enough to say something. Although she pretended concentration on her food Jessa saw everything that Noah did with Gideon. He was enormously gentle with the infant but not in the least uncomfortable. Cradled as he was in Noah's arm, Gideon was secure and content. Noah coaxed and teased but didn't coddle. "You're fond of him, aren't you?" she asked.

"Gideon? I'm more than fond of him." That was true and Noah had no trouble admitting it aloud. He was not so bitter that he held the child at fault for Jessa's plotting. "Did you doubt it?"

Jessa shook her head. "Not many people would take the interest you do in another man's son."

But whose son? Noah wondered. He bit back the question with difficulty. Go carefully, he told himself. He shouldn't rush his fences. There was time to learn the truth and ways to do it that would not raise Jessa's suspicions. "I wouldn't have brought you with me if I hadn't wanted to help Gideon," he said stiffly.

"I'm sorry," she said quickly. "I didn't mean . . ."

Noah waved her apology aside. "Clearly you love him above all others."

"Yes. I love him." But above all others? She wondered if that were still true. It had to be, she thought. The alternative did not bear scrutiny. Jessa's fingers trembled. She picked up her glass in both hands and sipped the sweet wine, a faintly troubled look in her eyes.

"Jessa?" Noah covered the top of Jessa's wineglass with his hand. He gently pushed downward so that Jessa was forced to set it on the table again. "Is something wrong?"

"What?" Jessa realized that after one sip of the wine she had simply been staring at her glass. "Oh. N-no. I was just thinking, that's all."

Noah nearly groaned aloud as the tip of her tongue touched the corner of her mouth. He wanted to taste the wine on her lips. Inwardly he railed against the unfairness of it. It wasn't right that she could move him with an unconsciously seductive gesture. He caught himself. When had Jessa ever done anything unconsciously? She calculated everything like the shrewdest New England merchant. "Anything you care to share?" he asked, cursing the involuntary huskiness that remained in his voice.

Jessa shook her head. "No. Nothing."

Gideon was getting restless in Noah's lap so Noah set him down on the floor. The infant crawled to the lacquered table set between the two lounging chairs, clapped at the edge a few times, then pulled himself up. "How long has he been doing that?" Noah asked, watching Gideon waver upright for a few seconds then plop back on his bottom. Undaunted, Gideon pulled himself upright again, this time shuffling a few inches along the table.

She turned in her chair to see what Gideon was doing. "It started today," Jessa said, smiling. "Watch him. He doesn't seem to know how to get down again. Poor baby, he stands there all wobbly and uncertain until his legs are simply exhausted, then he falls. I helped him down once, but there was such a wail of protest that I thought I'd better let him do it his own way. I didn't do much of anything today except watch him go up and down and up again. He never stopped." Her smile faded as she became more thoughtful. "I doubt there is anything in all the world more courageous than a child," she said softly.

Noah turned away from Gideon and stared at the pure lines of Jessa's delicate profile. "Aren't you courageous?"

"Me?" Jessa stood and began stacking their plates and silverware. "Hardly," she scoffed. "I've been beaten down so many times I know when not to get up."

Beaten? Jessa? She didn't seriously expect him to believe that. "You surprise me."

"Why?"

"The way you spoke to me yesterday, after Ross Booker's attack, that wasn't the defense of a woman lacking in courage."

"Oh, that," she dismissed lightly. "Well, I was angry then."

"And you left the Granthams," he prompted as if he believed her story. "That took courage."

"Not courage. I was frightened."

But of what? Of whom? "You were part of the robbery," he reminded her. "You knew that was dangerous no matter how well you thought it was planned. Surely that speaks to courage."

Jessa laughed. "It speaks to my desperation and nothing else. Really. Noah, you're looking for substance in my character where none exists."

Noah thought she was overplaying her role as the helpless young widow. Physically, Jessa might remind him of a willow, resilient and supple, whipping and bending in the wind, never breaking, never beaten, but when it came to Gideon she bent for no one. She had a spine of steel and a single-mindedness that allowed no retreat. She did not care who she compromised. If he had not been her victim Noah might have admired her courage in taking him on. As it was, he looked forward to revenge.

"Ma. Ma. Ma," Gideon said, interrupting Noah's thoughts. He had managed to climb onto the low table.

"I think he wants you," said Noah, moving swiftly to keep Gideon from falling.

"No. He only wanted to get down." She took him from Noah's arm, hugged him, and set him on the floor.

She watched him for a moment then began clearing the table.

Noah stopped her. "Leave them. I want to talk to you." His palm slid up and down her arm with a casual proprietal air. His fingers circled the fragile bones of her wrist and his thumb brushed the delicate underside. He watched her confusion with satisfaction, knowing he had her off balance. Drawing on his advantage, he led her away from the table and into the living area. He did not give her time to think or form a protest. He sat down and placed her onto his lap. If she were vulnerable at all it was at times like these. "I meant to tell you earlier. Booker's been transferred to another ship. You don't have to worry about him any longer."

"He was? When?" Why was he telling her this now, in this way?

"This morning."

It was difficult to think clearly when he was touching her. She gently tried to pull away and found herself held fast. He was giving no quarter yet he was being very tender. She wondered if she would ever fathom his moods. "What will happen to him?"

"He'll be released when the ship docks in England."

"You don't believe I flirted with him, do you?"

"No," he said, squeezing her wrist gently. "But I don't think it's the first time something like that happened to you." He felt Jessa stiffen and he knew his instincts had been right. "Was it?"

"It's not important."

To Noah's way of thinking Jessa was still zealously guarding her secrets. Well, dammit, something had to give and this was the one he had chosen to single out first. He held a tight rein on his anger. "I think it is. Can't you trust me at all, Jessa?" He held his breath, waiting for her answer, wondering if he could believe her if she gave one.

"That's not fair. I've trusted you with everything. Gideon's life. My own."

Noah said nothing. He merely continued to stare at her, pinning her with his green-gold eyes.

"It did happen before," she said finally, resigned to the fact that she could only tell him half-truths at best.

"How long ago?"

"After Robert died."

Noah nearly shook her then. She never had any damn husband! At least not one who took her to bed and gave her a son. And that was too much for Noah to swallow without choking. He couldn't begin to imagine the man who could be married to Jessa and not want her intimately. After all, he had his own experience to draw on. The question of Gideon's identity, and perhaps Jessa's own, remained to be answered.

"What's wrong?" Jessa asked. Noah had been quiet for so long that she believed he didn't want to know anymore. The longer he thought the deeper he scowled. Jessa could not help but worry.

Her voice broke Noah's reverie and he picked up the threads of their conversation. "Who was it?"

"Lord Penberthy," she answered truthfully. "The man in the carriage. Remember?"

"Very well," he said succinctly, recalling Jessa's panic. He never doubted her fear had been real. If the Granthams were no real threat to her then somehow the Penberthys were. He had not imagined that incident on the London streets. He tried to remember what Jessa had told him about Lord Penberthy. Sifting through truth and falsehood was going to be a Herculean task. "You said he was married."

"He is. I don't think he was concerned with his vows when he cornered me."

"Where did it happen?"

"At Grant Hall, in Gideon's nursery. Lord Penberthy came to pay his respects."

"He was offering condolences to the grieving widow, I take it," he said, trying to keep the cynicism out of his voice. Her explanations remained consistent if nothing else.

Jessa shivered. "Yes, something like that. Noah, I didn't encourage him. I swear it!"

He wondered. "I know you didn't," he said, wanting her to think he believed her. He hesitated, then his hand strayed to the ribbon in her hair. He undid it, letting it fall to the floor, and wound his fingers in the silky beauty of her hair. "Were you hurt?" he asked.

"No, not the way you mean. He didn't . . . you know, he didn't . . ."

"Rape you," Noah finished for her. He knew better than anyone that Penberthy hadn't used her that way, but he had wondered if she would tell the truth. "How did you stop him?"

"Gideon helped me." She sensed his disbelief rather than saw it. "No, it's true. There was some noise and he woke and began to cry. His lordship reacted to it and lifted his head."

"He was kissing you." Noah's fingers tightened in her hair.

"Yes, I suppose that's what he was doing." Jessa's hand slipped forward and curved around Noah's neck. She could feel the quickening pulse in his throat. "But it wasn't a kiss . . . not like yours."

Noah's breath caught. She was a temptress, a witch. As long as he knew her for what she was how could it be wrong to turn the tables on her? Why shouldn't he thoroughly enjoy what she was clearly offering? She may not have encouraged Edward Penberthy—and Noah had his doubts—but she was showing no such reticence with him.

Jessa went on hurriedly, realizing what she had said. "When he broke away I clawed his face. I don't think he believed I wasn't interested in him until then. Nothing I said before seemed to make an impression. My nails did though. From the corner of his eye to his jaw."

Noah's fingers dropped away from her hair. He

reached for her wrists, held them, and examined her small hands, turning them over in his. Her nails were not buffed. Neither were they long. Months of hard work at Mary's cottage had left an indelible mark. Washing Gideon's diapers in salt water almost daily made her skin dry. Still, Noah thought somewhat reluctantly that they were beautifully sculpted hands, slender, delicate, and capable of giving him great pleasure. Because it amused him to do so, he raised her hands to his lips, kissing the back of each one in turn.

Jessa's heart thumped madly. When Noah released her hands it seemed natural to curl her fingers around his neck and raise her head until her mouth met his. She initiated the kiss but she reveled in Noah's response. She felt a curling of desire deep within her as her lips parted and gave him the entry he sought. His hands were at her back again, pressing her close. His fingers tripped along her spine then threaded in her hair. The delicious ache she felt in her middle became a shiver that made her clutch his shoulders for support.

She pulled away, breathless. Even through the material of her gown she could feel Noah's arousal against her hip. It wasn't fair to continue. She knew that now. "I'm sorry. I shouldn't have done that. We can't . . ." Her voice drifted into nothingness.

"I hadn't forgotten," Noah said. He had been prepared for her to use her monthly flow as an excuse not to finish what she had started. How clever she must be feeling to be able to keep him at a distance. He decided to give her something to think about. Slipping one hand behind her neck, Noah pulled her toward him. Her startled gasp gave him the opening he sought. He kissed her deeply on the mouth. Once. Twice. When he felt her response and knew that she wanted to linger, renew the sweet kiss, deepen it again, he gave her a nudge and released her. She stood on her feet and now it was Noah who smiled. Jessa was nearly as wobbly as Gideon.

"I think I'll ready Gideon for bed," she said, a husky

tremor in her voice. Jessa reached hastily for Gideon, who seemed to have understood her intent and was now crawling full speed for the relative safety of the dining table. She gave him a little squeeze as she lifted him. Hiding her warm face against the baby, Jessa whisked him away to his room.

When she returned nearly an hour later, Noah was already in bed. The lamps had been turned back save for one near the basin. Thinking him asleep, Jessa crossed the room to wash her face and brush out her hair. If only Gideon had gone to sleep so easily, she thought wistfully. She had wanted to be with Noah. In her most vulnerable moments she wove fantasies about living a lifetime with him. Jessa brushed her hair with long hard strokes, punishing herself for her dangerous dreams. She set the brush down, and as was her custom when she was having her monthly courses, she readied for bed in the privacy of the washroom.

She was glad she had taken the precaution because when she slid into bed Noah turned on his side and cuddled against her. He immediately would have been aware if she had not worn anything beneath her nightshift and he must never guess at her subterfuge. Jessa felt as inviolable as a medieval maiden wearing a chastity belt. Noah must have thought so, too. He made a soft grunt that sounded like dissatisfaction as he touched her hip.

"Do you always pretend to be sleeping when you're not?" she asked looking up at him.

"I like watching you when you don't think I am," he told her.

Jessa wasn't certain she liked the sound of that. "Why?" she asked baldly.

"Because you're so lovely to watch." There was more truth to his answer than he cared to admit, but it was better than telling her that he suspected everything she did. He saw Jessa's frown. "Hasn't anyone told you that before?"

Without thinking, she shook her head.

"Not Robert?"

Jessa wished she wouldn't keep forgetting that she was supposed to have been married. Now she searched for something to say. "Robert wasn't very, umm, expressive. If he thought those things, then he kept them to himself."

He marveled at her ability to prevaricate so quickly. "How long were you married, Jessa?"

"Almost two years."

"Were you happy?"

"Y-yes."

"Did you love him?"

"Why must we speak of Robert? Can't you see that it distresses me? It was a lifetime ago. I wish to put it behind me. Can't you do the same?"

"I find it odd that you rarely speak of your husband," he said casually, intent on provoking her further.

Jessa realized she could not remain defensive. She had to attack. "Why should you? What are we to one another after all? I'm the woman you want in your bed because Hilary isn't here. You may dress it up and say I'm your wife—"

"You *are* my wife," he said coldly. How dare she bring Hilary into this! She wasn't fit to speak Hilary's name! The tiny voice of conscience that had not been entirely suppressed berated Noah for anger that was out of proportion to Jessa's words. In truth, his anger was born of guilt. He hadn't thought of Hilary in more than a casual way for weeks. For whatever reasons, Jessa occupied more and more of his thoughts.

"We both know it's a temporary arrangement," she continued. "Frankly, I wouldn't want it any other way." She was so furious with Noah that when she spoke the words she believed them. It was as if her dreams had never existed.

Noah was convinced she spoke the truth as well. It gave him a perverse sort of pleasure to tell her he had decided otherwise. "That's too bad," he said tightly. "I've changed my mind."

"What!" She couldn't have heard him correctly.

"You heard me. I've changed my mind. The events of last evening convinced me that our peculiar marriage has something to recommend it after all." Noah knew how she would construe his words and he wasn't disappointed. Beside him he felt her stiffen and try to move away. He held her fast. She didn't have to know that the marriage would continue because he needed to protect his back. What was it he had said to Drew ages ago? "She'd stab me as soon as look at me." How prescient he had been. He couldn't dismiss her until he knew what she was involved in. But she was welcome to believe his interest in her was physical. In some ways she was not so far off the mark.

"You're disgusting." She wiggled again, trying to get away. At her back she felt the heat and hardness of him. "Let me go."

"When I'm ready." He paused. "And, Jessa, I mean that now and in the future."

She gritted her teeth. "I want an annulment."

"No."

"A divorce, then."

"When I decide."

"What about your family? What will they think?"

"It's unfortunate that I'm committed to go to the landing, but there's no reason they shouldn't know the truth, or at least some part of it."

"What about Hilary?" she demanded with a hint of desperation. "How can you do this to her? What will you say?"

"What I choose to tell Hilary is my concern, not yours. She has nothing to do with you." Hilary was less of a problem than Jessa thought. His fiancée would support him because she cared about his political career. She had a vested interest in his future and she wouldn't let Jessa stand in her way any more than he would. As long as Hilary knew he was going to marry her after he eliminated Jessa as a threat, she would stand by him. "Hilary will wait for me," he said with a trace of cockiness.

"You arrogant swine! I feel sorry for her. Maybe she should know how you take her for granted. I wonder what she would think if she knew how you've sniffed after my skirts." Jessa didn't begin to understand how close to the mark she was. Noah's anger was volcanic.

"You bitch!" He pushed her on her back and pinned her wrists. She was every bit as vindictive as he thought. "By your own admission I didn't force you last night! You threw up your skirts as willingly as any London doxy."

Jessa felt his verbal thrust as a physical blow to her middle. "That's not the way I remember it, but you can be certain it won't happen again!" She had to bite her lip to keep from blurting out the truth—all of the truth. Oh, God, she thought despairingly. What would Noah do if she told him everything about herself and Gideon? The answer was swift in coming and it effectively sealed Jessa's lips. He'd set her adrift in the Atlantic for making him an unwitting accomplice to Gideon's abduction.

Noah released her. He forgot all about playing the gallant to gain her trust and learn her secrets. Cursing her, cursing himself, he thumped his pillow. At the moment he only cared about showing her that whatever he wanted to happen *would* happen. "How long will your flow last?" he demanded roughly, using her own lies against her. The waiting, the anticipation would be an agony for her. That he would have his way was a foregone conclusion for Noah.

A lifetime, she wanted to say. "Four days," she bit out.

"Then you have four days to accustom yourself to the idea that on the fifth I will be touching you again!"

"I'll scratch out your eyes!"

"Don't mistake me for Edward Penberthy," he growled softly.

Jessa shook with anger. "I despise you!" she whispered harshly.

Noah's short laugh was humorless. "You should have considered it might come to that when you married me!"

"I told you—I married you because I thought you were going to die!"

"I regret I was not more accommodating," he practically snarled.

"Bastard!"

Realizing that they had finally come to the point of childish name calling, Noah reined in his anger. "Go to sleep, Jessa," he said tiredly, turning on his side away from her. But Noah had difficulty following his own advice. He was awake long past the moment when Jessa had finally cried herself to sleep. He had begun to suspect that revenge was indeed a double-edged sword.

Ross Booker's views on revenge were decidedly different. In the dark and airless brig on board the *Sargus* he had had time to give the matter considerable thought. He would savor revenge; Jessa McClellan would feel its sting. He could not conceive of a different outcome.

His plans were made and revised and revised again. There was a great deal of satisfaction in creating new scenarios in which he invariably had the upper hand. He liked to imagine her reduced to begging him. Sometimes he thought of making love to her, teasing her, touching her, grinding his hips against her until she pleaded with him to take her. Other times he considered having her beg for her own life or the life of her child. He wanted humiliation to score her soul the way the whip had scored his flesh. Nothing he decided to do to her would be done quickly. He wanted her to feel the effects of his revenge for a lifetime. He wanted to make her very life a hell.

Ross leaned against the wall of his cell and rubbed his aching shoulders and back on the roughhewn planks. His wounds were healing slowly and his skin felt too small for him. Pain was merely a minor annoyance to him now. It served to keep his mind focused on the woman who had brought him to this pass. In some ways he welcomed it.

It occurred to Ross that neither Jessa nor her husband might have taken his threats seriously. He wasn't bothered by it. The element of surprise would be his, as would the last laugh. He knew how to find them. The crew talked freely about Noah McClellan's family, his practice in Richmond, and the work he would be doing in Philadelphia. It wouldn't be difficult to run them to ground.

Returning to the United States was the largest obstacle Ross Booker faced. He could pay for his passage or sign with another ship—all under an assumed name. He did not relish the idea of being part of another crew. The thought of booking a cabin on a packet ship appealed to him. The fact that he had no money was simply a temporary deterrent. There were whores he could pimp, pockets he could pick, and taverns he could rob. He would not be so careless as to get caught this time. Even his present accommodations were preferable to Newgate.

The rat scurrying across the floor did not make Booker revise his opinion. In Newgate he had shared a cell with companions far more dangerous than the poor creature sniffing at his toes now. Ross nudged the rat and sensed that it had become still and watchful. He waited. He wished Jessa McClellan could see how he exercised patience and planning. With the swiftness of a striking cobra Ross reached out in the darkness and caught the rat by the scruff of its neck. He held it up, trying to get a glimpse of its eyes, trying to sense its fear.

When he imagined he had seen it, felt it, he let the squealing animal go. "I can kill ye any time I want," he whispered, his flat eyes cold. "Any time."

In his mind's eye he was speaking to Jessa McClellan.

On board the *Clarion* there were no thoughts spared for Ross Booker. Whatever fragile promise existed in the relationship between Noah and Jessa was being slowly and painfully destroyed. Noah was rarely in the cabin. He rose early and stayed away in the morning and afternoon. If he joined Jessa at dinner it was to snipe at her for playing with her food instead of eating it. In the evening he pretended to read while Jessa pretended to sew. He never read more than a few pages, and Jessa reworked the same stitches night after night, never satisfied with what she had done. The dark circles under Noah's eyes were proof of the succession of nights he spent tossing and turning. They had their counterpart in the faint violet smudges beneath Jessa's eyes, a testimony to the nights she laid awake staring out the cabin window while Noah moved restlessly beside her.

They rarely argued; neither had the inclination nor interest. But the ugly, unsaid words and accusations were there, trapped in the pauses of their stilted and cautiously polite exchanges. Noah's features took on a gaunt, haunted look. There were hollows beneath his cheeks and an unmistakable pallor just below the surface of his skin. His mouth was permanently set in a single grim line. A muscle in his jaw worked almost constantly, the only visible sign of anger kept on a tight leash.

In Noah's presence Jessa's face was devoid of emotion. She didn't smile. She didn't not smile. The placement of her lips was exact, a midpoint that expressed nothing so much as indifference. Her eyes were shuttered, vague, pale to the point of being mirrors, reflecting Noah's most penetrating glance and effectively shielding her soul. Though her mood was more suited to the dull mourning hues of her own wardrobe, she continued to wear the more vibrantly colored gowns Noah had selected for her. The ironic contrast between her temperament and the spring colors she wore amused her because it set Noah's teeth on edge in a way he was helpless to explain.

For once, Gideon seemed oblivious to the tensions between Noah and Jessa. This was due in no small part to the undivided attention he received from each of them. Because they studiously avoided one another Gideon was in a position to command their complete interest. By the evening of the fifth day he was pampered and coddled within an inch of his life.

Her nerves frayed beyond bearing, Jessa returned to the main room after putting Gideon to sleep and began making a bed for herself on the window seat. She got as far as arranging the blankets before Noah found his voice.

"What in hell do you think you're doing?" he asked harshly. He was sitting up in bed, a pillow propped between the small of his back and the wall.

Jessa turned on him, clutching a pillow in front of her. Her voice was calm, patient, but her eyes avoided his and fixed on a point beyond his naked shoulder. "I think even someone with your intelligence can see that I intend to sleep here."

"Are you deliberately trying to provoke a confrontation?"

"No."

"Damn you, look at me!"

She did. Her mirrored eyes flashed in the candlelight. "No, I'm not trying to provoke anything."

"Then you'll sleep here, just as you have these past weeks."

"No."

If anything, the set of Noah's mouth became grimmer. "I probably didn't hear you correctly."

"You know you did. I said no. I'm not going to sleep in that bed, not as long as you're there too. You made yourself quite clear as to what I could expect tonight. I'm telling you now, I'm not willing."

"Sharpened your claws these past days, have you?" he asked, his eyes narrowing.

Her fingers bit deeper into the pillow. "Yes."

"Then I suppose I've been forewarned. I'll take my chances. You've scratched me before, little cat, and I don't remember complaining."

Jessa's mouth went dry. The memory of her nails digging into the solid muscle of Noah's back was so vivid that she felt a rush of heat burn her from the inside out. She dropped the pillow on the window seat. Turning away from Noah, Jessa went to the wardrobe and took out her nightshift. She slipped off her shoes and stockings, struggled with the lacings at the back of her gown, then eased out of it stiffly, conscious of any small movement she might make that Noah could interpret as provocation. Still giving Noah her back, she slid her chemise over her shoulders, but before she tugged it further than her waist, Jessa pulled the nightshift over her and finished undressing beneath it. She washed her face and brushed her hair until it crackled, keeping her face averted all the while. When she finished she turned back the last lamp and moved toward the window seat.

Noah's voice was quiet and, like the darkness, faintly threatening. "Don't do it, Jessa."

Jessa stopped. She looked at him over her shoulder. "Please, Noah, let me be."

"You're my wife."

"I'm a convenience."

"Hardly that," he mocked. "There's nothing remotely convenient about the sleeping arrangement you're proposing."

Ignoring him, Jessa began walking toward the window seat. Behind her she heard Noah throwing back the covers on the bed. She closed her eyes, bracing herself

for his assault. When it didn't come as soon as she
expected, she turned. It was a mistake.

Noah was standing directly in front of her. Jessa's eyes
were at the level of his bare chest. She hazarded a glance
downward and was only slightly relieved to see his cotton
drawers slung low on narrow hips. Biting the soft underside of her lip, Jessa raised her face. There was no defiance in the slender line of her jaw, no rebellion in the
hollow depths of her eyes. Nothing about her stance
indicated she was daring him, yet she knew it had ceased
to matter. The challenge had been issued days ago and
unless one of them surrendered now, real conflict was
inevitable.

"You can't despise me more than you already do,"
Noah said heavily, in the manner of a man who had
reached the powerful, dangerous conclusion that he
had nothing to lose. Without giving Jessa the opportunity to deny his claim, one hand swiftly encircled her
neck, the other her waist, and held her immobile for
his punishing kiss.

Jessa offered nothing in return, pressing her lips
closed until Noah forced them apart with his tongue.
Even then she didn't struggle, though she barred a
deeper kiss by clenching her teeth together. His mouth
ground against hers and pain was something both of
them shared. Jessa knew better than to suppose Noah
was enjoying the kiss.

It wasn't until he lifted her and began carrying her
toward the bed that Jessa resorted to the tactics she had
promised. Twisting, she freed her arms and landed a
hard blow to Noah's jaw with her fist. He lost purchase
just as he reached the bed and Jessa was dumped uncere-
moniously on the feather tick. She started to scramble
to the other side but he grabbed her nightshift, then
her ankle, and pulled her back. It enraged her that he
managed the thing with one hand while the other
nursed his sore jaw.

Jessa kicked at him violently, narrowly missing placing

the heel of her foot squarely in his groin. Noah side-stepped the blow, taking it in the thigh instead. Grunting softly, he dropped to his knees on the bed and trapped Jessa's flailing arms in his hands. Slowly he increased the pressure on her wrists and lowered them so they were flattened to the bed above her head. He then avoided her kicking legs by straddling her hips. He rested very little of his weight on her, supporting himself on his calves.

Noah studied Jessa's face for long, deeply charged moments. Her features were composed again, her expression grave. Her eyes were dark, intense. Her mouth was slightly swollen from the pressure of his kiss. Breath shuddered in and out of her, drawing his gaze to the neckline of her gown and the rise and fall of her beautifully shaped breasts. When he spoke his voice was rough and husky, his breathing still not quite steady. "This marriage was not my doing, Jessa, but in my own way I've accepted it. That's much more than I can say for you. You have never asked me, nor concerned yourself with what I might want in return for giving you protection. I'm going to tell you now. There are only two things I want from our marriage: the privilege of seeing that Gideon is provided for regardless of our situation and . . . and the use of your body. Tonight. Tomorrow. Anytime." He paused briefly, then finished, "In any manner."

She could not register any happiness that Noah had made a commitment to Gideon. For once the child's welfare was not uppermost in her thoughts. "You want a whore," she said tonelessly.

"Yes," he said slowly, "I suspect you're right. I merely want you as my whore."

Jessa's throat felt thick with the pressure of unshed tears. "Then have done with it. I'm not my father's daughter in at least one respect. I honor my debts."

Noah slid off Jessa and rolled onto his back, cradling

his head in the palms of his hands. "Well?" he said finally.

Confused, Jessa sat up, massaging her wrists where Noah's fingers had twisted her skin. "What is it you want?"

"My pleasure, Jessa. A whore sees to the man's pleasure and doesn't worry about her own."

"Damn you!" she gritted.

One of Noah's brows arched in a lazy curve of mild interest. "Reneging on your debt so soon?"

"No!" She drew in a deep breath and released it slowly. "What should I do?"

"You could begin by lighting the lamp on the table then removing your shift."

Trembling, Jessa slid off the bed and lit the lamp, adjusting the wick so the room was cast in muted yellow light and soft-edged shadows. She went back to the bed and stood uncertainly on the side closest to Noah.

"The shift," he repeated. "I want to see your breasts, not imagine them."

Jessa eased the straps of her shift over her shoulders, held the material against her for an indecisive moment, then let it fall away. It drifted downward with all the insubstantial softness of a cloud, touching her breasts, her stomach, the length of her thighs.

"My God, you're beautiful," Noah whispered lowly.

Jessa didn't hear the reverence in Noah's tone. She felt his eyes on her naked shoulders, her breasts, then felt his stare sweep along the curve of her body and come to rest at the juncture of her thighs. As she struggled with the urge to cover herself, Jessa felt anything but beautiful. She sat down on the edge of the bed, swiveled toward Noah, and drew her legs up and to the side. Her silky hair fell across her shoulder and down her arm as she leaned to the opposite side and rested her weight on one hand. When she bent her head slightly the soft corn silk strands slipped forward, covering one breast.

"I'm not certain what I'm supposed to do," she admitted tightly. "I've never played the whore before."

Noah's narrowed eyes lifted to her. "And I've never instructed one. Use your imagination."

Jessa did. She leaned forward and imagined plucking the hair from Noah's head, strand by strand. Her fingers threaded through it instead. She lowered her mouth and considered biting his ear until he howled in pain. But Noah only felt her lips nibbling at his lobe. When Jessa wanted to strangle him for every cruel thing he had ever said or done, her hands curved around his throat, tightened briefly, then slid across his shoulders. Her mouth followed the path of her hands, brushing his cheek, his jaw. Her tongue made a damp trail down the strong column of his throat. Would that it were razor sharp, she thought.

Jessa's nails scraped lightly across the smooth expanse of Noah's chest. He had called her little cat. At the memory Jessa curled her fingers like talons and pressed harder.

Noah caught her wrists. "Easy, Jessa. I'd prefer you didn't draw blood."

You drew my blood, she wanted to say. Virgin's blood. My heart's blood. She held back her cry of pain, her soul as raw as an open wound, and relaxed her fingers. Gently she kissed the tiny half-moon indentations, pressing a feral smile to his heated skin when he groaned softly in response. She felt a measure of triumph having drawn the response. Her nails flicked across his nipples and she felt him suck in his breath.

"You like that, don't you?" she whispered, echoing a phrase he had said to her before. "No? Then I won't do it again. I'll do this." *This* was moving her head lower and darting her tongue across the hard nub of his nipple. "Hmmm? Is that better?" She repeated the action on the other nipple. One hand slipped down the taut plane of his abdomen, then beneath the band of his drawers. She teased him, dipping, retreating, dipping again. When he stirred restlessly, arching so her hand would caress him, Jessa pulled away and languidly stretched along Noah's length until her body partially covered his. She considered the agony she could cause him by plunging her knee between his thighs. Instead, her bent knee nudged his loins just enough to feel the hot, hard evidence of his arousal.

As Jessa's mouth brushed Noah's lips he was moved to wonder what erotic thoughts guided her every action. Her touch was deft, skillful. There was rarely any hesitation on her part. She seemed to know exactly what he wanted, precisely where to touch him. Now her lips moved sweetly over his and he responded, opening his mouth and answering the ache she had stirred within him.

Meeting no resistance, his tongue plunged into her mouth. His hands cradled her head, keeping her close. His kiss was hard and demanding, still faintly punishing. Jessa accepted the kiss and returned it with passion born of anger.

Noah's hands slipped from her head and stole along the length of Jessa's back, silky with the fall of her hair. His fingers lightly stroked the side of her breasts. Gradually he insinuated his hands between their flushed bodies and cupped her breasts in his palms.

Jessa despised her body for responding to his touch and she began to retreat to a secret place inside herself where Noah could not reach her. It was as if he were caressing another woman's body, for Jessa felt no connection with the flesh he stroked and aroused.

Noah didn't sense Jessa's withdrawal. He was too awed, too overwhelmed by the fullness of her passion. He had called her a little cat. He was wrong. She was a lioness, breathtakingly feline as her body moved over his with sensuous, sinuous grace. Her kiss, as wholly satisfying as it had been, made him want more. Noah wanted to be inside her, sheathed by the hot, moist center of her, feeling the rhythmic pulsing of her body surrounding him.

Rubbing her leg against him, Jessa slid down Noah's body, trailing kisses along his throat, his chest, tracing a path to his navel with the tip of her tongue. Her fingers worked swiftly, unfastening the buttons on his drawers. Noah arched as she began to ease the material over his hips, swallowing a moan when her hand brushed his hard arousal. She paused, then caressed him deliberately, stroking the length of him, imitating the motion of him inside her. Just when he was on the point of grabbing her wrist to still the rush of desire that threatened his control, Jessa released·him and continued to tug at his clothes. Her hair was a pale silky curtain on either side of her face. It mingled with the dark, rougher hairs on his thighs and calves as she bent her head, intent on her task. Tossing his drawers over the side of the bed, Jessa ran her palms over the length of his legs, moving upward until her body lay flush to his. Her hand sought him again, fondling, teasing, making him ache until he thought he would die of wanting her.

Noah grasped her buttocks, twisted so that she was under him, and ground his hips against her. Jessa pushed at his shoulders, fighting the embrace because she wanted control. It was a futile gesture, and gradually her hands slipped over his back. She closed her eyes and remembered that she was his whore and that what control she had was granted to her by Noah. Anytime, he had said. In any manner.

She felt the brush of his lips on her eyelids, then her cheeks. His tongue traced the whorl of her ear, followed the curve of her cheek, then sought entry into her mouth. Her thighs were nudged apart by the insistent pressure Noah applied with one leg.

In a deep, whiskey voice that was at once smooth and raw, he demanded her attention. "Look at me."

Dutifully Jessa obliged, holding his dark gaze without seeing him at all.

Satisfied with her response, perceiving the wide, black centers of her eyes to be an indication of desire, Noah slid between her parted legs. Jessa raised her knees, slipped her hand between their bodies and guided him into her. His powerful thrust made her wince but she bit off the soft inside of her lower lip rather than let him hear her cry out.

Noah was already moving rhythmically inside her when he realized her dark stare was vacant rather than desiring. Swearing softly, he began to pull away, but Jessa guessed his intention and grasped his hips and curved her legs around him.

"Just finish it," she said emotionlessly. "I don't want anything from you."

"Damn you, Jessa!" There were pauses between his gritty words as Noah's control slipped away and he thrust into her again and again. Even now Jessa lifted her hips, matched the driving rhythms of his body, and caressed his shoulders and back. And Noah hated it. His pleasure was there; sparks of heat skittered across his skin, ribbons of white-hot flame uncurled inside him. But it was hollow pleasure. The satisfaction was for his flesh, there was none for his soul. He had not realized until now that it was important to him.

Noah's body shuddered with the force of his climax and he buried his face in the curve of Jessa's neck. She made no attempt to remove his weight from her, nor did she touch him now. Her fingers twisted in the sheeting beneath her and she closed her eyes, waiting for Noah to withdraw. When he did, Jessa climbed out of bed and padded over to the basin. Making no attempt to hide what she was doing, Jessa scrubbed herself just as she had after Ross Booker's assault. Though Jessa did not realize it, insult was inherent in her lack of modesty, her proud posture, in every deliberate stroke of the rough cloth across her skin. She only knew that she wanted to be clean again.

Noah had asked for a whore and Jessa thought she could play the role for him as long as he wished. She even acknowledged there was a curious sense of power in urging responses from his body when she felt nothing herself. But it was not what she wanted.

Jessa stared at her reflection in the mirror, looking for some evidence of what she had become. She was faintly surprised to find her features unaltered by the experience. Perhaps by the time they reached the landing there would be some subtle change, she mused indifferently. And then? Then it would be over, Jessa promised herself. She thought it odd that tears suddenly glistened in her pale gray eyes, and she hastily blinked them back before they softened her resolve.

Anything Noah did to her now wouldn't matter once she reached the landing. As soon as the opportunity presented itself she was going to leave him, taking Gideon with her. It was the only thing she could think to do to make Noah happy again. He didn't seem to understand how much he had changed and how much he hated her, how much he hated wanting her. She didn't owe him the use of her body; she owed him peace of mind. Leaving him was the surest means of giving him that gift.

CHAPTER NINE

"Just around this bend in the river," said Noah. The *Clarion's* bow cut cleanly through the blue-green water of the James. Lush, emerald-leaved trees thickly lined the opposing banks. The breeze was fresh, no longer redolent with the salty fragrance peculiar to the ocean. The scents that captured Noah's attention were pine and sweet tobacco, the earthy smells of dark, rich soil turned for planting and the fine, light fragrance of the woman who stood in front of him. "You won't be able to see the house from the river, but we've already reached the McClellan boundary."

In other circumstances Jessa might have smiled at the boyish excitement in Noah's voice. But not now. Now she was scared. McClellan's Landing was minutes away and Jessa was so frightened that she actually leaned into Noah for support. His large strong hands rested just below her shoulders, massaging lightly. Jessa wondered if Noah sensed her fear or if his touch was part of what he called his Strategy to Convince Others of Wedded Bliss. Believing it to be the latter, Jessa shivered in spite of the warm afternoon sun.

Noah bent his head slightly so that his words were a caress across Jessa's ear. "There's nothing to fear, Jessa. As long as you follow my lead my family will never know what we are to each other."

To the casual observer, of which there were many on deck, Jessa knew that Noah appeared everything solicitous. The way he held her, the manner in which his mouth brushed her ear, the way his eyes always sought her out, were carefully calculated to give the impression he was the doting husband. His words, edged with bitter dissatisfaction, told a far different story.

Jessa glanced sideways at Cam, who stood only a few feet away. He carried Gideon on his back in a sling Noah had fashioned for the infant. The boy was more concerned with Gideon's persistent tugging on his hair than he was by any conversation. "I'll do whatever you want," Jessa said wearily.

Noah's laughter was short, and to Jessa's ears, humorless. "Just like you did this morning."

It was Noah's tightened grip on her arms that kept Jessa upright. Her legs buckled under the weight of the painful memories he evoked. Four nights ago she had become Noah's whore and each evening since then was a repetition of the first. Holding herself aloof, Jessa made his pleasure her sole concern. She caressed him with her hands, her fingers, her mouth. She began to know his body better than she did her own, had learned exactly where to touch him in order to wring a cry of pleasure from his lips.

They never exchanged any words. In the darkness he would reach for her and Jessa would turn and surrender her body to his needs. Guarding against feeling anything herself, Jessa's thoughts were never connected with what she was doing. She could kiss him deeply, press her body flush to Noah's, and be considering which of her gowns to wear when she met his family. While her fingers stroked his abdomen, caressed his chest, or tightened in the bunched muscles of his arms, Jessa contemplated her escape from the landing. She recited poetry, counted to one hundred by threes, and imagined herself in any place but Noah's bed, doing anything but what she was.

Until this morning.

This morning she had been wakened by Noah's caress and retreat was out of the question. He wouldn't permit it. Every time he sensed her withdrawal he pulled her back to reality, describing in very explicit, erotic terms precisely what he intended to do to her and what he wanted her response to be. It was a complete assault on her senses. His fingers threaded in her silken hair. His lips traced a line down the length of her neck. The tip of his tongue stroked the hollow of her throat. Then he moved lower and her breasts were treated to the hot suck of his mouth. Stroking, caressing, he wouldn't let her deny her own pleasure. His mouth and hands tormented her, his desire teased her, and he created a wild rush of heat in Jessa she could not hide from him or from herself. He made her vulnerable to him, arousing her until she had surrendered to each of his demands, including telling him that she wanted him.

Noah had taken her then with a force that nearly left her breathless, yet there was no pain, only an answering need on her part. Her arms and legs clung to him. She moved with him, matching his rhythm and his hunger, and by slow degrees she was lifted, and lifted again, to another plane of excitement more intense than the last.

At the end Jessa cried out his name. Then she simply cried.

Turning from him, she had buried her face in her arm and released all the anguish and guilt caused by her response to his possession. Gone completely was the feeling of power. In its place was a terrible awareness of her own vulnerability, and she despised herself for it. In the aftermath she did not hate Noah even a tenth as much as she hated herself.

Drawing a ragged breath, Jessa attempted to take a

step back from the taffrail, but Noah's body blocked her. His hands slid along her arms, then circled her waist. She could feel his chin against her hair, moving back and forth in its softness.

"You're not crying, are you, Jessa?" asked Noah.

She shook her head, wishing he would not pretend concern when none existed. "No. Don't worry. I won't shame you."

Noah supposed he deserved that, but it still had the power to smite his conscience. Not that Jessa would realize it. Noah was of the opinion that Jessa thought he was long past the point where anything she said or did touched him below the skin. He had thoroughly humiliated her, not once, but time and time again over the past four days . . . and nights. Each evening he drew her to him, perversely hoping it would be the night that he would reach her with pleasure. But she withheld her responses, giving everything, accepting nothing. She behaved like the whore he had said he wanted and he could never find the words to tell her that he was not satisfied with the arrangement he had forced on her.

He tried to tell her in other ways, with his hands, his mouth, his body. It was as if her flesh were deaf to the whispering of his fingers. She remained remote, unaroused, which only made his own excitement more difficult to bear. Sometimes he wished he could join her at the basin when she washed herself of his touch. Each evening she satisfied him beyond anything he had ever known. Each evening she left him aching with a loneliness he had never expected to feel.

It was little better during the day. Noah had devised the Strategy to Convince Others of Wedded Bliss because Jessa would never accustom herself to his touch without it. She was closed to him and so were her secrets. The harder he pushed her the more guarded she became. Clearly another strategy was called for, and Noah thought he had come upon it, if only he could keep his temper in check. Calmly, patiently, he explained to Jessa that in order for her to be accepted by his family it would be necessary to persuade them the marriage was a lovematch. Jessa was skeptical at first, but there was enough truth in Noah's explanation that she was easily brought around to his way of thinking. Noah was actually less concerned with how his family received Jessa than he was with avoiding their damnable interference. He considered it very likely that everyone would be more accepting of Jessa than they had been of Hilary Bowen. This, of course, was his own secret to keep, and thus he began his war on Jessa's senses.

He resumed taking her for afternoon strolls on deck, finding it entirely appropriate to hook his arm in hers, whisper in her ear, or sometimes slip his arm about her shoulders. Noah persisted in spite of Jessa's discomfort, and over time he felt her relax, no longer stiffening when his hand "accidentally" brushed hers. He spent more time with her in their cabin, and though she made no objection, Noah was well aware that she wished him gone. He found small ways to make himself invaluable, hooking the back of her gown when she could not reach the fasteners, pacing the floor with Gideon when the infant was fussy, drawing water for the wash when Cam was unavailable.

Still, Jessa was unresponsive to his overtures, distrustful and wary, and Noah knew she had every right to be. He had given her a multitude of reasons to maintain the invisible barriers she had erected.

Then this morning he had awakened and found Jessa still deeply asleep, turned trustingly in his arms, defenseless, open, guileless. He was a little astonished to realize she could still stir some protective instinct in him. And she stirred something else as well. Slowly, with great care, Noah set about drawing her from sleep, intent upon waking the desire she kept shielded from him. He succeeded. And he failed.

Jessa's response was more than he could have hoped for. She came alive in his arms and matched his hunger, not mechanically as she had done previously, but with genuine feeling, leaving no doubt that she wanted him, needed him. When she realized what was happening, when the last dregs of sleep disappeared, she had tried to retreat only to discover it was too late.

Noah remembered the wicked, erotic things he had said to her, the husky, throaty murmurs that fell across her skin like a caress. He encouraged her response, fed it with the touch of his fingertips, stroked it with the flat of his palms. He made her say she wanted him, not to humiliate her, but because he needed to hear it, had needed to hear it for days. Hindsight was all knowing. Noah understood now what it had cost her pride to admit that need. He understood it the moment she turned away from him and sobbed out her grief and pain in the curve of her arm. Had her own misery been any less she would have seen the tortured look in Noah's eyes, the grim, self-punishing set of his jaw.

"I know you won't shame me," Noah said, responding at last to Jessa's statement. Silently he added, I'm more than able to do that to myself.

Jessa felt a measure of strength return to her legs. "Will anyone be at the dock to welcome you?"

"Probably not. No one's expecting us. When we docked in Norfolk I thought about sending a skiff upriver with word that we were coming, but I decided against it. I didn't think you would appreciate my entire family swooping down on you, which is precisely what would happen. This way we'll surprise them. I'm thinking we'll have about five or six seconds of blissful silence before pandemonium erupts. As I've said, after you become acquainted with them you'll thank me for those few seconds of quiet."

Jessa didn't believe him for a moment. Although his life had taken an incredible turn since he last saw his family, she knew he was still looking forward to seeing them. He wanted to be part of the confusion and noise and laughter. He'd never convince her otherwise. "It was kind of you to think of me," she said. "After all, you could be introducing me as your whore."

Behind her Noah shook his head, grimacing. Jessa could say something like that in her quiet, unobtrusive manner and cut Noah to the quick. "Jessa," he began, wanting to make one last attempt to set a better balance between them before they reached the landing. "I know I've made a—"

"Look, Mrs. McClellan!" Cam's excited cry cut Noah off. "That's the landing! See the dock! And there's Miss Courtney, fishin' off the last piling! Hey! Courtney!" Cam began waving his hands wildly, trying to get the young girl's attention.

"Careful, Cam," Noah said, tempering his smile as the boy fairly danced on the deck. "You've still got Gideon on your back."

Cam's thin face reddened. His eyes pleaded with Jessa. "Can you take Gideon now, ma'am? I don't want . . . that is . . . Miss Courtney would laugh if she saw me carrying a papoose."

Jessa's heart went out to the boy. "Of course I'll take him!" Noah released her so that she could unfasten the sling. She took Gideon in her arms and flushed slightly as Noah renewed the embrace. She would have liked to trod upon his toes. Courtney's dark head had swiveled in the direction of the *Clarion* and she was peering intently at the bow, one small hand raised to shield her eyes from the glare of the sun on the water. Jessa knew the moment she spotted Noah. Courtney had jumped from the piling and was calling happily to Cam, then she stopped, stared harder, and her mouth opened wide in astonishment. She let out a whoop of joy that carried across the water. "I think she's quite glad to see you," Jessa said dryly.

"She's a minx. Look at her," he added, laughing as Courtney ran back and forth along the wharf. "She can't decide whether to run to the house and alert everyone or stay here and be the first to welcome us."

"She's a lovely little girl," said Jessa. Courtney's ebony hair whipped around her small oval face as she ran. The folds of her russet-colored dress kept tangling in her legs and she lifted the hem impatiently, revealing that she was without shoes or stockings. "How old is she?"

"Eleven. She's Salem's daughter."

Jessa had remembered that. "It seems as if she's decided to stay and greet us," she said as Courtney plopped herself down on one corner of the wharf. She glanced sideways at Cam and saw his rapt look centered on Noah's niece. The look of youthful longing brought a sigh to her lips.

Noah heard Jessa's sigh and knew the reason for it. "You've been replaced in his affections."

"I didn't encourage him."

"I never said you did. But the fact that you're so quick to deny it makes me wonder."

"Don't Noah. Please don't start with me. I can't . . ."

Sensing her despair, he brushed his lips against Jessa's temple, simply because it seemed the most natural thing to do. For the span of a heartbeat it was as if no animosity existed between them. Jessa's stiff smile for the benefit of the crew reminded him otherwise.

The *Clarion* laid down its gangboard some fifteen minutes later and Noah escorted Jessa along the narrow ramp. Courtney was still on the wharf, carrying on an excited conversation with Cam at the taffrail above her. She broke away as soon as Noah's feet touched solid ground.

"Whoa!" Noah said as his niece's arms circled his neck. "You're going to knock me in the water!" He caught Courtney by the waist, lifted her, and twirled her around while she clung like a limpet.

"Oh, I've missed you!" she cried breathlessly, laughing. "Did you have a splendid time? Isn't England lovely? How was your voyage? Were you terribly sick? Did you miss us?" She took a deep breath, seeming to notice Jessa and Gideon for the first time. "Who are they?"

Noah set her on the wharf, tapping the end of her pert nose with his fingertip. "All in good time."

Courtney stuck out her lower lip, disappointed. Almost immediately the expression vanished and she stepped closer to Jessa. "Hallo," she said guilelessly. "I'm Courtney McClellan. Is that a boy or a girl?"

Jessa bit back a smile. "He's a boy," she said gravely. "His name is Gideon." Gideon sputtered something and smiled widely. "I think that means he's very happy to make your acquaintance."

Courtney nodded, sighing. "All the babies like me. It's a curse."

"Brat," said Noah, not unkindly. He gave her backside a little swat. "Why don't you lead the way to the house and you can tell us all about your new sister. Or is it another brother?"

"A brother," Courtney said, disgust rife in her tone. She began walking backward, waving farewell to Cam. "His name is Christian and he's fat and when he cries his face is all red and ugly."

"That's much how I described you," said Noah, his eyes dancing.

"Uncle Noah! That's a horrible thing to say!" She looked at Jessa. "He's an awful tease, you know. Everyone says so. You're very pretty. I should love to have hair like yours."

"Watch where you're going, Court," Noah interrupted, saving Jessa from replying. "Why don't you turn around and walk right?"

Courtney spun on her heel and found herself directly in front of a tree. "Ooops." She sidestepped it, shooting Noah a grateful look, and skipped along the path to the house.

"Where are your shoes and stockings?" asked Noah.

"If Tildy hasn't found them they're still on the veranda."

"Tildy is our cook," Noah told Jessa. "And when she finds things where they don't belong she spirits them away. Sometimes you get them back and sometimes you don't. She's still in possession of three of my very best slingshots and one corncob pipe . . . and she's had them for twenty-five years."

"Really?" Jessa asked skeptically.

"I swear it!' '"

Jessa's heart turned over. She laughed at his earnest expression because she couldn't help herself. Often during the last few days she had been reminded of the first time they met, how he had captured her interest with his open friendliness and easy charm. Given time she believed she could have confided in that man. Now she was careful not to dwell on those thoughts, preferring to remember the times when he was far less than kind. She made herself recall one of those instances now and answered a trifle coolly, "Then I shall be careful not to mislay anything."

Noah frowned at the sudden change in her mood, wondering if he would ever be privy to the thoughts that altered her feelings with lightning swiftness. He decided to ignore her, concentrating on Courtney instead. "Why were you fishing alone, Court?" he called. "Where is everyone?"

The girl's head turned just enough so Noah could see the woeful expression on her face. "They're eating dinner."

"Then why aren't you with them?"

"Because I don't like venison and I honestly said so, but Papa thought I was rude so he said I should excuse myself and catch my own dinner then." She took a deep breath. "So that's what I was doing, only the fish aren't biting, and I suspect I shall be very hungry at breakfast."

"I suspect you shall," agreed Noah, one corner of his mouth lifting in a smile. He glanced at Jessa and saw she was smiling also. "I hope you like venison," he whispered conspiratorially.

"I wouldn't dare complain," she said lowly, shooting him a wry glance. "Even if we were served rice and animals."

Noah's handsome head was thrown back as he gave a shout of laughter. "Oh, Jessa, you're wonderful!"

Jessa's eyes widened at this spontaneous accolade. On the heels of the momentary thrill came the inevitable suspicions.

"Let me take Gideon," Noah said as they came to the foot of a grassy knoll. "I'll carry him the rest of the way. The house is just beyond this rise."

Jessa considered objecting. There was a measure of security in holding Gideon and she wasn't certain she wanted to relinquish it. "All right," she said after a moment's hesitation.

"If you'd rather I didn't . . ."

"No," she said quickly, realizing Noah had taken offense. Jessa couldn't let him think she didn't trust him with Gideon. However he had treated her, she could not fault his care for the child. "No, my arms are aching. I'd be grateful."

With sudden insight Noah understood the reason for Jessa's reluctance. He took Gideon, balancing the infant in the crook of one arm, and placed his free hand at Jessa's back. "There's no reason to be afraid as long as you keep to our strategy." Then he urged her up the hillock where Courtney was waiting impatiently.

Jessa felt an odd stillness encompass her when she saw the house. She had not formed any expectations regarding it because she knew it had nothing to do with her, yet upon seeing it she wished that it could be otherwise. Set against a backdrop of towering oaks, Noah's family home was impressive but not imposing. Four white columns supported the portico entrance and the white roof fairly gleamed in the late afternoon sunlight. Used to the dull gray stone of the manor homes in England, Jessa found the red brick appealing and warm. Four chimneys rose above the roof, vying with the trees for command of the sky, and the white-shuttered windows on both floors caught the sun and seemed to wink a welcome. There were two verandas at the east end of the house, one opening from each floor, and beyond them was a meticulously manicured garden.

"Don't become too enraptured," Noah said a little roughly. "We won't be here long."

Some of Jessa's joy faded. She had not meant to be so obvious. "Yes," she said quietly. "I know."

Before Noah could reply Courtney interrupted, urging them to hurry. "If we don't follow her quickly, she's going to spoil our entrance." Even as he spoke Courtney began running down the hillock and across the wide lawn toward the veranda. "This is important to me, Jessa. I've given it a lot of thought. It would be best all the way around if my family believes we're happy."

"We've been over this before," she said dully.

"Just so you understand."

She felt compelled to protest. "This is so unfair to them, Noah. It would be better if you sent me away now."

"When I'm ready," he said, holding her pale gaze. "Not until then."

Noah and Jessa caught up to Courtney at the house's east entrance. She was hastily putting on her shoes and stockings and begging them to wait for her now. Once dressed, Courtney led them into the hallway, pressing a finger to her lips so they would know to be silent. Feeling rather like childish conspirators themselves, Noah and Jessa followed.

Courtney parted the heavy double doors to the dining room just enough to stick her head through the opening. Affecting a penitent expression, she waited for someone at the crowded dining table to notice her.

Ashley McClellan caught sight of her daughter out of the corner of her eye and gently nudged her husband. Salem looked up, bit back a smile when he saw Courtney's tiny face framed by the doors, and addressed her in a mildly interested tone. "Are you ready to join us, Court?"

"Yes, Papa," she answered solemnly. "I've caught my dinner."

"A big fish?" he asked, one dark brow kicking up.

"Oh yes! A very big fish!"

A single dimple appeared at the corner of Salem's mouth. "I hope you've given it to Tildy to prepare. I don't think your grandmother wants you to bring it in here."

"That's true, darling," Charity agreed, setting down her fork. Her deep blue eyes twinkled as she turned toward her granddaughter. "Please say you've given it to Tildy."

Courtney glanced about the room, delighting in the fact she had everyone's attention. At the head of the table her grandfather was regarding her with amusement. Rae and Jericho, with their two oldest girls between them, had turned toward the door hoping to get a glimpse of the fish if there was one. Even Courtney's brothers, Trenton and Travis, were looking at her with admiration.

"I don't think Tildy wants this fish," said Courtney. "I don't even know what sort it is. Mayhap it wouldn't be good eating." At her back she heard Noah's soft chuckle. "I should like it very much if someone would tell me what I've caught."

"Very well," said Charity. "But please hold it up in the doorway. I don't want it in here unless it's on a platter."

Smiling gleefully, Courtney threw open the doors and scampered out of the way.

Noah placed one hand at the small of Jessa's back and stepped forward. Grinning roguishly, he counted the seconds of stunned silence under his breath for Jessa's benefit, stopping at five.

"Uncle Noah!" cried Trenton, sliding off his chair before his mother could grab him. He was immediately joined by his brother and his young cousins. All four of the children danced around Noah, waiting to be picked up, scarcely noticing the babe he held in his arms.

Hunkering down, Noah gave each of them a squeeze with his free arm and added kisses for Elyse and Katie when they demanded them.

"Courtney," Salem called sternly. "This is most definitely *not* a fish for eating!"

Jericho had risen to his feet. Scooping one daughter under each arm he pulled them away from Noah before they toppled him. Their squeals of protest went unheeded. "I say we throw it back in the river," he drawled, glancing back at Salem.

"Do you hear the abuse I must take?" Noah asked, looking up at Jessa. He gave Trenton and Travis a pat on the behind and sent them back to the table. Standing, he circled Jessa's shoulders with one arm and pulled her closer. "This is my family," he said, pride evident in his voice. "And for all they may want to pitch me in the river, they won't do it until their curiosity's been satisfied."

Jessa smiled weakly under the curious, interested stares of so many eyes. She was grateful when Noah gave her Gideon to hold again. She squeezed him so tightly that he gave a little yelp and her cheeks reddened with embarrassment. "I'm very pleased to meet you," she said.

The uncertainty in Jessa's voice and the wariness in her beautiful pale gray eyes brought a burst of laughter from nearly everyone at the table.

"I don't know how you could be," Ashley said sympathetically, coming to her feet as the laughter quieted. "Be pleased to meet us, that is. I remember my arrival at the landing and it was nothing short of frightening to be subjected to all these McClellans." Her bright emerald eyes turned on Noah. "Would you kindly put her at ease by making introductions?" she asked.

"Very well," said Noah. He left Jessa's side and went to the foot of the table. "This is my mother Charity McClellan." He bent and kissed the finely lined cheek that was raised to him.

"It's so good to see you, son," Charity said feelingly, taking Noah's hand and squeezing it to reassure herself of his presence. She smiled warmly at Jessa and smoothed back her coffee-colored hair as Noah moved on.

Noah stood behind both of the boys. "Trenton and Travis McClellan."

"Hallo," said Trenton. "I'm six." He nudged his brother who automatically held up three fingers.

Chuckling, Noah ruffled their dark heads and stepped beside Ashley. "I'm sure you realize this is my sister-in-law Ashley McClellan," he told Jessa, delighted to see the boys had coaxed a genuine smile to her lips. He brushed a light kiss on Ashley's mouth. "You're looking very well," he said sincerely, taking in the color in her cheeks and the shining coronet of her thick ebony hair. "Courtney tells me it's another boy."

She laughed brightly as she sat down. "I'm certain I know precisely the tone she used. She wanted a sister so badly." Her eyes fell on Jessa then dropped to the babe. "Christian will be delighted to have company in the nursery."

Noah gave her shoulder a light squeeze and went to his older brother. "This is Jerusalem," he told Jessa. "Though I'd advise you to call him Salem. He has no liking for the name our parents settled on him."

As Salem caught his brother's hand in a firm grip Jessa was struck by the similarity between the two men. The resemblance was not immediately apparent on the surface. Salem's hair was several shades darker than Noah's and his eyes were pewter gray, yet he and his brother shared the same classic bone structure that Jessa thought set them apart from ordinary men. She found her eyes moving to the head of the table where Noah's father had come to his feet just a moment before Noah got there.

"My father," he said, taking his father's hand, then abandoning it for a fierce hug. "Robert McClellan."

Jessa dipped a small curtsey, thinking she would have known this man anywhere. He was as broad-shouldered as his sons, and though his hair was graying at the temples it was still dark and thick at the crown of his head. His smile was faintly bemused but welcoming.

"My brother-in-law Jericho Smith," Noah went on, tapping Jericho on the back.

"M'lord," Jessa murmured, remembering this was Geoffrey Hunter-Smythe, Earl of Stanhope.

Jericho's mouth turned up in a lazy smile and a lock of sunshine yellow hair brushed his forehead. "No one here calls me that," he said, darting a wicked glance at his wife. "Except Red when she's being sassy."

Noah intervened quickly before his flame-haired sister could take exception to her husband's teasing. "This is Elyse," he said, pointing to the fair headed little girl on Jericho's left knee. "She's nearly five. And the carrot curls belong to Katie who's three." Both girls pressed their faces shyly against their father's chest. "Where's Garland?" asked Noah.

"Napping," said Jericho, coaxing his daughters back into their chairs.

"Well," Noah drawled, looking around the table, pointedly avoiding his sister's efforts to be noticed. "I suppose that's everyone then. Gareth and Darlene are at their own home it seems," he said, turning to Jessa. "And I told you that Leah and Troy live in New York."

"Oooh! I knew you were going to be beastly, Noah!" Rae said, jumping to her feet. She flung herself into her brother's arms and hugged him with only a little less enthusiasm than the children had shown.

Laughing, Noah lifted her off her feet and kissed her cheek, then set her down, putting his arm around her.

Take **4 FREE** Books!

We created our convenient Home Subscription Service so you'll be sure to have the hottest new romances delivered each month right to your doorstep — usually before they are available in book stores. Just to show you how convenient Zebra Home Subscription Service is, we would like to send you 4 Kensington Choice Historical Romances as a FREE gift. You receive a gift worth up to $23.96 — absolutely FREE. There's no extra charge for shipping and handling. There's no obligation to buy anything - ever!

Save Up To 30% On Home Delivery!

Accept your FREE gift and each month we'll deliver 4 brand new titles as soon as they are published. They'll be yours to examine FREE for 10 days. Then if you decide to keep the books, you'll pay the preferred subscriber's price. That's all 4 books for a savings of up to 30% off the cover price! Just add the cost of shipping and handling. Remember, you are under no obligation to buy any of these books at any time! If you are not delighted with them, simply return them and owe nothing. But if you enjoy Kensington Choice Historical Romances as much as we think you will, pay the special preferred subscriber rate and save over $7.00 off the bookstore price!

We have 4 FREE BOOKS for you as your introduction to
KENSINGTON CHOICE!

To get your FREE BOOKS, worth up to $23.96, mail the card below or call TOLL-FREE 1-888-345-BOOK
Visit our website at www.kensingtonbooks.com.

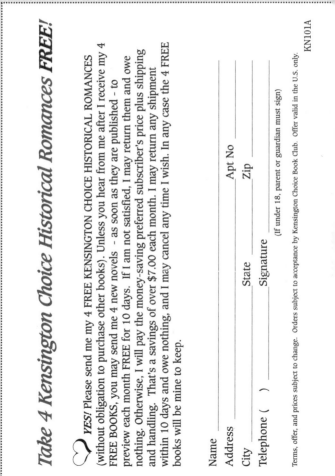

Take 4 Kensington Choice Historical Romances FREE!

YES! Please send me my 4 FREE KENSINGTON CHOICE HISTORICAL ROMANCES (without obligation to purchase other books). Unless you hear from me after I receive my 4 FREE BOOKS, you may send me 4 new novels - as soon as they are published - to preview each month FREE for 10 days. If I am not satisfied, I may return them and owe nothing. Otherwise, I will pay the money-saving preferred subscriber's price plus shipping and handling. That's a savings of over $7.00 each month. I may return any shipment within 10 days and owe nothing, and I may cancel any time I wish. In any case the 4 FREE books will be mine to keep.

Name _____

Address _____ Apt No _____

City _____ State _____ Zip _____

Telephone ( ) _____ Signature _____

(If under 18, parent or guardian must sign)

Terms, offer, and prices subject to change. Orders subject to acceptance by Kensington Choice Book Club. Offer valid in the U.S. only.

KN101A

4 FREE

Kensington
Choice
Historical
Romances
are waiting
for you to
claim them!

*(worth up
to $23.96)*

*See details
inside....*

"This is my sister Rahab. We call her Rae. Jericho calls her Red—for obvious reasons."

Rae stamped her foot and elbowed her brother in the ribs. "Enough! We have all been very patient, but you must give over." Rae pulled out the chair and motioned to Jessa. "Please, we've been so ill-mannered. Won't you sit down? It can't have been very comfortable for you standing there, listening to Noah rattle on, and no one even moving to offer you a chair."

Grateful for Rae's thoughtfulness, Jessa sank down onto the ladderback chair. Sunshine filtered through the large bay window and caressed her face. She would have been shocked to know that individually the McClellans were thinking she looked very Madonna-like in that moment, possessing a serene and tranquil beauty. "I suspect you all were a trifle surprised to see that Noah had brought home a guest," she said, not thinking for a second anyone had been rude to her. Quite the opposite, in fact. Under the circumstances, they were incredibly gracious. She turned Gideon in her lap so he could see everyone. His eyes were wide and his smile wavered as he examined the unfamiliar faces. "Two guests, actually."

"Well?" asked Salem, giving his brother a dark look. "As Rae said, give over. And I surely hope I hear what I want to hear."

Noah moved to stand behind Jessa, placing his hands lightly on her shoulders. "This is Jessa ... McClellan. My wife. And her son ... no, *our* son Gideon."

There was a brief silence then everyone began talking at once.

"Thank God," Salem said feelingly.

"Oh, Noah! That's wonderful!" Ashley added from her heart.

Rae hugged her brother again. "I'm so happy for you!"

"Congratulations, Noah!" Robert said, going to the sideboard to bring out the liquor.

Jericho slanted Noah a grin. "Joined the fallen at last, did you?"

Tears sparkled in Charity's eyes as she looked at her son. "This is wonderful news!"

Jessa was more than a little surprised by their easy acceptance of Noah's marriage. She did not understand, as Noah did, that their enthusiasm came in part because he had not married Hilary Bowen. Guilt pressed at her heart and the trick Noah was playing weighed heavily on her mind.

"May I?" Charity said, holding out her hands to Gideon. "Will he come to me?"

"I think so," said Jessa, lifting Gideon. He went into his new grandmother's arms without the least protest.

"He's beautiful," Charity said happily as the infant chortled. "I do so love babies. And Gideon is such a fine name."

Noah's smile was wry as he glanced at his brother and sister. "Did you have any doubts but that she would approve of it?"

"Not a one," they answered simultaneously.

Ashley called to her daughter who was still hovering by the door. "Courtney, will you take the children away now? Perhaps outside to play?"

Salem saw Courtney look longingly at the remains of the meal set before them. "Did you catch anything at all in the river?" he asked.

"No, Papa."

"Well, since you brought back your prodigal uncle, as it were, I think it would be all right if you asked Tildy to fix you something in the kitchen."

"Oh, thank you! I shan't be rude again. I promise!" She rounded up her brothers and cousins and hustled them out of the dining room, grinning impishly when Noah winked at her.

"That promise is just as worthless as a Continental," Salem said, shaking his head as Courtney fled.

"Don't be too hard on her, dear," Ashley said, patting

her husband's arm soothingly. "She has your penchant for honesty, and if she seems a bit rude at times it's because she never learned to mince words."

Salem sighed, biting back a smile. "I suppose you think she inherited that from me."

"If the shoe fits," she said sweetly.

Chuckling, Robert served up glasses of dark red wine as Noah seated himself beside Jessa. Rae took the empty chair at her husband's side. "I think we should toast the newest members of the family," he said serenely. "Before Salem and Ashley take up cudgels." He raised his glass. "To Jessa and Gideon McClellan. Welcome."

"Welcome," everyone added.

Under the table Noah's hand sought Jessa's and he squeezed it warningly. He could see very clearly that she was puzzled and overwhelmed by his family's warm reception. The sincerity of their welcome rankled more than a little. How was it they had taken such an instant liking to Jessa and could barely thaw to Hilary? Was he the only one who could recognize Jessa for the jade she was? Because it was necessary to do so, Noah put his sour thoughts to the back of his mind. He lifted Jessa's hand to his lips. "They mean it, Jessa. Welcome to the landing."

"Thank you," she said softly, staring deeply in Noah's eyes. There was no mistaking the cautionary look he returned. He was measuring her every response. When he released her hand it hovered uncertainly in the air a moment, then she let it fall on her lap. "Thank you all. I didn't expect you to be so kind." She gasped, her cheeks flushed, as she realized what she had said. "Oh, I didn't mean that the way it sounded," she said quickly. "I knew you would be kind, but I didn't think you would be so accepting. I know about Hilary, you see, and it must be very shocking to you that Noah married me when he was planning to marry her."

"Hardly shocking," said Salem, setting down his glass of wine. "Your presence here is the first indication I've had that my brother's senses have returned. And I probably speak for everyone at this table."

"Except me," Noah said coolly, leveling Salem with a dark glance. "I'd prefer not to discuss Hilary."

Salem shrugged, seemingly unaffected by Noah's hard stare. "As you wish." He turned his attention back to Jessa and caught the nervous look she darted at Noah. It's almost as if she's afraid of him, Salem thought, his eyes narrowing slightly on the taut, pale skin of Jessa's face. The flush of her earlier embarrassment had vanished, and though she schooled her delicate features quickly, Salem was not deceived by her composure. He found her reaction odd and wondered at it. "How did you become acquainted with my brother?" he asked kindly, changing the subject, hoping to draw her out.

"We shared a coach on the post road to London," she said. Lifting her glass of wine, Jessa took a deep drink and prayed that Noah would intervene.

Rae looked at her brother in amazement. "You rode in a coach! I thought it made you ill, just like sailing."

"It wasn't too bad," Noah said, stretching his legs beneath the table. "And I didn't have much choice. My horse came up lame as I was riding to Stanhope and I couldn't get another one. Therefore I took the coach. Jessa and Gideon were among the passengers. Jericho, do you know someone named Gilton . . . Gilly . . . Gil—"

"Gilmore," Jessa supplied. "Lord Gilmore."

"He's a twit," Jericho said succinctly. "I played cards with him once. His father managed to pull him away from the tables before he lost his last quarter's allowance to me. Never say he was riding the coach, too."

"I think his pockets were light again," explained Noah. "Though he did have a very fine watch on his person." Out of the corner of his eye he saw Jessa take another hasty sip of her wine and he smiled a little darkly, letting her know he was repaying her for bringing up Hilary. "As it happened, he lost the watch when our coach was stopped by highwaymen. Let me finish," he added quickly when it seemed as if everyone was going to interrupt. "We were robbed and I took a pistol ball in the side. I'm fine, Mother," he said reassuringly. "And you can thank Jessa. After the robbery she cared for me in her home and stole me from the very clutches of death," he finished dramatically, raising a smile to everyone's lips. He paused a beat and added softly, "She stole my heart as well."

Jessa could almost believe he spoke the truth. A surreptitious glance around the table told her that his family accepted his word. The happy smile she forced began to falter at Noah's next words.

"She's quite an accomplished thief, you see," he told them. "I was forced to marry her else lose my heart forever."

If Jessa could have kicked him without attracting attention she would have done so. He thought he was so clever, playing at his double-edged words. She knew what he meant when he called her a thief, and it was equally true that she had forced the marriage on him. She drained her glass of wine shakily.

"And now I have a son as well," Noah said easily, watching Gideon pluck at the bows on his mother's dress.

Robert cleared his throat a shade uncomfortably. "I've been wondering about that, Noah," he began, trying to broach the subject of Jessa's son tactfully. Was Noah—heaven forbid—the cause of a divorce, or had Jessa been widowed?

"I was a widow," Jessa answered, seeing Robert's distress and sensing the cause. "My husband died shortly after Gideon's birth."

"Did you know Robert Grantham?" Noah asked, watching Jessa carefully. "Ashley? Jericho?" Of course they couldn't know a man who did not exist but it was amusing to see Jessa squirm a little.

"No. I don't recall any Granthams," Ashley said. "But

that isn't surprising. I didn't know many people when I lived at Linfield."

"I'm not familiar with the name either," said Jericho. "Was your first husband much of a gambler?"

"N-no," Jessa stammered. "He never gambled at all."

"Then I probably never met him. The brief part of my adult life that I spent in England was almost entirely consumed at the gaming tables."

"We're very sorry to hear of your loss," Charity said, tickling Gideon's dimpled chin. "But you can understand that we're happy Noah has you now, and that in turn we have you, too." She frowned slightly and pressed her hand under Gideon's bottom. "Oh dear. I think this young fellow wants changing. No, stay where you are, Jessa. I'll take him to the nursery. I need to have a room prepared for you and Noah anyway. I'll take care of everything at once." Charity swept out of the room, cooing to Gideon all the while.

Ashley laughed when she saw the play of emotion on Jessa's face as Gideon was taken away. "She's wonderful with children," she said. "And after a few days you'll wonder how you ever managed without her. Charity has more energy than Rae and I together."

"I'm afraid Jessa won't have time to become accustomed to Mother's command," Noah put in before Jessa could respond. "We're here because I promised Ashley and Jericho a report on their estates. I have to go to Philadelphia in a few days. The convention, remember?"

"So soon?" Rae protested. "But you just got here! Surely it won't hurt to arrive at the convention late. The word here is that a number of delegates aren't even going to attend."

"All the more reason for Noah to be there," Robert said, supporting his son though it pained him to do so. Charity was going to be disappointed. "And to be there on time. The sooner those damnable Articles are revised, the better for all of us."

"Your father's right," Jericho told his wife. "And you know it."

"Oh, very well. But that doesn't mean I have to like it."

"That's very gracious of you, Red," he returned dryly.

She made a face at him, then turned to Noah. "How long do you think the work will take?"

"I have no idea," he said honestly. "Is Patrick Henry going to be there?"

"No," answered Salem. "He wants no part of it. Thinks the entire idea is ill-conceived."

"Then I suspect it won't take long to rework the Articles. A few weeks perhaps."

Robert disagreed. "Just because he won't be there to argue every point with Madison doesn't mean that others won't. I think you're being optimistic about the length of time the work will take."

"I hope not." His commitment to the convention would sidetrack him from discovering what manner of trouble Jessa had embroiled him in. "I'm not looking forward to spending the summer in Philadelphia, nor the fall and winter."

"Lord," Robert said fervently. "Let's all pray it doesn't take *that* long."

Ashley stood, clasping her hands in front of her. "At great risk to myself for interrupting this discussion, I'd like to offer you something to eat. Are you hungry, Jessa?"

"Starving," she said artlessly, bringing a smile to the lips of the men.

"Good. You, Noah?"

"This cold venison is looking very good to me."

"There's no need for you to eat a cold meal," she said. "I'll see what Tildy can do for you in the kitchen. Anything but rice and animals, isn't that right?"

"Anything but that," he agreed heartily, thankful she remembered.

Laughing, Ashley cleared some dishes then left the room in search of the cook.

Rae began collecting the dishes and platters that Ashley left and stacked them at Charity's end of the table. "So, Jessa, we know why Noah married you, but uppermost in my mind at least, is how you were persuaded to marry him."

"Well, thank you very much for that, Rae," Noah mocked. "I think I have a few qualities to recommend me."

"I don't want you to enumerate them," she said tartly, her green eyes amused. "I want to hear from your wife. Jessa? How ever did Noah convince you to marry him?"

"Actually," Jessa said lowly, darting a quick look at Noah, "I proposed to him."

Salem's dark head reared back as he laughed out loud this time. Seconds later he was joined by his father. Even Noah began to chuckle.

Jessa's face was a study in bewilderment and Rae took pity on her. "I don't suppose Noah ever thought to tell you," she said. "That's just like him. You see, Jessa, Mama proposed to Papa and Ashley had to propose to Salem. The McClellan men are notoriously reluctant to offer marriage. Even Darlene had to twist Gareth's arm, though not too hard in his case. You did the right thing by asking him, else it may have been months before he came to his senses."

Jessa's smile was faint. If only it were as simple as that. She doubted very much that Charity and Ashley had proposed marriage after the fact.

Noah took Jessa's hand again and brought it to his lap, threading his fingers through hers. Only she knew the pressure he applied was not for reassurance. "I told her once," he said to the others, "that strange things have happened in my family. I don't know if she really believed me."

"Let's not regale her with those stories now," said Robert repressively, pouring himself another glass of wine. "Jessa, we're very happy to have you among us. Please, believe that. You've been very gracious to put up with our ill manners."

Before Jessa could reply Charity and Ashley entered the room carrying large trays filled with warm biscuits, fried eggs, thick slices of ham, an assortment of jellies, and spiced applesauce. Jessa's mouth fairly watered as they placed the trays on the table.

"Don't be shy," Ashley said, setting clean dishes and silverware in front of Jessa and Noah. "Eat as much as you want. That instruction was for your wife, Noah. I *know* you won't be backward."

Noah merely grinned. He took Jessa's plate and filled it. "This should quiet your stomach," he said. He heaped food on his own. "Salem, you really ought to do something about the cook on the *Clarion*. I had better food during the war."

Salem's snort conveyed his disbelief. "I know better. Other than the food, how was the voyage?"

"Not difficult. No storms . . . for which I am eternally grateful." Noah slathered a biscuit with raspberry jelly and plopped half of it into his mouth. "Jessa likened the ship to an oversized rocking chair," he said, rolling his eyes. "She was completely comfortable and Gideon loved it, of course."

"And you were sicker than—"

Noah held up his hand, cutting Salem off. "Don't remind me."

"Gideon's a darling," Charity said, changing the subject. She winked at Noah when he sent her a grateful look. "He was a little fretful upstairs, though. I like to use a touch of spirits on a child's gums when he's teething."

Noah nearly choked on a mouthful of food. Swallowing painfully, he said, "The last time I tried that remedy, Mother, I was shot for it."

"It's true," Jessa added when they all regarded Noah

disbelievingly. She explained to her rapt audience exactly how Noah had been shot during the robbery.

"And afterward," Noah finished, arching one brow wickedly, "she took me home and wouldn't let me out of bed . . . even after I was well."

"Noah!" his mother chastised. "You're embarrassing Jessa."

Under the stern gaze of his mother Noah raised his hands in a gesture of surrender. "I'm teasing," he said. "Jessa knows that." God, he thought, if ever a woman guarded her virtue it had been Jessa.

Jessa thought he was taunting, not teasing, and her distress was evident to everyone even after Noah apologized. She was making a pretense of eating now, cutting her food into tiny pieces and only lifting a few to her mouth. Robert McClellan looked to his wife, a question in his eyes. He also noticed that the others were equally puzzled, though Noah continued his meal as if nothing were wrong.

Jericho broke the silence, encouraged by Rae's gentle kick under the table. "Tell me about Stanhope, Noah. Were you able to straighten out the problem with the deeds?"

"It's all taken care of. I don't think you'll be having any problems holding onto the estate. It would be better, of course, if you went there every few years."

"We'll see," Jericho said, refusing to commit himself. "And Drew Goodfellow? How does he fare?"

"Very well, considering his crippling condition."

"What of Linfield?" asked Salem.

"I've put Ashley's papers in order," Noah answered. "My advice to Jericho is the same for you, Ashley. You and Salem need to return every few years to maintain your claim on the estate. I took the liberty of hiring a new manager for you because the old one was bleeding the tenants. The house is in good repair though I ordered some minor work done."

"Thank you, Noah. I'm certain you handled everything admirably."

"We can talk more about it later," he said agreeably, looking around the table. "If you wouldn't mind, I'd like to show Jessa the nursery and our room. Is it ready, Mother?"

"Certainly. Everything's been aired and freshly dusted. Your belongings have already been brought up from the ship and they should be unpacked by now. Go on, Noah. Jessa's looking a trifle tired."

Jessa would have liked to protest, but it would have been such a patent lie that she didn't dare. She felt incredibly weary.

Noah pushed back his chair and stood up. He wavered unsteadily on his feet and he almost knocked Jessa's chair sideways as he grabbed it for support. His face paled and when Jessa looked up at him, clearly alarmed, he could only grimace.

"Noah? What is it?" Jessa stood quickly and put one arm around Noah's waist, offering her shoulder. She didn't notice the knowing glances everyone else exchanged or the smiles that hovered near their mouths. "Are you ill?"

"I'll be fine. Just give me a moment." But he made no effort to stand without her assistance.

"It's land sickness," Salem explained to Jessa. "After a long voyage it takes a little while to become used to walking on solid ground. You expect the floor to come up and meet your feet and when it doesn't it throws off your balance. A lot of people aren't bothered by it at all."

"And then there's me," Noah said ruefully. "I thought it wasn't going to happen this time." His temples were thudding now and he was regretting every bit of the meal he had just consumed.

Robert looked at his son sympathetically. "Salem, Jericho, help Noah to his room. Jessa can't take him up the stairs."

"I'm not a damned invalid," Noah gritted, stepping away from Jessa. "It will pass."

Robert's dark brows rose nearly to his hairline at Noah's sharp delivery, but he also suspected his son was embarrassed by his weakness, especially in front of his wife. "Very well," he said quietly, motioning Salem and Jericho to stay in their seats.

"I can manage," Jessa said softly, her eyes apologetic. "He doesn't mean to be insufferable." Not to his family anyway, she thought.

Noah groaned, rubbing his temple with his thumb. "Thank you for that spirited defense," he said sarcastically. He took her small hand in his with enough strength to make her wince. "Come along, Jessa. I'll apologize for my rudeness when you've taken away this headache."

CHAPTER TEN

"Aren't you going to say something?" Noah demanded. "Take me to task for my behavior?"

Jessa's fingers paused in their gentle rotation over Noah's temples. His head was in her lap and his hair looked especially dark against the pale rose fabric of her gown. His eyes were closed but Jessa was not lulled into thinking he was relaxed. Even before he spoke, his voice tight and faintly accusing, she could feel the rigid tension in his shoulders as they rested on her thigh. He was lying across the high tester bed diagonally, his feet crossed at the ankles, but he hadn't even spared a moment to remove his shoes. The ivory counterpane was wrinkled where he held it bunched in the tight curl of his fists.

Leaning wearily against the headboard, Jessa refrained from comment and resumed massaging Noah's temples. Her fingers sifted through his hair, rubbing his scalp, then kneaded the taut cords of his neck and shoulders. She attended her task without concentration though the movement of her hands was sure and deft.

Jessa glanced about the bedchamber, really seeing it

for the first time since Noah had fairly dragged her across the threshold and onto the bed. The room was cheerful and warm, a marked contrast to her husband's black humor. The ivory walls were dappled with the late evening sunlight not contained by the drawn window curtains. The hardwood floor and woodwork were all dark walnut. There were patterned area rugs around the bed and one in front of the brick hearth. Logs were stacked on the hearth's apron in anticipation of a cold spring night. The wardrobe and highboy stood against the wall at opposite sides of the room and the brass pulls on the dresser drawers gleamed from a recent polishing. A large rocker sat at an angle in front of the window, and Jessa could imagine sitting there with Gideon in her arms, sunlight streaming over her shoulder and resting on the infant's dear face.

Jessa's gentle musings were shattered by Noah's impatient interruption. "Well?" he demanded again, annoyed by her continued silence.

"What is it you want, Noah?" she asked, striving for calm. "I can hardly credit you want me to rail at you. I know you don't feel well. If I can find it a reasonably acceptable excuse for your rude and churlish manner, I'm certain your family can also. You can make your apology tonight or on the morrow and all will be forgiven. They know you well enough. They must be used to you blowing hot and cold by now."

"But they're not," Noah said testily. "I'm the even-tempered McClellan, the peacekeeper."

All the more reason to leave him, Jessa thought. It seemed obvious to her that she brought out the worst in him, made him unrecognizable to himself and his family. "Then I shall have to be very careful around the others, won't I?," she said tartly. "They must have been on their best behavior earlier. If you're even-tempered, I can't imagine what *they* must be like."

Noah's eyes opened and he looked up at Jessa, searching her face. "I've been spoiling for a fight, haven't I?"

"It's nothing new."

Perhaps not, he thought, but he was supposed to be trying to win her confidence, not give her another reason to throw up more barriers. His hands unfolded around the bunched counterpane as some of the tension seeped out of him. "God, you have the gentlest touch," he said feelingly, closing his eyes again.

"Feeling better?"

"Mmm. The room's not spinning any longer." One of Jessa's hands had come to rest on his chest. Noah reached for it, lacing his fingers in hers. "I'm sorry for dragging you out of the dining room the way I did. I'm surprised no one leaped to your rescue. That would be just the sort of thing they would relish doing."

"I doubt anyone but me thought you were bent on murder."

"Did I hurt your hand? I know I grabbed it hard."

"It's all right now," she said, dismissing his concern. "No bruises."

"That doesn't mean I didn't hurt you. I know better." He paused, turning his head in her lap while her free hand continued to stroke the side of his neck. Her fingers were light as they moved upward, tracing the outer edge of his ear. "Do you like the room?"

Jessa hesitated. She liked it very much but she wondered if he would be angry if she said so. He hadn't been pleased when she expressed enthusiasm for the landing. "It's fine," she said, carefully noncommittal.

"I want you to be comfortable while you're here, Jessa. You should know that our bedchamber in Philadelphia is similar to this one. Only larger."

But she wouldn't be going to Philadelphia with him. In Jessa's mind it was a certainty. "Has it always been your room?"

"Since the time I moved out of the nursery. If you look along the baseboard near the door you can still see where I carved my name into the wood. Salem and

Gareth put me up to it, then they both went straight to Mother and told her what I had done."

"What happened?"

"You have to know my mother. She was suspicious of my brothers immediately, probably because they had been doing that sort of thing to one another for years. She congratulated me for having spelled my name so neatly and made the three of us polish every bit of woodwork in the entire house."

"How wonderfully just."

"None of us thought so at the time."

"She was very good with Gideon."

"There was never any doubt of that. You don't have to worry that she'll take the upper hand where Gideon is concerned. We'll only be here long enough for her to spoil him. She'll enjoy that."

"Would you mind if I looked in on Gideon now?" Jessa asked after a moment's pause. She needed to get away from him. His sharing of childhood memories made her uncomfortable. It was the sort of thing he might do if he really cared about her, and Jessa was not about to be duped by that unlikely fancy.

Noah wanted her to stay with him. He felt as if he had just begun to make some small headway. But perhaps there was more to be gained by giving her a measure of freedom. "The nursery's two doors down on the left. Do you want me to come with you?"

"No," she said quickly, panicked by the thought. "I can find it. I should think you would feel more the thing after you've slept a little while."

Raising her hand to his lips, Noah's lips brushed her knuckles. He felt her stiffen but didn't take issue with it. He knew he had a great deal to answer for in regard to his treatment of Jessa. She was correct when she said he blew hot and cold with her. It was no longer a matter of simply trying to keep her off balance; he couldn't seem to control his reactions any longer. If he didn't completely understand it how could she?

He dropped Jessa's hand and lifted his head so that she could ease away from him. When she was gone Noah slammed his fist into the headboard. The force of the blow shook the bed, the canopy fluttered above him, and a sudden wave of nausea turned his muscles to butter. Groaning, Noah stretched out on his stomach and closed his eyes. He fell asleep praying that he would never have to make another ocean crossing in this lifetime.

Ashley McClellan looked up as the nursery door was cautiously opened. It could only be Jessa. No one else in the household would have shown such reticence. "Please, come in," she called, biting back a smile. "I'd welcome adult company." She guided her young son back to her breast and motioned to Jessa to enter.

"You're certain?"

"Most certain," she said, starting the rocker in motion again. She pointed to the small child's bed in one corner of the room. Gideon wasn't in it. Rather he was under it playing with several brightly colored cloth balls he had found on the nursery floor. "I've tried to coax him out but he seems to like it under there."

Laughing, Jessa pulled Gideon from under the bed and rolled the balls to other parts of the room. Gideon immediately set out to get one, churning his chubby legs along the polished floor with amazing speed. Jessa looked around the room and noticed the larger bed behind Ashley's rocker "Does someone sleep with the children at night?" she asked

"Hm-mmm. Ruth stays here. She's Tildy's granddaughter so she's fiercely protective and naturally bossy."

"I've heard Tildy is a force to be reckoned with."

"That would describe her," Ashley said with undeniable affection. She lifted Christian away from her breast and righted her scooped bodice. Laying the infant across her lap, she began patting his back to make him burp. "How is Noah?" she asked casually while Jessa wandered about the room.

Jessa's fingers stilled on the carved mane of the wooden rocking horse she had been examining. "He's feeling better," she said, giving the horse a nudge to set it in motion. The daffodil yellow wallpaper was flocked with tiny white flowers. It lent a golden hue to Jessa's hair as she moved through a pale beam of sunlight. She bent, picked up a ball, and tossed it in Gideon's direction. "I massaged his head and shoulders for him. It seemed to help."

"I'm happy to hear it. I've never witnessed Noah so out of sorts before. He usually takes his illness in stride, making light of it along with everyone else. It's been something of a family joke for years."

"Perhaps he finally tired of it," she said, sitting down on a three-legged stool at the foot of Gideon's bed. "It can't be very pleasant for him to appear so weak. Not with his stubborn male pride."

"Another McClellan trait, I'm afraid," Ashley sighed, shaking her head ruefully. "I wish you luck with it. I haven't been able to beat it out of Salem in twelve years of marriage." She winked playfully. "Though I've humbled him on occasion."

Jessa smiled weakly. "I can't imagine humbling Noah."

"Oh, I don't know," Ashley said, lifting Christian to her shoulder. His dark head lolled sleepily against the slender stem of her neck. "A man in love is remarkably vulnerable."

"Oh, but—" Jessa caught herself before she told Ashley that not only wasn't Noah in love with her, he intended to divorce her as soon as he tired of her.

"Yes?"

"I never thought of Noah as vulnerable." Jessa smoothed the fabric of her gown over her knees and avoided Ashley's thoughtful regard by attending to Gideon's antics. He had gathered all three of the cloth balls and was determinedly nudging them toward the haven of the underside of the bed.

"How does he seem to you?" Ashley asked, unable to check her curiosity.

"Well, he's enormously fond of Gideon, so he's very kind and generous in that regard."

"Of course. Noah's like his mother. He loves children though we despaired of him having any of his own. But you haven't precisely answered my question."

"I don't really know what you mean," she prevaricated, raising her hands in a helpless gesture. "Noah's . . . Noah."

"Forgive me," Ashley said, rising from the rocker. She went over to the window and drew the drapes. "I didn't mean to pry. It's just that after you and Noah left the dining room Salem remarked that you seemed a little afraid of Noah."

"He said that?" Jessa asked, swallowing hard. "How odd."

"I thought so, too."

"I'm hardly likely to be afraid of my husband."

Ashley nodded in agreement, though she was not deceived by Jessa's denial. "I know. Who could be afraid of Noah? He has rather a calming effect on the rest of us. I can't recall hearing him raise his voice above two or three times, though I understand he's something of a firebrand in the courtroom."

And the bedroom, Jessa wanted to say. That's where I'm on trial. "You'll have to tell your husband he was wrong. I can't imagine why he would think Noah frightened me."

"I can't either." Ashley put Christian in his cradle and covered him with a thin blanket. "Why don't I find Ruth and have her sit with Gideon? I know Noah intended to take you on a tour of the landing, but I don't think he'd mind if I did it instead."

Jessa glanced at the clock on the mantelpiece. "I promised him I wouldn't be long," she invented, unwittingly confirming Ashley's suspicions that Noah kept a tight leash on his new wife. "Perhaps if he's sleeping I could come with you."

"All right. Why don't you see if that's the case?" Ashley plucked Gideon off the floor. "I'll find Ruth and give her this sweet young man." She watched Jessa go and turned a thoughtful frown on the child in her arms. "Something's not quite right, is it? But I'm damned if I know what it is."

"Dam. Dam. Dam," Gideon cried happily, waving his fists.

"Oh, dear," Ashley laughed. "Don't tell anyone where you heard that."

Ten minutes later Ashley found Jessa waiting for her in the foyer. "I take it Noah is sleeping," she said.

Jessa shook her head. "No, that is, he was, but I woke him up when I opened the door. He asked us to wait while he washed and shaved. You don't mind, do you?"

"Of course not. Actually, if Noah's rousing himself out of bed perhaps he would like to show you around himself."

Thinking Ashley would act as a buffer, Jessa opened her mouth to say that she was more than welcome to accompany them. The words never were voiced, for just then she saw Noah at the head of the wide staircase.

Ashley followed the direction of Jessa's eyes and looked over her shoulder as Noah jauntily descended the steps. "You're looking well," she said. "I don't think I've ever known you to recover so quickly."

Noah grinned as he stepped behind Jessa and folded his arms about her waist. He kissed the crown of her head. "That's because no one has ever cared for me the way Jessa does. I swear she has magic in her fingers."

"She must," Ashley said. "I was just saying that now that you're up again, perhaps you'd rather show her around yourself." Though Noah and Jessa immediately replied she was welcome to join them, Ashley found the real message in their eyes, and it was a decidedly mixed invitation. Jessa's clear eyes were unconsciously pleading with her to come along; above her, Noah's green-gold eyes were also pleading, but in a manner that let Ashley know he wanted to be alone with his wife. Her heart went out to Jessa, but she couldn't allow herself to interfere in Noah's personal life, not in front of him anyway. She had known him nearly as long as she had known Salem and trusted him without reservation. "That's very kind of you, but I remember what it was like to be newly married at the landing. There wasn't nearly enough privacy. If you don't mind, I think I'll try to find my husband and see if that's changed."

Slipping his arm in hers, Noah led Jessa down the steps and along the curved driveway. There was only a hint of sun left on the horizon, backlighting the trees in the distance with a bright orange wash of color. Noah pointed to a row of small whitewashed houses bordering on the immense tobacco field. "Most of the field workers live there. There are vegetable gardens behind the houses that extend back to the woods."

Noah steered Jessa away from the drive and around the northern corner of the house. "Come on. I want to show you the stables."

There were in fact two buildings that held animals. The first quartered the animals used on the plantation itself, draft horses and riding animals. It also held carriages, wagons, and farming implements. The second building held the thoroughbreds, beautiful sleek animals that Jessa admired with unrestrained enthusiasm, stroking their necks, talking to them, and feeding them bits of dried apples.

"Do you ride?" asked Noah, pleased by her reaction.

"I haven't for some time, and never anything so fine as these animals."

"Then we'll find you a mount from the other stable. Would you like to go riding in the morning?"

"If you wish it." When had he ever cared what she wanted? Why was he asking now? She almost begged him to stop being kind. In some ways his cruelty was much easier to bear.

"I do," he said succinctly. His arm slipped naturally around Jessa's waist as they left the stable and walked along the paddock fence. He pointed out the cow shed, the barn where the tobacco seedlings were nurtured and eventually dried and packed, and the newly built summer kitchen. As they got closer to the house they could hear laughter coming from the lower veranda. Noah abruptly steered Jessa away, wanting more time alone with her.

"Where are we going?"

"Do we have to be going somewhere? I thought you were enjoying the walk."

Jessa dug in her heels so that Noah was forced to stop or drag her along. He stopped. "I want to go back to the house," she said. "Please, Noah. Your parents are going to be disappointed if we don't join them soon."

"All right," he relented ungraciously. He pushed the thought of the little clearing near the river to the back of his mind along with his plans for seduction. "But we'll go back to the front of the house and I'll show you the main floor. You'll need to know where everything is. *Then* we'll join the others on the veranda."

The last part of Noah's tour was over too quickly as far as he was concerned. Jessa felt differently. She had known exactly what he had on his mind as soon as he altered their approach to the house. Being alone with him in one room after another made her distinctly uneasy. Not that he didn't behave himself. He did. It was the casual touch of his hand in the library, the manner in which his fingers brushed her hair in the music room, the way he stood within touching distance as they went through the front and rear parlors, the kitchen, and the significant pause at the pantry door, that kept Jessa's teeth on edge. There was no one around he had to impress, and Jessa began to believe he was playing the doting husband just to shred her nerves. She didn't thank him for it.

By the time they reached the veranda Jessa's smile was a brittle parody of genuine feeling. Robert, Salem, and Jericho all came to their feet and offered her a chair when she stepped out onto the flagstones. Jessa thanked them and refused, taking a seat instead on the first step where Courtney was sitting.

Noah was ready to sit beside her when he was embraced from behind by a fierce hug that almost sent him tumbling down the steps.

"Sakes, boy! I thought yo' was never gonna stop long enough to say hello!"

Turning, Noah grasped Tildy by her wide shoulders and placed a kiss on each of her coffee-colored cheeks. "Where have you been?"

"In the nursery takin' a look at the fine son of yours!" She stepped out of Noah's arms, straightened her mobcap, then smoothed the front of her dress over her ample bosom. Hands resting on her hips, she stared at Noah expectantly. "Well?" she asked, tapping her foot. Behind her she could hear Rae's giggle.

Noah pretended ignorance. "Well what?"

"Introduce me, brat!"

"How is it that you can still make me feel like a green youth?" he asked grinning.

"Practice," she said succinctly.

Over the top of her head Noah saw Salem encouraging him with gestures and silently mouthed words to argue with Tildy. Noah was not so stupid as to fall for that trick. "Not me, brother," he said, holding up his hands in surrender. "I've no desire to tangle with her."

Tildy shot a quick, suspicious glance behind her, but Salem had already settled back in his chair and was looking completely innocent. "Well?" she asked again.

Noah reached down for Jessa's waiting hand and drew her to her feet. "Jessa, this is Tildy, the woman who can make me confess to stealing her Sunday pies just by looking at me. Tildy, my wife Jessa.''

Tildy surveyed Jessa up and down. ''My, aren't you an itty bit. Tinier than Miss Ashley, I'll wager. How you came to take up with this piece of timber, I'll never understand.''

''She felled me in one blow,'' Noah said gallantly.

Tildy snorted. ''More likely yo' jest carried her off, little thing like her. I'm afraid to hug her. Might break something.''

''I'm not all that fragile,'' said Jessa. ''I'm very glad to meet you, Tildy. Everyone says you're wonderful.''

Tildy felt a warmth creep over her skin. ''Ain't no one here likely to have said that. But yo' are kind to say so.'' She studied Jessa again. ''I like her jest fine, Mr. Noah. Yo' be good to her.'' Without further ado she walked back into the house.

''You've made a conquest, dear,'' Charity said, responding to Jessa's complete bewilderment.

''But how can that be? She doesn't even know me.''

''Tildy knows,'' said Rae wisely. ''She has a way of peering in someone's eyes and seeing their soul.''

Noah nearly groaned aloud. Usually he had great respect for Tildy's perceptions. In this case she was as easily misled as the others. Jessa made a hell of a good first impression. It was the knowing of her that gave one pause. He thought of the letter he had written to Drew Goodfellow. It would be sent on the next packet out. Surely Drew would find some evidence that would bear out his own suspicions.

''And besides that,'' Jericho put in, ''we've already told her how you saved Noah's skin. That went a long way to impressing her.''

''And she fell in love with Gideon,'' Ashley added.

''And you're not Hilary Bowen,'' said Courtney.

Salem looked sharply at his daughter. ''That's unkind, Court. It's not flattering to Jessa, Hilary, or your uncle.''

"But you all were saying before Uncle Noah got here that—"

"Enough," said Salem abruptly.

Courtney pulled a face. "I don't understand."

Noah sat down on the steps beside his niece and pulled Jessa down with him. "It's a matter of do as I say and not as I do, Courtney. You're not meant to understand, just accept it."

"It's not fair," she pouted.

"No, it's not." He chucked her lightly on the chin while he looked meaningfully at the rest of his family, telling them with a narrow glance exactly what he thought of them making comparisons between Hilary and Jessa the moment his back was turned. "Where are your brothers and cousins?" he asked, changing the subject.

"In their rooms. I'm the only one allowed to be up this late," she finished importantly, bringing a smile to everyone's lips.

"And I've already cause to regret it," Salem sighed, his mouth twitching.

"Did you have a chance to visit with Cam?" asked Jessa.

Even in the blue-gray twilight, Courtney's blush was evident. "Just for a little while. He went downriver to Norfolk with some of the crew."

"Salem," Noah said. "I was wondering if you'd let me steal Cam from you for the length of the convention. I'd like to take him to Philadelphia with me. He made himself invaluable to Jessa on board ship."

Jessa swallowed her protest. Cam would be more than welcome if she had any intention of going with Noah. Since she didn't, the discussion was absurd. There was also nothing she could say without giving herself away.

"That's all very well," said Salem, "but it's up to Cam. I always had the impression he left home to get away from playing nursemaid."

"And an abusive, drunken father," said Jessa. When

everyone looked at her in surprise she added, "Cam told me. He and I spent a great deal of time together while Noah was working. He . . . he was easy to talk to and . . . we had something in common—fathers who drank too much. Not that mine ever hit me. It wasn't like that. Mostly he just . . . ignored me." At her back she felt Noah's fingers caress the curling ends of her hair. It was a sweet, light touch, and if he had pulled her into his arms in that moment she wouldn't have shied away, even if they had been alone. "That sounds so self-pitying, doesn't it," she said, smiling faintly. "I'm sorry. I just thought you should know. My family wasn't quite like this one."

"There aren't many that are," said Robert reasonably. His face glowed briefly as he lit a cheroot.

Noah's fingers tugged a little as they continued to sift through the near colorless fall of Jessa's hair. She was about to feel the sting of more of her lies. "I imagine Jessa feels compelled to explain because her first husband's parents were bothered in the extreme by her background."

Jessa wished she could call back everything. She didn't care if the McClellans knew about her own family, but she despised herself when she heard Noah bring up the fictitious Granthams. Somehow she had imagined those lies would remain between Noah and her.

"Then it's their loss," Charity said firmly. "Really, Noah, you should have made it clear to Jessa that we don't set much credence by bloodlines and the like. That was very bad of you."

Jericho leaned forward in his chair, placing his elbows on his knees. A frown puckered his forehead as he studied Jessa's face. Rae reached over and brushed back a wayward lock of his bright hair. "D'you know, Jessa, you have the look of someone I've met. I just can't—"

She had been afraid of this since Jericho first mentioned that he had done more than his share of gambling during his brief stay in England. Noah, for all his probing and prying, had never once expressed an interest in her maiden name, or in her past beyond her fabricated marriage to Robert Grantham. Yet now it was going to come tumbling out because Jessa had no doubt Jericho Smith had played cards with her father. "You probably knew my father," she interrupted. "Baron—"

"Winter!" Jericho finished triumphantly. "Of course. Lord Winter. My God! You have his hair, his eyes. I don't know why I didn't realize it immediately. Lord, yes, I played cards with him on several occasions."

"That, I imagine, did not bode well for my father. Noah says you're an exceptional player."

Jericho leaned back and stretched his long legs, crossing his feet at the ankles. "That was a lifetime ago. I don't play much these days. Tell me, Jessa, what could your in-laws find objectionable? As I recall, your father is well-liked, titled, and has considerable resources."

"My father is dead," Jessa said. "Mother also. There was a fire on the estate. It killed my parents and destroyed our home as well."

"Oh, God," Jericho groaned softly. "I'm sorry. I didn't realize."

Jessa waved his apology aside. "You couldn't have known. And yes, my father was well-liked and titled. However, his considerable resources were something of a sham. After the fire there was nothing left. That's what others found objectionable."

"How did you manage?" Ashley asked. "It couldn't have been easy for you."

"It was . . . awkward," Jessa said truthfully. "I took a position as a lady's companion in London. I met the Penber—er—Robert there and we married later." Had Noah caught her faltering? He was always so quick to suspect a lie and too often he was right. She was glad when Courtney blurted out a question.

"Was this lady mean and overbearing and pompous? And did she use you as a drudge?"

Jessa blinked in surprise at the young girl's earnest question. "Why ever would you think that?"

"Because it's so romantic that your husband should rescue you from that sort of life."

"Oh, I see. Well, I'm afraid you'll be disappointed. Lady Howard was very kind to me and I didn't have the least sense of being rescued."

"Oh."

"God, Courtney," Salem said feelingly. "The way your mind works. You have the most cork-brained notions."

Courtney drew herself up defensively. Her silver eyes, so much like her father's, flashed. "Everyone knows you carried Mama away from her wicked uncle at Linfield," she said, waving her arms dramatically. "And Jericho saved Aunt Rae from certain death in a seedy redcoat tavern. I'm not cork-brained!"

"I don't think I ever used the word seedy," Rae said calmly.

"And you *are* cork-brained," Jericho added, "because there was nothing the least romantic about it."

Ashley rose from her chair and motioned to Courtney. "Come with me, young lady. It's past your bedtime. And I think it's time I explained to you those tales you've heard are only romantic in the telling." She took Courtney's small hand in hers. "Good night everyone. I imagine I'll have this child's muddled head cleared by morning." Courtney pulled away from her mother long enough to kiss her father good night, then she followed Ashley into the house.

When Salem was certain Courtney was out of earshot he let out the laughter that was rumbling in his chest. "Truth, Jericho," he said, nudging his brother-in-law in the arm. "Wasn't it the least bit romantic?"

"Have a care how you answer," Rae cautioned.

Jessa never heard Jericho's answer. She was intrigued by the easy play between husband and wife, the happy comraderie between all the McClellans. Their laughter was infectious, their humor slightly ribald, and anyone who feigned shock was instantly reminded of something outrageous he or she had done. Charity and Robert presided over the gathering with amused calm, Charity invariably serene, Robert with a certain amount of pride. Noah took his fair share of ribbing and added his share as well. Jessa realized she was the only one who was exempt from the good-natured barbs, and the knowledge was accompanied by an odd, lonely feeling.

Noah leaned back against one of the veranda's white columns and without quite knowing how he accomplished it, Jessa found herself sitting between his parted thighs, her head resting lightly on his shoulder. The candlelight from the interior of the house was all that lit the porch, but even in the shadows Jessa could see Robert and Charity exchange knowing glances. Jessa placed her hands over Noah's as they stole around her waist. It was not the loving gesture the others thought, but rather it was designed to keep Noah's wandering hands respectfully distant from her breasts. Noah seemed perfectly satisfied with this arrangement, and somewhat disconcertedly Jessa realized the sense of loneliness had passed.

Gradually the laughter and storytelling subsided. Ashley rejoined them on the veranda and conversation became focused on the growing season, absent family members, the new mare Robert had recently purchased, and finally politics. Just as the last subject was provoking a little heat and the participants were choosing sides, the lines clearly defined by sex rather than spousal or familial affection, Tildy appeared on the threshold and offered everyone hot buttered rum.

"Excellent timing, Tildy," Robert declared. "We were just—"

"I know, Mr. Robert," she said in long-suffering accents. "I could hear y'all at the back of the house. How's a body to concentrate on her Bible readin' with you folks carryin' on?" Ignoring their laughter she continued to complain and huff as she disappeared into the house again.

Twenty minutes later Noah narrowly caught Jessa's empty glass before it slipped from her nerveless fingers. He set it down beside his own then looked at Jessa closely, smiling wryly when he confirmed that she had fallen asleep. He turned her a little so she could rest against him more comfortably.

Jericho's lips twitched. "I don't think there's any question that Jessa doesn't have her father's tolerance for alcohol."

So that much of her past was true, Noah thought. Wonder of wonders. "I take it the baron was everything she described."

"Worse," Jericho said, his smile fading. "I never saw him without a glass in his hand. He never cut his liquor when he was gaming and he drank continuously. Truth is, if he hadn't died in that fire, drink would have killed him eventually."

"But to your knowledge he was never abusive, was he?"

"No, not that I ever saw. Quite the contrary, though I didn't know him well. We only met a few times over a period of weeks and never anywhere but the gaming hells. I didn't know then that he had a daughter. I'm not certain if he ever mentioned his wife. The thing of it is, one would hardly know he was foxed even after he had been drinking heavily."

"Jessa told me once he could charm anybody."

"That would describe him," Jericho agreed.

"Noah," Rae ventured quietly. "I know you don't want to discuss it, but I'm going to risk your wrath anyway. What have you told Jessa about Hilary?"

"Very little. Why?" he asked, his suspicions aroused. "Has she asked you about Hilary?"

"No, of course not. This is the first I've been with her since dinner. It's just that you've been very touchy about Hilary. It seems a little odd, that's all."

"I don't think there's anything odd about asking you not to speak ill of my ex-fiancée," he said a trifle stiffly. "Until I met Jessa I fully intended to marry Hilary when I returned." It was all he could do to keep from telling them it remained his intention. "Hilary didn't deserve such shabby treatment at my hands."

"Then Hilary has no idea that you've married?" asked Charity.

"None. A letter would not have reached her much before my arrival, and in any event, I would hardly inform Hilary in that cold manner. Obviously I'll speak to her in person. Frankly, I'm not certain I understand the nature of your concern. Is it for Hilary or Jessa?"

"Jessa," Rae answered immediately. "I know you don't want to hear this, Noah, but Hilary has a tendency toward, umm, spite."

"That's ridiculous."

"It's true," Rae whispered harshly. "I would have told you before if I thought there was the remotest chance that you would heed me. She is a vicious, nasty woman beneath that well-mannered, butter-wouldn't-melt-in-her-mouth exterior, and I'm telling you now so that you can properly protect Jessa from Hilary's cutting tongue."

"I don't know the woman you're describing."

Rae threw up her hands, exasperated. "Salem, you tell him! If you don't, I will."

"God, Rae," Salem sighed, "you do choose your moments."

"Tell me what?" Noah demanded, cutting off his sister before she snapped at Salem.

Salem's hands tightened around his mug of rum. "The first time you brought Hilary here," he began lowly, "Ashley and I were in the midst of a quarrel, the nature of which neither of us can remember now. I only mention it because there was obviously some friction between us at the time. Naturally, since you came home with your guest we did our very best to be civil to one another. We were less successful than we might have wished. Hilary must have sensed the tension. She let me know, in her discreet way, of course, that she was, er, available if I had need of her.''

Noah's eyes narrowed dangerously. "You must have misunderstood her intent,'' he gritted. "If she sensed something wrong between you and Ashley, then she was willing to listen. She was offering her help.''

"She may have been discreet, Noah, but she was clear. Any help she was offering was carnal in nature.'' Salem's upper lip curled derisively. "I did not mistake her meaning.''

"I don't believe you.''

Salem shrugged. "That's of no consequence to me. You're the one likely to be hurt by your lack of judgment. Jericho? It's your turn.''

Jericho's boots scraped against the flagstones as he shifted in his chair. "Dammit, Noah,'' he said roughly. "On one of her other visits Hilary cornered me in the library one afternoon while I was working on the accounts. She came on the pretense of finding a book but soon made it evident that she had something else in mind. At first I could hardly believe what I was hearing. When I realized she was serious, I ran like hell.''

"Why didn't you say anything to me then?'' Noah demanded.

"Because I was embarrassed. Believe me, I regretted my silence when you wrote and told us that you and Hilary were engaged.''

Noah's smile was bitter. "So you all got together and conspired to send me to England, knowing full well that Hilary wouldn't marry me before the voyage.''

"We didn't know that for certain,'' Charity said, her voice soft with regret for her son's pain. "We merely suspected that would be the case, knowing her abhorrence of the English. It's just not natural, Noah, not with the war behind us these five years.''

"Her abhorrence, as you call it, seems hard to credit if she was willing to throw herself at Jericho."

"You're missing the point," said Salem. "She didn't really want Jericho any more than she wanted me. What she wanted was to destroy our marriages. Hilary completely overlooks the fact that Jericho and Ashley both did their part for America during the war. Hell, Jericho was even wounded at the same battle that took her brother's life. The only thing she cares about is that my wife and Jericho both have holdings in England, and she'll do her damnedest to punish them for it."

"That's quite a theory," Noah sneered. "I had no idea you were given to contemplating the motives of others."

"It's hardly a theory," replied Salem, making an effort to gather the threads of his patience. "It didn't matter to Hilary that her advances were spurned, first by me, then by Jericho. She deliberately set out to make Ashley and Rae think that something had happened, and she intimated that we were the ones to express interest in her. Had their trust in us been any less than what it was, Hilary could very well have been successful in making herself believed."

Salem drained the last of his rum. "I think you know Rae well enough to realize she doesn't let something like that go unconfronted. I'll spare you the details of that scene except to say that Hilary confessed to Rae what she had been about. Rightly or wrongly, we decided among ourselves to let it rest because Hilary swore she wasn't trying to make you a cuckold. Her actions had nothing at all to do with you and everything to do with her twisted notions of revenge."

"So why tell me now?" Noah demanded. "I could have done very well without ever hearing it."

"Surely that's obvious, Noah," said Rae. "You're about to leave for Philadelphia in a few days, and not only are you going to tell Hilary you've married, you're presenting her with an *English* bride! Can you possibly begin to imagine how she will take that news?"

"She's going to be hurt. And she has every right to be."

"She's going to be *furious!* And if you think she won't exact some sort of revenge, then you haven't heard a word we've said."

Noah was silent a moment, choosing his words carefully. When he spoke his voice was low, slightly strained. "I think you're being melodramatic, Rae, and your talk of revenge is premature. I can accept your reasons for raising this issue were prompted by genuine concern, and I can appreciate that. However, your meddling— and I'm addressing this to everyone, not Rae alone— has already had profound consequences on my life and I am heartily sick of it. I want—"

"Meddling?" Charity asked. "Do you mean the voyage to Eng—"

"What profound consequences?" Rae wanted to know.

Robert laid his hand over his wife's knee. "Let him finish, Charity," he said both gently and firmly. "Rae, that's enough."

"Thank you, Father." Noah drew in a deep breath, let it out slowly, and continued. "I want you to know that I love you all. More than that, I like you as well. I suspect you return those sentiments else you would not have felt compelled to tell me these things tonight. Yet I find myself resentful because you weren't honest with me at the outset. I knew you didn't approve of Hilary, but no one saw fit to tell me the real reason you withheld that approval. You hinted. You shared glances you thought I didn't notice. And you conspired behind my back. Do you think I should thank you for that? You maneuvered me into making a trip I despised to deal with problems that could easily have been handled by any lawyer of your acquaintance."

"But you wouldn't have met Jessa," Ashley pointed out softly.

"No, Ashley, I wouldn't have," he said, almost without inflection. Noah paused then, lifting Jessa in his arms as he stood awkwardly. He could feel the press of her soft cheek against his shirt. "And you can make of that what you like." Bidding them only a cursory nod, Noah turned on his heel and carried Jessa into the house.

No one on the veranda spoke for several minutes. The nightsounds they had not noticed before seemed abnormally loud now. Crickets in the hedgerow clicked incessantly. Wildlife moved in the wood, shaking the underbrush. Leaves fluttered overhead as a cool breeze swept up from the river.

"I don't think I've ever seen Noah so angry," Salem said finally, running his fingers through his dark hair. "Certainly never so quiet *and* angry."

Rae nodded slowly, her eyes glistening with unshed tears. "God, I shouldn't want to face him in the courtroom," she said, her voice a mere thread of sound.

"What do you think he meant by that remark about meeting Jessa?" asked Ashley, worrying her lower lip, her emerald eyes troubled.

Robert lit another cheroot and drew on it deeply. "I fear any speculation on that matter would serve no purpose. Noah was deliberately vague, and given his experience with our interference, he chose exactly the right course. I suggest we let it rest."

Once inside the bedchamber Noah laid Jessa on the bed and lighted two candles on the nightstand. She stirred but did not wake as he loosened the laces in her bodice and eased the gown off her shoulders. Taking off her shoes, he dropped them lightly on the floor, then managed to get Jessa under the covers with a minimum amount of rolling her this way and that. He could feel himself begin to resent the way she continued to sleep, oblivious to his hurt, his bitter disappointment, his frustration. Not that she would have cared, he thought. He had certainly given her no reason to concern herself with his problems, but still he resented it.

Noah undressed, blew out the candles, and slipped into bed, careful not to touch Jessa. He lay on his back, cradling his head in his hands, and stared unblinkingly at the snowy canopy above him. God, when had he lost control of his life? How was he supposed to cope with this overwhelming sense of aloneness? Tears welled in his eyes. The canopy blurred. Breath shuddered through him.

"Jessa?"

The sound of her name spoken so softly, so uncertainly, accomplished what all the movement beforehand could not. Jessa woke. "Yes?"

Noah found himself saying words he never thought he would utter—and saying them with absolute sincerity. "I need you, Jessa. Please . . . I need you."

And Jessa misunderstood. "All right," she said. She hardly knew where she was but it didn't matter. Noah had said anytime, in any manner. Easing herself across the space that separated her from Noah, Jessa slipped one arm across his chest and curved her body into his. Catlike, she rubbed her cheek against his naked shoulder. Though Jessa's senses were dulled by sleepy exhaustion she still felt Noah stiffen when she touched him. His response, the kind he would make if he were trying to shrug her off, struck her as odd. But because he had said he needed her and because her body was the only thing he had ever needed, Jessa persisted, raising herself until her mouth hovered above his.

She wet her lips in a way that usually made Noah suck in his breath with the first urgings of desire. This time he did nothing. A frown puckered Jessa's brow as she lowered her mouth to his, tracing the line of his lips with the tip of her tongue. One of her legs slid between his. Her knee nudged his inner thigh and she was vaguely aware that she was still wearing her stockings.

Jessa wondered if Noah disliked the slightly abrasive sensation.

While she was kissing the corner of his closed mouth the tips of Jessa's fingers threaded through Noah's thick hair, stroking the sensitive curve of his ear with her thumbs. When his lips did not part under the gentle persuading pressure of her tongue, Jessa's mouth moved lower and trailed along his jawline. She waited for his hands to touch the small of her back, cup her buttocks, or sift through the wave of hair which fell over one shoulder. None of those things happened.

What did he want?

Confused by his lack of interest, Jessa sat up and removed her stockings then pulled her shift over her head. Tossing the garments to the foot of the bed, she leaned over Noah so the tips of her naked breasts just brushed his chest. Finally she got a response.

Noah's fingers curled around Jessa's upper arms in a bruising, hurtful grip and in a single motion filled with contempt and disgust he pushed her away from him. "God, you make me sick," he said tightly, bitterly. "Get away from me."

Stricken, Jessa scrambled to the far side of the bed and snatched the counterpane to cover herself. She was fully awake now and wishing she were dreaming. Tears clogged her throat and the enormity of her shame left her mute. She stared hard at Noah, trying to discern the reason for his anger in the rigid set of his profile.

Noah sat up, threw his legs over the side of the bed, and reached for his breeches, which were lying over the arm of the nearby rocker. He jammed his legs into them, stood, fastened the laces at the back with stiff, quick motions, and walked over to the window. Drawing back the curtains, Noah leaned forward, pressing his palms and forehead to the cool panes of glass. Beads of moisture formed on the glass.

"I make myself sick," he said at last, his voice strained. He turned away from the window and looked at Jessa's curled figure on the bed. With the curtains pulled aside a sliver of moon cast pale bluish shadows in the bedchamber. Noah's face was gray and drawn in the beam of light. He ran a hand through his hair. "I'm going to Philadelphia in the morning, Jessa. In spite of what we've discussed before I think it would be best if you remained at the landing. I need to be able to concentrate on the work I have to do."

Jessa pressed her knees closer to her chest, closed her eyes, and wondered why she wasn't rejoicing. Wasn't he giving her exactly what she wanted? Hadn't she already decided to leave him? Then why did she feel so horribly empty at the thought of him running to Hilary? Surely that was his intention.

"I'll return in a few weeks," Noah continued, "and perhaps then we can discuss how we mean to go on. I meant what I said before about providing for Gideon. You needn't worry on that account. And I'm not making a decision about divorce now. I need some time to think."

As far as Jessa was concerned he had already decided. But then, hadn't she?

"You mustn't think that you won't be welcome here, Jessa. I'll tell my parents that I want to make some changes in my home to accommodate you and Gideon. No one will find it odd. We have just spent the better part of six weeks in each other's pockets."

Jessa didn't doubt that she would be welcome to stay at the landing. But how could she? All the time Noah was gone she would know the truth, know that he would be with Hilary, know that he would only return to end the marriage. How could she stand to be with his family, perhaps even come to feel part of them, then sever every tie when Noah made it clear he wanted a divorce? She was tired of the lies that governed her life, and though she could not be free of them, she could free herself from others.

Noah's thumbs hooked in the waistband of his

breeches. "There's an empty room down the hall," he said, rocking slightly on his heels. "I'm going to spend the night there. I'll be back in the morning before anyone's up. No one will know. Good night, Jessa." At the door he paused. "For what it's worth, I regret what happened tonight. I should have realized you thought I only needed one thing from you."

Shortly before dawn Noah returned to the bedchamber. He leaned wearily against the door, his face devoid of expression as he stared at the neatly made bed and felt the emptiness of the room.

Jessa was gone.

CHAPTER ELEVEN

Only the clothes Jessa had before their marriage were missing from the wardrobe and highboy. Her traveling cloak was gone. She had left her trunk and taken one of Noah's valises instead. Lord Gilmore's timepiece, the gold fob, rings, and coins from the robbery had also vanished. Noah noticed that his valuables, which had shared the same teakwood case as her booty, were untouched. On a whim he opened the trunk. It was empty, but the cloth lining had been ripped jaggedly across the length of the base. That gave him pause. He could only assume she had always had something hidden under there, something he neglected to find when he unpacked the trunk on the *Clarion* and discovered the spoils of the robbery lying among her clothes and Gideon's things. Whatever could she possibly own that was so important to her she kept it secreted away all this time?

Rubbing his forehead with one hand, deep in thought, Noah closed the trunk lid and sat heavily on top of it. He couldn't see that he had any choice but to go after her. How like her to take flight rather than discuss the terms of dissolution of their marriage. Hadn't he made it clear that he intended to provide for Gideon?

Noah splashed water on his face at the basin but did not take the time to shave. He dressed quickly, choosing practical riding clothes and boots, then ran his fingers haphazardly through his hair rather than pause long enough to use a brush. He retied the black grosgrain ribbon at his nape as he strode toward the nursery.

Ruth and Christian were still sleeping and, as he expected, Gideon was no longer there. Noah closed the door quietly then hurried down the hall, taking the stairs to the main floor two and three at a time. He glanced in all the rooms on his way to the rear of the house, just in case Jessa had not left yet. They were empty and silent.

The kitchen, however, was neither.

Noah had forgotten how early the day began at the landing. Robert, Salem, and Jericho were all sitting around the large, scarred oak table drinking coffee while Tildy prepared their breakfast. The kitchen was filled with the aroma of frying bacon and warm loaves of fresh bread.

Tildy saw Noah first. She clicked her tongue and shook her head slowly from side to side, darting him a disapproving glance before she went back to beating eggs. Whatever she muttered under her breath Noah was not meant to hear. It didn't matter. He caught the gist of it anyway.

Salem stopped in midsentence, setting down his mug, when he realized Noah was in the room. "Morning," he said casually, though his eyes had become watchful, even shrewd. "We've been wondering when you would rouse yourself. Or were you out all night? You look like hell."

"How long ago did she leave?" asked Noah without preamble.

Salem's brows drew together thoughtfully. "I'm not

certain. Jericho, what time did you say the stable boy woke you?"

"Must have been about three this morning," Jericho said, rubbing his chin. "Not much earlier than that. 'Course that's when he woke me, not when she left. Billy says he spent thirty minutes calling for someone to untie him before he was heard by one of the other grooms and released."

"Untie him?" asked Noah disbelievingly. He spun a chair away from the table and straddled it, sitting down slowly. Tildy set a mug of steaming coffee in front of him. Hard. "Jessa tied Billy? *Big* Billy?"

Robert watched his son out of the corner of his eye. "It seems Billy did most of the work."

"But how? He'd make three of Jessa."

"Billy's a trifle slow-witted," Robert said calmly, "but he understands what to do when a pistol's pointed at him."

"A pistol?" Noah rubbed his brows with his thumb and forefinger. "Jesus, that must be what she had under the lining of the trunk. A damn pistol. How did I miss it?" He dropped his hand, resting it on one of the rungs of the ladderback chair. It was something of a miracle, he thought distractedly, that she had never turned it on him. "Never mind," he said when he saw their curious expressions. "Why the hell didn't you come and get me when this happened, Jericho?"

"I did. You weren't in your room."

"Dammit! I was only down the hall. Didn't you think to look around a little?"

"No. I woke Robert instead. He reminded me we weren't to interfere. End of story."

"Father! How could you think I wouldn't want to know that Jessa left?"

Robert shrugged carelessly. "It seemed to me, after listening to what Billy told Jericho, that she was quite serious about leaving. And you did give her opportunity. How was I to know you cared one way or the other?"

"Care!" Noah shouted. "Of course I care! Dammit, I—"

"Yes?"

The stiffness went out of Noah's spine and he closed his eyes briefly. He had almost said the words aloud, almost admitted them to himself. It frightened the hell out of him. If it were true, then he had been deceiving himself, and Noah had not thought himself such a fool as that. No. It couldn't be true . . . could it? Did he love her? "I don't want anything to happen to her," he said instead. That was certainly the truth. Sighing softly, he reached for his coffee mug, warming his cold hands around it rather than lifting it to drink. "There are things about my marriage to Jessa that . . . that are rather difficult to explain. More difficult to understand. She hasn't been entirely honest with me, nor have we been honest with you. I can't tell you more than that."

"But you *are* married," said Salem, confused. "The separate bedchambers . . . I wondered . . ."

"We're married." For now.

Tildy set plates heaped with scrambled eggs, bacon, and buttered bread in front of them, clicking her tongue all the while. "Never heard the like before. Separate bedchambers. Hmmpf."

Robert cleared his throat in the charged silence that followed. Noah looked as if he would cheerfully strangle Tildy. "Have you, er, that is, have you consumma—"

"Yes," Noah finished. "And I won't welcome any more questions on that score. What I would welcome is some assistance in bringing Jessa back to the landing. Did Billy say which direction she went?"

Salem nodded, biting off the end of a strip of bacon.

"Well?" demanded Noah caustically. "Do I have to pay you for the information?"

Swallowing, Salem pointed his fork at Noah. "Your manner leaves me a trifle raw, Noah. If this is how you speak to Jessa, it's no wonder she thought better of staying with you."

The lines of Noah's face hardened as he glared at his older brother. Jericho stepped into the fray before they came to blows. "Jessa took one of the wagons," he said. "And she's on the road to Richmond. She can't have gone far, not during the night at least, and not with the wagon Billy harnessed for her. It has a rear axle that was in need of repair."

"Wonderful," Noah said, throwing up his hands. "Now you're telling me she's probably had an accident along the road. Jesus!" Noah stood up and shoved his chair back in place. Without another word he stormed out the back door.

Jericho winced as the door slammed. "Maybe we should go with him," he suggested. "In his mood there's no telling what he'll do to Jessa when he finds her."

"If he wanted us along, he'd have asked," Robert said practically.

Salem stabbed at his eggs. "It's not as if Jessa left here at breakneck speed. Not with that wagon, though why she took it is beyond my reasoning powers. And she's not going to be hurt if the axle breaks. Noah should be happy that he doesn't have to chase her the entire way to Richmond. Damn, but I wish I knew what's gotten into him. He's acting like a complete idiot."

One corner of Robert's mouth lifted in a wry smile. "I remember another son of mine acting much the same way," he said, pinning Salem with his dark green eyes. "Have twelve years of marriage made you forget what it was like in the beginning?"

Salem's smile was sheepish as he recalled his courtship with Ashley. "Everyone knows I behaved like an ass, not an idiot. There's a difference."

"Of course," Robert said, mildly amused. "Eat up. We have work to do."

Behind them, Tildy continued to make disapproving noises though she hid her laughing eyes from everyone.

The morning was cold and gray. The river road was banked in thick fog that showed no sign of burning off quickly and the grass gleamed wetly with dew. Noah's mount was a skittish chestnut stallion whose restlessness matched Noah's mood perfectly. Noah had a strong desire to have control over something, and the high-strung thoroughbred beneath him proved a worthy opponent in a test of wills.

Noah didn't give the stallion his head until he was sure they had established who was master. Even so, as soon as Noah's thighs relaxed and he kicked the stallion's flanks, General charged forward in a wild gallop that nearly unseated his rider. "Wily beast," Noah swore, pulling up the mount after a quarter mile. "It's her neck I want to break, not my own." General snorted, pranced, and continued down the road at a less danger-ous pace once Noah snapped the leather reins.

Noah estimated they had ridden just under ten miles when he sighted the wagon. It was abandoned on the side of the road, resting askew on three wheels. The nag Billy swore he had harnessed for Jessa was nowhere around. Noah shook his head, his eyes bleak as he exam-ined the empty bed of the wagon. How did Jessa hope to manage her journey with a valise, an infant, and a horse with no saddle? Her determination to be gone from him was not to be questioned. Under the circum-stances, she was making her very best effort.

"Let's go, General," Noah said, his voice strained and unhappy. "She can't have gone much further."

The gray mist that still cloaked large sections of the road caused Noah to pass directly in front of Jessa's hiding place in the trees. It was Gideon's cry that halted him. Noah jerked General around and made straight for the spot where the wailing had originated and now continued in intermittent, angry bursts. When he saw Jessa crouched in the shelter of some low-hanging boughs, he didn't dismount immediately. Instead, Noah wove General through the trees until he and the horse blocked her best route for escape.

"It would seem that Gideon is not so anxious as you to leave," he said, his expression and tone glacial.

"He's hungry," Jessa said lowly.

"Didn't you bring any food for him?"

She shook her head and raised dull, near colorless eyes to him. "I thought we would be in Richmond before morning. I didn't know it was so far."

"You should have inquired. I could have told you it's forty-five miles. There's also the small matter of crossing the Chickahominy River, but you couldn't have known about that. I imagine you would have found the ferryman eventually."

Jessa huddled closer to the trunk of the tree, sheltering Gideon in the warmth of her cape. He had stopped crying, lulled by the quiet drawl of Noah's voice. He sucked on his thumb and buried his face in the curve of Jessa's breast.

"Where's your horse?" asked Noah, glancing around.

"She ran off."

"Ran? That's doubtful. Billy says he gave you Dorey. She hasn't run in years."

"Well, she gave a very good imitation of it when I released her from the wagon," Jessa said, a little of her spirit returning.

"I see."

Jessa frowned, worrying her lower lip. "I don't understand why you aren't angry."

"Oh, Dorey will come around," Noah said, deliberately misunderstanding her. "She'll find her way back to the landing sooner or later. Where is your valise?"

"I'm sitting on it."

"And your pistol?"

Jessa gave a tiny start of surprise. "In the valise. I suppose the stable boy told you about it."

"Actually, Jericho told me about it. Billy confirmed it when I talked to him before I left. That wasn't very kind of you, Jessa, to involve Billy in your escape."

"Billy just happened to be there. I didn't involve him

on purpose. If he hadn't made his presence known and tried to stop me, I wouldn't have done what I did."

"But to hold a pistol on him," Noah said, shaking his head in a disapproving manner. "You didn't make a friend there."

"It wasn't loaded. Do you really think I would point a primed pistol at someone?"

"Jess," he sighed, "I really don't think I know what you would do." He dismounted in a smooth, fluid motion and hunkered down beside her. "Let me have the valise. I'll fasten it to General's saddle. I'm afraid we'll have to walk back to the landing. General won't carry all of us and I don't think he'll respond very well to having you and Gideon on his back." He reached for Jessa's arm to help her to her feet but she shied away. Noah's hand was suspended for a moment in midair. Slowly he brought it back to rest on his knee. "Let me have Gideon then. You can't possibly carry him all the way."

"We're not going back with you, Noah," Jessa said, her voice barely audible. "You must have realized that. I left the road as soon as I heard the horse coming because I thought it might be you. I didn't want you to find me. If Gideon hadn't cried, you wouldn't have. Leave us alone. We'll make our own way."

"Jessa, even if I didn't give a damn what happens to you, I wouldn't let you take Gideon," he said grimly, straining to keep his voice and temper in check. He was not particularly successful.

"You're not taking him! I won't let you! I didn't come all this way to lose him now!"

"Dammit!" he snapped. "Listen to me. You're both cold, at least one of you is hungry, and this road isn't much safer than the posting road to London. If you haven't any concern for yourself, then for God's sake, think of Gideon! Of all the nod-cocked, scatterbrained notions that you've taken into your head, this one is the worst. I can hardly credit your selfishness!"

"My selfishness?"

Noah stood, grasping General's reins as the horse started to meander away. "Yes, by God, your selfishness! That you would risk Gideon's life on this ill-conceived journey simply because you hate me is hardly the act of a loving mother!"

"How dare you!" Trembling with cold and rage, Jessa got to her feet and faced him squarely. "How dare you suggest I don't care about Gideon!"

"I dare because it's true! You may as well pitch him in the river, because he's not going to survive what passes as your caring for him!"

Tears sparkled in Jessa's eyes. Without giving any thought to the consequences she raised her free hand and swung the flat of it against Noah's cheek. Her palm stung but it was nothing compared to the pain that darkened Noah's eyes. He stared at her for long moments, making no move to retaliate, then, just as she thought he was going to leave her, he dropped General's reins and tore Gideon free of her cradling arm. Stunned by the swiftness of his action, Jessa stumbled backward, grasping at the tree behind her for balance. She cried out as Noah turned on his heel, took up the reins again, and began leading the stallion through the trees to the edge of the road.

Though Noah held the infant gently, Gideon's thumb had been dislodged and he sent up a distressed wail at being so brusquely handled.

Jessa lifted her skirts and ran after Noah. "Let me have my son! You're hurting him!"

Noah stopped long enough to give her the benefit of his icy stare. "As you pointed out earlier, he's hungry. I fully intend to feed him at the landing. You're welcome to come, or not. The choice is yours." He continued walking. "I suggest you come. Once I have Gideon home I have every intention of riding back for you. I'll be a damn sight angrier then than I am now."

"Please, don't do this, Noah!" She tugged on the

sleeve of his soft leather jacket, her eyes pleading. "Let me have Gideon."

"You're not thinking clearly," he said, shaking her off. "If you intend to come with us, get the valise. I'll wait."

Jessa knew he was right. She wasn't thinking clearly. She wasn't thinking at all. Until last night her first concern had always been for Gideon. Somehow, even as she prepared to leave the landing, she had deluded herself into believing it still was. Noah knew differently and he had made her realize it as well. She was endangering the child's life because *she* was the one who had the need to go. Defeated by the complete insanity of the position she had taken, Jessa swiped at the tears streaking her face. "All right," she said hoarsely. "I'll only be a moment."

When Jessa returned with the valise Noah told her how to attach it to the saddle. After those curt instructions he said nothing. Gideon more than made up for the silent void between the two adults, whimpering fitfully with each step Noah took. His every cry wrenched at Jessa's heart and filled her soul with guilt. She didn't have to look at Noah to know that he was blaming her for Gideon's unhappiness, but surely, she thought dismally, no more than she was blaming herself. When they reached the abandoned wagon, Noah tugged on General's reins and halted him.

"I'm not certain I can listen to Gideon cry for the next ten miles, Jessa," Noah said, straightening Gideon's blankets and adjusting the child's bonnet. He didn't spare a glance for Jessa. "Not at the rate we're making progress. He's hungry *and* wet and it's too damn damp and cold to change him out in the open. I think it would be better if I took him to the landing on General. I want you to wait here by the wagon. I won't be much above an hour in returning."

Jessa nodded, holding out her hands, expecting him to give her Gideon while he mounted. Noah did no such thing. Somehow he managed to swing into the saddle without the slightest disruption to Gideon. Jessa's hands fell uselessly to her side and she released the breath she hadn't known she was holding.

"Be here, Jessa," he said curtly. Then he nudged General's flanks and started on his way.

Desolate, Jessa stood in the middle of the road until Noah, Gideon, and the stallion disappeared in the gray mist up ahead. When they were no longer visible she sat down in the slanting bed of the wagon, wrapped her cloak closely about her shoulders, and waited.

She regretted letting Noah leave with the valise. What if he should look inside it? It didn't matter about the pistol. He already knew she had it. But what about the papers? She hadn't taken any pains to hide them, not as she had when she ran from Penberthy Manor. They were there, in plain view, among a few items of clothing and the valuables from the robbery.

What would Noah make of Kenyon Penberthy's will if he saw it? What would he think of the pages torn raggedly from the family Bible, detailing the births and deaths of generations of Penberthys? And then there was the letter from Claudia Penberthy, addressed to Jessa when she was still a companion to Lady Howard in London, asking Jessa to leave her post and accept a position at the manor as Adam's nanny. That letter held the key to her relationship with Claudia, Kenyon, and Adam, but would Noah understand what it meant?

The documents could damn her in Noah's eyes, yet, she reflected, what choice did she have but to carry them with her? When Gideon became of age she was obligated to give him proof of his birthright. He would need the evidence if he wanted to claim the manor as his home. Even with the will, the Penberthy lineage, and her letter he would have a difficult time making himself believed, but it was all Jessa could offer him. The will and the pages from the Bible had been stolen from Edward's study at no little risk to herself. She hoped some day Gideon would appreciate that.

There were moments of doubt when she feared Gideon would not believe she had taken him from the manor because his life was threatened, still worse, that by not believing he would come to hate her. She could imagine him thinking she had stolen his birthright rather than tried to protect it for him.

"Oh, God," she whispered forlornly, leaning her head against the rough side of the wagon. "After today anyone would suspect I don't care a whit for Gideon's interests." Gradually complete exhaustion eliminated Jessa's tortured thoughts. She fell asleep, huddled in one corner of the wagon, and gradually drifted into dreams of what might be rather than of what had been.

Noah carefully climbed into the wagon and hunkered down in the corner opposite Jessa. He had removed his leather jacket and his white linen shirt billowed lightly in the breeze. Jessa was still wrapped in her cloak, but the tiny beads of perspiration on her upper lip and forehead were proof that the day was no longer cool. The fog was gone now. Even the clouds had scattered. The sun was still low in the clear morning sky, but it shone brightly and warmly, and a scorching afternoon seemed inevitable.

Watching Jessa sleep was one of the most peaceful things Noah had ever done. She appeared incredibly young to him, her expression untroubled and trusting. Her flawless complexion was faintly sleep-flushed and her dark lashes fanned pale shadows against her cheeks. Tendrils of silky hair that had escaped the braided knot at the nape of her neck fluttered about her ears and temples. Had Jessa but known it, her slightly parted lips, soft and pink, invited kissing. Noah wished with all his being it was the sort of thing he could do without frightening her or perhaps causing her to raise the flat of her hand again. He knew he had given her sufficient reason to react either way.

Smiling wryly, he touched his cheek on the spot where she had slapped him. Her hands were so small and delicate compared to his, her movements graceful, her long fingers beautifully shaped. Yet he had felt his teeth rattle when she delivered the blow. He'd remember that. Not that he intended to retaliate in kind the next time she lifted her hand. What he intended to do was duck.

"I know you're awake, Jessa," he said softly, amusement deepening his smile. His hand fell away from his cheek and rested on his knee. "I saw you peek."

"Have you been here long?" Jessa straightened her head, massaging the back of her cramped neck.

"Not long, no."

She blinked several times and rubbed her eyes with the back of her fingers. "Gideon?"

"He's fine. He's being cosseted and coddled within an inch of his young life. When I left, Tildy, Ruth, and Mother were all fighting over him. You realize, don't you, that no one's particularly happy with you?"

Jessa nodded, biting her lower lip.

"Jericho's the most put out. He's blaming himself for not going after you." At Jessa's questioning look, Noah explained. "When Billy freed himself he went to Jericho and told him you were gone. Billy's a trifle thick-witted and never mentioned you had Gideon. Jericho never thought to ask. He looked for me in our bedchamber and when I wasn't there he went to my father. They decided the best course was not to interfere and let it rest until I found you missing this morning. Then they pointed me in the right direction. However, last night neither of them thought for a moment that you had taken Gideon. Even when I left the landing to come after you, they still didn't realize you had Gideon. I thought it was an obvious fact. They, on the other hand, couldn't credit you with such—"

"Stupidity.

"I was going to say lack of judgment."

"It amounts to the same thing," she said tonelessly.

Noah could see she was punishing herself more thoroughly than he ever could or wanted to. He decided it was time to take some of the responsibility on his own shoulders. "If it makes you feel any better you should know that I'm not exactly in the family's good graces at the moment either. It was pointed out rather forthrightly that a man's wife does not run away without thinking she has good cause. My parents are wondering how they whelped such a complete fool. Salem wants to thrash me. Rae and Ashley think I'm an ogre, and when Jericho's done kicking himself, I'm his next target."

"It doesn't . . . m-make m-me feel any b-better," she stammered, fighting the tears that were clogging her throat. "I d-don't want them t-to hurt you. It's m-my fault."

"Oh, Jessa," Noah said sadly. "Let's not speak of fault." He stood, rocking the wagon slightly as he jumped out. Going to the corner where Jessa crouched miserably, Noah's hands slid beneath her cloak and curved on either side of her tiny waist. With hardly any effort he lifted her from the wagon bed and brought her to stand directly in front of him. His hands steadied her then slipped around her back as she leaned into him. Her ragged sobs tore at him. He could feel the wet press of his shirt against his skin where her tears dampened the material. "Jessa, you're going to make yourself ill crying like this." His gentle words had quite the opposite effect he intended. Jessa merely sobbed harder.

Noah patiently waited her out, stroking her back laying his cheek on the silky crown of her head in much the way he would have offered comfort to a child. Only against his body Jessa did not feel like a child and Noah did not feel very paternal. Her body curved sweetly into his and her palms warmed his skin through his shirt, yet she aroused feelings that were less sexual and more protective in nature.

Drawing a shaky breath, Jessa pulled away and fumbled for the handkerchief she had tucked under one sleeve of her slate gray dress. Her head bowed, she wiped her eyes and blew her nose. "I suppose we should be going back now," she said, tucking the handkerchief away. "Your family is probably . . . they'll begin to wonder where we are."

"No, they won't," he denied. "I told them that you and I were going to sort some things out between us. They don't expect that to be accomplished in minutes. Neither do I." He lifted her chin and pointed her face in the direction of the wood where he had tethered a pair of horses. "I left General at the landing in favor of a fresh mount. Willow is for you. That's the bay. The roan is mine. That nag Billy gave you, by the way, is already back at the stable. Now, I'm thinking we can have that ride we spoke of last night, but first, there's the matter of breakfast."

"Breakfast? But—"

Noah redirected Jessa's gaze so that it fell on the cloth-covered basket laying on the ground beside the roan. "Are you hungry?"

Jessa nodded.

"Good. Tildy packed a feast." His hand dropped away from her face. "The river is only a short walk through the woods. I have a blanket and we can sit on the bank and no passersby will disturb us. Why don't you throw your cloak over Willow's saddle? It's warm enough that you don't need it now. And no, that wasn't an order. Only a suggestion."

It was a good suggestion. She slipped the cape over her shoulders and draped it on her arm.

"Here, your pins have come loose." Noah plucked one of the hairpins from where it had fallen on her shoulder and handed it to her. "Don't bother with it now,'' he said when she began trying to straighten her hair. "In fact," his fingers pulled the rest of the pins out before she could protest, "I rather like your braid like that." He drew it over her shoulder. "Isn't it more comfortable now instead of having all that weight at the back of your neck?"

It was, but why he should care bewildered Jessa. More to the point, she found his entire manner odd. When Noah started for the wood she held back uncertainly.

Noah picked up the basket and took the rolled blanket from behind the roan's saddle. He turned, frowning, when he realized Jessa wasn't with him. "Aren't you coming?"

Jessa's hands gestured to the horses, the basket, and blanket. "Why are you doing this, Noah?"

"This?"

"This. You. Everything. Why are you being so . . . so *considerate?*"

Noah's brows raised a fraction. "Yes," he said slowly, "I can see that it would seem out of character to you, but the truth of it is, this is much more my nature than scrapping and fighting. Would you rather I were angry?"

"Yes . . . no . . . I don't know," she finished weakly. "It's just that you'll be kind now and as soon as I'm lulled into thinking you mean to remain pleasant, you'll become furiously angered. I can't go through it any more. I suppose I'd rather that you didn't pretend with me."

"I'm not pretending, Jessa. I didn't choose a picnic by the river because I planned to pitch you in. Neither did I choose it because I planned a seduction. I imagine both those thoughts crossed your mind."

She looked away guiltily, revealing that she had indeed considered both those things.

"I thought it might be something like that. Actually, I'm hungry. Therefore, the basket. I also hoped we could talk. The river is quiet and calming and we'll have privacy we would never be afforded at the landing. I've had a lot of time to think this morning, Jessa, and my mother is right about one thing. You wouldn't have left me without believing you had good cause. Not when I already promised we would discuss our situation after a brief separation. I'd like to find out why the urgency."

Jessa took a few steps into the wood and regarded Noah curiously. "I thought it was obvious."

"Come on," he said. "You can tell me while we eat." He turned and began walking, hoping Jessa would follow.

Jessa threw her cape over Willow's saddle and caught up to Noah, relieving him of the blanket he carried. He shortened his stride so she could keep up with him, and that small token of thoughtfulness lifted Jessa's heart more than he could have possibly realized.

When they broke through the woods, Noah pointed out a place where the grassy bank leveled off. It was shaded in part by the trees behind them but it was also dappled by prisms of sunlight and looked warm and dry. Jessa laid out the blanket, smoothing the edges neatly to give herself something to do. Noah watched the fluttering of her nervous hands and smothered his grin. She would probably be amused to know that he was just as nervous, but he had a picnic basket to clutch and therefore it wasn't quite as obvious.

"I think that's fine, Jessa," he said, sitting down cross-legged on one corner. He placed the basket in front of him and Jessa sat on the other side of it, maintaining a safe distance as he had known she would. Noah lifted the basket's cloth cover and tossed it aside. "We have hard-boiled eggs, fresh bread, a crock of sweet butter, two kinds of jam . . . elderberry and grape, I think, cold drumsticks, ham slices, apples, cheese, wine, and . . . no glasses." He glanced over at Jessa. "It's a wine skin" he said, holding up the leather pouch. "If you don't mind sharing, we can drink out of it."

"That's all right. I don't think I care for any, thank

you. In case you hadn't noticed, I don't have much of a head for drink. It only makes me sleepy."

"I had noticed. You slept through quite a family disagreement last night."

Jessa reached for an egg, cracked it on the edge of the basket, and began peeling it. "No, I didn't."

"You didn't?"

"I was awake while you were discussing politics. Remember? That was before Tildy brought out the rum."

Noah relaxed and rummaged through the basket for a drumstick. "Arguing politics is a favorite pastime. No, you fell asleep before we started sparring in earnest." He took a bite of chicken. "I'm glad you didn't hear us. There were things said I'd rather tell you myself."

"Oh?" Her eyes were wide, uncertain.

"But not just yet," he said quickly. "I'd like to hear why you felt compelled to leave in the middle of the night. You may think your reasons are obvious, but they're not. Not to me, at least."

Jessa swallowed her first bite of egg and cleared her throat. "Tell me why *you* think I went," she said. "You must have some idea."

"All right. I think it's because I've treated you abominably, subjected you to my black humor on more occasions than I care to remember. I've criticized, badgered, and hurt you. Those would all seem sufficient reason to go."

"They are," she said as unwelcome tears gathered in her eyes. "But they're not precisely my reasons. Do you think I don't know that you treat me differently than other people? With Gideon you're patience itself. You're firm with him, but never harsh. You show every kindness to Cam. Captain Riddle respects you. You were attentive to Drew Goodfellow, polite to Mary. On the coach, when I was still a stranger to you, you were solicitous and friendly. I haven't forgotten that." Jessa tossed her half-eaten egg into the river, plucked out a blade of grass, and rolled it back and forth between her hands. "It may have been better for you if you hadn't been so kind then. God knows, nothing's been right for you since."

"What about you?"

She shrugged, avoiding Noah's thoughtful eyes by choosing a point beyond his shoulder. "My feelings are of no consequence. Whatever's happened I've only myself to blame."

"You take too much on yourself," he said. "And you haven't the shoulders to support such weight."

"Please, Noah, let me finish," she said, looking at him long enough to plead. "This marriage was none of your doing, certainly not to your liking. I was prepared to accept your protection, but on my terms, not yours. That was not a very reasonable position to take and I shouldn't have been surprised when you made your objections known. Day after day I watched you grow increasingly bitter and unhappy. You acted in ways that were foreign to you, and I could see it in your face that you were alarmed by what was happening, even shamed. Then . . . the night on the *Clarion* when you said you wanted a whore . . . I knew then that I would have to leave you. I hated what I was becoming; I hated what I had made of you."

Jessa flicked away the twisted blade of grass and picked another. "Last night seemed the perfect time to go. You said you needed me, yet you didn't want me. I made you sick, you said." Jessa heard Noah groan softly as if in pain. "You said the same thing of yourself. I didn't—I still don't—understand what happened, but then you were telling me you were going on alone to Philadelphia and I knew you were going to Hilary. Which is the way it should be since you love her," she added a shade breathlessly. "We've always agreed that our marriage should be temporary, though we've never quite agreed on how and when it should be ended. I couldn't remain at the landing knowing how things are between us. I suppose I could have waited until you had gone, but it

seemed wrong somehow to do that to your family. I
thought it would be better if you were still there to
explain why I left."

Noah was silent for a long time. His green-gold eyes
followed the meandering progress of a box turtle dragging itself along the river's edge. Noah found himself
wishing that he might have such an uncomplicated existence. Almost instantly he called back the wish, knowing
that he would be bored in a sennight. "Do you want
our marriage ended, Jessa?" he asked finally. He tossed
his half-eaten chicken leg to the turtle and wiped his
fingers on the cloth which had covered the basket.
"Please, look at me. I need your honesty now." Don't
lie to me, Jessa, Noah prayed silently. Please don't lie
to me.

"I want you to be happy again," she said, holding his
steady gaze. "The way you were when I first met you."

"And you believe dissolving the marriage will accomplish that?"

"Yes." She frowned slightly, her pale gray eyes pen-
sive. "Wouldn't it?"

"No."

"No?"

"No," he repeated firmly. Since breakfast this morning some things had become astonishingly clear. "I want
to be happy *with* you, Jessa, not without you."

Jessa said nothing. She stared at her hands. Finally,
with a touch of wariness, "I don't see how that's possible."

"Do you hate me?" he asked baldly.

"N-no," she stammered, startled into honesty by his
bluntness. "That is, sometimes I think I do. Not always."

"That, at least, is something. Though why you
shouldn't all the time is beyond my comprehension.
Tell me, do you think I hate you?"

She shook her head. "Not hate, precisely. I think you
feel contempt for me. I think you resent me for the

trick I've played you. There will always be Hilary between us."

"She doesn't have to be. Don't you think there were times when I felt the same way about Robert?" Noah's eyes pleaded with Jessa to take the opening he offered and tell him the truth about the husband who never existed. Seconds ticked by before Noah accepted that she had no reason to trust him with the truth. Her eyes, the set of her shoulders, the way her fingers plucked at her skirt spoke to her wariness. Given her experience with him she had every right to doubt his sincerity. "I was jealous. There! I've finally said it. God, that I should be so stubborn! It's not to be borne." He leaned forward a little, resting his elbows on his knees. "Jessa, you cannot conceive how jealous I am of Robert Grantham. Do you know what it's like to battle a ghost? A veritable saint?"

Caution stayed Jessa's tongue. Noah's confession surprised and confused her. "He wasn't a saint."

"You made him sound like one. Sometimes I wanted you to wonder about Hilary and I wanted the wondering to hurt."

"It did."

"Then can I hope that there were times, though I suspect too few of them, that you liked me enough to be jealous?"

He had her so off balance that Jessa didn't know which way to turn. Her lashes lowered momentarily and she nodded quickly.

"Well," Noah said with something akin to triumph. "We've established that you don't always hate me and that you occasionally feel jealousy. I've already admitted to being extremely jealous. I don't believe that's necessarily a bad thing. I think we're making progress."

"This is an odd way of going about deciding the fate of our marriage."

Noah considered that while he looked through the basket again. Suddenly he was ravenously hungry. Probably, he decided, because Jessa, in spite of her words, was looking at him hopefully. He found an apple and bit into it. "Perhaps it is," he said offhandedly, "but then we have collected a lifetime of misunderstandings between us. I think we have everything to gain by muddling through them, don't you?"

The knot in Jessa's stomach was uncoiling also. "All right. Then tell me what you wanted last night when you woke me." She tipped the basket and took out a slice of bread, buttered it, slathered it with grape jam, and began eating while Noah stretched out on the blanket and considered how to answer her.

"I wanted nothing more than what we're doing right now," he said. Sunlight flickered over his hair and his mouth was relaxed, his eyes contemplative. "Just this. To talk. I needed you to listen to me. I don't blame you for misinterpreting my intent—that's the next wrinkle we'll iron out—but last night I only wanted you to hear me. After you fell asleep on the veranda my sister decided it was time for a few home truths about Hilary. It seems Salem and Jericho at different times had to fend off her advances. Hilary deliberately tried to destroy their marriages by carrying tales back to Ashley and Rae. I didn't believe them at first, I suppose because I thought Hilary's actions were a reflection on me. I wondered if I hadn't been attentive enough, not attractive enough, not . . . man enough for her. Salem and Jericho, well, you've seen them. They can turn a woman's head." Noah took another bite of apple and chewed thoughtfully. "Anyway, perhaps to salve my pride, or perhaps because it was true, they convinced me that Hilary's designs on them were nothing but a means of revenge."

"Revenge? I'm not certain I follow."

"Hilary despises the British. It doesn't really matter why, suffice it to say she thinks she has reason. Ashley and Jericho both have holdings in England. Therefore,

Hilary took it in her head to hurt them. At least that's what they told me."

"But you're not completely convinced," Jessa said shrewdly.

"I don't suppose I am. Last night I felt betrayed and hurt by what she had done. And that was odd because I suddenly realized I hadn't felt truly loving toward her for a long time. My mother once asked me if I was being perhaps too coldhearted in my decision to wed Hilary. I didn't think so then. I know differently now. What I learned last night didn't change my feelings toward Hilary. It merely confirmed that my feelings had already changed. I pitied her." His short laugh was self-mocking. "That's rather revealing, isn't it? I felt sorry for her because *she* was going to lose *me*."

"Is that why you chased me down today? Did you decide that since Hilary no longer suited perhaps I would fill in for her?"

"No," he said gravely. "It wasn't—isn't—like that." The glance he darted Jessa was wry. "I'm beginning to think Hilary should be rejoicing at her narrow brush with marriage and that you should be running like hell. Clearly I have a number of undesirable qualities."

"Pride isn't always undesirable," Jessa said. "And I've known about yours from the very beginning. But it might not be such a bad thing to have it bruised on occasion. It keeps one human."

"Then I'm feeling very human," he sighed, biting his apple again. He stopped mid-bite, reflected on the humanness of another man in a certain other garden, and smiled with a touch of self-derision. *"Very* human."

Jessa didn't comment. She wiped bread crumbs from her hands and searched the basket for cheese. "Why didn't anyone tell you what Hilary had done when it happened?"

"That's less difficult for me to understand. We McClellans are born campaigners. Every challenge requires a strategy."

"Like the Strategy to Convince Others of Wedded Bliss?" she asked arching one brow.

"Precisely," he said, chagrined. He finished off his apple and tossed the core into the river. A fish jumped at it and the water rippled. "No one thought the truth would serve; in part because they hoped to spare me, in part because they were afraid I would think them liars. They believed I only required time and distance to view Hilary in the same light they did. Hence, the voyage to England." He ran his fingers through his hair in an absent gesture. "I let them know what I thought of their meddling. That's why my father and Jericho were reluctant to interfere when you left the landing. Hours earlier I told them to allow me the privilege of handling my own affairs." He sighed. "I was furious with them. Disappointed by their maneuvering, disgusted they didn't trust me to deal with the truth."

"And you wanted to tell me that last night."

"Hmm-mm." He crossed his legs at the ankle, leaned back on his elbows and looked at Jessa consideringly. "That brings us to the wrinkle I mentioned earlier. Jessa, please don't look away. That's better. I *know* why you misunderstood. Your response was in keeping with what we have made of our peculiar marriage. But I don't think it's what either of us want. The question remains, what are we going to do about it?"

Jessa's words tumbled out in a rush. "I can't go on being your whore, Noah. I thought I could, but I can't. At first it only hurt, and then the hurt vanished. It makes me feel hollow inside, dead, . . . and dirty." She drew in a shallow breath, her eyes wide and earnest. "It's all very well that I don't hate you all the time or that your resentment of me has perhaps lessened, but what do we have? I know I'm supposed to perform certain, ummm, wifely duties, but perhaps we might go on if you sought your, er, pleasures elsewhere. If you want a child, well, we could talk about that. I'm not opposed to, you know, laying with you for the purpose of having a child. But more than that . . . Oh, God, this is so difficult.'' She fidgeted with the folds of her skirt. "Help me, Noah. You know what I'm trying to say.''

He sat up and moved the basket so it was no longer between them. Reaching across the space that separated them, Noah took one of Jessa's hands in his and squeezed it reassuringly. "Indeed I do, and I think you've expressed yourself very well.''

"Then you agree?''

"No.''

Jessa frowned. "Oh.''

Withdrawing his hand, Noah laid on his side and propped himself on one elbow. "I don't want to find my, er, pleasures outside of my marriage. But I'm no more satisfied with our current arrangement than you are. I'm not proud of what has passed for loving between us. There are so many things I've said and done that I regret, but none so much as demanding intimacy against your will. There was no satisfaction in it.''

Jessa's eyes widened slightly. "But—''

"I'm not speaking only of physical satisfaction,'' he interrupted, shaking his head. "You gave me that, yet any pleasure you felt was against your will. I didn't think it would bother me. I thought I could use you because I believed you owed me. I was wrong, Jessa. Terribly wrong.'' Would she believe him? "It was only yesterday morning that you turned from me and cried because you despised the pleasure you felt. Do you think I found any satisfaction in that? Or on any other occasion when you gave and took nothing in return?''

"I don't know.'' Jessa couldn't look at him. She fiddled with the end of her braid. "Once you said my . . . my pleasure was unimportant. Now you say that's not true. I doubt you know your own mind.''

"I've given you every reason to believe that,'' he said. "But it's *not* true. I know precisely what it is I want. I've always known it, though I haven't always admitted it. Not to myself, certainly never to you.''

Jessa dropped her braid and regarded him steadily, a question in her eyes.

"Affection," Noah said. "Sharing. Commitment." He paused a beat. "Trust."

Jessa merely blinked.

"Are those things so impossible between us?"

When Noah smiled at her as he was doing now, encouraging and somehow hopeful, Jessa thought anything was possible. Still, she was reluctant to give in. Noah had trampled her feelings too many times for her to surrender everything now. "I suppose those things would come in time," she said carefully. "They would be important if our marriage were to be more than the sham it is now."

"I think so," he said solemnly. "I care about your happiness too, Jessa. Could you be happy married to me?" *Please say yes,* he whispered to himself.

"Sometimes I think I could."

Noah's heart skipped a beat. It was a start. "We'd still argue, you know."

"I know."

"And on occasion we'd probably still hurt one another."

"But not intentionally," she said quickly.

"No, not intentionally."

Jessa thought about that. "Then it wouldn't be quite so bad."

Noah lay back on the blanket, cupping his head in his palms. He stared at the cloudless blue sky. "For all that we've done it backward, we've made some sort of beginning, haven't we?"

She nodded slowly, uncertainly. "It seems as if we have."

"And I don't have to worry about you running away in the middle of the night any longer?"

"No. That is, I don't think so."

It wasn't what he wanted to hear, but upon reflection he realized it was honest. "I suspect there will be times when I provoke you," he said, playing the devil's advocate.

"I suppose I could stand my ground."

"Oh, God, Jessa," he said feelingly. "I hope you will. I want this marriage . . . I want to be your husband."

Jessa was much struck by the obvious sincerity of his tone, yet her doubts were not so easily laid to rest. "How can that be, Noah, when I've complicated your life beyond reason?"

"I find I like the complications," he said. "Some of them anyway."

"You mean Gideon."

"In part. You must know I've come to love him. I should continue to love him even when we have children of our own." He opened his eyes just enough to catch Jessa's reaction. The dreamy smile on her face boded well, he thought. She was definitely not repelled by the idea of having his children. Perhaps she would not be repelled by what they had to do to conceive them. "You'd like children, wouldn't you?" he asked, closing his eyes again.

"Oh, yes! Dozens!"

Noah was definitely encouraged. "I was thinking of one at first," he said. "But your enthusiasm has been duly noted."

Jessa's cheeks pinkened. "You're teasing me."

"Yes, I think I am. Do you mind?"

"No."

"Good." He stifled a yawn and smiled sheepishly, rolling on his side. "I wouldn't be opposed to napping a bit before we returned to the landing. I didn't sleep very well last night. I imagine that brief nap you had in the back of the wagon wasn't restful either."

"It wasn't," she admitted, eyeing the space beside him warily.

Noah felt rather than saw her hesitation. "Just sleep, Jessa. Nothing else. You've nothing to fear."

How could he possibly know what she feared? She

wasn't certain herself. Jessa covered the picnic basket again and moved it off the blanket entirely. Without a word she lay on her side, her back to Noah, and rested her head on her forearm. He made no move to narrow the space that separated them and Jessa acknowledged a keen sense of disappointment. She wanted to be held.

She waited until she heard the even cadence of his breathing then she moved closer to him. Reaching behind her, she found his arm and drew it about her waist, threading her fingers in his. She never saw the contented smile that lifted Noah's lips nor realized she fell asleep before he did.

CHAPTER TWELVE

Something brushed Jessa's cheek. Sleepily she turned her head away and burrowed deeper into her pillow. As pillows went, this one was rather uncomfortable. Worse, the tickling continued. She wrinkled her nose and frowned slightly. Noah's low chuckle woke her.

"You look like a rabbit when you do that," he said, his voice not much above a whisper. "Twitching your nose, I mean. It's even a little pink."

Jessa came awake by slow degrees. She realized somewhat hazily that her pillow was Noah's shoulder and that one of her arms laid completely across his chest. The annoying tickling wasn't a bothersome insect at all. It was the tip of her braid which Noah was feathering over her skin. "Pink?" she asked, making no effort to move.

"Hmmm. Pink. A touch too much sun. I'm afraid some of the shade deserted us while we slept."

Jessa stretched leisurely and opened her eyes. She was aware that her gown had ridden up above her knees and that she had kicked off her shoes while she slept. One stockinged calf lay flush to Noah's. The other covered Noah's legs with proprietal intimacy. "Oh!" She sat up quickly, pulling her braid from Noah's grasp. Her attention was caught by Noah's soft groan as he also sat up and shook out his right arm.

"It fell asleep along with the rest of me," he told her.

Jessa realized it was the arm that had been supporting her head. "You should have pushed me away."

Noah's eyebrows shot upward and he slanted her a disbelieving look. "It was never a consideration. I like having you in my arms. Did you doubt it?"

Rather than answer, Jessa busied herself by unwinding her braid. She combed her hair with her fingers, smoothed it, and began plaiting it again. Noah caught her wrist, stopping her.

"I like it loose best of all," he said. "Leave it that way." He glanced away, feeling much like a schoolboy under her startled, yet direct stare. "Please."

It would have been much cooler to keep the braid but Jessa relented because she found herself willing to please him, not so much for Noah's sake as for her own. It had been so long since she truly *wanted* to do something he asked of her that it was almost a pleasure to acquiesce. Her hands dropped away from her hair and fell quietly in her lap. She searched for something to say. "It's hot," she said finally, wondering why conversation was so difficult. Perhaps it had something to do with the way she had abandoned herself in his arms while they slept.

"Very hot," Noah agreed. He turned to her suddenly, his eyes bright with eagerness. "Would you like to go swimming?"

"Sw-swimming? In the river?"

"Of course in the river."

"Won't it be cold?"

He laughed. "That's the idea."

"But I don't know how to swim."

"You don't?" That hadn't occurred to him. He'd been swimming almost as long as he had been riding.

Both activities were as natural as walking. "Then you should learn," he said confidently. "It's not difficult." He stood up and pulled her with him. "Come on. You can wear your shift."

She shook her head. "Perhaps another time. You go on. I'll watch."

Noah looked over his shoulder at the river. It was very inviting. "You wouldn't mind?"

"Not at all." She smiled. "Really. Go ahead."

Noah didn't require any more encouragement, though he was disappointed Jessa wouldn't join him. "Very well. But you're missing a treat." He hopped about on one foot while he took off one boot, then the other. Dropping them on the blanket, he quickly stripped down to his drawers and tossed Jessa his shirt as soon as he pulled it over his head.

Jessa tried very hard not to notice certain things about Noah as he walked to the river's edge. She failed miserably. It was not possible for her to be unaware of the breadth of his shoulders or the tapering of his waist. He might not have been wearing drawers at all for the way the material clung to his hips and thighs. And when he came out of the water—oh, God—it would be worse! She busied herself folding his clothes into a neat pile and missed the moment he waded into the water and dove in.

"Jessa!" he called, swimming on his back away from her. "You should at least get your feet wet! It's splendid!"

"And you're a splendid liar, Noah McClellan! I can see your blue lips and hear your teeth chattering from here." He merely laughed and ducked under the water, resurfacing a few moments later farther downstream. Jessa had already moved down the bank, anxiously awaiting his reappearance. "Don't do that! I haven't the least idea how to save you if you don't come up again!"

"All the more reason you should learn to swim," he

said, using powerful strokes to move upstream against the current.

"I've no desire to become fish fodder."

"Coward," he goaded.

"Hah! You won't get me in that way! I warned you long ago that I was a coward!"

Noah wondered if she could see the gleam in his eye. Apparently she could because she was backing away slowly from where the water lapped at her stockinged feet. Jessa held out her hands to ward him off as Noah swam closer to the bank. She laughed shakily, darting a glance around her, looking for escape when Noah began wading toward her.

"Noah! Don't come any closer!"

He ignored her.

Jessa ran for the blanket, picked up the picnic basket, and whipped off the cover. Watching Noah's purposeful advance, she dug her hand blindly into the basket and pulled out a hard-boiled egg. "Stop right there, Noah! I'll throw this at you!"

Noah paused, grinning. "You wouldn't."

"I would!" Lord, she thought, what his smile did to her insides. Her eyes grazed over his figure. Droplets of water glistened on his shoulders and chest. And his waterlogged drawers were precariously close to falling past his narrow hips.

Seeing the direction of her gaze, Noah squeezed some of the water out of the fabric and retied the drawstring tightly. "Better?" he asked.

"I wouldn't know," she said tartly. "I wasn't looking."

Noah's taut belly rippled with laughter. "And you called me a liar? Methinks you deserve a dunking for that."

"You wouldn't!" She retreated a few more steps, holding the egg aloft, prepared to throw it. "You promised you wouldn't pitch me in the river!"

"I've changed my mind." He advanced on her, ducking as the egg whistled past his head.

Jessa realized she was enjoying his play, more than that, she was unafraid of his threats. "Change it back, Noah!" she warned, digging into the basket again. This time she pulled out a drumstick. She felt so ridiculous holding it that she threw it at him immediately. He sidestepped it easily and lunged at her just as her fingers curled around an apple. "Put me down!" she cried out as she was heaved over his shoulder. Jessa dropped the basket and the apple. Laughing, she flailed at his back. "Noah! You're carrying *this* too far! You're carrying *me* too far! Stop! Where are you taking me? Noah! You wouldn't! Don't you dare drop me in the water! There are *things* in there!"

"*Things*, madam?" he asked, choking on his laughter. He continued to walk into the river until the water reached the level of his knees. "What sort of *things*?"

"Fish and snakes and turtles and, oh, there's something now! It wants your ankle!"

Since it was very doubtful that Jessa could see through the water to his ankles, Noah ignored her. He lifted her off his shoulder and cradled her in front of him, one arm under her knees, the other across her back. Jessa's arms circled his neck, hanging on tightly. Her eyes were squeezed shut.

When he didn't do anything she risked a peep at him. "Are you going to drop me?" she asked.

"I'm still thinking on it."

"I see. When will you make a decision?"

Noah's arms relaxed a little, lowering Jessa a few inches closer to the water. Her arms gripped him more closely and her eyes shut again. "Don't hurry me. This requires some consideration."

"Consider that you made a promise."

"I also promised not to seduce you, but I'm afraid it's very much on my mind." Really, he thought, she shouldn't look so deliciously kissable.

Jessa felt her heart swelling. Against all reason she wanted this man. She wanted him now, in the bright heat of day, on the blanket in the grass, nothing covering them but sunshine. "Oh, that," she said airily "I won't hold you to it. Only don't pitch me in the river."

Noah stiffened, hardly believing that he had heard her correctly. "Jessa?"

"Hmmm?"

"Do you mean it?"

In answer, Jessa raised herself in his arms and touched her lips to the rough stubble of his chin. The day's growth of beard tickled her mouth. "I mean it," she said against his skin. "Even if you weren't dangling me over the water, I'd mean it."

Noah turned his face toward her and brushed her mouth with his. Her lips parted and his tongue quickly accepted her invitation. He kissed her deeply and hard, unable to get enough of her sweet, honeyed mouth. Jessa's fingers tangled in his wet hair and held him close, returning the kiss with eagerness and abandon.

Noah was never certain how he found the strength to carry her back out of the water. His legs felt as wobbly as a foal's. She must have sensed it, because her eyes expressed a certain amount of relief when he set her down. "That look in your eyes is not very complimentary," he said, brushing a strand of hair from her cheek. She stood on tiptoe and kissed him full on the mouth, pressing her body against him. When Jessa broke the kiss her eyes were dark with the strength of her arousal. "On the other hand," he said softly, *that* look is very complimentary."

"It is?"

"Yes."

"Show me."

Noah was glad to demonstrate what her siren's smile did to him. Cupping her face in his hands, Noah held her still while he teased her with kisses that whispered across her skin. Her response was everything he could have hoped for. She tried to get closer, whimpering softly as her fingers closed over the taut muscles of his upper arms. His hands dropped away slowly, his thumbs caressing the slender line of her neck, pausing at the pulse at the base of her throat. Her fingers slid along his arms and came to rest on his wrists. She nudged his hands downward until they hovered over her breasts. The material of her bodice was damp from being held against Noah's water slick chest. The outline of her nipples was evident.

"Touch me," she said. "Please."

Noah's palms curved over her breasts and he felt Jessa's breath catch. She pressed into him, easing her arms around his waist. Her mouth spread kisses along the line of his collarbone, branding him with the hot, hard outline of her mouth. Noah's hands slipped from her breasts as he drew her against him. His fingers tangled in her hair, brushing it to one side as he fumbled with the laces at the back of her gown. He yanked at them impatiently and thought he heard her giggle.

"Are you laughing?" he asked.

"A little." She drew away. "Here, let me help." Her hands went behind her back and she tugged at the laces. "Oh, Noah! I think you've made a knot!"

Jessa looked so desperately unhappy that Noah found himself laughing. He turned her around. "Lift your hair out of the way. That's better." He kissed the exposed back of her neck.

"Noah! Pay attention to what you're doing."

"I am. Stop dancing or I'm just going to say damn to these laces and throw up your skirts."

At that moment Jessa wouldn't have cared. Perhaps it was because of the laughter they had shared, the cheerful play and teasing. Or perhaps it was because of the quiet moments they had shared earlier as they untangled so many misunderstandings. Jessa believed for the first time that he desired her, truly desired her, and she returned that feeling with an intensity that she refused to question now.

"There!" Noah nibbled on the curve of her neck as

he pulled the laces free and eased the sleeves of her gown over her shoulders. The wide straps of her shift followed and when he turned her around again she was naked to the waist. There was sunshine in her hair and on the pale slope of her breasts. The backs of Noah's fingers traced the length of her collarbone. His touch was reverent. "You can't possibly know how beautiful you are to me," he said. "You can't possibly know how much I want you." He looked down at himself, at the hard arousal he couldn't deny or hide. His quick smile was rueful. "Then again . . ."

Jessa's smile was more self-conscious as she tore her eyes away from the evidence of Noah's desire. She slipped her gown and undergarments over her hips then sat down on the blanket and removed her stockings. Drawing her knees modestly toward her chest, she glanced up at him. "I'd rather that you were down here."

Noah dropped to his knees beside her. Touching her shoulders, he gently pushed her back until she unfolded beneath him, her arms circling his back. "Better?" he asked, his mouth hovering above hers.

"Hmm-mm." Involuntarily her hips rotated against him as she stretched, curving one leg along the length of his. "You're dripping water everywhere." Her fingers tripped along his spine and pushed at the edge of his wet drawers. When they wouldn't budge she found the knot he had tied in the drawstring and tugged at it— which only made it tighter. "Oh, dear," she murmured. "I think we have a slight problem."

Noah sat up and wrestled with the knot. It wouldn't give. He rolled his eyes. "Of all the damn . . . what are you doing? Jessa! Put that knife back in the basket! I'm serious, Jessa! Don't come near me with that thing!"

"Be still."

"At least let me do it."

"Don't you trust me?"

"That's not a fair question right now." Noah sucked

in his breath as Jessa ignored him and brought the tip of the knife against the drawstring. "For the sake of any future children, Jessa, turn that blade upward—not down!"

She giggled. "Oh, of course. I see what you mean."

"Witch," he said softly. "Stop laughing or you'll—"

"All done," she interrupted. She tossed the knife in the direction of the basket and out of Noah's reach. Her eyes dropped to Noah's thighs. "It seems as though you've cooled a bit."

"A knife pointed at my vitals will do that to me," he said dryly. Noah slipped out of his drawers, squeezed the water out of them, and threw them on the grass to dry. "You'll just have to do something about it."

"I fully intend to." Drawing on his hands, Jessa pulled him with her as she laid down again. Her mouth met his hungrily, proving that her ardor hadn't cooled a whit. The kiss was really a dozen kisses, some teasing, some deep. Her tongue whispered across his upper lip, touched the ridges of his teeth. She loved him with her mouth, inviting him one moment, making demands in the next.

Noah's responses echoed her own. When he broke the kiss his mouth trailed over her face, touching her closed eyes, the soft pulse at the temples, the pink tip of her nose. When her throat arched the tip of his tongue made a damp line across her skin. His hands cupped her breasts and his thumbs made gentle passes across her nipples.

Jessa bit back a moan as her breasts swelled in his hands and her nipples hardened under his touch.

"Don't hold it in," Noah whispered against her skin. "This is something to share." His mouth trailed lower, circling one breast in a slow spiral until his lips closed over the rose-colored nipple. He felt Jessa's fingers stiffen on his shoulders. After a moment they relaxed and she cupped the back of his head, holding him to her breast as her body arched and stretched beneath

him. When Noah lifted his mouth he saw the pinkish
abrasions his beard had made on the pale skin of her
breast. "Oh, God, I'm sorry." He rubbed his chin. "I
never shav—"

Jessa's fingers pressed at the back of his neck and
urged him toward her other breast. "It only hurts when
you stop, Noah," she whispered.

Noah required no more encouragement than that.
He suckled her breast, drawing the tip into his mouth,
laving it with his tongue. His hand slipped between their
bodies and he caressed the smooth plane of her stomach
and the inward curve of her waist.

Jessa released a startled gasp as his lips began to follow
the path of his hand. He pressed a kiss to the hollow
between her breasts, his mouth warm and faintly damp
over her heart. His kisses went lower and her flesh tingled as it was warmed by his touch, then by the sun.
She felt his mouth on her inner thigh, circling, taunting
her with kisses that were not quite as intimate as they
could be. Of their own accord, her legs parted. Noah
cupped her buttocks and lifted her slightly, raising her
to his mouth.

Sweet sensation flooded Jessa. Her hands fell to her
sides and clutched the blanket beneath her. The
strained, staccato whimpers that rose in her throat were
hardly recognizable as her own voice. Pleasure coiled
around her, drawing her limbs tight. The sun was bright
behind her closed eyes and her lids swirled with hot
colors. Fiery orange. Brilliant crimson. The frissons of
excitement were as liquid as those colors, like flames,
darting and dancing. Heat flickered along her spine
and beads of perspiration glistened in the curve of her
elbows and on her face and neck.

A soft cry exploded from her lips as pleasure shot
through her and the colors merged and light was blinding white. Her breathing was shallow and her heart
seemed to thud erratically as if it could no longer keep
pace with the quickening of her excitement. Jessa felt

a shadow cross her face and she welcomed the coolness, the protection. Then Noah's mouth descended on hers and his kisses were light, soothing, and tender.

Jessa raised her knees, inviting his entry as her hands caressed his shoulders and back. When he didn't move to position himself between her thighs she opened her eyes and blinked up at him. The aura of sunlight behind him cast his face in a faint shadow. The centers of his eyes were wide, dark and probing. Lines of self-imposed denial marked the corners of his mouth. The effort to maintain control showed on the taut planes of his face.

"That was for you, Jessa," he said, brushing her lips with his own. His voice was thick and husky. "I don't always want to take from you."

She shook her head, a faint frown creasing her brow. "I thought you said we would share?"

"Is that what you want? Are you certain?"

Her smile was sweet. "Dear, foolish man," she sighed. Pushing against his shoulders, Jessa rolled Noah onto his back and straddled him. She leaned forward, allowing her breasts to brush his chest before the pale curtain of her hair fell on either side of his face. "Your gallantry is misplaced in this instance," she said. "Are you going to deny us both?"

Mutely, Noah shook his head. His hands curved under her buttocks. He lifted her and with Jessa's help, guided her onto him. She kissed him, easing her tongue back and forth in his mouth, foreshadowing the movements of her hips. His groan was muffled against her lips. He closed his eyes as she raised herself up and began to move.

Noah's fingers skittered along her thighs, stroking her, matching her rhythm. His hands lifted to her breasts, fondling them. He saw her clearly in his mind's eye. He could imagine the way her teeth played with her lower lip as she sucked in her pleasure. He could see the dark liquid centers of her eyes widening until her eyes were more black than gray. When she moved, the silky ends of her hair caressed his skin. The sensation made his skin ripple. He thrust into her and she into him. He held her buttocks again and urged a faster rhythm. A harder one. She surrounded him with warmth, with soft velvet heat.

Jessa never took her eyes from Noah's face. The planes of his skin were even tighter now. His lips were drawn back in a hard thin line as he denied release in order to increase his pleasure and her own. Jessa knew almost the same moment as Noah that he could not hold back any longer. His fingers tightened in her flesh and his throat arched. She heard her name carried on a puff of air. Every muscle in his body seemed bunched with tension.

Jessa felt his shudder as it passed through him and into her. He was part of her. His pleasure was hers. What they shared between them now was different from everything that had come before it. The first time she had been frightened. Later she had felt used. Yesterday morning she had cried because she thought he was trying to trick her, prove that he could make her respond against her will. Today was the beginning of something so special that Jessa hugged the feeling to her heart to keep it safe.

Noah rolled them on their sides so they faced one another. "Jessa?" His forefinger traced the outline of her beautifully shaped mouth.

"Hmmm?" Her lips caught his finger.

"I don't want you to panic. . . ."

Whatever was he talking about? She was too drowsy and content to panic. "Panic?"

"Hmm-mm. Panic. Do you hear that sound?"

To humor him, she listened. Behind them there was the gentle rustling of leaves. A bird cried out. Another answered. Farther away, in the direction of the river, she could hear something snapping and flapping as the fickle breeze faded and swelled by turns. Her eyes widened. She sat up, hugging her knees to her chest, and stared openmouthed as a two-masted schooner raced down the river. The distance between herself and the ship was not so great that she couldn't see most of the crew had gathered at the rail. She hoped their eyes fell out of their heads and their ship ran aground. Grabbing Noah's shirt, she yanked it on and ran for the relative privacy of the woods.

"You weren't supposed to panic!" Noah called after her, jamming his legs into his trousers. The catcalls from the passing ship were explicit and ribald. Noah couldn't find it within himself to be embarrassed. The situation was too funny. He waved to the ship then hurried after Jessa. He suspected she would be less than amused.

Noah found her crouched behind a thick knotty oak. Her head was bowed, her shoulders shaking. He bent down and touched her knee lightly. "Please don't cry, Jessa. I'm sorry it happened. I should have been more circumspect."

"You didn't have to make a bow to them," she said tartly. "As if you had been performing."

"I didn't bow," he defended himself. "I waved." He listened to her choke back the sound that rose in her throat. "Are you crying or laughing?" he asked, suddenly suspicious.

Jessa looked up at him. Her attempt to pull a frown failed as laughter bubbled to her lips. She swiped at the tears glinting in her eyes. "I know I should be mortified . . . b-but it was so ridiculous. Please tell me you didn't recognize any of the men on that ship!"

"Nary a one." He knew the schooner belonged to the Flemings farther upriver, but he wasn't going to tell her that.

"You're certain?" she asked, eyeing him steadily.

Noah crossed his heart, his expression earnest. "I swear it."

Jessa stood, brushing off his shirt. "I'm not stepping out of these woods until I'm fully clothed, Noah McClellan. You'll have to bring everything here." Noah straightened, but other than lifting a piece of dry bark from her hair, he didn't move.

"Why are you looking at me like that?" she asked, feeling herself go still beneath his searching eyes.

"Like what?"

"Like that. All peculiar and funny. Do I have a smut on my nose?" Self-consciously she brushed at her face with the sleeve of his shirt.

"I love you, Jessa."

"Because if I have a smut it's your—." She blinked owlishly. "What?"

"I love you."

She sagged against the tree behind her. "You do?"

"Hmm-mm." He braced his hands against the tree trunk on either side of her head. He ducked and stole a kiss from her parted lips. "Don't say anything," he cautioned quietly. "I don't expect anything in return. I just thought you should know what I felt." He pushed away from the tree and without another word he went to get their things.

The ride back to the landing was completed largely in silence. Occasionally Noah would point out something he thought would interest Jessa. She listened politely, asked questions, but it was clearly an effort on her part to make conversation. Mostly Noah left her alone to the privacy of her thoughts.

Gideon was playing with Rae's youngest daughter on the veranda. Charity was watching the babies while she instructed Courtney on stitching a sampler. Courtney laid down her sewing when Garland crawled off the blanket and headed toward the steps. She picked up the infant as her grandmother grabbed Gideon to keep him from following.

"It looks as if you have your hands full," Noah said, rounding the corner of the house. He jumped up on the veranda and whisked Gideon from his mother's arms. The boy gurgled happily. "Fat as a dumpling. That's what you are." He glanced at Charity. "Do you want to say something, Mother? You look fit to have an attack of apoplexy."

"Courtney, take Garland up to the nursery. The things I have to say aren't suitable for young ears."

Flashing Noah a sympathetic grin, Courtney disappeared into the house.

"You didn't have to send her inside," said Noah as he tickled Gideon's belly. "Jessa's upstairs, if that's what you were preparing to upbraid me for. She went in the front door and she needs some time to herself. I came around here because that's where Ashley said I'd find Gideon." At the sound of his name Gideon's eyes widened. "Yes, you're Gideon. Can you say that? Mmmm? Can you?"

The twin spots of color in Charity's cheeks faded a little. "Dare I inquire why Jessa requires time to herself?"

"Of course," he said easily. "Firstly, she is a bit daunted at the thought of facing all of you after what she did. Secondly, she wants to change her clothes. They're a bit, ummm, rumpled. And thirdly, just above an hour ago I told her that I love her and she doesn't know what to make of that." He kissed his mother on her furrowed brow and before she could ask anything else, he carried Gideon into the house.

Dinner that evening was not as uncomfortable as Jessa thought it might be. If the McClellans were curious as to what had taken place between her and Noah, Jessa decided they were to be credited for their discretion. Even when Charity suggested they take drinks in the music room no one pulled her aside to ask any questions.

Jessa sat beside Noah on one of the small sofas. His arm circled her shoulders as she leaned into him. She wondered if he were as contented as he looked or if he were hiding the same frayed nerves as she. The short, abrupt musical tones of the harpsichord became the background of her thoughts as Noah occupied all of her senses. His touch, his fragrance, the sound of his laughter as he responded to a query from his father, held Jessa's complete attention. By slow degrees she began to relax, less from the wine she was drinking and more from the serenity Noah projected.

When Ashley paused in her playing Charity turned to Noah. "Do you really have to leave on the morrow?"

"I'm afraid so," Noah said. "The trip will take longer with Jessa and Gideon. And Cam if he wants to come."

"You could take the *Clarion,*" Salem suggested. "It's not making another Atlantic run for several weeks."

Noah rolled his eyes. "No, thank you. Father's already offered me use of one of the carriages. The best sprung one, I might add, not that it will make much difference on the roads. Henry's going to be our driver and I'm taking General along."

"Take Willow, too," Robert said. "You're not the only one who might enjoy riding outside the carriage occasionally, and I wouldn't put Jessa on General's back until he takes a gentler turn."

Jessa flushed with pleasure at the thought of having her own mount. "That's very kind of you. I should like it above all things." She glanced at Noah. "That is, if it's all right with you?"

Before Noah could answer, Rae snorted lightly in response to Jessa's uncertain question. "Did Noah beat you this morning?" she asked forthrightly.

"Rae!"

"Rahab!"

"Red!"

Drawing herself up defensively, Rae shrugged off her family's censure. She held Jessa's startled eyes. "I know my manners leave much to be desired, but no one else will ask and they want to know as much as I do. Did Noah drag you back or did you come of your own free will?"

"You don't have to answer that," Jericho told Jessa while he shot his wife a dark look.

"No, it's all right," Jessa said quietly. "Actually, I was wondering why no one said anything. I've rather been on pins and needles waiting. I thought perhaps Noah had already made some explanations."

"He's been extremely closemouth," said Rae. "And unbearably smug."

"That's because it's really none of your affair," Noah said, his voice dripping honey.

Jessa nudged Noah lightly in the ribs to halt his exchange with his sister. "I don't mind Rae's concern," she said. "In truth, Rae, Noah didn't drag me here. I wanted to return with him. I don't know what he would have done had I wanted otherwise, but it didn't come to that. We managed to settle some of our . . . differences. This is where I want to be."

Noah anticipated Rae's next question and held up one hand to stop her. "Don't ask what our differences were, Rae. Suffice it to say that you all were correct this morning when you told me Jessa must have thought she had very good reason to leave. I'm afraid I gave her a number of reasons. You'll have to be satisfied with that."

"We're satisfied," said Jericho, laying his hand firmly on his wife's forearm. "Aren't we, Red?"

"I suppo . . ." She felt Jericho's fingers tighten a bit and smiled brightly. "Oh, yes. We're satisfied."

Jessa watched the interplay between husband and wife. Without hinting at the amusement she found in Rae's immediate capitulation, she asked, "Does he beat you?"

"What a novel idea," Jericho interjected dryly.

There was an explosion of laughter as Rae had the grace to look shamefaced. The light sprinkling of freckles on her nose disappeared beneath the flush that warmed her complexion. Rae's smile was sheepish as she looked at Jessa. "Touché," she said. "I deserved that."

"Beautifully done," Noah whispered in Jessa's ear. He leaned away again and caught Ashley's eye. "I think you'd better play something, Ashley. Jericho still seems to be considering the merits of beating his wife."

Happy to oblige, Ashley swiveled on the bench and struck a series of dramatic minor chords. Everyone laughed at Rae as she played along and looked warily at her husband. Ashley's fingers began a lighter melody and good humor reigned for the rest of the evening.

Jessa was still enveloped in a warm glow when she and Noah retired to their own room. She flitted about the room, humming to herself as she lit candles and drew the drapes.

Amused, Noah leaned against the door and watched her, his arms folded across his chest. "You enjoyed yourself tonight, didn't you?"

"Enormously," she agreed, sitting on the edge of the bed. She kicked off her shoes. "I don't remember the last time I laughed so much."

"I do. It was this afternoon when you were hiding from . . ."

Jessa's smile was prim. "You're wicked to remind me of that."

"Perhaps I am." He pushed away from the door. "You handled Rae very well."

"I like her, Noah. She's so . . . so—"

"Inquisitive? Aggravating?"

"Lively," corrected Jessa. "In fact, I like all your family. I'll be sorry to leave them."

Noah went to the wardrobe, slipped off his jacket, and hung it up. His back was to Jessa as he spoke. "Would you rather remain behind for a few weeks? I suppose it would give me time to set the house in order and—" He stopped when he felt Jessa's arms slide around his waist. He hadn't even heard her cross the floor. The pressure of her cheek against his back felt good.

"I want to go with you. So does Gideon."

Noah turned and searched Jessa's face. "Do you mean it?"

She nodded. "I'll miss your family when I go, but I'd miss you more if I stayed."

Bending his head, Noah kissed her warmly on the mouth. "That pleases me greatly."

It was an odd feeling, this wanting to please him. She smiled as her hands dropped away. "Will you help me with my gown?"

Turning her around, Noah undid the laces then gave Jessa her nightshift from the wardrobe. By the time he was ready for bed Jessa was already in it, curled on her side in the middle. He blew out the candles and slipped under the covers.

Darkness gave Jessa the courage she had been seeking most of the day. As soon as Noah was settled she touched his forearm lightly. "Noah?"

"Hmm?"

"I have to talk to you about what you said this afternoon."

"I said a lot of things." He felt his heart give a little lurch. He had almost given up hope that she would broach the subject. Her thoughts had been a mystery to him since they left the river. "Are you referring to something in particular?"

She sighed. "Please don't make this difficult for me. I think you know what I mean."

Noah brought his knees up. They nudged Jessa's. "Jessa, if what you have to say to me is difficult, then perhaps you're not ready to say it. I meant it when I said I loved you. As much as I would like to hear those words from you, I can appreciate you might not return my feelings or even believe me. I can hope that will change one day."

"You don't understand," Jessa said miserably. "I don't want to talk about what I feel. I want to talk about what *you* feel. It's not right, Noah. You can't love me."

Noah's brows raised a notch. Here was a twist he hadn't expected. "I can't?"

"Well, you can. But it would be wrong."

"Why wrong?"

"Because it would be dishonest. Not for you, but for me. I don't want you to love me, Noah. I thought I did, but I don't. At least I don't think I do." She took a deep breath. "I'm not explaining this well, am I?"

"No, not well." He rolled away and lit one of the candles on the bedside table. "There. That's better. I don't like it above half trying to understand you when I can't see your face." When he turned back to Jessa he saw she had pulled the counterpane over her head. He suppressed his laughter. "Jessa! What maggot have you taken into your head this time?"

Her voice was muffled. "It's no good, Noah. I've lied about so many things and you'll hate me if I tell you, so I can't. But I don't want you to love me either, because it isn't fair to you and I don't know what to do any more."

Noah propped himself on one elbow and gently gave the covers a tug. "What lies, Jessa?"

She shook her head, her eyes pleading with him.

The smile vanished from his face. He thought that hiding under the covers had simply been a bit of silliness of her part. Now he saw it wasn't the case at all. She really was frightened. "Do you trust me?" he asked.

"I want to," she admitted. "You don't know how much I want to. I told you before, Noah. I'm a coward. I'm afraid of what will happen."

Noah's fingers stroked her hair on the pillow. He felt her faint trembling. "Let's suppose you did set these lies straight," he said. "What is it you think I would do?"

"Besides coming to hate me, you mean?"

"Besides that."

"I can't tell you," she said forlornly. "I would give myself away."

"I see."

"No. You don't. That's just it. And I don't know how to set it right."

Noah was silent for a long while. Finally he said, "Perhaps I can make it easier for you if I tell you a few things first."

Jessa looked at him hopefully. "What things?"

"I didn't love you when I offered to take you on the *Clarion*." He put a finger to her lips when she would have interrupted him. "I felt sorry for you and . . . and I felt drawn to you. Those emotions were as compatible as a spark and gunpowder. I wanted you and then I despised myself for taking advantage of the need that brought you to me. No one, least of all you, could have forced me to accept a marriage I didn't want—even a temporary one. I chose not to tell you these things because I had no wish to appear vulnerable to you. It was enough that *I* knew my vulnerability. I was not unafraid that you would use or trick me again. After all, you were merely looking for a way to flee England."

"Then you discovered my part in the robbery."

He nodded. "And it seemed that hardening my heart against you was the best course. Unfortunately, it was a plan more easily conceived than carried out. You drew me to you in ways no woman ever has. Jessa, I fell in love with you in spite of the lies you told me. You need to know that because anything you tell me now isn't going to change the way I feel."

"Don't say that, Noah. You don't know enough to say something like that."

"I know more than you think I do."

Jessa's eyes widened slightly. "What do you mean?"

"I know Gideon isn't your child," he said, watching her carefully. "I've known it for a long time. I wanted you to tell me yourself."

"You know?" Jessa sat up, hugging her knees to her chest. She rested her back against the headboard. "But how could you—"

"Does it really matter how I came to realize it?"

"No, I suppose not, but if you know then someone else might—"

Noah's soft chuckled interrupted her. "It's highly unlikely that anyone else will find out the way I did." At her frown, he continued. "It was because you were a virgin, Jessa. I know what you told me at the time, but after a little reflection and a little counting, I knew your story wasn't true."

"But you never let on."

"I told you, I wanted you to tell me. Tonight is the closest you've ever come to it." He sat up and faced her, holding a pillow against his midsection. "And actually I did let on," he said, smoothing the pillowcase. "In a number of ways. I was furious with you. I felt betrayed again. It's one of the reasons I was determined to assert my rights over you. I needed to feel in control, take my revenge. The only thing I accomplished, however, was hurting both of us and making it even more difficult for you to tell me the truth. For my part, I vowed never to trust you again." He shook his head slowly, sighing. "I want that to change, Jessa. I want to believe in you. I've never felt as . . . as desolate as I did this morning when I realized I had finally pushed you out of my life."

"I don't understand you," Jessa said, absently twisting her braid. "This matter of trusting can't be one-sided. Just this afternoon you pretended to be jealous of Robert Grantham. You lied to me as well. You knew all along he didn't exist."

"I wasn't pretending," Noah denied. "Not entirely. There was a time that I did believe in him. You used his name to stop me from making love to you. Can you begin to imagine how much I hated him then? You spoke of him as if he were real. I began to think he was your fairytale hero. You were so convincing whenever I asked you about him. Hell, you even described him to me!"

"How can I tell you more? You haven't even heard

the worst of the lies and I know you're getting angry just thinking about it. This is never going to work."

Noah drew in a deep breath and let it out slowly, calming himself. He got out of bed and sat in the nearby rocker. Distance helped. "Are you giving up already? What happened to standing your ground?"

"You made it sound so simple."

"What are you afraid of? That I'll send you and Gideon on the next ship back to England?"

She nodded jerkily.

"That isn't going to happen," Noah said, leaning forward in his chair. "I know you're running from something, Jessa. It's your way. And I'm not going to send you back to it, no matter what it is."

"You can't promise that . . . you don't know."

"I know I'm not going to turn my back on you. I know I want to help you. You asked for protection. If you won't allow me to give you anything else, allow me to give you that."

"Why would you want to?"

"Because I love you."

Jessa could hardly believe what she was hearing. "It doesn't make any sense that you should."

One corner of Noah's mouth lifted in a half-smile. "Well, there you have me. It may not make any sense, but it's true nonetheless." He got out of the rocker and sat on the edge of the bed, drawing his legs up and crossing them in front of him. "Actually, Jessa, it does make sense to me. I happen to think there is a great deal about you worth loving. More, apparently, than you yourself realize. You're brave and gentle and fierce and vulnerable, all at the same time. You are exactly what you need to be in any situation. You adapt and survive and grow stronger. I didn't always want to love you. Lord knows, I fought what was happening time and time again. In the end, all my struggling came to nothing. I love you, Jessa."

"I don't deserve you," she said, working the words past the tight lump in her throat.

"You don't have a choice any longer. Like it or not, you have me." He lifted one corner of the counterpane and gave it to her so she could dry her eyes. "Now tell me about Gideon."

Jessa collected herself, wondering how she would unravel all her lies. "His name is Adam Penberthy," she said. "I was his nanny."

"Penberthy? That was the name of the people in the carriage that almost ran us down in London." His eyes narrowed. "Didn't you tell me Edward Penberthy was the man who accosted you at Grant Hall?"

She nodded. "It's true that he made advances," she said, regarding Noah anxiously, willing him to believe her. "Most everything I told you about that was true, except the incident did not take place at Grant Hall. It was at Penberthy Manor. And of course, Edward did not come to the nursery to comfort a grieving widow. He came to take advantage of someone in his service."

"Edward is Gideon's . . . Adam's father?"

"Don't call him Adam. And no, Edward is not his father. They are third cousins. The relationship may even be more distant than that, I'm not certain. Edward was named guardian after Gideon's mother and father were killed in a carriage accident. Kenyon and Claudia Penberthy had hired me only weeks after Gideon was born. I met them in London. They were acquaintances of Lady Howard."

"So you *were* a paid companion."

"Yes. That was true. I realize you have reason to suspect everything I've ever told you, but there are fewer lies than you might think. Mary helped me with much of my story. We rehearsed it together. She warned me not to stray far from the truth because I would only tangle myself."

"Wise advice," he said dryly. "It served you well."

Jessa grimaced at his tone. "You're not making this easy."

"I'm sorry," he said sincerely. "That wasn't kind. Is it safe for me to assume that everything you told me about your own family is true?"

"Yes."

"And that everything about the Granthams is a lie?"

"Yes. There never were any Granthams."

"All right. Go on. You were saying that Gideon's parents hired you. . . ."

She nodded. "Claudia specifically requested that I take the position at the manor. She was sympathetic of my circumstances and thought I was better suited to dealing with Gideon than working for Lady Howard. I was happy to accept her offer. I enjoyed Lady Howard's company, but living in London was an awkward existence at best. Too often I was reminded how my life might have been different if my father had been anything but what he was. Penberthy Manor offered seclusion. It was also not far from where Mary lived, and the Penberthy's had no objections when anyone in Mary's family visited me. I felt as if I had family again. It was a good arrangement all around."

"And then Gideon's parents were killed."

"Hmm-mm," she murmured, her eyes pained. "It was a horrible time for everyone at the manor. The servants were grief stricken as well as uncertain about their future. No one knew who would be named as Gideon's guardian because Kenyon's will was vague on that account. It was quite possible the staff would be cut to a minimum and that Gideon would be raised elsewhere. Penberthy Manor was his, of course, but it seemed likely he would not grow up there. In the midst of all the uncertainty, Mr. Leeds, Kenyon's man of affairs, located Kenyon's cousin Edward. Edward and his wife returned from the Continent, agreed to accept guardianship, and moved into the manor house. For a while we all were relieved."

Jessa smoothed her nightshift over her knees. "It didn't last long. That Lady Barbara was difficult is the kindest thing I can say about her. She was never satisfied. Often she was cruel. I had very little contact with her because she had no interest in Gideon, and until her husband began making excuses to visit the nursery, she had none in me."

"She knew of Edward's interest in you?"

"Yes. I realize now that she knew it before I did. I was naive enough to believe Edward simply liked Gideon, and I maintained that belief for months. There came a time when Edward began to hint that Barbara wanted me gone. He said if I was *kind* to him, he could save my position. It was soon after that he cornered me in the nursery and wouldn't listen to my refusals. He was so *certain* I wanted him. You know what happened then. He didn't approach me for days after that incident, and I thought everything was going to return to some semblance of normalcy."

"Obviously it didn't."

"No. Far from it. One evening—I remember it was raining terribly—Edward came to my bedchamber. I was prepared to scream for help but Edward clamped his hand over my mouth and told me to listen to him, then scream if I wanted. Noah, there was so much pain in his voice, so much agony in his face, that I agreed to hear him out. He told me that Lady Barbara was planning to murder Gideon and that he had, in effect, given his consent. It was the estate, you see. It was entailed, and Barbara wanted everything. If Gideon were dead, Edward, as the closest male relative, would inherit it. Barbara would have it through him."

Noah swore softly. "You believed him?"

The question startled Jessa. No one, not Mary nor Davey nor any of their kin, had ever asked her that. "Yes. Yes, of course I did. I wouldn't have taken his advice and left the manor with Gideon if I hadn't."

"I see," he said, his green-gold eyes thoughtful. "He helped you leave then?"

"No. He only encouraged me to do so."

"Did he know where you went?"

"No! I believed him, when he told me about his wife's threats, but I didn't trust him so far that I would tell him where I was going. On the contrary I let him think that I wasn't going to take his advice. It took several days to get everything in order, and it was Davey Shaw and his brothers who helped me get away."

"You realize, don't you, that by leaving you were falling neatly into Barbara's, and perhaps Edward's, hands? The outcome was the same. Why didn't you go to the authorities?"

"The outcome was *not* the same. They may have the estate, but Gideon is alive. And how could I go to the authorities? There was no proof. Edward would have denied that he had spoken to me. Certainly Barbara would have denied everything. My accusations would have meant my dismissal and Gideon would have been left unprotected. I'm sure his life would have been safe for a while, years perhaps, but eventually there would have been an accident. I chose the only course open to me. I fled."

"How did the Penberthys explain Gideon's disappearance?"

"They said I abducted him, which was the truth. There was an extensive search." She frowned. "I don't know how this escaped your attention while you were in England. The London papers had the story."

"I didn't read the papers often."

"But people were talking about it."

"Not to me they weren't. Mayhap they thought I wouldn't be interested. When did you leave the manor?"

"In January."

"I was at Linfield then." He paused, thinking back. "I remember something about an infant. . . . Wasn't there a child who was abandoned in the wild? The child died, I believe."

"Yes. That was Mary and Davey's son. He died a few days after I arrived at their cottage with Gideon. He had never been well." Jessa's hands knotted together. "Please, believe that I didn't ask them to do what they did. It was Mary's idea to take little Davey's body to the Penberthy estate. She laid him in the woods, dressed in Gideon's clothes, wrapped in one of Gideon's blankets, and when his body was discovered Lady Barbara identified it as Adam Penberthy. It's possible Edward may have known differently, but he never said otherwise publicly."

"So you are considered a murderess," he said heavily, "and Edward Penberthy legally claimed the estate."

She nodded. "I've made quite a tangle of everything, haven't I?"

"A veritable Gordian knot."

"But do you believe what I've told you?"

There was no hesitation. "Yes."

Relief shuddered through Jessa. "Then you understand why I had to marry you? And why I created Robert Grantham and his family and all the other lies?"

Noah's eyes shut briefly. He rubbed his lids with his thumb and forefinger. Weariness was rife in his voice. The truth was finally out and it was every bit as complicated as Jessa's lies. Noah firmly believed he had never been given more than he could handle at any one time. Had he learned all of this on board the *Clarion*, before he understood his own feelings, he may well have made good on his threat to abandon Jessa on the high seas. "I'm not prepared to sort through all of that tonight. I know how much you love Gideon and that explains many of your actions."

"But—"

He held up his hand, effectively cutting Jessa off. "We'll talk on the morrow, Jessa. We have a long journey ahead of us. I suspect I'll understand everything by the time we reach Philadelphia." He leaned toward the nightstand and blew out the candle.

"You're right," she said quietly, staring straight ahead in the darkness. "This probably isn't the best time to say I love you as well." She stretched and slid under the covers. "It can wait."

CHAPTER THIRTEEN

Noah was still in a happy state of confusion eight days later. Time and the tedium of travel had provided him with the opportunity to put many of the things Jessa told him into perspective. He began to understand how events unfolded from her point of view, and the impact of this new awareness was staggering. He recognized how deeply her fear of discovery ran, and how often she risked her own well-being in order to protect Gideon's identity. Her bravery, though sometimes foolish, was not to be questioned.

Noah sifted through the lies she had told, the actions she had taken, and realized time and again she had deceived him for Gideon's sake. The post road robbery, the marriage, her refusal in the beginning to be intimate, and the invention of Robert Grantham were all motivated by her singular desire to keep Gideon safe.

In hindsight, Noah realized that deception was something that did not come easily to Jessa. She had been reluctant to accept the clothes he had provided for her because she believed she had no right to them. Guilt kept her silent on the matter of his fiancée. She disliked speaking of Robert because it enmeshed her in more lies, and she had been compelled by overwhelming remorse to refuse his own declaration of love. Jessa's fundamentally honest nature was battered and bruised by the necessity of lying, her nerves stretched to the point of snapping.

While Noah was able to reconcile his thinking in regard to Jessa's actions, adjusting to the fact that she loved him was another matter entirely. At times he felt oddly giddy and would discover he was grinning without apparent cause. His heart would give a faint lurch when Jessa touched him casually to get his attention. He laughed more frequently, often over the most trifling things. He felt bemused, light-headed, and unequivocally happy. More than that, Noah felt blessed.

The closed carriage rumbled along Philadelphia's paved streets at a leisurely pace. The sun bore down relentlessly and a hazy screen of heat rose from the cobblestones. Cam, feeling very self-important, rode with Henry in the driver's seat. Lowering his cocked hat a notch, he pretended not to see the shy interest of three young serving girls gathered at one of the public water pumps. Inside the carriage, Jessa's face was pressed childlike against the window while Noah dangled Gideon on his knee and made an effort not to be obviously amused by his wife's enthusiasm.

He directed her attention away from the tidy row of brick buildings where shopkeepers displayed their goods toward the gleaming white steeple of Christ Church that towered above the city. Jessa pronounced it beautiful. Of course, she said much the same thing about the simple elegance of the State House and Carpenter's Hall. She even found something to admire about the rows of dockside warehouses along the Delaware and the open markets and sidewalk stands. At the end of their brief tour it was her firm opinion Philadelphia had much to recommend it, not the least of which was its enterprising and engaging citizens.

The carriage slowed on Chestnut Street and finally stopped in front of a row of three-story red brick dwellings. Jessa drew back from the window as Cam leaped from his perch and opened the door to the carriage. He helped her down and she waited somewhat nervously on the narrow sidewalk while Noah alighted with Gideon.

"Our home is the one with white shutters," he said, searching his pockets for a key.

Jessa glanced over her shoulder at the houses. Fused as they were, it was difficult to tell where one house began and another ended. "Noah, they all have white shutters," she said.

"So they do," he said, pretending he had never noticed it before. "But only one has the shutters closed. Therefore it is unoccupied and therefore it is ours. Also, Henry had the foresight to stop the carriage directly at our front door." Triumphantly he held up the key. "This way." At the door he paused. "Be warned. I only arranged for it to be cleaned periodically in my absence. There's no telling what you'll find."

Noah's fears had not been without substance. While Henry and Cam carried in trunks and valises, Noah took Jessa through the rooms on the first floor. The furniture in the parlor was draped protectively in sheets. Dust motes scattered in the still air when Noah pulled off one cover with a bit too much flourish. The dark hardwood floor was dull, and Jessa noticed a trail of telltale footprints as they moved about the room. Noah's study, the dining room, and the kitchen were in no better condition. The master bedchamber, with a large dressing room adjoining it, was on the second floor. The smaller, unfurnished bedroom was to be Gideon's. On the third floor were rooms for Cam and the house servants Noah intended to rehire as soon as time permitted.

Back in the parlor Noah checked his watch and wound the clock on the mantel. Jessa was sitting on the only uncovered chair while Gideon cut a swath through the dust by bouncing along the floor on his bottom.

"You won't need to hire anyone," she said, pointing to Gideon "He's quite happy to polish the floors for us."

"You're not too disappointed, are you?" he asked, an anxious note in his voice.

Jessa was genuinely bewildered. "Disappointed?"

Noah waved one hand indicating the room they were in and beyond. "The house," he said. "I'm only renting it. Perhaps I could find something larger."

"Don't you dare," she said firmly. "I'm far from disappointed. In fact, I couldn't be more pleased. There's nothing wrong with this house that a little airing and dusting and scrubbing won't eliminate."

"You really think so?"

"I really do."

Noah felt unburdened by her pleasure. Crossing the room, he placed a swift kiss on her lips. "I'm going to help Cam and Henry bring in the furniture for Gideon's room," he said.

"Shouldn't you be going to the State House?" she asked. "I thought your meetings began today. By my reckoning you're already hours late."

"They do and I am. But I can't very well leave you within minutes of arriving."

"Why ever not? There's nothing to do here that I can't accomplish. If you leave me some coin I'll send Henry to market for foodstuffs. Cam and I will begin airing the rooms." Her smile was amused as she looked up at him and saw the protest that hovered on his lips. "Very well, Noah. Argue with me for a minute longer then be on your way. I knew what you were about when you glanced at your watch and set the clock."

He laughed. "I didn't realize I was so obvious. I thought I managed to look calm and indifferent."

"Hardly," she said dryly. She held out her hand, palm up.

Sighing, Noah pulled out a small leather pouch out of his jacket pocket and dropped it in her hand. "Now that you've separated me from my money, wife, I'll take my leave." Gideon tugged at his leg. Noah bent down and ruffled the infant's dark hair. "I'll call on Mr. Bowen at the bank, Jessa, before I go to the meeting. The small staff I let go when I went to England work for him now. Charles employed them as a favor to me. Perhaps I can persuade him to part with Sally and Mrs. Harper to help with the housework and cooking."

Jessa focused on only a small part of what he said. With the exception of one name Noah's words simply washed over her. "Bowen?" she asked. "A relative of Hilary's?"

"Her father." He stood, brushing off his sleeves. "I have to meet with him sometime. Hilary as well. You understand, don't you?"

She nodded, keeping her features carefully closed so he would not guess at the depth of her insecurity. "You'll see Hilary tonight, then?"

"I think it's for the best. I don't want her to hear about my marriage from anyone else. Her home is on Arch Street, only a few blocks from here, and rumors fly in this city. I shouldn't be surprised if all our neighbors know that I didn't arrive alone." His smile strived for a lightness he was not really feeling. "That means there is a story circulating somewhere along Market Street by now."

Jessa stood, slipped her arm through Noah's and escorted him to the door. "I know you're not looking forward to your meeting with Hilary, but you're right not to let her learn of our marriage from anyone else." She stood on tiptoe and kissed his cheek. "You're a fine man, Noah McClellan, and I love you."

The embrace that Noah planned was aborted as Cam pushed through the door carrying a valise under each arm. He glanced guiltily from Noah to Jessa then mumbled a pardon and shot up the stairs.

"I'll expect you for dinner," Jessa said, giving Noah a playful shove toward the front stoop.

Once Noah was gone, Jessa set herself to the task of restoring some sense of order to the house. The first thing she had to do was find a place for Gideon to play where he would be out of harm's way and not underfoot. She caught Henry as he was carrying in the footboard for Gideon's bed.

Henry puzzled over the problem while he wiped the dark, shiny crown of his head with a kerchief. Beads of perspiration glistened on his upper lip, testimony to the heat of the day and the work he had already done. His breath whistled softly between the gap in his front teeth. After a moment's thought, he rearranged the parlor furniture into a formidable blockade, laying some of the pieces on their side so Gideon couldn't get out. Cam found Gideon's toys and tossed them into the pen. Everyone was satisfied with the arrangement except Gideon. He cried soulfully for several minutes, waiting for someone to rescue him. When he finally realized that confinement was going to be his lot for the time being, he was content to chase his ball and suck on his string of beads.

Jessa changed clothes, discarding her violet gown in favor of something more serviceable. The coarsely woven brown dress she wore had sleeves that were pleated at the cuffs and fell just below her elbows. It was a dress eminently suited for work because it left her hands and forearms free. After breathing the stale air of the house and sweeping dust with the hem of her gown, Jessa fairly itched to be elbow deep in sudsy water. Mary Shaw would have thought her mad. Smiling wistfully as she thought of her friend, Jessa pinned an apron to her bodice and tucked her hair under a mobcap.

Cam was envious that Henry was sent to market, but he accepted his fate stoically. He found brooms, dusters, and oil soap, drew water from the pumps, and opened windows and shutters that refused to budge under Jessa's lighter touch. He carried the sheets into the backyard and snapped the dust out of them— though he was inclined to cough overmuch as a way of attracting Jessa's sympathy. He helped Jessa wash the woodwork and floors, rub down the furniture with beeswax, make beds, clear the corners of cobwebs, and sweep the front stoop. He was careful to mention only a few times and in a casual way that Henry seemed to be overlong at the market.

When Henry finally returned, Cam was relieved of his duties, yet he felt so guilty as Jessa continued to work that soon he was down on his hands and knees, scrubbing the kitchen floor while she wiped the pantry shelves.

The knock at the front door startled Jessa. She dropped her rag into the bucket at her side and water splashed her dress. "Oh, damn," she swore softly, smoothing her apron and straightening her limp mob-cap. Her damp fingers merely streaked the material, making the dirt more obvious. "Cam!" Distressed, she fairly wailed the boy's name. "I can't go to the door like this." She knew her face was smudged with dirt and strands of hair clung damply to her neck. Her gown and pinafore were hopelessly stained. "Would you see who it is, please?" She raised her eyes heavenward, praying it was the help Noah said he would send.

Cam jumped to his feet and pitched his scrub brush into his pail, wishing Henry weren't plucking their main course for dinner in the backyard. The older man made a more dignified doorman than he did.

Jessa strained to hear Cam's conversation at the door, but she couldn't make anything out. Gideon's whimpering in the drawing room attracted her attention and as soon as she heard the front door close she hurried down the hallway to look in on her son. She was brought up short in the entrance hall when she saw Cam was not alone.

The woman engaged in earnest conversation with

Cam was easily one of the most beautiful women Jessa
had ever seen. Her coal black hair was thick and lustrous,
arranged in ringlets that fell lightly against her slender
neck. Her face was a near perfect oval, her features
sculpted and pared as though crafted by a fine hand.
Dark, luminous eyes were feathered by heavy lashes and
her brows were faintly winged.

Her form was less spare than the delicate planes of
her face, but she was tall, long of limb, and her curves
seemed less generous than they actually were.

There was no evidence the woman was in the least
troubled by the oppressive late afternoon heat. The
sheer white lawn mobcap she wore, trimmed with lace
and a blue taffeta ribbon, showed no signs of wilting.
The bodice of her printed linen dress was decorated
with bows, and she wore a gauze apron over her skirt.
In one hand she carried a parasol, in the other, a basket
of fruit.

Jessa felt herself growing cold as the woman became
aware of her presence in the entranceway. It did her
little good to hope this stranger might be some neighbor
come to wish Noah well. She knew differently. This
beautiful, poised woman was Hilary Bowen.

"May I help you?" asked Jessa, stepping forward.
"Cam, will you see what's bothering Gideon?"

Cam hovered uncertainly for a moment, reluctant to
leave his mistress alone. It took an almost imperceptible
nod from Jessa to get him to move.

"Oh, good," the woman sighed when Cam was gone.
"I wasn't able to make that boy understand me. I'm
Miss Bowen, Mr. McClellan's fiancée. Perhaps you can
tell me where I might find him?"

Jessa was careful to swallow her nervous laughter. Cam
must have been playing at being very slow-witted if he
couldn't answer that question. "He's gone to the State
House," she said.

"The State House," Hilary repeated, giving no indication whether she was displeased or satisfied with this

information. Her eyes were coolly polite, their regard thorough, as she studied Jessa. "Papa sent a message to the house saying Noah had need of Sally Boley and Mrs. Harper. They'll be here directly, though I can't imagine why Noah should require more staff. You seem to have everything well in hand."

"Cam and I have made a good beginning, but I'll appreciate the help."

Hilary's eyes narrowed faintly. "Have I seen you before? At the landing perhaps?"

Gideon's fearful howl cut off Jessa's reply. "Excuse me," she said and hurried into the parlor. She scooped Gideon out of the pen. "What happened to him, Cam? How did he get this mark on his head?" She soothed Gideon, cuddling him against her shoulder, whispering sweet nonsense in his ear while she awaited Cam's reply.

Cam rocked on his heels and cast a sideways glance at the entrance where Hilary had come to stand. Her curiosity made him uneasy. "He got his head stuck between the seat and the arm of that chair," he said, pointing to the Chippendale turned on its side. "He was trying to get out. He's not hurt, is he?"

"No, just a little frightened."

"What have you done to the furniture?" demanded Hilary, tapping the rounded point of her parasol against the floor. "This is outrageous. Mr. McClellan prizes these pieces."

Jessa's eyes widened a little and she looked questioningly over Gideon's head at Cam. He shrugged his thin shoulders as if to say he didn't know whether Noah set great store by his furniture or not.

"That child's not likely to have any answers," Hilary continued in frigid accents. "I'm telling you Mr. McClellan will *not* approve. Where precisely did Noah find you?"

Hilary couldn't have been more than six years Jessa's senior, but she made Jessa feel as awkward and graceless as a schoolroom chit. "In England," she said, wiping tears from Gideon's rosy cheeks with the corner of her apron.

"That's obvious, but I cannot imagine what he was thinking." She set down her basket of fruit on a mahogany end table. "Well, I don't know whose service you were in before, but I doubt they had very exacting standards if you were permitted to rearrange their furniture in this manner. I shouldn't wonder if your brat hasn't drooled on the seat covers. He *is* your brat, isn't he?"

Jessa's chin lifted a notch. "He's my son, yes. And generally he prefers chewing the chair legs to drooling on seat covers."

Hilary's eyelashes fluttered at this insolent riposte from a servant and her poise noticeably faltered. "Have a care with your tongue," she said, managing an even tone though her eyes pinned Jessa in place.

Cam drew himself straighter and stepped in front of Jessa as if to protect her. "See here, Miss Bowen, you oughten to—"

Placing her hand on Cam's shoulder, Jessa silenced him. "It's all right, Cam." For all that Hilary's assumptions and attitudes rubbed her the wrong way, Jessa couldn't help but feel sorry for her. It was obvious she had yet to learn of Noah's marriage. "Would you take Gideon in the kitchen? I saw that Henry brought back a stoneware jug of milk. I think Gideon would like a cup. And have some yourself if you'd like."

Cam was happy to leave the room and he hurried out, avoiding Hilary's disdainful stare as he did so.

When Cam was gone Jessa began righting the furniture. "It's unfortunate you have arrived at this time, Miss Bowen. I regret that I seem to have misrepresented myself to you and I have no wish to do that. You should know—"

Hilary tapped her parasol impatiently. "It makes no difference to me if you are in charge of the staff or a kitchen drudge," she said. "I understand there exists such a class distinction in England, even among the servants. However, it matters not at all here. You will find that I deal fairly with all the help. In return I expect the work to be satisfactory. *This,*" she said, waving her hand in a gesture that was at once graceful and scornful, "is not satisfactory."

"I beg your pardon, Miss Bowen," Jessa said with calm dignity, "but I am not *your* help. And it seems to me that some sort of class distinction does exist or you would not speak so rudely to me when none of this is your affair."

"How dare you! Don't think I'll let this pass. You may be assured I will speak to Mr. McClellan. You will discover your position in his home is very much *my* affair!"

Jessa was astonished to see that Hilary's anger merely accentuated her beauty. Her cheeks flushed becomingly, her midnight blue eyes sparkled. It was only the clipped, superior tone of her voice that was repulsive. She spoke as if her words were spittle, ridding herself of them quickly, uncaring, or perhaps unconscious, of giving offense.

Seeing that she had effectively silenced Jessa, Hilary turned on her heel. "I can find my own way out, thank you."

Jessa blinked as the door closed behind Hilary. "Good," she whispered, "because the exit I had in mind was a third floor window." Shaking her head, not quite believing what had just taken place, Jessa went to the kitchen.

"Is she gone?" Cam asked.

"Yes. She wasn't very, umm, pleasant, was she?"

"If you'll pardon me for saying so, she's a bloody bi—witch," he corrected quickly. "Ask anyone at the landing."

Jessa was already thinking she shouldn't be discussing Hilary with Cam, but her curiosity got the better of her. "How do you know her?"

"Don't really know her. I saw her a few times at the

landing with Mr. Noah. Miss Courtney and me, well, we saw her hit Billy with a riding crop once when he didn't move quick enough for her. You have to understand, Billy didn't do nothin', he's just a little slow sometimes." Cam tapped the side of his head. "I gave her a wide berth after that. Told Court to do the same."

Jessa didn't know what to say. She could hardly cast stones when her own treatment of Billy was little better. "Did you tell anyone?"

Cam shook his head. "Court and me thought Billy'd be the one in trouble if Miss Hilary lied about what happened. Billy thought so too. He's smart about some things."

"Yes, he is." She smiled, recalling Billy had given her a nag and a broken wagon when she was bent on leaving the landing. "Very smart. Here, let me have Gideon. If you'll draw me some water and heat it, I'll give Gideon a bath. He's a sight dirtier than either you or I—and that's saying something." She plucked Gideon from Cam's arms and went to the back door. "Henry, have you finished with the chicken? Mr. Noah's going to be home soon and I promised him dinner."

Grinning his wide, gap-toothed smile, Henry held up his work by the feet. "A plump one it is, Miz McClellan. I'm skinnin' some taters now and directly I'll shell the peas."

"Do you cook, Henry?"

"That be a matter of some debate betwixt me and Tildy, ma'am. She don't think so. I do."

Jessa laughed. "Well, I'd certainly be willing to judge the matter this evening. Could I prey on your good will and ask you to make dinner?"

"Be more'n happy to."

"Thank you," Jessa said with heartfelt relief.

Gideon's bath was delayed because Cam had to leave to buy firewood, kindling, and coals for the kitchen hearth. During his absence Sally Boley and Mrs. Harper arrived. Jessa could have cried that she had to greet them looking no better than a chimney sweep. They were obviously shocked to discover she was the mistress of the house and not one of the staff. Sally's dimpled smile wavered unsteadily as her mouth kept opening and closing. She dipped half a dozen curtsies before Mrs. Harper—definitely the more restrained of the pair—clamped her hand over Sally's plump forearm and held her still. It was subtly clear in a matter of minutes that they were pleased to be in Noah's employ again.

Mrs. Harper was a diminutive woman with clear blue eyes that seemed strangely beautiful in a face otherwise so plain. She had a score of years on Jessa, but at the moment she radiated more energy in her little finger than Jessa had in her entire body. She was also sympathetic to this fact, taking charge almost immediately. While she and Sally sniffed around the kitchen, Henry was dispatched to carry their bags to the third floor. It was their opinion that Henry could *not* cook, given the way he had cut the chicken and allowed the potatoes to brown in the hot sun while he shelled the peas. Sally stood militantly in the center of the kitchen and threatened him with the flat of a skillet if he set foot in there again except to take his meals.

"That's what Tildy always say," he said, accepting the situation good-naturedly. "If you don't need me here I'll see about getting Mr. Noah's rig and horses stabled."

Cam returned shortly after Henry left. He was a little overwhelmed with activity in the kitchen. Sally was banging kettles, searching for what she needed, and Mrs. Harper was slicing potatoes and dropping them into the water he had drawn for Gideon's bath.

"More water, ma'am?" he asked Jessa.

"I think so," she said, pushing away from the wall where she had been leaning, too weary to take Mrs. Harper's earlier suggestion that she retire to her room. "I'm taking Gideon upstairs with me. If you'd bring up the water when it's warm, I'll wash him there." As Cam turned to go she added, "I promise you won't have to lift a finger tomorrow. You can sleep till noon or fish along the Delaware or tour the city."

"No lessons?" he asked. Ever since they left the landing Jessa had been helping him with his letters and reading.

She shook her head. "No lessons." The spring in Cam's step was not comforting. "We'll begin again the day after," she called as he bounded out of the house.

Noah eased himself down on the edge of the bed. Gently tugging at Jessa's mobcap, he lifted it away from her head. The spill of her pale hair on the pillow was burnished with candleglow from the nearby lamp. There were smudges of dirt on her chin, cheek, and temple, smudges of exhaustion beneath her eyes. She lay on her side, knees drawn toward her chest. Her skirt was twisted around her legs and she still wore her shoes.

"Slugabed," Noah whispered, bending low to her ear. He brushed her hair aside and kissed the soft spot behind her ear.

She stirred vaguely. "Hmmm?"

"Jessa." He placed his hand on her shoulder and gave her a small shake. "I dislike waking you, but you'd dislike it more if I didn't."

Yawning, she pressed her hands to her eyes and rubbed them. "Is dinner prepared then?"

"Sweet lady, dinner was prepared some hours ago and eaten by everyone but you. I've brought you a tray. Sally kept your meal warm."

Sitting up quickly, Jessa's head almost collided with Noah's. She blinked owlishly, throwing off the dregs of sleep, and looked about the room anxiously. "Where's Gideon? I brought him up here to bathe him."

"Gideon is down for the night," Noah explained gently, easing her fears. "Apparently Cam came in with the water and you were already fast asleep. Our son, however, was rearranging our belongings in the bottom drawer of the highboy."

"Oh, Lord," Jessa sighed. "I must not have closed the drawer tightly. It's a miracle he didn't bring down the chest on his head."

"Not to worry. Cam rescued him and gave him a bath. He cleaned up very nicely, too."

Jessa remembered her own dirt-streaked face and wiped at it with her apron.

Noah's hands closed over her wrists and pulled them away from her face. "Don't bother with that now. There's water warming for you downstairs, and you can have a bath as soon as you've eaten something." He reached for the tray on the bedside table and held it in front of her. "You'd better sit up a little more. That's better." He placed the tray on her lap. "Anyway, you look adorable."

"Liar. But you're sweet to say so." She speared a slice a buttered potato with her fork and began eating. "What time is it?"

"Nearly eight o'clock."

"Eight!"

"Don't fret yourself. You deserved your nap. I came home at six to a near immaculate house and mistakenly congratulated Mrs. Harper and Sally for their outstanding efforts. I can tell you, I got an earful. They took great delight in informing me that you and Cam had done most of the work and that I was the most negligent husband for not sending word that I was returning to the city and having the house prepared."

Jessa's mouth gaped a little. "They didn't say that."

"Well, I could tell they were thinking it. A guilty conscience needs no accuser."

Jessa picked some tender white meat away from the breastbone and dropped it in her mouth. "You've nothing to feel guilty about."

Noah gave a small snort. "Liar. But it's sweet of you to say so." He took a warm roll from her tray, broke it in half, and buttered each piece for her. "I understand from Cam that you had a visitor this afternoon."

She nodded. "You haven't been to see Hilary yet, have you?"

"No." He placed the roll halves back on her plate. "I'm going in a little while. What happened while she was here? Cam couldn't—or wouldn't—tell me much."

Between bites Jessa told him what had taken place. By the time she had finished Noah's scowl had deepened the lines around his mouth. "It was a natural mistake, Noah," she said, apologizing for Hilary's behavior. "And mayhap it was for the best. I don't think I should have been the one to tell her I'm your wife."

"But you did make an attempt to explain."

"Yes. Once. She wouldn't let me finish."

"Then she has no one to blame for her mistake but herself," he said. "I'm sorry you met her this way. When I talked to her father at the bank he told me Hilary was gone from the house for the afternoon. He sent a note to the house asking that Sally and Mrs. Harper come here. Hilary must have returned unexpectedly and learned they were leaving."

"How did Mr. Bowen react to your news?" she asked.

"Charles was naturally upset at first. Livid is a word that comes to mind. Hilary's his daughter after all. But he's also a practical man and he knew there was nothing he could do about it. He expressed regret, asked me to deal with Hilary gently, and before I left he wished me happy."

"Quite a turn in his thinking."

Noah agreed. "I've often thought Charles rides the fence too easily. It must be deuced uncomfortable for him, never taking sides, always straddling the middle ground. The truth is, he can't offend anybody. He sincerely meant it when he wished me happy, but you can be certain that when he's consoling Hilary, he'll tell her I should be sent to perdition. He'll mean that sincerely as well."

"You will deal with her gently, won't you?"

"I'll try, though why you should want me to is a mystery. Even if you were a servant, you didn't deserve the edge of her tongue today."

"*I* have you, *she* doesn't," she said softly. "I can afford to be generous in regard to her feelings."

Noah leaned forward, kissed Jessa's butter-moist lips, and flicked away a crumb from the corner of her mouth with his tongue. "Aren't you just the tiniest bit jealous that I'm going to see her?" he asked. "After all, I've bathed, changed my clothes, and I'm looking remarkably well even if I must point it out myself."

"I noticed," she said dryly. "But if you can kiss me when I'm looking no better than a street beggar, I'm not worried." She slapped his hand away as his fingers began to walk up her forearm. "Tell me about the convention today. Did it go well?"

Noah moved from the bed and sat in the rocker by the window. The drapes were open, and though it was dark outside, light from the street lamps filtered into the room. "Today we argued about the need for secrecy in our work. We made a unanimous pledge, a gentleman's agreement as it were, not to discuss the meetings with anyone."

"Even wives?"

"Most especially wives," he chuckled.

"Well I like that," she said tartly.

"Actually wives were not mentioned at all. Most men in the assembly believe we have a responsibility to make the revisions, complete the writing, and present the work to the public all in a piece. If today's idle talk was any indication, there is going to be much dissension in the ranks. It wouldn't serve to have the state assemblies riled on each issue before we settle them ourselves. The pressure is enormous to do the right thing by our individual states, and yet we have an obligation to create a central government capable of keeping us united. We've agreed not to publish any details of the debates nor to keep a record of how we vote on the issues. Thus, we're given the freedom to change our minds and are protected from embarrassment should we choose to vote in ways the public might take exception to. We'll be able to talk freely without fear of reprisals."

"Your family will be outraged," she said. "They were looking forward to hearing everything that goes on."

Noah rolled his eyes. "Can you imagine what it would be like if I hinted anything to them? I may as well publish the proceedings in the *Gazette.*"

Jessa laughed. "You do them a disservice. They would be discreet."

"Jessa! You met Rae. Discretion is not among her virtues. Speaking her mind is."

"Oh, very well," she said, giving in. "I only took their side because they're not here to state it for themselves."

"I'll be sure to tell them that when I write," he said dryly. "Anyway, the agreement is for the length of the convention, which looks to be months rather than weeks, and we are not committed to silence after that. Not a man among us would have agreed to such a thing. It violates the principles we hold most dear. Even now our agreement carries no force of law. It wouldn't be treasonous to speak of what we do, but neither would it be in the best interest of what we're trying to accomplish."

Jessa held up her hands as if in surrender. "You've made your point beautifully. If this is how you speak in the debates then I'm sure you will have no difficulty drawing others to your views."

"Hah! If only it were so simple as that. There are many men more eloquent than I with convictions just as strong." He rose from the rocker, kissed her cheek, and relieved her of the empty tray. "But I appreciate your confidence." He was warmed by her pleased smile. "I'll send Cam up with the water. You probably already know there's a tub in the dressing room. I think a leisurely bath is in order and then sleep. Don't wait up for me. I have no idea how long I'll be with Hilary. I shouldn't like to be there above an hour, but I'm not making promises."

"I understand," she said gravely.

Noah gave her a brief, encouraging smile and left the room. The night was warm and balmy, and Noah chose to walk to Hilary's. His shoulders were hunched, his head lowered, as he tested the tone of certain phrases in his mind. He was so deeply in thought he didn't hear Ben Franklin call to him as he passed his house. He deliberately hurried past the taverns where he knew he might see some of the delegates. His steps slowed after he walked by Christ Church and turned the corner onto Arch Street. When Noah realized he was only delaying the inevitable he quickened his pace until he stood squarely in front of the Bowen House. Raising his hand, he loudly rapped the heavy brass knocker against the door.

He was shown to the drawing room on the second floor where, as the doorman informed him, Miss Bowen was in expectation of his arrival. Noah would have chosen a less grand place to make his announcement, somewhere less formal and spacious than the room Hilary and her father used for entertaining large numbers of dinner guests. As Hilary drew him into the room and the doors closed behind him, Noah saw they were reflected in the half dozen gilded mirrors which decorated the walls. Noah had never given much thought to those mirrors before, but now their heavily scrolled borders seemed ostentatious, their very presence a sign of vanity.

Hilary caught Noah's gaze in one of the mirrors. She smiled at him. "We're striking together, aren't we? Everyone says so."

The comment startled Noah. It had never occurred to him that Hilary might see him as some sort of complementary bookend. "Do they? How odd of them."

Hilary pushed out her lower lip in a beautiful pout as she turned in his arm. "Aren't you going to kiss me?"

Noah placed a perfunctory kiss on her cheek.

"Noah! Is that the best you can do after being gone all these long months?" She leaned into him and raised her mouth to his.

Shaking his head, Noah grasped her elbows and took a half step backward. "No, Hilary. I have something to say and I want you to hear me out."

"What is it?" she asked, searching his face, uncertain for the first time in their two year courtship.

"May we sit down?"

Frowning now, Hilary pointed out a chair near the barren fireplace. "Would you like something to eat? I have sweetmeats and tarts." She started for the silver salver ladened with fresh pastries. "I thought it was safe to assume you ate dinner at home, what with Sally being back in your employ, but I know how you like desserts. I had Mrs. Corning make these especially for you."

Actually, Noah didn't like desserts. Hilary assumed that he did because of some idle comment delivered long ago. It had always seemed like such a small thing; he had never bothered to correct her assumption. Now it struck him that he had been dishonest. "Nothing for me, Hilary. I'm not hungry."

Hilary set the tray down again and nervously smoothed the folds of her lavender taffeta gown. "Did you just arrive in the country today?" she asked striving for calm.

"No. I arrived in the city today. I spent two days at the landing before I came here."

He knew, she thought. He knew about Salem or Jericho. Perhaps both. That's why he was acting so strangely. Someone in his family had said something to him, poisoning his mind against her. Oddly, the realization lifted Hilary's spirits. This was a matter she could handle. She felt a measure of calm returning. "Tea, then?"

"No, thank you. Nothing for me. Will you please come and sit down?"

"You're so serious this evening," she said lightly, trying to coax a smile to his lips. "Such gravity doesn't suit you, Noah." She sat opposite him, her hands folded neatly in her lap. "Papa has retired to his room for the evening so you mustn't think that he'll interrupt us as he has in the past. Of course, we *are* engaged, and I'm past the first bloom of youth, when one must accept the chilling eyes of chaperones."

Noah knew precisely the response she was seeking, and dutifully he gave it to her. "You're looking lovely as ever, Hilary." And she was. The choker of pearls she wore emphasized the slim length of her neck. Her ebony hair was coiled becomingly at the back of her head and several dark ringlets brushed her ears as she tilted her head. It occurred to him the only jewelry Jessa had was stolen, and that her soft, fine hair would never obey the dictates of fashion.

"Then perhaps I have a need of a chaperone after all," she said lightly.

"That won't be necessary," Noah said. This was the side of Hilary she did not present publicly, the side of her that was slightly flirtatious and coy. Noah used to find it amusing that she reserved this part of herself for him alone. Her passion was a secret they shared. He had liked it that way. There was something powerfully fascinating in the contrast between Hilary's public reserve and her private passion. "I understand you visited my home today," he said.

"Oh, so she *did* tell you I came by. I was concerned that she wouldn't. But I suppose you saw the basket of fruit and wondered about it. Did she tell you I sent it?"

"Actually, I didn't know about the fruit. But it was kind of you."

Hilary stiffened. "You didn't see it? What did she do with it?"

"I couldn't say. And the fruit is not the issue here."

"I should think not. The issue is that woman's rudeness. I don't know what she told you, but her manner was wholly insolent. I paid a call at your home to welcome you. She informed me that you were at the State House—we can speak of that later—then she left me cooling my heels in the entrance hall while she ran after her sobbing child. I'm afraid I was curious so I followed her. Oh, Noah! You can't imagine my thoughts when I saw how she had abused your beautiful furniture! I know you must have your reasons for hiring her, but I wish that you had written to me of your intent. She is totally unsuitable. I would be reluctant to have her working for us after we're married."

"You would?" Noah asked casually, permitting himself to be diverted from his main concern.

"Certainly I would. I'm not suggesting that we let her go without making some arrangement for her future. Perhaps her husband can find other employment first and then she can follow."

"Her husband doesn't work for me."

Hilary's brows raised slightly. "I hadn't realized that. I thought he must have been somewhere about. She's married, isn't she?"

"Yes."

"And her husband's working here in the city?"

"Yes."

Hilary's head bobbed once as if the matter were settled. "Then there is no problem. You can dismiss her at once. There's no reason she should be working for you, not with her unpleasant demeanor, and not with a child underfoot."

"It's not so simple as that, Hilary, but I take responsibility for approaching this matter in a backward fashion. You mistook Jessa's position in my household. She is not an employee. She is my wife."

Color flooded Hilary's face. Gradually it receded, leaving her complexion pasty white. "That is a cruel jest,

Noah," she said finally. "I cannot help but think less of you for—"

"It's no jest," he said gravely. "I deeply regret having injured you in this reprehensible manner, Hilary. It is beyond the bounds of forgiveness. I came tonight because it is only right that you should hear it from me and no one else."

Hilary's hands unlocked. Like talons her fingers spread and curved as she grasped the arms of her chair. Her knuckles were bloodless, her skin like veined marble. She was perched on the edge of the chair, a cold stony figure more reminiscent of medieval demons than anything human. "You bastard," she said tightly. "You great bloody bastard!" She rose from her seat slowly, crossed the distance between herself and Noah in carefully measured steps, and slapped him with all her considerable strength across his left cheek.

Noah was prepared for the blow and he accepted it without flinching. Only when Hilary backed away, gripping the folds of her wide skirt to keep her hands still, did he allow himself to relax. "Do you wish me to leave?" he asked.

Hilary's hip bumped the edge of a table. An oil lamp teetered. She managed to still it before it toppled. This small action, the normalcy of it, rooted her in reality again. "No," she said, crossing her arms in front of her to quiet their trembling. "No. You owe me more than what you've given me. I deserve and demand an explanation." Her bottom lip quavered slightly. "How could you do this to me, Noah?" she asked plaintively.

"I'm sorry, Hilary." The inadequacy of the words struck him on the raw, and he knew they did nothing to salve her wounds. "I fell in love."

She sucked in her breath. "You said you were in love with *me!*"

"I thought I was," he said, meeting her fiery eyes directly. "Jessa made me realize otherwise."

"Is it because you made her pregnant? Is that it?"

Hilary demanded, grasping at straws. "If you married her out of some gallant sense of obligation I can accept that," she went on quickly. "In time you can divorce her and we can still be married. We can weather the scandal. I'm willing to do that for you!"

"Then you should know I am unwilling. I love my wife, Hilary. I have no intention of divorcing her. Also, I am not Gideon's father. He is Jessa's child and I love him like a son, but he is not mine."

"You're going to accept someone's bastard child as your own?" she asked disbelievingly.

"Gideon is no one's bastard, Hilary," Noah said with more calm than he was feeling. "His parents were married."

Hilary turned away, clutching the table for support. "I cannot credit what you're telling me," she said lowly, her head bowed. "Why didn't you write? Why did you marry her there? Couldn't you have waited until you returned, shown me the civil courtesy of speaking with me first?"

"I didn't write because I thought it was an unacceptable means of communicating my intentions. In any event, the letter would not have reached you much before I arrived. Jessa and I were married very near the end of my visit to England, and no, I could not have waited to speak with you first."

Hilary spun around. "What you mean is that you were sniffing after her skirts! I salute the chit for demanding marriage before she allowed you to spread her legs! *I* should have been so uncompromising!" Her midnight blue eyes glittered coldly when Noah remained silent. "Well? Have you nothing to say?"

"I didn't believe your remarks deserved a response," he said evenly, "but if you insist, I will remind you that at no time did I ask you for something you were unwilling to give. More to the point, I don't remember asking on the first occasion. You were flatteringly eager to be intimate with me and you were not without experience."

Noah regretted having said that last as soon as the words were out of his mouth. He had not come to pitch stones at Hilary, yet that was precisely what he had done.

Her cheeks flushed and her indrawn breath hissed. "Damn you! How dare you say that to me now! No, you weren't my first lover! Or my second. Or even my third! Shall I tell you about my lovers?"

Noah forced himself to look at her though her pain cut through him. "Don't do this to yourself, Hilary. You don't have to make explanations to me. If you think for a moment you'll realize I cared nothing about men you had known before me."

"And you think that's flattering?" she asked, her voice rising.

Pressing one hand to his forehead, Noah released his breath slowly. "I put that very badly." But there was some truth in what he said, he realized unhappily, just as Hilary had divined. He had never been jealous enough to ask about her former relationships. "I meant that what happened before you met me was placed properly in the past. It had nothing to do with us. I asked you to marry me before I went to England, more than seven months ago." Belatedly he wondered if Hilary had heard him. She had gone to the window facing the street and was staring vacantly into the night. The lamplight below threw her beautiful profile into stark relief.

"Ah, yes," she said tonelessly, once more under control. "Your marriage proposal. How clever you were to make the offer *before* you went to England. A wedding trip, you said. Yet you knew full well that I would not take such a voyage."

Had he been clever? he wondered. Had he known even then, in some secret part of him, that he shouldn't marry Hilary, that he didn't love her enough? "I would have wed you before I left." That was true. He would have married her if she had agreed. It also would have been a grave mistake. He realized that now.

"So you said," she answered, implying she believed otherwise. "Since I refused we'll never know, will we?" Her short laugh held no humor. "I spent these months planning our wedding." She turned to face him. "I can't even tell people I broke with you before you left for London. It would be such a patent lie that I would seem more of a fool than you've already made me."

There was nothing Noah could say. He remained silent.

"Shall I tell you why I wouldn't go to England with you?"

"You've never made it any secret that you dislike the British."

"That's true, but you don't know why."

Noah wondered why she was addressing this now. He felt compelled to listen to her because it was all he had to offer. "I don't? You always said it was because your brother was killed at Yorktown."

"Yes, that's what I've said. And I've always been amazed that people accepted it so easily." She sneered. "You included. Evan and I were never even particularly close. We had one thing in common though. We were our father's pawns and during the war Papa played his pieces well."

"Hilary," he said gently. "Are you sure you want to go on?"

"Very sure," she answered. She returned to the table where the pastries were laid out. Smiling, she poured herself a cup of tea and added a dollop of sweet cream and sugar. "Tea makes it all seem very civil, doesn't it?" she asked, taking the chair opposite Noah once more. "I remember serving many cups of tea during the war," she continued quietly. "I was seventeen, no, I'm sorry, I was eighteen when British troops occupied the city. In general, the redcoats made their quarters where they pleased, but in some homes, like this one, they were welcome. Did you know that? Papa welcomed them in our house. You and I didn't know one another then, but I know where you were during that winter. Valley Forge. You see, Evan was there also. That's what I meant about Papa playing his pawns. Evan was his patriot. I was his Tory. Papa claimed to the British that he had disowned his son, that Evan was an irresponsible ruffian. To his revolutionary friends he said the British were quartered in his house against his will and that Evan was acting on principles he had learned at home."

Hilary sipped her lukewarm tea, her hands shaking ever so slightly. "In the midst of war Papa had found a way to show favor to both sides. No matter what the outcome, Papa believed he was safe from reprisal. He lost his son, of course, and I was . . . ," she shrugged with a forced air of indifference, ". . . and I was raped. But those were reprisals Papa could learn to live with. He still had his bank, his friends, his home . . . his slightly soiled daughter."

"Oh Jesus, Hilary," Noah said softly. "I don't—"

The dainty china teacup clattered against the saucer as Hilary set it in place. "Let me finish, Noah. And then I want you to leave."

He nodded, his eyes pained.

"All during that winter, while Evan was wondering where his next meal would come from, wondering whether his uniform would withstand the bitter cold, I played hostess to well-fed, warmly clothed British officers. It seemed ironic to me even then that the roles Papa forced on Evan and me suited neither one of us. I believed in the cause Evan would eventually die for. Evan never stopped hoping for eventual reconciliation with England. But gender, not ideology, determined our fates.

"Papa said I should be pleasant to the soldiers. He would later say, after the rape, that I was too pleasant, that I encouraged their attention in an unseemly manner. It had to be thus, he said. Why else would it happen not once, but twice? Two different men on two separate occasions."

Noah closed his eyes briefly. "Were the soldiers—"

"Punished? No. Papa asked me not to speak of it to anyone. And I haven't . . . until now." She set her cup and saucer on the nearby table. "I wanted you to know about those lovers, Noah, because I want you to understand how deeply I despise the British. Unreasonable, perhaps, to hold an entire people responsible for the vile acts by two of their red-breasted representatives, but that is my feeling, and nothing will change it." Hilary's eyes were bright with unshed tears. "There were other men after the war, but I was not an indiscriminate whore. Far from it. I earned and deserved my reputation as a snow queen. I relished it." The corners of her mouth lifted. Her smile was malevolent. "And occasionally I was able to have my revenge as well. Do you know that I took your brother Salem and your brother-in-law Jericho as my lovers?"

Noah's head shot up. It was on the tip of his tongue to say that she was lying, that he knew she had only attempted these things. He held himself back. She was lying because she wanted to hurt him, and strangely Noah realized he could only hurt *for* her. He stood. "I think I should go now, Hilary."

"It was the merest dalliance," she said, ignoring him. "I shouldn't want you to think my affections were engaged. My affections rarely were. I saved those for you."

"I regret I wasn't worthy of them."

She shrugged. "You can leave, Noah. I only ask that you support whatever story I give out."

"As long as Jessa and Gideon are not hurt by it, you may say what you will to salvage your pride. I would not deny you that."

She covered her mouth with the back of her hand to stifle a sob. "Generous to a fault."

"Good night, Hilary."

Hilary didn't move until she heard Noah leave the house, then she slid out of her chair and slumped to the floor. Burying her face in her hands, she cried brokenly, choking as tears clogged her throat. "This won't go unpunished, Noah McClellan," she whispered, her voice harsh. "You'll find I'm as worthy an adversary as any you've ever faced."

CHAPTER FOURTEEN

June, 1787

Lady Barbara Penberthy stared out the drawing room window, a vacant, distant look in her eyes. She did not see the gardeners trimming the boxwoods or the sheep grazing in the far field. The clear, cloudless beauty of the day was lost on her. Unconsciously her fingers twisted and knotted the lace handkerchief in her hands. When she spoke her voice barely broke a whisper. "I'll see her in hell for this."

"Damned if those ain't my words exactly," Ross Booker said, slapping his knee. "Imagine her bein' the one wot took the baby. It don't set right with me, spendin' all those months in Newgate for a little thievin' and her jest dancin' out of the country, fancy free and all."

Barbara slowly turned from the window. Not sparing a glance for the rough, ill-mannered man who had muddied her carpets and stained her seat covers, Barbara's cool emerald eyes sought her husband. "See that he's paid for his information, won't you?"

Edward Penberthy rose from his chair, nodded briefly to his wife, and motioned to their visitor to follow him. When he returned, Barbara was sitting down, her head resting against the scrolled, curving back of the chair, her eyes closed. She held a glass of red wine in her hands though it appeared she had not taken more than a few sips from it. Edward went to the sideboard and filled a crystal tumbler with whiskey. "Well," he demanded sharply. "Do you believe him?"

She took exception to his tone but did not remark on it. "Yes," she said. "I believe him, don't you?"

Edward merely shrugged. "This isn't the first story we've heard about Miss Winter since you decided to offer the reward. God, how I wish you had let the matter rest! By my count you've interviewed no less than two dozen people who say they know Miss Winter's whereabouts."

"True," she said, raising her head languidly. The tumbler in Edward's hands caught her attention as sunlight glinted off its edges. A prism of color flashed on the wall behind him. "Although this is the first story with the ring of truth. I believe Mr. Booker was very well acquainted with Jessica. He described her in vivid, though crude, terms."

"Most of the people we spoke with previously related similar descriptions," said Edward. "That information was given out to the papers at the beginning of the year."

Barbara's upper lip curled derisively. "Do you really think that foul man reads?" she asked. She held up her hand to stop him from pointing out that the same could be said of many of the others they had interviewed. "More to the point, Mr. Booker was released from Newgate the same day we saw Jessica in London. He says he sailed on the *Clarion* within hours after being released. Those things are easily checked, Edward, but I believe it would be prudent to use our time in other ways. You and I both knew it was very likely that Miss Winter was leaving the country that afternoon, and that is not something we shared with anyone. Mr. Booker could only know it because he saw her on board himself. The timing in his story is exact. Furthermore, he was able to describe the man accompanying Miss Winter. No one else was able to do that." Barbara's smile was faint but somehow managed to convey superiority. "Admit it, Edward. Mr. Booker is speaking the truth."

Edward sat down opposite his wife and plucked at a piece of lint on his blue satin breeches. "I admit that the timing would seem to support his story," he said after a moment's pause. "However, he knows the woman he spoke of only as Jessa McClellan. And apparently she is the wife of the owner of the *Clarion.*"

"I have heard Jessica is called Jessa by her friends. Come, Edward, you are flailing at the wind. Can you not grasp what has happened? She has somehow managed to inveigle this Noah McClellan into marrying her, or perhaps lured him into pretending marriage. The details are unimportant What is, is that she has a child. A *boy,* Edward."

"That should be proof that Booker's story is the merest coincidence of timing and detail. McClellan's wife is named Jessica, a common enough name. He calls her Jessa, simply a pet endearment. That she resembles Miss Winter is only wishful thinking on your part. They have a son. What of it? Many people do. This child's name is Gideon, not Adam. Adam Penberthy is buried in the family vault. You don't really think otherwise, do you?"

"I certainly do," she said, sipping her wine. "I have no idea how she managed it, but I will stake my life on the fact Adam Penberthy is very much alive. I only wish I had known it when we saw her in London. I would have allowed you to give chase." She placed her glass to the side and held her husband's probing stare without flinching. "You are forgetting that *we* saw the man she was with that day. He was exactly as Mr. Booker described this Mr. McClellan. Do you think that is a coincidence as well? I'm afraid it's you who is entertaining some wishful thinking. If you persist in these doubts I will make further inquiries, though I believe it will only delay us in acting on the facts."

"What inquiries could you possibly make?"

Barbara's hand turned upward in a graceful gesture. "Mr. Booker heard many things while on board the *Clarion* that can easily be checked. He knew, for instance, that Mr. McClellan had some sort of family business at Linfield and Stanhope and that his marriage was a recent one. Someone at one of those estates will give us more information. I'm certain we will discover that Mr. McClellan's bride was none other than Miss Winter. Do you really think it is necessary to involve so many people?" Her eyes narrowed shrewdly. "Perhaps even the authorities?"

Involvement with the authorities was the last thing Edward wanted. There were too many explanations to make, none of which boded well for his claim on the Penberthy estate. He drank deeply from his tumbler. "What is it you want to do, Barbara?" he asked tiredly.

"I should think you know the answer as well as I. Our position is not secure as long as Adam is alive. He can make a claim at any time."

"He's a *child*. It will be years before he can claim the estate, and it's doubtful he will be believed then. As far as everyone is concerned, Adam is dead. Indeed, you thought so until Booker mentioned the child."

"Miss Winter may make a claim on his behalf."

"Do you really think that's likely? Who will believe her? It's our word against hers. Isn't it better to leave affairs as they stand?"

"I think not, Edward. I can't go through the rest of my life looking over my shoulder. It was all very well when I thought Adam was dead, but now that I know differently I see things in a different light. It has always struck me odd that Miss Winter should abduct Adam days after we had our discussion concerning his ...

welfare. I've ofttimes wondered what you might have said to her that prompted her flight."

"I assure you, I said nothing," he lied easily. "It is more likely that she was listening at the door while we spoke."

Barbara didn't believe that for a moment but she let it pass. "I suppose it doesn't matter how she found out," she said. "But it seems clear to me that she knew Adam's life was threatened. No other explanation for her flight makes sense. And because she knows something she shouldn't, she is a constant danger to us. Seeing her in London made me realize we had been incautious in abandoning the search for her. Do you think I would have offered the reward for information about her otherwise? Knowing that Adam is alive only compounds the reasons we must do something about her. I tell you, Edward, the estate is not secure while she and Adam live."

"Bluntly stated," he said dryly. "What do you propose to do? If Booker has his facts in order, Miss Winter and Adam are an ocean away."

"True enough." She picked up her glass again and sipped thoughtfully. "But Mr. Booker knows their destination. I certainly don't suggest that we do anything so reckless as travel there ourselves. I propose that we allow Mr. Booker to take the matter in hand. I believe he will leap at the opportunity to revenge himself on your dear Miss Winter. She played him a nasty trick, didn't she? Leading him on, then crying rape. You are somewhat familiar with her penchant for that game, are you not?" She laughed shortly, humorlessly. "Aah, that still rankles. I can see it in your face. How fortunate you were that she did not scar you permanently. I suspect Mr. Booker was not so lucky."

"That man is a cretin."

"Of course he is, darling. How it must goad you to know that Miss Winter found him fascinating enough to give him a second glance." She stood up, making a pretense of smoothing her dark hair, though not a strand was out of place. "Well, m'lord? Do I have your permission to proceed?"

"I don't like this, Barbara."

"I know you don't," she said soothingly. She touched his shoulder as she walked past him. "It is a credit to your conscience that you entertain doubts. I don't require an answer today. Mr. Booker told us where he is lodging. It shouldn't be difficult to locate him. Reflect at length on what I've told you, Edward. I am confident that you will come to realize our choices are really very limited."

When Barbara was gone from the room Edward finished his whiskey and poured another. He was very much afraid his wife was correct. Jessica was biding her time, willing to wait years if need be in order to make Adam's claim on the estate. That would be her way. Edward believed he knew her well enough to make that judgment of her character. She had gone to enormous lengths to make them believe that Adam was dead. He had been less certain than Barbara that the infant found in the woods was Adam, but in time he had come to accept it. Now he realized that Jessica had made a fool of him. She couldn't possibly believe that he would protect her forever, could she? Not when she had allowed herself to be seen in London.

It seemed immaterial to Edward whether or not he gave approval to Barbara's scheme. It was highly doubtful that he could stop her from dealing with Ross Booker on her own. His wife was nothing if not resourceful. The dilemma for Edward was of a different nature, one that Barbara only suspected. He had to decide if he should warn Jessica. He had done so once. Should he do so again?

The question only formed in his mind a moment before the answer echoed resoundingly in his head. *No.* He could not warn her in person, and to commit anything to paper was to give Jessa proof she did not now

Jo Goodman

possess. A letter would incriminate him, and Edward was not so foolish as to take that course of action.

Tossing back his whiskey, Edward threw the tumbler into the cold hearth, shattering it. Having made his decision, he left the drawing room in search of his wife.

June fell away into July, July into August. The summer days were unrelievedly hot, the nights muggy. Though the weather took on a sameness that left many Philadelphians irritable and weary, Jessa did not count herself among them. Her life had never seemed so full, rich or comfortable.

In June, Gideon found his land legs—as Cam and Noah were inspired to call them. The infant traveled helter-skelter about the house after that, never crawling when he could walk, never walking when he could run. He barreled forward on the balls of his feet, usually stopping because he ran into something. The top and bottom of the stairs were barricaded with furniture until Henry fashioned gates for each end.

Gideon had his first birthday in July and made a pig of himself with the lemon ices Noah brought home to celebrate the occasion. There were gifts for him from the landing in addition to those shyly given by Cam, Henry, Sally, and Mrs. Harper. Overwhelmed by these kindnesses, Jessa held back her happy tears until the beautifully carved rocking horse was delivered, only minutes after Noah's arrival. Then she flung herself onto Noah's lap and told him he was the most generous man on the face of the earth. Noah pointed out the horse was for Gideon, not her, and she responded to his dry humor by pinching him lightly on the thigh. That night he gave her a gold wedding band. They did not sleep for making love.

Gideon developed four more pearl-white teeth, stopped chewing on furniture, and learned how to say no and mean it. He understood his name, dropped blocks in a box, and gleefully dumped them out again. He loved noise, loved making it even more.

While Gideon's accomplishments, large and small, marked many of Jessa's days, there were other moments she remembered with equal clarity, moments filled solely with the things Noah had done. There was the Sunday he took her out in the country and they picnicked by the banks of the Schuylkill, an afternoon reminiscent of the one they had spent at the landing. This time there was no passing schooner to interrupt their pleasure.

Some days he would come home ineffably tired, weary of the endless disagreement among the delegates at the State House. The plans for revising the Articles had long since been abandoned in favor of drafting an entirely new document. The challenge was enormous because nothing quite like it existed anywhere in the world.

There were occasions when Noah would grumble that he should take his leave as most of the New York delegation had done. When he was especially disgusted he wished aloud that Virginia had been as wise as Rhode Island and never sent a delegation at all. He complained because, in spite of the heat, Ben Franklin wouldn't let them open the windows in the assembly room. A combination, Noah said, of their need for secrecy and the horseflies, though he was inclined to think the horseflies were the deciding factor. Rarely was Noah's dissatisfaction wasted on some petty issue, however. The discord among the delegates was a constant source of discouragement. Compromise seemed the order of the day, and he despaired of ever creating a constitution the states would ratify. Once he had gotten as far as taking out his valises in order to pack. Jessa saw them and hurriedly sent Cam to find James Madison and bring him to the house. Mr. Madison, small of stature and large in purpose and principle, convinced Noah to stay.

Noah was not grateful for Jessa's interference. Quite the opposite. He brooded for two days before he had the grace to accept that she had acted in his best interests. The arguments at home were more intense than anything occurring on the assembly floor. The compromise, when reached, was infinitely more satisfying.

Jessa, feeling secure in Noah's love, accepted there would always be disagreements, even rows. Never once was she tempted to run. The unhappy moments were far surpassed by the happier ones as they both made adjustments to married life.

She engraved memories for a lifetime that summer. There were carriage rides after sunset, evening strolls along the thoroughfares. They attended plays and entertained delegates in their home. There were quiet conversations in the front parlor as they discussed their future plans. Frequently they shared laughter over some silly antic of Gideon's. Jessa wrote often to Charity and Robert, sharing with them the happiness she had found with their son.

"Would you look at this, Jessa?" Noah complained, showing her his neckcloth.

Jessa moved toward the edge of the bed and squinted at the small, greenish stain on the white material as he waved it in front of her. "What is it?" she asked, propping a pillow behind her back and leaning against the headboard. Languidly she fanned her neck and face with the Chinese fan Noah had purchased for her. "Would you open the window please?"

"It's peas," he mumbled, groaning as he struggled with the heat-swollen window frame. "That's what it is."

"Yes, dear. I think you're right."

Noah batted at a fly that buzzed past his head as soon as he opened the window. "I know you're laughing at me," he said. "I take strong exception to that."

"Of course you do," she said serenely. "No man likes to be laughed at."

"Hah!" he snorted, jerking off his neckcloth. "No

man likes to entertain a half-dozen guests with pea stains on his person. You should have said something to me."

"I would have, if I had noticed."

"Franklin noticed."

"Did he? I hadn't realized. What an odd man he is to point it out to you. But then he is so old that he can say the most outrageous things without anyone taking exception. Surely you explained that you and Gideon had a small battle of wills earlier at dinner." Her laughter broke to the surface. "Did you tell him who the winner was?"

"He divined that from the state of my neckcloth," Noah said, hard pressed not to grin. "I refuse to give our son a spoon again until he sports his first whisker. Gideon can eat with his fingers until then. He is simply not to be trusted." Noah slipped off his jacket and unbuttoned his vest, then dropped into the rocker and kicked off his shoes. "What do you think of that?"

"I think in a week or so you'll be trying to teach him how to use the spoon again. And when he succeeds you'll take the lion's share of the credit for raising such an intelligent, well-mannered little boy."

Noah chuckled. "You know me too well." He rolled down his stockings and dropped them over the arm of the chair. Sighing, he stretched and wiggled his toes.

Jessa smiled at him. "You look utterly exhausted," she said. "Come to bed."

"In a moment. I can't garner the energy to move from this chair. Actually, I'm a bit surprised to find you still awake. When you retired earlier I thought you meant to go to sleep."

The fan stirred Jessa's hair. Short, fine strands tickled her face. "I meant to. I couldn't. I hope your guests did not think ill of me for leaving them so early."

Noah shook his head. "They were disappointed, Ben in particular. He admires your, er, charms greatly."

"He's a rogue."

"A discerning one." He frowned slightly. "Did we overtire you, Jessa? James seemed to think we had."

"Not at all. I knew you were anxious to discuss strategies for tomorrow's debate. I felt I should allow you the opportunity to do so."

"That's what I told them. Now I'm wondering if that's true. Of late you seem tired."

"It's the heat. I'm still finding it difficult to adjust. England is never so hot as this."

Noah's brows drew together thoughtfully. His eyes glanced over Jessa's face, the serene purity of her features. "Is there something you're not telling me, Jessa? Something . . . I don't know? . . ."

Jessa took pity on him because he looked at once anxious and hopeful. These were not the surroundings in which she had planned to tell him. She had envisioned a romantic dinner or perhaps a return to their picnicking spot. She had definitely not foreseen the possibility that he would be slumped in the rocker, his long legs stretched in front of him, his beautiful face drawn equally with fatigue and concern. "You're bent on spoiling my surprise, you terrible man."

Noah rose from the chair and sat on the edge of the bed. "Surprise?"

"Yes, my surprise. Though it shouldn't be one as often as we've . . . well, you take my meaning."

"You can be irritatingly indirect at times, Jessa. Can you explain yourself more clearly?"

She folded her fan and tapped him on the back of his wrist with it. "You know very well what I'm saying. I'm going to have your child, Noah."

Noah blinked. "Do you mean it?" he asked, his voice not much above a whisper.

Snapping open her fan, Jessa waved it in front of his face a few times. "Of course I mean it. Has the heat addled your senses?" She laughed when he growled playfully, grabbed the fan, and tossed it aside. Taking her delicate wrists in his, he drew her close. "Aaah," she said wisely, her lips a mere moment from his. "I see you do believe me."

Noah kissed her, reverently at first, then with deep adoring passion. "How long have you known?" he asked, his hands framing her face. Her pale gray eyes reflected color from the candlelight as she held his gaze.

"Only a few days. I wanted to be certain before I told you."

"And you are? Certain, that is?"

"Very certain. I visited Dr. Markum this morning. He was quite happy to tell me that my fatigue, weepy moods, and upset stomach had a reasonable explanation."

"You've had morning sickness, then?"

"No. In the afternoon. Dr. Markum assured me it is as normal as the other."

"I hadn't noticed you being particularly weepy."

"That's because I've done most of my crying when you were gone from the house. It's really the most annoying thing, Noah. It happens with almost no warning, aggravated by the merest trifling occurrences. I think Mrs. Harper suspects my condition, though she has refrained from saying anything."

"How many weeks are you?"

"I make it to be ten."

Noah digested that information. His eyes dropped to her abdomen to see if he could make out any swelling. He grinned happily as Jessa divined his thoughts and drew his hands to her belly. "You're still flat," he said, vaguely disappointed.

"Give us time," she laughed. "And enjoy it while you can. I'll be as big as a cow before long."

"Hardly," he scoffed. "Are you pleased about the baby, Jessa?"

"Yes. Very much. And you?"

"I think it's wonderful."

Jessa squeezed his hand, her eyes anxious. "This child won't make a difference, will it?"

"A difference? In what way?"

"In the way you feel about Gideon." Almost immediately Jessa realized her doubts had hurt Noah. "I'm sorry. I know that you love him. I just don't want that to change when we have children of our own."

"Gideon *is* our child," said Noah. "I don't anticipate loving him any less, and I can't imagine how I could love him more than I already do. All my life I shall be in his debt."

Jessa's head tilted to one side. "What debt?"

"He's responsible for bringing us together."

She laughed. "And all this time I was thanking the horse that came up lame on your way to Stanhope."

He tasted the laughter on her lips. "Him, too." He kissed her again, this time sliding his arms around her.

"Noah?"

"Hmmm?"

"It's too hot."

Noah drew back. "What's that again?"

Jessa groped among the covers for her fan. She opened it and began fanning herself. "I'm miserably uncomfortable. If you could propose a way to make love without touching, I'd be happy to participate. Before you came in I was daydreaming about thundershowers and blizzards and was giving serious consideration to throwing myself in the river."

Noah plucked at his shirt, which was clinging damply to his chest. "Point taken." He took the fan from her. "Lean back. That's good. Raise your chin a notch." He was tempted to kiss her exposed throat. Instead he fanned it. "Better?"

Jessa closed her eyes. "Wonderful," she sighed.

"You know, the river's not a bad idea. What do you think of a midnight swim?"

"It's well after midnight."

"Don't quibble with details. We can take the carriage."

"We'd have to wake Henry to get it from the stable, then we'd have to tell Mrs. Harper or Cam that we're leaving so one of them can listen for Gideon in the event he wakes. I think we should simply stay here and you should fan me forever. Or at least until I fall asleep."

He dropped a kiss on the curve of her shoulder. When he drew back Jessa had roused enough energy to open one eye, raise one brow, and manage a credibly suspicious look. "Sorry," he said with absolutely no remorse. "I couldn't resist. You look delicious."

"You're ridiculous." Still, she felt pleased.

"Here," he said. "Take the fan. I've been inspired." He jumped off the bed.

"Where are you going?" she asked when he opened the door.

"I'll be back."

"But that wasn't . . ." Noah disappeared into the hallway. ". . . what I asked," she finished lamely.

Noah returned ten minutes later awkwardly toting four buckets. Water sloshed on the floor as he carried them into the dressing room. "One more trip," he said, stopping her question. The second trip took less time. He filled the copper tub in the dressing room, lighted all the available candles, then scooped Jessa up from the bed and carried her in. "Madam's bath," he said grandly setting her on her feet. "Cool water, I may add."

Jessa dipped her toes in the tub. "Cold water," she corrected him.

"Too cold?"

She shook her head, raising the hem of her shift and stepping into the tub. "I can get used to this."

"Good." Noah stripped off his shirt and loosened his breeches and drawers.

"Noah! What are you—But there's no room for—"

Noah braced his spine against the sloping back of the tub and his legs against either side. Jessa sat facing him, knees drawn toward her chest. She could feel Noah's toes wiggling beneath her buttocks.

"You were saying?" he asked pleasantly.

"It appears I was wrong." Her voice was dry. "We've

room enough for guests if we want them." She flicked water at him. "Stop that!"

"What?" He nudged her with his toes again.

"That! How would you feel if I did that to you?"

"Tickled?"

Pursing her lips, Jessa tried to look stern. The effort was wasted on Noah. He merely grinned at her, his expression boyish and sly. Jessa took the washcloth that was folded over the edge of the tub and dipped it in the water. She raised her face, squeezing droplets of water on her neck and shoulders.

"I think the baby's made your breasts larger," Noah said conversationally.

Jessa was tempted to throw the washcloth at him, but she was afraid that's what he wanted. She'd have to fight to get it back. "Oh? How can you tell?" Her knees were modestly covering her chest.

"They're spilling over."

Jessa glanced down at herself. Her breasts were indeed curved above the rounded caps of her knees. "So they are. But that's not because of the baby. That's because you have me squeezed in this tub the way fish are packed in a barrel."

"Are you that uncomfortable?" he asked, concerned. He put his hands on either side of the tub and started to rise.

"Sit down!" she laughed. "I'm just fine."

Jessa eased her legs forward a bit and leaned toward Noah. She wiped his forehead, cheeks, and throat with the damp cloth. "You're not sorry we didn't go to the river?"

"Flexibility is one of my virtues."

Pausing, Jessa looked at the manner in which Noah was folded in the tub. "It certainly is."

He peeked at her through his lashes and saw she was admiring his form. "I was speaking of flexibility of thought," he said, closing his eyes quickly when she glanced at him. "Not of body." The temperature of the water did nothing to stop the heat that was uncurling inside him. If Jessa's hands dipped a fraction lower from where they rested on his thighs, she was bound to notice. He nearly came out of his skin as she dragged the wash-cloth over the inside of his leg to his knee.

"Yes," she said thoughtfully. "I realize that now. Your body is not as flexible as it first appeared. In fact . . . parts of it are, umm, quite rigid." One hand slid under the water. Delicately her fingers curled around him. "You don't suppose that we could . . . umm, you know . . . here in the water?"

Noah's response was a slow, lazy smile. *"Umm, you know?* You're phrasing lacks much in the way of clarity. Strive to be less ambiguous, please."

Jessa rearranged herself in the tub so she was sitting on her knees between his parted legs. She placed her hands on his shoulders, bent forward, and whispered in his ear.

Noah's brows shot up, his eyes opened wide. "Jessa!"

"You wanted clarity," she said defensively, flushing deeply.

"Well, I certainly got it. And to think you want all that here in the tub. It quite boggles the mind. The logistics alone would require weeks of planning."

"Fool," she said, shutting him up by kissing him soundly. "Take me to bed."

"Happily."

They didn't make it that far. Jessa's water slick body rubbed against him invitingly as he helped her out of the tub. Without a word passing between them they unanimously decided the dressing room floor would serve as well as any bed.

Noah's body cushioned Jessa as she spread kisses over his face and throat, loving the salty-sweet taste of his skin. Her tongue flicked at droplets of water on his neck. Her fingers teased his flat nipples into hardness. The palm of her hand was filled with his heartbeat.

She was not neglected while she touched him. Noah

stroked her skin, raising sparks of heat along Jessa's spine. His fingers pressed the dimples at the small of her back and she wriggled against him. Their legs tangled, rubbed. The contrast in textures, the friction, was delightful.

Jessa sat up, straddling Noah's waist. The backs of his fingers lightly caressed her breasts. Her hair fell over her shoulders, mingling with his fingers.

"Do you remember that dream you once had?" she asked, dipping her head quickly to place a fleeting kiss on his mouth. "The one about us?"

"I've had a lot of dreams about us."

"Have you? How nice." She kissed him again. "But I'm talking about the one where we were making love like this. The one you had when you were healing from your wound."

"Aah. That one. I remember it vividly."

"There's good reason for that," she said, shifting her body lower. She gasped as Noah turned suddenly so that she was under him. His lips worried the tip of each breast in turn, making her nipples pearl-hard and achingly sensitive. Jessa nearly forgot what she had been saying. "It really happened," she managed to get out just as Noah's teeth tugged gently.

Noah looked up, bracing himself on his forearms. "What?"

"It really happened."

"That's not possible. The first time we made love was on the *Clarion.*"

Jessa wound her arms around Noah's neck. She pulled him close, kissing him deeply. "Mmmm. It was." He kissed her temples, her cheeks, pressed his mouth to the soft spot directly behind her lobe. "But the first time I was with you like this—naked as the day, I mean— was in Mary's cottage. I pretended that we were lovers for the benefit of the sergeant who was searching for the highwaymen."

"You did?" he murmured, raising his head. "How

enterprising of you." He fanned out her hair with his fingers. "And what did I do while you were taking advantage of me?"

"Nothing," she said cheekily. "You just lay there. Still, you were very convincing." She tilted her head to one side and rubbed her cheek against Noah's hand. "The sergeant thought Mary's cottage was a trysting place and that I was a great lady conducting an illicit affair with my virile gardener."

"Groom."

"What?"

"If I had to be your, *er virile* anything, I should much prefer to have been your groom. Snipping hedgerows and plucking posies doesn't bring to mind an image of robust manhood." He moved slightly so that she could feel his hardness against her belly. "Anyway, you were riding me then. Just the sort of thing a grand lady would do to her groom."

"I . . . umm . . . take your meaning."

"Like that, do you?"

"I'd like it better if you were inside me."

"Your servant, ma'am." Noah kissed her. Once. Twice. She moved impatiently beneath him, her thighs parting for his entry. Noah teased her, entering her slowly, testing her control as well as his own. Jessa didn't seem to care that she lost. She raised her hips, taking him fully into her, and wrapped her legs around him.

"Have a care to please your lady," she said huskily as Noah began to move.

He did. Noah drew out their pleasure just this side of forever. The hot night air lay like a blanket on their bodies, but it was nothing compared to the shimmering heat that passed between them. Her hands caressed his back, and the pads of her fingertips pressed into his shoulders. Her body moved with him in rhythms as ancient and natural as the ebb and flow of tide. The shape of their world changed so that they alone existed. They did not hear the town crier announcing the hour, nor the clatter of a carriage on the cobblestones below their window. There was nothing or no one who mattered beyond the moment. Their souls were filled, their bodies embraced the loving in their hearts.

Noah held himself back until Jessa shuddered beneath him. He tasted his name on her lips as she cried out then he joined her, whispering the words that gave meaning to the pleasure they shared.

"I love you," she echoed softly, her eyes shining

Noah eased himself off her and turned on his side. One leg still held her possessively. "I take it milady was well pleased."

She laughed shyly. "Yes. But that isn't why I love you."

"I know," he husked, bending his head to nuzzle her neck. "But it's awfully nice, isn't it?"

"Wonderfully nice," she sighed. "I barely noticed the floor."

"Praise indeed." He caressed her hip. "Come on, back to bed." He sat up and pulled her up as well. "Think you can sleep now?"

"For days."

Noah got to his feet and held out his hands to Jessa. When she took them he helped her up with a quick movement that brought her flush against his body. "Your breasts *are* larger," he teased, scooping her up in his arms.

"Noah! I can walk!"

"I know. But why should you when I enjoy this so much?" He dropped her on the bed and was instantly contrite as she groaned and rolled away, rubbing her bottom. "I didn't hurt you, did I? I forgot about the babe."

"Idiot. The babe's fine. It's my posterior that's been sorely abused."

Relieved, Noah padded back to the dressing room and snuffed out the candles. When he returned to the bed Jessa was already under the thin sheet. She held it up for him. He slid in beside her, not too close because the heat was oppressive again. "It would have been worse in the tub," he told her. "You'd ache all over."

Jessa yawned. "Yes, but so would you."

Chuckling, Noah turned back the bedside lamp. "Good night, Jessa."

"G'night."

Jessa's soft-edged rosy world lasted until dinner the following evening. Gideon had already eaten by the time Noah returned home, so Jessa and Noah had the dining room to themselves. A basket of fresh flowers claimed the center of the table. Their fragrance was appealing, yet elusive. Mrs. Harper had taken care to set places for Noah and Jessa at the same end of the table. She breezed in and out of the room, her eyes sparkling as she served up their dinner.

Noah looked at Jessa over the rim of his wineglass. "Whatever has set Mrs. Harper in this mood?" he asked. "She's been smiling at me since I walked in the door. I think she was humming when she left."

"She thinks you're a wonderful man." Jessa raised her glass to his and touched it lightly. "So do I."

Noah felt his smile fading. "You told her about the child, didn't you?" His voice was not as casual as he hoped it would be.

Jessa's eyes clouded with confusion. "I didn't know it was meant to be a secret. I told you I thought she suspected. I simply confirmed it."

He set his glass down. "I wish you hadn't." He picked up his knife and fork and attacked the thin slices of rare roast beef on his plate. "Who else knows?"

"Sally. Henry. I told Cam this afternoon. I wrote to your mother but I haven't posted the letter yet. Why don't you want anyone to know? Are you ashamed?"

"That, perhaps, is the most ridiculous thing you've ever asked me. Of course I'm not ashamed. In other circumstances I'd have the town crier announce it to Philadelphia at large."

Jessa frowned. "What circumstances prevent you from doing that now?"

"Hilary," he said tersely. "I don't want her to know."

Jessa didn't understand, but she accepted it. "All right. I won't tell her. Not that I was thinking of it in the first place. Hilary crosses to the other side of the street if she sees me coming."

In Jessa's collection of summer memories Hilary Bowen was the single person Jessa wished she could forget. Most days she did not think at all of Hilary, then she would see her unexpectedly on the street or in a passing carriage, and Jessa would scarcely be able to think of anything else. Hilary had not honored Noah's wishes not to use Jessa and Gideon to salvage her own pride. She was not only a vicious gossip, she was a subtle one, telling her lies as if they were merely unfortunate slips of the tongue. She let it be known that Gideon was a bastard and Jessa had required a name for her child. She managed to leave the impression that Jessa had schemed to be alone with Noah so it might appear she had been compromised. The marriage was a forced one. She also told the tale of how Noah, upon his arrival home, had confided all and begged her to be his mistress. A shocking proposition, she said, and one which she unequivocally refused.

Jessa had known a certain amount of notoriety during June and part of July as the stories were spread and elaborated upon. Commenting on them seemed tantamount to admitting there was truth in the tales. Jessa preferred to keep her silence. Then Hilary had gone to nurse her grandfather at his country home in Germantown, and without her presence in the city to provide fodder for the gossips the rumors had quietly died.

"I hadn't even realized Hilary had returned to the city," she continued when Noah kept scowling. Really, she thought, dismayed by his mood, he could look positively menacing when he scowled like that.

"She arrived today. Don't you recall? Her grandfather died a week ago."

"I'm sorry to hear that," she said sincerely. "But this is the first I've heard of it."

"I told you Quincy Hearn passed on. Mrs. Harper and Sally even attended the services."

"What all of you neglected to mention, perhaps intentionally, was that Mr. Hearn was Hilary's grandfather. How should I be expected to know that? Their names aren't the same."

"That's because he was her mother's father."

"I surmise that now," she snapped, adopting Noah's attitude. She stabbed a potato with her fork. "So. How am I to keep Hilary from learning of my condition? It's certain to be obvious to the meanest intelligence in a few months."

Listening to Jessa's waspish tone, Noah belatedly realized how surly and short-tempered he must appear to her. She did not suspect that he was more afraid than angry. "God," he drawled feelingly. "I hope we're not here as long as that. I make it to be three or four weeks before the delegation is disbanded—perhaps in middle or late September." He dropped his fork and touched Jessa's wrist lightly as she was cutting her meat with angry, measured motions. "I'm sorry, Jessa. I've been behaving badly."

Not sparing him a glance, she shook off his touch. "Yes, you have. And for no reason I can comprehend. What can it possibly matter if Hilary knows I'm going to have a child?"

"It shouldn't matter, but I fear that it will. I can't imagine Hilary accepting the news graciously, can you?"

"Her gossip need not touch us."

"It touched us before. I came within a hair's breadth of strangling Sally for repeating Hilary's tales to you. She should have had better sense. I don't doubt that she's told half a dozen friends by now that you're expecting.''

"She's happy for me."

"I'm sure she is. However, Hilary won't be. And she's certain to find out. This is going to cut her to the quick."

Jessa picked up her wineglass and drank deeply, troubled by this turn in the conversation. "I didn't think you cared any longer for what Hilary thinks or feels."

"Don't misunderstand me, Jessa," Noah said quickly. His green-gold eyes searched her face. "I'm only trying to anticipate how Hilary may react to this news. She tried very hard to make people believe that I wanted her as my mistress. She took to following me, running into me when I was out alone or with friends, then making it seem as if I were doing the chasing. She—"

"You never told me that," she interrupted, her voice faintly accusing.

"Perhaps I should have. But at the time I didn't want to further complicate our lives. I didn't want to bring Hilary's name and her sharp little viper's tongue into this house. It seemed pointless to trouble you with her actions. Then she left for her grandfather's and there was no reason to speak of her at all."

"Surely it's better that she know about the baby, Noah. She'll see it's quite hopeless to entertain thoughts that you'll go back to her."

Noah shook his head. "If only I could believe that. I think it's far more likely that she'll feel the fool. She delicately implied that you and I were not the loving couple we portrayed to others. She purposely allowed people to believe we were not intimate. Since I couldn't very well make love to you in the center of town, Hilary enjoyed her lies without fear of being found out. I don't think she ever considered that you might become pregnant."

"Because she never did," Jessa said softly.

"I wasn't going to say that," he said, looking away, "but you're correct."

Jessa didn't respond immediately. She touched the centerpiece, brushing her knuckles across the petals of a blood red rose. "I can't help but feel sorry for her, Noah," she said finally. "After all that she's been through I can scarcely hold her accountable for the things she says or does. She's been hurt very badly—and not only by you. Perhaps it's not right, but I blame Hilary's father for what she has become. He failed her far more than she imagines you did. As I recall, you expressed much the same sentiment when you returned from her house that night. Yet your feelings seemed to have changed with time. I can only surmise it's because you perceive Hilary has hurt Gideon and me with her lies."

"Hasn't she?"

"Gideon's not a whit troubled," she answered, smiling faintly. "None of this has touched him. As for myself, the hurt is only a small one. I care more that your reputation has been sullied than anything else." Her shoulders straightened a little and she went on tartly, "I find it incredible that anyone, knowing your intelligence and your cleverness, could possibly credit Hilary's story that I tricked you into marrying me."

Noah's brows rose slightly and his lips twitched with amusement. "Did you hear what you just said? If Hilary only knew how close she came to the truth!" Trust Jessa to make him want to laugh. God, how he loved her!

"Yes, well, *we* know what the truth is, but that anyone else should believe such rubbish is beyond my comprehension. I wouldn't care that people think I'm a schemer if it did not reflect so poorly on you."

Noah shook his head, trying to clear it. Jessa's logic had a way of fogging his brain. "So you're saying that Hilary has only hurt you through me."

"Yes."

"And she has hurt me by saying things against you."

Jessa nodded. "They're only words, Noah. We can decide how much we'll let them bother us. If I didn't pity Hilary I'd have scratched her eyes out long ago. Sometimes I think that in her place I wouldn't behave half so well."

"You think I'm making too much of her return, don't you?"

"Hmm-mm. She's been out of the city for weeks and it's quite likely that she's had time to reflect. Why should she want to stir trouble again? If you like I'll ask Sally not to speak to anyone about the baby. She won't say anything."

"If she hasn't already."

"In that event we can be prepared for Hilary to hear of it, though what she can possibly do or say to hurt us is beyond me. The people who matter most to you don't attend to idle gossip."

Noah wished he were as confident and unconcerned as Jessa. He was less afraid of anything Hilary might say and more of something she might do. His sympathy for Hilary was increasingly overshadowed by examples of her vindictiveness. He could not find it within him any longer to make the same allowances for her spiteful behavior that Jessa did.

"You could be right," he said. "Nevertheless, I'll be happy to return to Virginia."

Jessa's eyes brightened. "I almost forgot!" she exclaimed, snapping her fingers and practically leaping out of her chair. She hurried from the dining room and returned moments later waving a letter in front of her. "This came this morning from the landing." She gave it to Noah and took her seat again. "I didn't want to open it since it was addressed specifically to you. That's not your father's handwriting, is it?"

Noah wiped his knife with a napkin then used it to break the seal on the packet. "No, it's Jericho's writing. Oh, there's more than one letter here. This is for you. From Mother." Noah handed it to her. "Here's something from Courtney as well. Ah, I see why Jericho put it all together. Apart from his note, there's a letter from Drew Goodfellow."

"Drew? How nice." Jessa leaned closer to Noah as he opened the missive. "What does he have to say?"

"Wouldn't you like to know?" he teased, holding the letter away from her. He scanned the first few paragraphs quickly. "All I can say, Jessa McClellan, is that it's a very good thing you told me the truth months ago, because you've been found out."

"What!"

"Calm yourself, darling. It's not what you think. Drew's not told anyone. I wrote to Drew while we were still aboard the *Clarion* and asked him to discover what he could about you. Don't fly into the boughs. I had my reasons. If you recall, you were less than honest with me then. Actually, I had forgotten about the letter by the time we reached the landing but Cam, being the helpful sort that he is, sent it out. It appears Drew had little difficulty in establishing your identity. Will Shaw has a loose tongue when he's deep in his cups."

"Will! How could he!" She threw up her hands in disgust. "What a brainless chatterbox he is. I should have strangled him after he shot you."

"That would have done the trick," Noah said dryly. He continued to read. "Drew says that the Penberthys had offered a reward for information concerning your whereabouts. It didn't mean anything to him then. It wasn't until he received my letter and talked to Mary and Davey Shaw, and eventually Will, that he assembled the pieces properly." Noah paused, checking the date on the letter. "He wrote this shortly after he heard from me, some six weeks ago. There's no indication that the Penberthys had any success with their reward."

"What if Will speaks to them?"

"I don't think that's likely. Drew gained Will's confidence because they share a bit of smuggling in their past. According to Drew, when Davey found out he threatened to cut out Will's tongue with a dull knife if he ever spoke of those things again.''

Jessa grimaced at the grisly image. "How did Davey know Will talked?"

Noah folded the letter and slipped it in his deep jacket pocket. "Drew told him. Drew wanted to be certain Will was not so easily taken in again. It would seem that Drew's become your champion, Jessa. He sends his best regards and begs that I find it in my heart to forgive you for—how did he put it?—oh, yes, the falsehoods occasioned by your complete devotion to the child. Very prettily said, don't you think?"

Jessa didn't care about that. "Have you, Noah?" she asked anxiously. "Have you forgiven me?"

Noah removed the letters from Jessa's hands. They were crumpled and limp from the tight hold she had had on them. His fingers encircled her wrists and he drew Jessa out of her chair and onto his lap. "There was never anything to forgive," he said.

Some minutes later Mrs. Harper peeked in the dining room to see if Jessa and Noah were ready for dessert. They definitely were *not.* She shut the door hastily and fanned her heated face. Certain appetites, she thought primly, should be confined to the bedroom.

CHAPTER FIFTEEN

September, 1787

It was not a coincidence that they met. Their intentions were similar, their goals shared. They were motivated by a singular purpose. That their paths eventually crossed was more inevitable than surprising. Still, at the first meeting, Hilary was naturally wary.

"I beg your pardon," she said coolly, tightening her grip on the parcels she held. "Did you speak to me?" The man tipping his hat to her was handsome in a bearish sort of way. His features had been molded with a rough regard for the details that made a man attractive to women. Short strands of hair that were neither brown nor blond, but some mixture of the two, fluttered across his broad forehead before he lowered his hat again. His eyes were deep set and so dark they appeared to be black. In spite of the smile that lifted the corners of his wide mouth, his eyes remained strangely flat and somehow cold. His jaw was square cut, his nose and the planes of his cheeks blunt. He had powerful shoulders and large hands. As Hilary's eyes glanced over him,

taking his measure, he shrugged and stuffed his hands
into the pockets of his navy blue jacket.

"Ye know I did," he said bluntly, rocking slightly on
the balls of his feet. "Ain't likely I was talkin' to meself.
I'm not daft."

Hilary turned to go. It was merely unfortunate the
man was rough spoken. That he was also English was
beyond bearing. His accent grated harshly on her ears.

Ross Booker fell in step beside her. "Yer not interested in what I 'ave to say?" he asked. She was a cool
one, he'd give her that. Lovely to look at, too. She
thought he was beneath her, of course, not worthy of
her attention, but Ross had seen the fleeting interest
in her eyes. He'd wager all the blunt Lady Barbara had
given him on that.

"Hardly." She stopped. "Will you kindly leave me
be. I have no qualms about calling a constable." She
waited, tapping her foot impatiently. Her figure was
reflected in the bakery shop window where Molly Wren
was placing a tray of fresh three-penny loaves. Hilary
returned Mrs. Wren's wave. "Well?"

"You can call the constable or that woman in the
shop if you've a mind to," Ross said. "But I'll be tellin'
anyone you call that Mr. McClellan is a mite tired of
you doggin' 'is footsteps and I'm 'ired to see that it
stops."

Hilary's head jerked up in surprise. "What are you
talking about?"

Though she strove to keep her voice calm the effort
was insufficient. Ross saw that she was visibly shaken by
his declaration. It was an encouraging sign. "Perhaps
we could speak somewhere more private," he suggested.

"I'm not going anywhere with you."

"Me carriage is over there," he said, pointing across
the street and down one block. He felt a surge of pride
every time he looked at his fancy rig and matched set
of cinnamon mares. Lady Barbara had been generous
with her coin, and Ross believed he was putting it to

good use. His clothes, his carriage, and his mounts made a pleasing first impression. He was no longer one of the rabble. "It's in yer best interests t'accept me invitation."

Hilary hesitated. "What did you mean that Mr. McClellan hired you?"

"I'll tell ye about it while we ride. Ye best come now. Mr. McClellan isn't one to spend long in a tavern. He'll be leavin' soon and nothin' good will come of 'im seein' us together."

That decided Hilary. She didn't want Noah to see her, not if he was already aware she was following him. "I'll choose the route we take."

"Fair enough."

"One more thing."

"Yes?"

"I don't know your name."

"Booker, Miss Bowen. Ross Booker."

Hilary sat back in the carriage, pleased that it was as comfortable as it was handsome. She did not mind being seen with Mr. Booker, his physical presence was agreeable, his clothes a cut above the common mode, but she despaired that he would speak too loudly and draw attention to his crude command of the language. After a few minutes she realized her fears were unfounded. Mr. Booker was not eager to have his conversation overheard. He explained as soon as the carriage was under way that he was not in Noah McClellan's employ. Somewhat to her own surprise, Hilary did not demand he stop the carriage. Instead she continued to listen to him, fascinated by the story he had to tell and, later, intrigued by the plan he proposed.

"Why did you stop me today?" she asked when he had finished. "And why share all this information with me? Aren't you afraid I'll go to Noah with it?"

"One question at a time, Miss Bowen," he said, grinning sideways at her. "I've been takin' yer measure a few weeks now, watchin' you watchin' 'im . . . sometimes watchin' 'er. That's 'ow I first noticed ye—when ye were watchin' 'is wife. Standin' outside their 'ouse, ye were. And when she came out, carryin' the babe, you moved on, jest like ye'd 'ad other business. I knew better, o'course. I followed ye 'ome . . . I asked a few questions. I'd 'eard yer name before. Men on the *Clarion* talked about ye, 'ow Mr. McClellan 'ad been plannin' to marry ye. A man simpler than me could understand why ye were so interested in Mr. McClellan. I *know* what a woman can do when she's lookin' to get back at a man.''

"And that's what you think? That I'm looking for revenge?''

"Wouldn't have stopped you otherwise. Didn't plan to do it so soon, but ye were callin' attention to yerself. Maybe ye wanted to, I don't know. But sooner or later ye were bound to call attention to me. That's not what I want. As for goin' to Mr. McClellan and tellin' 'im what ye know . . . ye could do that. I'm thinkin' that ye won't. I'm offerin' ye a chance to settle with 'im if that truly be yer desire.''

Hilary's eyes remained remote, giving nothing of her thoughts away. Ross Booker's plans were intriguing, but she wasn't certain she trusted him. "Turn left here,'' she directed. "And stop the carriage.''

Booker obliged her. "Ye'll think on what I've said?'' he asked as Hilary gathered her parcels. He helped her alight.

I'll think on it. How will I find you if I decide to help?''

"I'll find you.''

"Don't come to my home,'' she warned him.

"I won't.'' His obsidian eyes darted over her face and he saw her shiver slightly. He tipped his hat and bid her good day.

Jessa pirouetted in front of the mirror. The hem of her forest-green taffeta gown lifted as she twirled, revealing lace-edged underskirts, dainty damask shoes, and trim ankles. She stopped, looking past her reflection in the mirror to where Noah stood by the bed. He had paused in putting on his blue satin jacket while Jessa danced in front of him. His attention was caught by the trim ankles until Jessa's gown fell in place again. He looked up, holding her gaze in the mirror.

"Very nice," he said, slipping the rest of the way into his jacket. He straightened his waistcoat and brushed away something caught on the silver embroidered trim. Noah tried to catch a glimpse of himself in the mirror, but Jessa was blocking his full view. "In fact, you're looking quite lovely." She continued to stand there. "Radiant comes to mind." His head bobbed from side to side as he attempted to see himself. "Exquisite? Beautiful? Adorable?"

"Are you asking or making a statement?"

"I'm searching for the word that will give you enough confidence to move from that mirror."

"Try *ravishing*."

Noah's expression became solemn. "You're ravishing," he said sincerely.

She spun around and faced Noah, giving him a dimpled smile. "Do you really think so?"

Growling playfully, Noah advanced menacingly. "Out of my way, Circe." His hands circled Jessa's waist, lifted her, and set her down again when she had cleared the mirror. He turned to his own reflection, smoothing his cuffs, plucking a speck of lint from the knee of his satin breeches, and striking a series of casual poses solely for Jessa's benefit.

Watching him, Jessa feigned a yawn, tapping her open mouth lightly with her fingers. "You'll do," she said.

Noah stopped preening. "You overwhelm me with that complimentary turn of phrase," he said dryly.

She stood on tiptoe and kissed him on the cheek. "Sweet, vain man. Your handsome countenance quite takes my breath away."

"Say that again without simpering and I may believe you."

"Oh, do be quiet. Can't you see that I'm as nervous as a fox before the hounds?" She moved away from him, picked up her ivory shawl, and draped it over her shoulders. "Promise you won't desert me this evening. And that you won't dance with anyone else unless I already have a partner. And that you won't play cards with the delegation from South Carolina again. And—where are you going?"

"To get paper. I'm writing this down."

"Beast!"

He took pity on her. "Jessa, you're worrying over trifles," he said soothingly. "I'm not going to do any of those things—especially the one about playing cards. I nearly lost my shirt to them in my own home. There's no telling what would happen in someone else's." That raised a tremulous smile to Jessa's lips. "Are you sorry we accepted the Porters' invitation?"

She shook her head a little uncertainly. "No . . . that is, I don't think so. I wanted to go when we received the invitation. It's the first one we've had to anything so grand. I suppose I'm a bit wary."

"Think of it as a small dinner party. You enjoyed yourself at those."

"Hilary wasn't at those."

"She may not be at the Porters' either. I only know that Anne invited her."

"I wish I had known when I accepted."

Noah slipped his arm under Jessa's and gently nudged her in the direction of the hallway. "Smile, Jessa. We're within days of finishing the work on the Constitution. We'll be back in Virginia soon. Forget about Hilary and concentrate on enjoying yourself."

"All right," she said. "I suppose there will be so many people there that I'll hardly notice her."

She didn't sound very convinced but Noah let it pass. Tonight was the first time he and Jessa had ever been

invited to the same function as Hilary Bowen. Most
hostesses had taken special care not to create this
uncomfortable situation. Anne Porter, however, was a
mutual friend and she didn't want to offend either Noah
or Hilary. Noah thought she was probably hoping that
one of them would decline, or at the very least, decide
at the last moment not to attend. If that was the case,
then Anne would have to depend on Hilary. He had
every intention of being there, Jessa on his arm, and
giving Hilary the cut direct if she stepped even once
into his field of vision.

Henry had the carriage waiting out front. Jessa gave
last minute instructions regarding Gideon to Cam and
repeated them to Sally. She would have delivered the
same speech to Mrs. Harper but that woman was fortunate enough to be visiting her sister in Camden. "We're
only going to be gone the evening," Noah said, hustling
her out the door just moments before Gideon screwed
up his face and began crying for his mother.

The Porter residence was north of the city proper
on the eastern banks of the Schuylkill. Its imposing
columned entrance faced the river. Strains of music
coming from the ballroom greeted guests as their carriages turned up the wide, horseshoe drive. Lamps
burned in every window and light winked in the
entrance hall as the front door was opened and closed
at regular intervals and new arrivals were announced.

Jessa and Noah milled with other couples on the edge
of the ballroom until Anne and Harrison Porter opened
the dancing. After that Jessa felt as if her feet were never
still. Following the first dance, Noah despaired that he
would ever partner his wife again.

Noah lifted a glass of wine from a tray passed before
him by one of the servants, and his eyes followed his
wife's graceful movements as she went through the steps
of a country dance.

"Don't be so obvious," Anne said, tapping Noah's
forearm with the end of her fan. Her full mouth was

set sternly but her deep brown eyes were amused. "Your eyes are eating her up. People will talk."

"They already do," said Noah, glancing sideways at his hostess.

"Yes, but they're bound to start saying you're in love with her if you keep looking that way."

"I am in love with her."

Anne laughed and closed her fan, letting it dangle from her slender wrist. "Ask me to dance, Noah, and you can tell me all about it."

Noah set his drink aside and drew Anne out onto the floor. "Half of Philadelphia is here, Anne. You've outdone yourself."

"Why, thank you." Anne Porter was a handsome woman rather than a beautiful one, but when she smiled, as she was doing now, she was clearly striking. "I gather you're enjoying yourself then."

"Very much."

"And Jessa?"

Noah chuckled. "She asked me not to desert her this evening. It appears I should have extracted the same promise from her. I'm certain she's enjoying herself."

"That makes me very happy. I find that I like her, Noah."

"You say that as if it surprises you."

"Perhaps it does. I was prepared to dislike her ... because of Hilary. How horrible that sounds!" She shook her head sadly. "I hope you can understand how difficult it's been. I'm sorry there's been so much bitterness between you and Hilary."

"For the most part, the bitterness has all been Hilary's."

"I've come to realize it these past weeks since her grandfather died. She's been acting ... I don't know that I can explain it. Her moods are so changeable and she's been so secretive. I feel as if I don't know her any longer."

"You're frowning, Anne. People will think I'm crunching your toes. Let's speak of something else."

She smiled. "Of course. Forgive me. I've taken frightful advantage of our friendship and forgotten my manners." Anne's steps faltered as she looked past Noah's shoulder to the arched ballroom entrance.

"What is it?" he asked, helping her recover her balance.

"Oh, God! No, don't look!" She raised anxious eyes to Noah. "Hilary's just come in on her father's arm. Please, Noah, don't cut her dead."

"How did you know—"

"Because that's what Harrison said *he* would do if he were in your place. My husband's completely out of patience with Hilary and wanted me to cut her from the guest list. I couldn't do it. Hilary was so helpful in the planning. She's the one who insisted I invite you and Jessa. She promised to behave herself. Oh, dear. Harrison's going to greet her now. I suppose you'd better let me go so I can join him. You'll have to find another partner."

Noah escorted Anne to the edge of the dancing area. "There are no other partners," he said, pointing to the far corner of the room where Ben Franklin sat surrounded by a number of women, most of them a quarter of his age. "Dr. Franklin's got them billing and cooing, making sympathetic noises about his gout."

"So join them," Anne advised before she hurried away. "And limp!"

Noah didn't have to resort to that. The dance ended and he managed to claim Jessa before the next one began. Her face was flushed becomingly and her eyes were bright. Soft, featherlight strands of hair had come loose from her coil of ringlets and curled against the nape of her neck.

"Did I mention earlier that you look ravishing, wife?" he asked, taking her hand.

Jessa gave him a mischievous, sidelong look, fluttering

her lashes coyly. "I seem to recall goading you into saying something to that effect."

"So you did. How clever you are at wheedling the truth out of me."

They danced twice more before Jessa begged off. "I could do with a small glass of punch," she said, taking Noah in hand. "Would you be so kind?"

"Wait over there by Dr. Franklin," Noah suggested. "No one would dare steal you away from him." He watched her go then went for her refreshment. Charles Bowen was standing by the crystal punch bowl as Noah approached. For a moment he looked indecisive, as if he weren't certain he should stay or go. He looked uncomfortable in the extreme, though his round, ruddy features were incapable of expressing tension. "Good evening, Charles," Noah said pleasantly.

"Good, umm, evening," he replied. His eyes darted nervously about the room for his daughter. When he saw she was dancing with Mr. Rufus King of the Massachusetts delegation he relaxed. "It's a pleasure to see you again. Quite the squeeze Anne and Harrison have here."

"Yes, it is." Noah accepted the crystal cup a servant passed to him. "You're looking well, Charles. May I express my condolences about your father-in-law? I admired him greatly. I would have attended the services, but . . . you understand, don't you?"

"Yes, umm, yes. Certainly I do. I wish Hilary were taking this better."

"You mean her grandfather's death?"

"What? Oh, no. She's dealing with that admirably. She's been spending a great deal of time at his home, putting things in order. Dismissed all the servants because she wants to do everything herself. Don't know how she manages. Thing of it is, she plans to move there. Grandfather left it to her, you know." Charles raised his glass of white wine to his lips. "No, I was speaking of your broken engagement. She's not, umm, recovering in the manner I thought she would. Lately . . ." His voice trailed off as he saw Hilary coming up behind Noah.

"Really, Papa, you make it seem as if I've been ill," she said brightly. "I assure you I've never been in better spirits. Noah, how good it is to see you." She held out her hand, forcing Noah to make a decision whether to take it or ignore it. He took it politely, raising it a few degrees but making no attempt to kiss it. "I said to Papa weeks ago that it wouldn't do to accept Anne's invitation too quickly. I feared you and your dear wife might not attend if you knew I was coming. And I did so want to see you here, darling."

Noah bit back the caustic reply that came to his mind. He saw Anne Porter looking at him anxiously over the edge of her fluttering fan. He realized she was not the only person watching him. He and Hilary were the focus of a number of surreptitious glances and even a few wide-eyed stares. "Did you, Hilary? Anne said you were insistent that Jessa and I were invited. Why is that?"

"Because I want to show everyone I can be perfectly civil where you and your wife are concerned. I understand congratulations are in order. You're soon to have your first child."

"If you'd like to make small talk, I'd prefer to discuss the weather."

Hilary's smile faltered momentarily but she recovered quickly. "Oh, I forgot. You already have a child, don't you? A boy. What *is* his name?" she asked thoughtfully, then chattered on before Noah could interrupt. "Something Old Testament, I think. You McClellans have a penchant for Biblical names. Adam? No, that's not right, is it? Gideon. That's it. Gideon." Hilary's crimson gown rustled against her stiff petticoats as she turned to her father. "You'll excuse us, won't you, Papa? I want to dance with Noah."

Charles Bowen could not mask his bewilderment. Noah was a touch pale, his features drawn, and Hilary was smiling triumphantly as if she had scored a coup. "Of course, m'dear. Don't umm, mind me. I see George Garret I've been want—"

Noah's voice was low when he interrupted and the smile on his lips was forced. "Don't let your father leave, Hilary, else you'll be stranded in front of the punch bowl. I intend to return to my wife." He started to go but Hilary's fingers curved around his forearm and he nearly lost his purchase on the cup he held. "Take your hand off my arm, Hilary, before I damn the consequences and break it for you."

Hilary laughed gaily as if Noah had said something amusing. She also released his arm. "Come, Papa, dance with me. Noah doesn't want to make amends." Hilary swept her flustered father away.

Jessa's eyes asked a silent question when Noah returned to her side.

"Excuse us, please," Noah said, nodding to Franklin and his companions. He offered his elbow to Jessa. When she took it he gave her the glass of punch and led her toward the back of the ballroom where the doors to the veranda had been thrown open.

"You look like thunder," she said once they were outside. "What did Hilary say to you?"

"She knows," Noah said tersely.

Jessa's brows puckered. "What do you mean?"

"She knows about Gideon."

The glass slid easily from Jessa's nerveless fingers and shattered on the stones. It didn't seem as if her legs could hold her. "What *exactly* did she say?"

Noah slipped his arm about Jessa's waist and led her farther away from the house. "She wished me happy about the child we're expecting." Jessa's sigh was carried away in the breeze. "Then she made a pretense of forgetting Gideon's name. She fumbled for something Old Testament and came up with Adam."

Jessa's arms folded protectively about her middle. "It could be an honest mistake."

"Not bloody likely," he ground out. "Do you think I would have shared this with you if I thought there was any chance I was wrong? Hilary knows and she wanted me to *know* that she knows."

"It doesn't make any sense, Noah. We're not thinking clearly. How could she have possibly found out?"

"I have no idea."

Jessa stopped walking and held Noah back. "Please, I want to go home. Can we leave?"

"Do you think that's wise? Should we let Hilary see that she's rattled us? I probably shouldn't have even brought you out here. This is not something we can run from, Jessa. If Hilary goes public with what she knows, there's nothing we can do but come forward with the truth."

"Oh, God." Jessa closed her eyes, her face ashen. "We'll lose Gideon. You'll be ruined."

"Don't even think those things," he said quietly. Noah realized Jessa could not return to the ballroom. Her entire body was trembling and her eyes, when she opened them, were feverishly bright. "Walk with me to the carriages," he said. "You can wait with Henry while I get your shawl and make our excuses to Anne and Harrison. I'll only leave you a few minutes."

"No." She shook her head quickly. "No, you were right before. We shouldn't go just yet. I need a few moments to collect myself."

Noah was quite willing to give Jessa all the time she needed. Her force of will amazed him as she gathered the frayed threads of her thoughts and composed herself. When they reentered the ballroom her slightly swollen, cherry-red lips looked as if they had been thoroughly kissed. Noah accepted the winks and understanding smiles that greeted them upon their return. He alone knew that Jessa had bitten them to that state.

They stayed at the ball for the better part of another hour, waiting until several delegates and a few couples had departed before they took their leave. Jessa huddled beside Noah in the carriage, shivering in spite of the balmy night air. Neither of them spoke during the drive home. They held each other, sharing strength, offering comfort, their thoughts spinning wildly in different directions.

Jessa felt completely defeated, but Noah was gathering forces for the fight of his life. He thought his battleground would be the courtroom. It wasn't until he arrived home that he discovered how wrong he could be.

"Sally and Cam must have retired for the night," Noah said as they alighted from the carriage. "There's not a single lamp burning in the house." He managed to convey the air that he was unconcerned by this fact but the truth was far different. Sally or Cam, usually both, would stay up until he and Jessa had arrived home. A frisson of alarm made the hair at the back of his neck stand up. He glanced at Jessa. She merely looked weary, not worried.

Henry jumped down from the carriage and opened the front door for them. "Just give me a moment, Mr. Noah. I'll light some candles." He ambled inside the house while Noah and Jessa waited on the stoop. Henry had taken all of six steps when he tripped over a chair that wasn't supposed to be in his way. "Hell and damnation," he cursed loudly, shoving the chair angrily. He sat up and massaged his ankle which had been twisted badly beneath him as he tried to break his fall.

Noah and Jessa rushed into the house when they heard Henry take his spill. "Henry?" Noah asked. "What happened?"

"Fell over a chair. Have a care Miz McClellan," he said as he felt Jessa's skirts brush past him. "Gideon must'a rearranged the furniture."

Jessa fumbled in the dark for the candelabrum that normally sat on the table just inside the front parlor. Not only wasn't it there, the table had been turned on end. "Noah? Nothing's as it should be. Gideon didn't do this." She knelt and patted the floor with her hands, looking for the candles.

"Stay where you are, Jessa," Noah said. "Let me—" He couldn't finish. Jessa's scream paralyzed his own voice. Noah jumped from his place by Henry, kicked aside the chair, and felt his way in the dark to Jessa's side. She was whimpering softly by the time he reached her.

"Th-there's someone . . . hand . . . I f-felt it. Sally? I think it's S-Sally."

"All right, Jessa." Noah's arm encircled her waist and he gently moved her aside. "Wait there. Don't move. Let me deal with this." He dropped to his knees and let his hands sweep the floor. "It's Sally," he said as his fingers made contact with her curly hair. His hand roamed over her scalp. Almost immediately he found the bump at the crown of her bead. It filled the curve of his palm. He touched her throat and felt her steady pulse. "She's going to be fine, Jessa. She'll suffer a tremendous headache but otherwise she'll be fine."

"Did she fall?"

Noah didn't answer her. He found the overturned candelabrum. There were a few candles that hadn't fallen out of their holders. Noah righted the table, searched its single drawer for matches, and lit three of the candles. Holding up the light, he scanned the room. It was worse than he had expected. Two other chairs lay on their sides. The drapes at one of the windows had been pulled down. The tools for the fireplace were scattered on the apron and the poker was within a few inches of Sally's outstretched hand. She was sprawled face down on the floor, her skirts tangled in the awkward splay of her legs. Sally hadn't been rendered unconscious without a fight.

Henry hobbled into the drawing room and whistled softly as he looked around the room. "Lord! What's happened here?"

Noah took one of the lighted candles, cupping the

flame to keep it from going out, and shoved the candelabrum into Henry's hands. "See to Sally," he said tersely. "I have to find Cam. Jessa, stay with Henry."

Jessa ignored him. As Noah turned toward the staircase Jessa lifted the hem of her gown and hurried past him. He reached for her but she pulled away and ran up the steps, calling for Cam and Gideon. Noah went after her, taking the stairs two at a time until he caught her at the top.

"Take this candle," he said roughly. "And stay behind me. You can't go charging around here. There's no guarantee we're alone in the house."

The flame flickered wildly as Jessa's trembling hands closed around the candle. "I have to find Gideon," she said, her voice a bare thread of sound. "I *have* to!"

Noah said nothing. He couldn't bring himself to raise Jessa's hopes when he felt none himself. Nothing he had seen downstairs had led him to believe they had been robbed. The intruder's presence in their home had a far more sinister motive than simple theft. Noah opened the door to Gideon's room cautiously while Jessa held up the candle behind him.

Cam was slumped beside Gideon's bed. There was a livid bruise on the side of his face and a trickle of dried blood at the corner of his mouth. The deep basin where Cam had been bathing the infant was overturned. Cam was sitting in a puddle of water. His hair was plastered wetly to his head and the neck of his blue smocked shirt was soaked. Gideon was not in the room.

Jessa bit back the cry that welled in her throat. It wasn't difficult. She felt as if there were no air in her lungs. Jessa used the candle to light the oil lamp on the nightstand, then she knelt beside Cam as Noah bent over him. "Is he going to be all right?" she asked.

Cam moaned softly as Noah lightly touched his shoulder. A moment later he blinked owlishly though his stare, as it alternated between Noah and Jessa, was vague.

"Bring the lamp down here," Noah told Jessa. "Hold it in front of his eyes."

Jessa did as she was told. Cam's pupils contracted. "What does that mean?"

"It means he doesn't have an injury to his head," said Noah. "All right. You can put it back. Cam? What happened tonight? Where's Gideon?"

Cam drew his knees to his chest and cradled his head in his hands. His lower lip quivered slightly as he sucked in his breath. "I was putting Gideon in the wardrobe when I heard Sally shouting." He started to rise but Noah held him back by placing his hand firmly over Cam's shoulder.

"Let me look," he said. But Jessa was already ahead of him. He watched her open the wardrobe, feel blindly along the base of it, and step back empty-handed.

"Oh, God," Cam sobbed when he saw Jessa's white face. "I th-thought he would be s-safe there. I d-didn't know w-what else to do."

Henry's uneven steps in the hallway stopped Noah from responding. "Sally?" he asked as Henry came into the room.

"She's sitting up. Still woozy. How's the boy?"

"Cam will be fine."

"Gideon?"

"We don't know where he is." Noah turned his attention back to Cam, though he was very aware of Jessa's fragile state as she leaned against the closed wardrobe. "Tell us what happened." He squeezed Cam's shoulder as the boy steadied himself to respond.

"I was up here putting Gideon to bed when I heard someone at the door. I didn't give it a thought 'til Sally started hollerin'." He looked apologetically at Jessa. "It happened so quick, ma'am. All the noise and shoutin', and then it got so quiet and I didn't know what to do. I heard someone on the stairs so I put Gideon in the wardrobe, you know, to protect him, and I scooted under the bed. Only Booker sees me and drags me out and—"

"Booker?" Noah demanded harshly. "Ross Booker?"

Cam nodded. "The very same. We was both surprised to see each other. I kicked at him . . . tried to get free . . . but he walloped me with his fist and then he shoved my face in Gideon's bathwater. He kept pressin' me down and I couldn't get away. I just let go then . . . pretended I was beaten . . . and held my breath 'til I thought I would die for sure. Ross, well, he thinks I'm done in and he lets go. That's about all I remember. Things are fuzzy after that."

Jessa pushed away from the wardrobe and managed two shaky steps. Her eyes were anguished, her lips pale. "I'm sorry," she said, gravely polite. Then she fainted.

When she came around Henry was sitting in the rocker at her bedside. The drapes were drawn and the light from the candles on the mantel glowed orange-yellow on the bald crown of his head. "Henry?"

Henry leaned forward. "Yes'm?"

"Where's Noah?"

"He's gone, Miz Jessa. Gone back to the Porters. He's wantin' to speak to Miz Bowen."

Jessa sat up, refusing the glass of water Henry offered her. "How long ago did he leave?"

"Minutes ago. He put you t'bed and left. Went straight for the stables to get General."

"Then I haven't been out long?"

"No, ma'am. But Mr. Noah says you're to stay right where you are," he added when Jessa put her legs over the side of the bed.

"Where's Cam?"

"He's helpin' Sally to her room."

"Then Noah went alone."

Henry nodded. He chewed the inside of his cheek and forbid himself to mention that Noah had taken the pistol he had kept locked away since the war. "You're not to worry, ma'am. It ain't good for you, not in your delicate condition."

"Not now," she said impatiently, anger just below the surface of her sharp words. She slid off the edge of the bed and stood. "Henry, I want you to saddle Willow for me." Her eyes dropped to his foot and she saw that he was only wearing one shoe. His left ankle was grotesquely swollen. "Never mind. I can see you can't do it." Before Henry could utter a word to the contrary Jessa swept out of the room. She found Cam coming down the stairs from the third floor. He had changed his shirt but his hair was still wet. She blocked his path. "Cam, can you help me? I want to follow Noah. He can't have gone far. Will you go to where the horses are stabled and bring Willow here?"

"I can't do that," Cam said, his eyes wide and earnest. "Mr. Noah would be angry."

"*I'll* be angry if you don't," she said, glaring at him.

Even when she straightened stiffly to her full height Cam still had a half inch on her. The boy, however, cringed slightly at the implacable expression on her face. "Don't ask me t'do this, ma'am," he begged. "Mr. Noah wouldn't want you to go after him."

"That may very well be true and it makes absolutely no difference to me. If you won't get Willow for me, Cam, I'll go myself."

"You don't even know where Mr. Noah's going," he said, dogging her footsteps as she turned and started down the hallway to the other staircase.

"You're wrong. Henry told me." She stopped. "I don't have time for this now. Will you help me? Yes or no?"

Cam hesitated a fraction too long and he had to grab Jessa's sleeve as she started to go again. "I won't saddle Willow but we can take the carriage. I can drive."

"You can barely see out of your right eye," she said,

looking at his puffy lid. Flecks of blood were still on his mouth.

Cam wouldn't let her leave. "I'm going, Miss Jessa," he said forcefully. "Gideon was my responsibility."

Jessa gave him a long look, measuring his determination. "All right," she said finally. "But *I'm* driving."

Several more valuable minutes were wasted as Jessa overrode Henry's protests when she told him of her decision to go with Cam. The older man offered to join them, but Jessa saw that he was in considerable pain. She propped several pillows under his foot, told him to stay put so he could hear Sally in the event she needed something, and wait for Mrs. Harper's return.

Cam was already on the driver's box when Jessa came out. He handed her the reins without making another protest. A little tension seeped out of him after a few miles as he acknowledged that Jessa was able to handle the carriage and the pair pulling it. He spit on his forefinger and wiped the flecks of blood from his lips. "Why are we following Mr. Noah anyway?" he asked somewhat timidly.

"Because I'm afraid of what he'll do to Hilary when he finds her."

"Henry wasn't supposed to tell you about the pistol," Cam muttered.

The ribbons nearly slipped through Jessa's fingers as she looked sharply at Cam. "The pistol? What are you talking about?"

Realizing too late that he had put his foot in it, Cam told her about the weapon. "What I don't understand is why Mr. Noah was so hell-bent—pardon me, ma'am— so set on goin' after Miss Bowen. I told him Ross Booker has Gideon."

"Yes, but Noah doesn't know where Mr. Booker is and he can find Hilary. She knows something she shouldn't know, Cam. I can't explain it to you now—if ever. You'll have to trust me. Hilary Bowen and Ross Booker are in league. They have to be. Nothing else makes sense."

"Nothin' makes sense," he said glumly. "What's Booker doin' here at all? We sent him back to England."

If only that hadn't happened, Jessa thought. She remembered how relieved she had been at the time. Now she saw that his release in England had brought about Gideon's abduction. Somehow he had learned of the Penberthys' reward and he had responded. He couldn't have been certain she was Jessica Winter when he went to see Edward and Barbara, but it wouldn't have taken them long to assemble the facts. And now Booker was here. He had hurt Sally, who couldn't identify him, and attempted to kill Cam, who could. "He came here to take Gideon from me, Cam. Perhaps to—" She couldn't say the words. She didn't have to. Cam's shudder told her the boy understood. Jessa told herself that she had a thread of hope to hold on to. Gideon had only been abducted, not murdered. Ross Booker could have done that easily if that had been his intent. Yet he hadn't. There had to be a reason. "Did he say anything to you at all? You said he was surprised to see you. How did you know?"

"At first just by the way he looked at me when he got me from under the bed. Then I knew it for certain because he mumbled somethin' about how could he have missed me all these weeks. It made me think that maybe he had been watchin' the house."

"It certainly sounds as if that may be true." That meant that Booker had had ample time to make Hilary's acquaintance, though how that had been accomplished was beyond Jessa's comprehension. She couldn't imagine Hilary deigning to speak to Ross Booker. Yet somehow they *had* met. There was simply no other way Hilary could have known Gideon's true name. "Did you tell this to Mr. McClellan?"

Cam shook his head. "You fainted and then Mr. Noah was off in a hundred directions at once. He was shoutin' orders and me and Henry did what we were told. I tried to tell him about the other thing I remembered Booker sayin' but he wasn't still long enough to hear me."

"What other thing?" asked Jessa.

"He kept askin' me where the baby was. I didn't understand him then. I still thought he just wanted to steal somethin' from the house. I didn't tell him though. Even when he put my face in the water, I didn't tell him where I hid Gideon."

"I know that, Cam," Jessa said, striving for patience. "But what was it Mr. Booker said?"

"Well, he was talkin' under his breath and I was under water so I'm not sure I heard him right, but I thought he said he'd never make it to Germany in time if he—"

"Germany? That can't be right."

"I know," Cam sighed. "I told you I couldn't hear very well. But what if he's taking a ship somewhere tonight? We're goin' in the wrong way, Miz McClellan. We should be goin' to the docks."

Jessa pulled up the reins and turned to Cam, her eyes as silver bright as the moon overhead. "Could he have said Germantown?" she asked quickly. "Think Cam. Might he have said Germantown?"

"I suppose," the boy responded, shrugging his shoulders. "That would make sense at least. Don't know why I didn't think of it before except I was all fuzzy-headed."

"It makes complete sense, Cam!" She hugged him and kissed his forehead before she snapped the reins and applied the whip to the horses.

Cam was full of questions as the carriage lurched forward and Jessa urged the team to go faster. He held all of them back, holding onto his seat with a white-knuckled grip until Jessa altered their direction. "Where are we goin'?" he asked anxiously. "This isn't the way to the Porters."

"I know. We're going to Germantown."

"But—"

"Trust me, Cam. I know where Ross Booker's taken Gideon."

* * *

The squeeze of guests at the Porter home was only slightly less than it had been when Noah left the first time. Standing at the edge of the ballroom, Noah searched the room for Hilary. He found Mr. Bowen instead.

"Excuse me," Noah said as he approached the gathering of men which included Charles Bowen. The buzz of conversation stilled momentarily. "I need to speak with you, Charles."

"What?" Charles looked around, flustered, not certain who had spoken. When he saw Noah his eyes widened slightly. "Noah! What are you doing here? I thought you left."

"I need to speak to you, Charles," he repeated. He could feel the press of the pistol against the small of his back. "It's a matter of some urgency."

Charles made his apologies and separated himself from the group. When Noah turned to leave the ballroom he followed. "What is it?" he asked after Noah drew him into Harrison Porter's library. "I confess you don't look well. Not at all."

"Where is Hilary?" Noah asked without preamble. He jammed his hands into his jacket pockets so Charles wouldn't see how badly they were shaking. "I don't see her in the ballroom."

"She's gone home," said Charles, surprised by Noah's curt manners. "Shortly after you left, I think. Why are you looking for her? I, er, thought it was ended between you. You know I can't like the things she's told me, Noah. About you wanting her as your, umm, mistress. I hope that isn't why you've come here. Your wife is—"

"Shut up, Charles," Noah said coldly. "There's no time for your blithering now. I want you to listen to me and I want you to listen carefully. Hilary has involved herself in a matter for which she will pay dearly. Tonight, while I was here, my son was taken from his bedchamber and carried off. Your daughter knows something about Gideon's abduction, Charles, and I will have her confession *and* my son before the night's over. If you care at all for Hilary's welfare, you'll accompany me to your home and listen to what she has to say. I cannot guarantee her safety if I go alone."

Charles's mouth opened and closed several times before he found his voice. "Now see here," he sputtered, "you forget yourself. Hilary was here tonight. You spoke with her yourself. How could she—"

"I didn't say she took my son. I said she knows something about what happened. You heard what she said to me earlier. Has Hilary ever given you reason to believe she didn't know my son's name?" He saw the flicker of Charles's earlier confusion pass across his face again. "Well, did she?"

"No, er, that is . . ." His voice died under Noah's hard, probing stare. "No," he said with a certain weariness. "I don't understand why she did that. She doesn't speak of the boy often, but she never was at a loss for his name before."

"I know precisely why she did it," Noah gritted. "She couldn't help herself. Hilary is vengeful and she had to prove her superiority. Her accomplice in this nasty piece of business is not going to thank her for it."

"Her accomplice?"

"Not now, Charles. If you're coming with me I can tell you on the way." Noah didn't give Hilary's father time to weigh his decision. He started to leave immediately after he had spoken.

Charles's short, thick legs pumped furiously to keep up with Noah's long, fluid strides. "I don't have a horse," he told Noah once they were on the front porch. "Hilary took the carriage and I was going to beg a ride from Orrin Barton."

Noah swore softly at the inevitable delay this would cause. "Give me a moment," he said and disappeared back into the house. Minutes later he returned. "I tendered your respects for this evening's pleasantries to our hosts and have Harrison's permission to take a mount from his stable. Come. I fear I've already lingered here too long."

Charles was a man given to consideration. He despised being rushed. Still, because of his great need to be liked, to smooth life's rough edges with vapid diplomatic charm, Charles Bowen allowed himself to be hurried to the stable. He accepted the bay gelding Noah brusquely chose for him and didn't speak at all until he and Noah reached the end of the Porter's drive and Noah had turned his mount toward town. Charles pulled up and waited for Noah to realize he wasn't following. "It's likely you're going the wrong way," he said in response to Noah's query. "I don't think Hilary went back to the city this evening."

"But you're not certain?"

Charles shook his head. "No, I'm not. However, we're closer to my father-in-law's home. Remember? I told you she was spending a great deal of time there in preparation of moving permanently. I suggest we go there first."

It was the wiser course and Noah nodded a curt thanks to Charles as he turned General around and gave the horse his head. Charles had no choice but to match Noah's bruising pace.

"Well," said Cam as Jessa stopped the carriage a hundred yards from the Hearn residence, "I found Miz Bowen's house for you, but what do we do now?" Cam's bright hair fell over his forehead and he pushed it back with the heel of his hand. "If Gideon's in there, how do we get him out?"

Jessa wished she knew. She wished she had brought her pistol. She wished she had known how to load it. She wished . . . "Do you have any suggestions?" she asked, staring through a break in the silver-white birches that thinly lined the roadside. Only a few rooms in the Hearn home were lit. The gray stone house looked bleak in the pale wash of moonshine. For as long as she watched no one moved in front of the windows.

"I could peek in a few of the rooms," Cam offered a trifle reluctantly. "The ones on the first floor wouldn't be too hard to get to."

"They're too high off the ground. You couldn't see inside even on tiptoe. What if I lifted you?"

Cam snorted. *"I'll* lift you."

"That's fine."

Too late Cam realized she had tricked him. He had been going to argue that Jessa should stay with the carriage and yet somehow she had managed to make him forget that. He tugged on Jessa's pleated sleeve as she stood to get down from the box. "What if we do see somethin'? We still don't know what to do."

Jessa's face was without expression but her pale eyes were flinty and her voice was hard, her words clipped. "Cam, if I see Gideon in that house I promise you I'll know precisely what to do."

The first thing Jessa did when she reached the ground was to strip off her bulky underskirts. Cam politely turned his back while Jessa took them off and tossed them in the carriage. "I'm ready," she said, coming to stand beside him. She looked at him consideringly. "Do you have a cap? A hat? Something to cover your hair."

He shook his head. "But I can pull my jacket over my head a little. What about you?"

"I'll stay behind you as much as possible. You lead the way."

Cam and Jessa cautiously made their way through the trees and then across the open lawn. Cam chose a window on the side of the house rather than the front. He cupped his hands and steadied his legs. "Put your foot in here, ma'am, just like you were going to mount. Then grab the stone ledge with your hands and pull yourself up. Easy though. Don't let anyone inside see you."

Jessa kicked off her shoes and did as Cam instructed. "There's no one here," she whispered. "The candles are almost gutted in their holders. No one's been here for awhile."

Cam gingerly lowered her to the ground again. "What room is it?"

"A library . . . study. Does it matter?"

"I thought it would help us to know where to look next. The parlor's probably on the other side. We should circle round the back of the house."

Nodding her agreement, Jessa followed the boy. The rear of the house was dark, the kitchen and larder areas deserted. Cam tried the back door in the event they had need of it and found it locked. There was a rose trellis, bare of flowers now, on the north side of the house. Jessa rattled it lightly testing its strength as she and Cam passed it. The lighted windows on the second floor kept drawing her attention.

Cam lifted her to three more windows before their persistence was rewarded. "Hilary's here," she told Cam in hurried whisper. "Can you lift me a little more? That's good. Hold me steady. She's talking."

"Who to?"

"I don't know. Mayhap she's talking to herself. If there's someone else in the room I can't see who it is." Jessa cocked her head and strained to see the areas of the parlor on the periphery of her vision. "It's no good, Cam. I can't see who's with her. Let me down." She stumbled a little and fell against the house as the boy set her on the ground.

Cam grabbed her hand. "Are you all right?"

Jessa waved aside his concern. She eyed the trellis again. "Do you think you can climb that?"

"Sure. It ain't much different than climbing the ropes on the *Clarion*. Probably easier. Don't know if it will take my weight though. That could be a problem."

"We won't know until you try."

Cam walked to the trellis and tested its sturdiness himself. "Do you really think Booker's here? And Gideon?"

"Yes." Jessa put her foot on one of the lower wooden slats and lifted herself. The trellis creaked a bit but it held her. "Perhaps I should go up."

"It's too dangerous for you," he said. "And you may not be able to raise the window even if you get there."

"What if the window's locked?"

Cam reached in his jacket pocket and brought out a sheath knife. He opened it, grinning slyly, and showed her the shiny blade. "Every sailor's friend," he said. "I can jimmy the latch."

"I'll hold the trellis for you."

Placing the open knife between his teeth, Cam started up the latticework. He was light-footed, as quick and agile as a monkey. When he reached the top he cautiously peered inside the room. It was a bedchamber. A small fire had been laid in the hearth in anticipation of the night turning cold. There was no other light in the room, but even so Cam could see that it was deserted. For now. The window was also locked. Working swiftly he flipped the latch with his knife, snapped it closed and pocketed it. Nodding to Jessa that he was going in, Cam opened the window just enough for him to shimmy inside the room.

Once Jessa saw Cam disappear she thought better of her decision to remain on the ground. Cam's climb hadn't looked to be very difficult. Lifting the hem of her gown in one hand, Jessa stepped onto the trellis. Above her she heard Cam close the window and she cursed softly. Now she would never get his attention. The lattice trembled when she reached the halfway point. Holding her gown made it hard to distribute her weight evenly. The strips of wood creaked and shifted beneath her feet. Jessa dropped her gown so she could hold the latticework with both hands. A moment later the trellis began to shake violently and Jessa cried out as she briefly lost her footing.

The shaking stopped as suddenly as it had started and Jessa held herself very still. The unmistakable sound of light applause reached her ears. Startled, Jessa risked a look back at the ground. Ross Booker stood below her, clapping his hands in a bored, insolent manner.

"I did enjoy the view afore ye dropped yer skirts," he said. He stopped clapping and gave the trellis another shake. "Ye better come down. Can't 'ave ye takin' a fall."

There was nowhere for Jessa to go but down. Rushing for the window would solve nothing and it could endanger Cam. Jessa didn't think Booker had been outside very long and he might very well believe she was acting alone. She began her descent, cringing when Ross Booker's large hands rested on either side of her waist and he lifted her to the ground. He held her overlong, laughing huskily when Jessa tried to wriggle away.

"Was someone there?" Hilary called from the front porch. "Mr. Booker? Did you find anyone?"

"I'm comin' directly!" he yelled back. "We have a guest!" He pushed Jessa in the direction of the porch. "This way, Miz McClellan. Ye should 'ave come to the door. Not that ye would 'ave been anymore welcome by that route, but it would 'ave been safer for ye."

Jessa made no reply. She drew herself up sharply, avoiding his touch, and began walking quickly toward the front of the house.

Hilary's shock was real when she saw Jessa. "My God! How did you—"

"Inside, 'ilary," Ross ordered tersely. "Follow 'er, Jessa."

Jessa did as she was told. Hilary led the way into the parlor and Booker slammed the front door angrily before he joined them.

"This is insane," Hilary said, rounding on Booker as soon as he came into the room. Her eyes were blazing.

"You said no one would come here! You said no one would know! You don't think she's alone do you? Noah could be anywhere!"

"Calm yerself. There wasn't anyone with 'er outside. 'Er 'usband wouldn't let her climb the lattice if 'e was 'ere."

Jessa was careful not to show her relief. If Gideon were in the house, Cam would find him. She listened to the exchange between Hilary and Ross, wondering how she might drive a wedge between them.

"You'll have to do something about her," Hilary said impatiently. "I don't want her here."

"What do ye think I should do? Kill 'er?"

Jessa recoiled slightly at the dark look Hilary slanted her.

Hilary's response was a frigid smile. "Why not? Her presence here changes everything. Listen to me, Mr. Booker, this plan of yours is unraveling like the cheapest yarn. I did my part. I made certain Anne Porter invited Noah and his slut to the ball. I even advised her on the date, choosing the evening when I knew Mrs. Harper would be out of the house visiting her sister. You only had to deal with Sally, that miserable boy, and one infant. You never said anything about bringing the child here. That wasn't in our agreement. You told me you were going to take him away and sell him. You said you had found people to buy the brat."

Jessa's relief was so great that she very nearly began to cry. Gideon was alive! Booker was too greedy to kill him!

Ross shook his head slowly from side to side. When he spoke it was to Jessa. "She's makin' it very hard for me *not* to kill ye. Did ye ever 'ear a body talk so much as this one? Now ye, ye've been too quiet. I 'aven't 'eard a word that 'elps me understand wha's brought ye 'ere in the first place. And ye didn't look surprised to see me when I trapped ye on the trellis. That makes me wonder what ye might 'ave been told and who told ye."

Jessa remained mute. She refused to let him know Cam was very much alive. Booker's flat, opaque eyes regarded her coldly. When he rapped out a command for her to sit down she did so, her legs folding under her so quickly that she began to doubt that she could have stood much longer.

"Where's yer 'usband?" Booker demanded.

"I don't know."

"She's lying," Hilary snapped, agitated.

"Be quiet!" Ross ordered. "Sit. Stand. But stop yer damn foot tappin'!" He turned back to Jessa. "Where's yer 'usband?" he asked again.

"I don't know." Jessa thought Booker was going to strike her. One blow from his heavy hands could knock her unconscious. Thinking quickly, she elaborated on her answer. "I really don't know. He left the house as soon as we discovered that Cam was ... was dead ... and Gideon was gone. I think his intention was to find Miss Bowen."

"Why?" When Jessa only appeared puzzled he explained himself. "What reason did 'e 'ave for suspecting 'ilary?"

Jessa folded her hands in her lap. Her palms were scraped from grabbing the rough window ledges. She found herself welcoming the stinging pain because it reminded her she was still alive. "He's looking for Hilary because of something she said tonight at the ball. She mentioned Adam."

Ross raised his hand but it wasn't Jessa he struck. Hilary had no time to block the unexpected blow. She reeled backward and nearly fell over a footstool. "Ye stupid bitch!" he railed. "Ye stupid, bloody bitch!"

Tears stung Hilary's eyes. She put her palm to her cheek and stared accusingly at Ross. "Don't you ever touch me again! I know what you are, Ross Booker, and I won't hesitate to tell the authorities if you ever lift your hand to me again!"

"Don't threaten me with yer 'igh 'n mighty airs! Ye've

been in this from the beginning. Ye could 'ave said something long before now. But ye wanted yer revenge. Well, that's what ye've got. It's yer loose tongue that's brought 'er 'ere and it's only a matter of time before 'er 'usband will come."

Hilary could not be intimidated easily. Though she skirted the stool and took a few more steps back toward the window she squared her shoulders and lifted her chin regally. "Why don't you ask her why she wasn't surprised to see you? And why she's here by herself—if that's true at all."

"Do ye think that matters now? We 'ave to get out of 'ere."

"I'm not going anywhere. Take her! Take the baby! But you're leaving without me! I can handle Noah myself. *She's* the one you have to worry about."

"Not entirely," he said, oddly calm of a sudden. "Ye shouldn't 'ave threatened me earlier, 'ilary. It goes without sayin' that I'm honor bound to do something about you."

Bile rose in Jessa's throat as Ross Booker advanced on Hilary.

A quarter of a mile from Hilary's home Noah pulled General up short as he rounded the slight curve in the road. Charles followed suit. Dust hadn't even settled on the road surface before Noah was charging forward again, heading directly for the carriage stopped on the edge of the woods.

"This is my carriage," he said when Charles came up beside him. "What the *hell* is it doing here? If Jessa—"

"Mr. Noah?" The voice came from inside the carriage.

"Cam? Is that you?"

Cam drew back the window curtain and pressed his small face to the glass. "Come around to the door."

Noah dismounted and went to the other side of the carriage. He yanked open the door. The interior of the carriage was dark. He could only vaguely make out

Cam's profile. There was, however, no mistaking the soft gurgling cries that came sweetly to his ears. They belonged to Gideon.

Charles heard the cries also. He dismounted and came up behind Noah, peering in the carriage as Noah climbed in.

"Dear God, Cam!" He took Gideon from Cam's arms and cradled the infant in his own. "How—where—" He couldn't finish. Emotion clogged his throat.

"Papa!" Gideon giggled happily, trying to stand on Noah's lap. He waved his arms in an attempt to get them around his father's neck.

Noah hugged him until Gideon squealed in protest. "What are you doing here, Cam? Where did you find Gideon?"

"Please, Mr. Noah," he said urgently. "You can't stay here. You've got to get Miss Jessa. I think they found her."

Noah went very still. "They?"

"Booker and Miss Bowen. Up at the house. Miss Jessa and me went there. We figured it out for ourselves after you left. She was bent on comin' here, Mr. Noah. I couldn't stop her. I had to come along to help."

Cam spoke so quickly that his words were nearly unintelligible to Noah. "Slow down, Cam. Take a breath and tell me more slowly. And more loudly. I want Charles to hear this."

"Miss Jessa saw Miss Bowen in the front parlor. She was talkin' to someone—probably Booker, but we weren't sure then. We couldn't find Gideon in any of the rooms we looked in but Miss Jessa was certain he was here. I climbed the trellis for her and got in the house from an upstairs window. It didn't take me long to find Gideon. He was sleepin' when I came upon him. I think he was tuckered from cryin' but he seemed fine. I thought Miss Jessa would be waitin' for me. I carried Gideon out the same way I came in. When she wasn't there I supposed she'd come back to the carriage. I came here straight away, lookin' for her. It's been too long, Mr. Noah. Miss Jessa's in some kind of trouble. She'd have been here by now."

"All right, Cam," Noah said as gently and calmly as he was able. "Take Gideon and stay with him here. Mr. Bowen and I will go to the house. We'll find Jessa and bring her back as safely as you brought back Gideon. Do you understand me?"

"Yes, sir."

"Good." He turned to Mr. Bowen who was leaning heavily against one side of the open doorway. "Do you have any doubts now, Charles?" Without waiting for a reply Noah moved to the opening, forcing Charles to step aside or be trampled as Noah jumped down. "We'll leave the horses here. I don't want Booker or Hilary alerted to our presence." He started in the direction of the house. "This has changed things," he told the older man. "Your daughter is more involved than I first thought."

The brisk pace that Noah set winded Charles. "Perhaps this Booker person forced her to keep the child here," he puffed. "You don't have all the facts and you can hardly credit all that boy told you."

"That *boy* nearly died tonight because of Ross Booker," Noah said curtly. "And he saved my son's life. I trust his word more than I'll ever trust yours. I know what happened to Hilary while you quartered British troops in your home, Charles. She told me. You've earned my contempt. Nothing else." Noah broke into a run as he neared the house. At the porch he paused long enough to take out his pistol.

Jessa screamed. It was enough to startle Booker. He hesitated a heartbeat, giving Hilary the opportunity to evade him and thwart his advance by placing herself behind a large leather chair. Hilary's eyes darted around the room, searching for a weapon. Her anguished glance rested momentarily on Jessa.

Jessa didn't hesitate. She threw herself at Booker, tackling him from behind. He grunted, cursed, and faltered briefly, then he rid himself of Jessa's grasp by kicking backward, landing a blow squarely between her breasts. Jessa rolled away, gasping for breath. Ross reached for her, grabbed her wrist, and yanked her to her feet. Jessa stumbled and fell into the chair that Hilary was using to protect herself.

"Ye'll be sorry ye did that," Booker said, his black eyes narrowing on Jessa. "If I didn't 'ave a mind to take what ye owe me, I'd kill ye now." He lifted his eyes to Hilary. "Ye be another matter."

"I won't say anything," Hilary promised hurriedly. Her hands gripped the curved back of the chair until the tips of her fingers were white. "You mistook me earlier. Take her and the child. I'll never tell anyone you were here. I'll never admit to knowing you."

Booker laughed shortly. "That's 'ow ye repay 'er?" he asked pointing to Jessa. "She tried to save yer worthless life and ye tell me to do what I like with 'er?"

Jessa was not listening to their exchange. She was making every effort not to appear threatening to Booker. Her hands were clenched together to form a single fist, but she had held it close to her chest in an attitude of prayer. Booker's waist was at the level of her eyes. She couldn't credit what she was thinking and planning.

"I mean it," Hilary said, her eyes pleading. "You said yourself that I was involved since the beginning. I won't say anything to implicate either one of us."

"Why is it that I don't believe ye?" He took a short step forward, standing with his legs slightly apart for balance. With no warning one arm shot out, rising above Jessa's cowering form to grab at Hilary's wrist.

Jessa had been waiting, anticipating Booker's movements so that she wouldn't miss her target. She didn't.

Lightening quick, her arms unfolded and she brought her two-handed fist directly between Booker's splayed legs, jamming her fist upward against his groin. It was almost as effective as a knee. Ross howled, released Hilary, and bent over, clutching himself. Jessa leaped from the chair and shoved him, throwing all her slight weight against him. Booker fell victim to the footstool that had caused Hilary to stumble earlier. He thudded to the floor but quickly recovered and scrambled to his hands and knees. Jessa picked up the stool and threw it at his head. It glanced off Booker's shoulder and he started to rise.

"Run, Hilary!" Jessa yelled. "Get out of here!"

Hilary remained frozen behind the chair, too terrified now to respond.

Jessa picked up the stool again and prepared to throw it, raising it over her head as Ross began to straighten. "Hilary! For God's sake! Do something!"

"Back away, Jessa."

It was Noah's voice, calm and devoid of inflection, but it sounded like a tender lullaby to Jessa's ears. She didn't hesitate to obey him, moving swiftly to the far side of the room. Her eyes swept over him, grateful and relieved. "Gideon's here, Noah. Mr. Booker wanted to sell him."

Noah didn't spare a glance for his wife. "Gideon's with Cam in the carriage." He kept his pistol steady, targeting Booker's heaving chest. "Hilary, go to the window," he said.

"Do what he says, Hilary," Charles added, coming to stand in the arched entrance to the room.

"Papa!" Hilary started to move toward her father, careless of Ross Booker now that Noah's pistol was leveled at the man.

"No! Hilary!" Everyone shouted at once and all the warnings were too late. Booker lunged at her as soon as she passed within a few feet of him. They both toppled to the floor but Hilary landed on top, shielding her captor and preventing Noah from firing.

Noah shoved his pistol into Charles's trembling hands and immediately entered the fray, pulling Hilary away from Booker and roughly shoving her aside. He fell back, breath whooshing from his lungs as Ross kicked him between the ribs. A cherrywood table overturned. Noah jumped over it, knocking Ross back to the floor just as he was getting up again.

"Kill him, Papa!" Hilary cried out as Ross and Noah grappled and rolled. "Kill him!"

Noah shouted over Hilary's shrill scream. "No! I need him alive!"

But that was the last thing Hilary wanted. Alive, Booker was a danger to her. He would never remain silent about the part she had played in the Penberthys' scheme. Dead, she could say what she wanted and no one could gainsay her save Jessa. It would be her word against Jessa's, and Noah's wife had everything to lose by contradicting her. Jessa would have to admit that Gideon was not her son, that she had abducted him herself. Hilary refused to believe Jessa would willingly share the truth—not if Booker was dead and the secret was put to rest with him.

Hilary grabbed the pistol from her father's nerveless fingers and aimed it at Booker.

"Hilary!" Jessa shouted. "Don't do it!" She was certain Hilary wouldn't get a clear shot. Noah and Ross were both tiring, flailing wildly, missing as many blows as they connected. Their bodies were only apart for seconds at a time. Neither man could break away long enough to rise to his feet.

"Give me the pistol, Hilary," Charles pleaded.

Hilary shrugged off the hand her father placed on her forearm. "I want him dead." There were bitter tears in her eyes and the pistol shook in her double-handed grip. "He'll hurt me, Papa," she rasped. "He can hurt me if he lives. He'll tell lies . . . horrible lies."

Grunting with the force of his efforts, Noah straddled Booker's broad chest, pinning the man's upper arms with his knees. He could hear Hilary's pitiful childlike voice and he knew what she wanted to do. She thought by killing Booker she could save herself. That knowledge angered Noah beyond reason and the anger marshaled his strength. He slammed his fist into Booker's jaw and heard bone crack. It was much later that he realized it was the bones in his own hand. He was only immediately aware that he had finally rendered Ross Booker unconscious.

"Put down the pistol, Hilary," Noah's breathing was harsh, his head bowed as he leaned back and rested his weight on Booker's chest. "It's over," he said tiredly. Noah got to his feet, protecting Booker's limp form by standing in Hilary's line of fire. He approached her slowly and saw her arms waver slightly and her resolve weaken. "Let me have it," he said, forcing himself to be gentle as he watched her carefully. Her beautiful dark blue eyes were glazed and though she was looking at him Noah felt as if she were looking through him. He couldn't guess what she was thinking. "Please, Hilary, give me the weapon."

Hilary lowered the pistol and stifled a sob with the back of one hand. Her eyes shifted to all the occupants of the room, first Booker, then Noah and Jessa, and finally her father. "Oh, God!" she whispered forlornly, tears streaking her face. "I'm sorry. I'm so sorry!" She turned on her heel and ran from the room and out the front door.

Noah started to follow her but Charles stopped him. "Let her go," he said. "She needs me now. I know I've failed her in the past, but not this time. I'll see her through this."

Noah inclined his head slightly and held out his arm for Jessa as she crossed the room to his side. He embraced her, rubbing his cheek against the corn silk softness of her hair. "I hope you mean that, Charles.

She'll need someone to help her face what's ahead. Hilary won't—"

The pistol shot silenced Noah. In his arms he felt Jessa stiffen. Charles Bowen's face sagged and he aged visibly in that moment. None of them shared their thoughts aloud yet they shared the same thought: Hilary had decided not to face her future at all.

EPILOGUE

May, 1788

"Guilty!"

Jessa bolted upright in bed. "Guilty!" She could hear the pronouncement as clearly in her mind as she had in the courtroom. "Guilty!" Her hands shook and she clasped them around her legs as she drew her knees to her chest. Tiny beads of perspiration formed on her forehead and her stomach knotted with tension. "Guilty!"

She glanced at Noah beside her. He hadn't stirred. The cadence of his breathing remained soft and even. Jessa had an urge to wake him but she quelled it and took comfort from the fact that he could sleep peacefully. It was a statement of sorts, she supposed, that her own fears were unfounded. The voice inside her head was silenced and she listened to the soothing rhythms of water rushing against the hull of the *Clarion* as the sleek ship cut its path toward home.

Home. It was a wonderfully heady thought. They had been too long in England and painful memories of the trial were not easily dismissed. Jessa welcomed returning to Virginia. She could hardly imagine there had been a time when going to the landing had inspired nothing so much as panic. It seemed a lifetime ago that she had first shared the cabin with Noah. When moonshine lent its pale light to the length of the window seat Jessa could only shake her head in wonderment. Had she once really professed to prefer that bench to sharing Noah's bed? She could scarcely credit it now.

Slipping out of bed, Jessa padded to the wardrobe and took out her dressing gown. She lit a candle, cupping the flame to keep it from bothering Noah, and cast one last glance over her shoulder before opening the door to the adjoining room.

The night was cool but that hadn't stopped Gideon from kicking off his covers. Jessa rearranged the blankets that were bunched at the foot of his bed, oddly disappointed that he didn't wake. She stood over his bed for long moments simply watching him sleep. His perfect little mouth was parted enough to allow room for the tip of his thumb. His dimpled fist pressed against his face, skewing his nose comically to one side. Jessa lightly touched a lock of dark hair that had fallen over his forehead and pushed it back. The backs of her fingers brushed his soft cheek. After a few minutes she moved to the crib where his sister slept. Bethany was curled on her side with only the tip of her fair head showing. Jessa eased the blanket over her daughter's face and lightly traced the shape of one tiny ear with her fingertip.

Jessa never heard Noah's approach, yet moments before he slipped his arms about her waist from behind and rested his chin against the crown of her head, she sensed his presence in the room. She set down the candle and her arms slid over his. Jessa leaned back against his solid strength, hugging him to her. "They're beautiful, aren't they?" she asked. "I never tire of looking at them."

"Hmmm. The earl and the little princess," he said, his voice husky with sleep. "One's a blue blood and the other just thinks she is. That's rather unsettling, don't you think, for a man who put his signature to a republican document like the Constitution some eight months ago?"

It seemed he knew precisely what to say to coax a smile from her. "I think we'll all manage to live under the same roof," she said.

"We'll have to. I'm not giving anyone up. What brought you here?"

"I thought I heard one of the children."

Noah's own smile was pressed into the corn silk softness of her hair. He didn't believe her explanation for a moment. "Sweet liar."

Jessa would have liked to take exception to his words but she could not. There was no accusation in his tone, only an endearment. She could only love him more because he knew her so well. "Let's go to bed," she said.

When they were back in their own bed and cuddled warmly under the covers Noah repeated his earlier question and added another. "Was it a nightmare?"

Jessa's head was cradled in the curve of Noah's shoulder and one of her legs lay with a proprietal air over both of his. "I dreamed of the trial again," she admitted lowly. "The court's judgment echoed in my head even after I awakened. I kept thinking it was meant for me."

"Oh, Jessa," he said softly, aching for her. "That verdict was for the Penberthys."

"I know. In my head I know it to be true. Sometimes . . . in my heart . . . I can't help but feel that I'm at fault."

"The jury didn't think so," he reminded her gently. The trial had been months in preparation and lasted seven days. The jury had had a verdict in twenty minutes.

Jessa shuddered slightly and pressed herself closer to Noah. How differently the outcome would have been if the jury had believed the lies Barbara and Edward Penberthy had used in their defense. When they took the stand they had twisted the facts to suit their purpose, claiming they had hired Ross Booker to bring Gideon safely back to England. Lady Barbara had sounded so convincing that Jessa feared that the jury would forget all the contradictory testimony they had heard earlier from Cam, Ross Booker, and a still-grieving Charles Bowen. "It seems so ironic that Hilary's suicide should have helped discredit the Penberthys," she said sadly. "It was good as an admission that she was involved in something more than simply helping Booker take Gideon back to England."

"I know," Noah said softly, filled with the same regrets as Jessa. He still wondered what he could have done to prevent Hilary from taking her own life. That he could logically absolve himself of responsibility did not always clear his conscience. "But there is no blame to be laid at your door for what Hilary did. Furthermore, I don't think that's what decided the jury."

"You don't?"

He shook his head. "*You* made the difference, Jessa. The fact that you took the documents from the manor helped prove that you were not abducting Gideon in order to deprive him of his birthright, but to save it for him. Those papers and your own testimony satisfied the court as to your intent. You were magnificent in your own defense. We should never have been granted guardianship of Gideon otherwise."

"Do you really think so?"

"I really think so," he said. "It helped that Barbara and Edward had never informed anyone when they learned that Gideon was alive. It sealed their fate because it made the jury question their motives. Their silence convicted them as much as anything you said. I suspect that Barbara will find the accommodations in Newgate less than satisfactory. At least Edward and Ross Booker will have each other for company. They deserve

one another." Noah stroked Jessa's hair with his fingertips. "It still surprises you that you were believed, doesn't
it?"

"I suppose it does," she admitted, shying away from
thoughts of Newgate. There had been too many
moments when she thought it would become her residence. "I keep expecting to wake and find this reality
is but a dream and my nightmares are real. Sometimes
I have to assure myself of the truth. That's why I went
to see the children."

Noah smiled. "You could have reached for me," he
said. "I'm real enough."

"You were sleeping."

"So were they."

"I was rather hoping one of them would wake," she
said wistfully. "I wanted a cuddle."

"And I woke instead," he said. "How disappointing
for you."

Jessa's arm slid down Noah's chest. She lightly
pinched his side. "Actually," she said, "you cuddle better. Gideon squirms and Bethany kicks as much now as
she did when I was carrying her."

Noah's hand slid to Jessa's flat abdomen. "She was
impatient to be born," he said. Bethany had arrived on
a bitterly cold day in February three weeks before she
was expected. "It's a miracle she waited until after the
trial."

"You have a slightly different recollection of that than
I do," she said dryly. "My labor began before the jury
retired. Had they deliberated any longer your daughter
would have been whelped in the courtroom."

"And as I recall," he said, "you didn't mention a
word until after the verdict was in."

"That's not true," she objected. "I whispered to you
earlier that I was going to have the baby."

Noah laughed, rolling Jessa on her back and placing
a swift kiss on the corner of her mouth. "Madam," he
chastised her. "I *knew* you were going to have a baby.

What you neglected to make clear was that you intended to have one *then*. I've told you before that you have a regrettable penchant for ambiguity."

"I shall strive to do better in the future," she said solemnly. Her arms encircled Noah's neck and she brought his face closer to her own. "I should very much like it if you'd kiss me again."

Noah rewarded her forthrightness. His mouth closed over hers and his tongue teased her lips apart. He felt Jessa's eager response. "You are a contradiction, love," he told her when he lifted his head. Her beautiful gray eyes held his own darkening gaze. "Innocent. Seductive. Shy. Then bold of a sudden."

Jessa laughed and placed a finger to his lips. "You can expound on your theme later, Noah. I want you now."

The tip of Noah's tongue touched her finger and her siren's smile held him captive. She withdrew her hand as he lowered his head. Their mouths touched. Parted. Touched again. Held. The kiss deepened and their hearts thudded in unison until their bodies became as one. They were unselfish in giving pleasure, greedy in taking it, and replete in the aftermath of loving.

Much to Noah's amusement, Jessa fell asleep almost immediately, her body curved against the contours of his. She never heard him whisper that he loved the contradictions in her character. Neither did she hear him enumerate them. The tender smile on her face was there because he held her close, cocooned and protected in the circle of his arms, making her dreams and her reality one and the same.

Please turn the page for
Jo Goodman's
McClellan short story
Tidewater Promise

TIDEWATER
PROMISE

JO GOODMAN

December 24, 1796

Everyone had an opinion. It was difficult to be a McClellan and not have an opinion. It was impossible to be a McClellan and not voice it. Sometimes there was unanimity, more often not. It was difficult to tell how the lines of the argument would be drawn, who would support whom. There were family ties to consider, parental and sibling affection. Then there were all the spousal ties. Marrying into the family made one a McClellan just as certainly as if one had been born to the name. Finally there were bonds of gender, with the men lining firmly on one side and the women just as committedly on the other.

They had come together, more than a score strong, to celebrate Christmas and a wedding. Christmas was coming as scheduled. The wedding was off.

Courtney McClellan stood on the edge of the flagstone veranda, leaning against one of the white columns. She hugged herself. It was cold enough now that she should have had a cape, but not cold enough to encourage her to go back inside the house to get one. The cold, she thought, was more inside her than outside. Her faint smile was self-mocking. It was because of the cold inside her that she had broken her engagement with George Monroe.

Most of the stunned family was still crowded in the drawing room arguing the merits of her last-minute announcement to cry off. Closing her eyes, Courtney could see her father standing at the fireplace, tapping a poker against the marble apron as he presided over the family meeting. She imagined she could still catch the scent of the pine garlands and the baskets of oranges, decorated with ribbons and pinned with cloves. She remembered thinking that the heady fragrances she associated with winter, with celebration, had little impact on her father's thinking or disposition once he heard her news.

Unbidden, the discussion echoed in her mind and she felt the disappointment and censure of her beloved grandparents, parents, and a host of aunts and uncles. She cringed inwardly as their voices came to her one after another.

Her mother's soft voice addressing her father, "Our daughter has a mind of her own. You helped raise her that way. I don't think we can force her hand."

Her grandfather's concerned reprimand, "When a man asks a woman to marry him and she says yes, then by God, he has every right to expect that she'll still mean yes come the wedding day."

Aunt Rae's practical interjection, "At least Courtney's not pregnant."

A chorus of male voices had been raised in unanimous disapproval of Rae's plain speaking. For all of a minute Courtney had ceased to be the center of attention and she loved her aunt for that. But then it started again.

"This is the third engagement she's broken," someone said. "The *third.*"

"It's *her* future," it was pointed out.

"But it's a family scandal," came the objection.

"She's too stubborn by half."

The response had been quick. "That's a McClellan trait. You can't fault her for what she's seen all these years."

Courtney put her hands over her ears in an attempt to silence the voices. It was not enough. Her father's angry edict came to her clearly: "The next time she even thinks about marriage she should plan to present me with a *fait accompli*. I want to hear about her marriage *after* the fact.''

It was then Courtney had come to her feet and made her own opinion known. The drawing room had fallen silent as she stood. A pale wash of sunlight filtered in through tall, narrow windows, glancing off the powder blue walls and white woodwork. The curtains shifted slightly in the breeze coming up from the river. Shadows were scattered on the hardwood floor, across the walnut pie table, and on the back of the love seat. Someone rose to close the window. The shadows ceased to dance and the sunlight lay still, this time across the gentle slope of Courtney's shoulder.

She had her father's height and her mother's delicate features. Her silver-gray eyes were mirrors of Salem's own, but their provocative, mysterious slant was Ashley's. The shape of her generous mouth came from the Lynne side, the dimple at the corner was McClellan. From both parents she had inherited hair the color of midnight.

Courtney's hands were steady at her side, her shoulders straight. There was a touch of high color in her cheeks but her voice was calm.

''You're mistaken if you think I get engaged and break it with the lightness of feeling that one has for a school-girl prank,'' she said with quiet dignity. ''I didn't set out to hurt anyone. I want to know the kind of love Mama has with Papa, that Aunt Rae has had with Jericho, that Uncle Noah and Jessa have shared these last eight years. Why should I settle for less than Grandpapa and Grandmama have had, or Uncle Gareth and Darlene, or Aunt Leah and Troy?''

She had looked at her father squarely then. ''I'll never have that with George Monroe, Tom Broadwater, or John Rourke. I want to believe it's there, Papa, but it never is, not on my part.''

Her fingers had begun to tremble. Her chin had come up a notch and she had hidden her hands in the folds of her hunter green gown. "But if I have become such an embarrassment to my family, I'll accept your decision." Tears had gathered in her eyes and spiked her lashes. The trembling in her hands had become part of her voice.

Courtney felt a rush of heat to her cheeks as she recalled the threat she had made then. Before she could call back the words she had swept from the room, ignoring her father's command for her return. McClellan pride and the ache in her own heart kept her from returning to the family fold now.

She pushed away from the veranda column and started down the path that led to the river. In her childhood the path had been beaten-down grass and dirt. She had loved the feel of it beneath her bare feet. Now it was laid with gravel and the stones jabbed at her even through her shoes.

The sateen skirt of her gown swirled around her as she turned and looked back at the house. McClellan's Landing was set among a grove of regal-looking willow oaks. They had been there, vying for their share of the sky with the Landing's four chimneys as long as Courtney could remember. White shutters framed all the windows. Sunlight winked at her as it was reflected off the panes of glass. The red brick and slate roof absorbed the warmth.

As a child, sailing with her father and mother on the *Clarion*, she had run to the taffrail with her brothers as their ship approached the James River from the Atlantic. It was their game to see who could spy the Landing first. There were a dozen stately residences in the Virginia Tidewater, but none save McClellan's Landing made Courtney's heart swell with such fierce love.

McClellan's Landing was a small community unto itself. Besides the outbuildings for the servants, the summer kitchen, and a stable for the draft animals, there were curing and storage sheds for the sweet tobacco crop, stables for the thoroughbreds, and a dock for shipping the plantation goods and livestock.

It was also largely a family enterprise. Some members were responsible for the farming, overseeing the plantings and harvesting, the crop rotation, the curing, and packing. Other members managed the raising of prime horseflesh. Her Uncle Noah, practicing law in Richmond, kept everyone apprised of the regulations that were thorns in the side of all McClellans, and it was Courtney's own father who was responsible for every aspect of the shipping.

The graveled path took Courtney to a knoll. She paused on its gently curving crest and breathed deeply. Even in winter there was a certain lushness to the Tidewater, a substance that could be felt in the salty air, heard in the rhythmic lapping of water against the shore. Loblolly and pond pines shaded her, bare black willow branches whipped at her as the wind swept off the river.

Courtney's skirt beat against her legs and her hair blew back from her face and shoulders. She stood there a long moment, staring at the blue-gray expanse of water, the bright white curve of the tidal waves, and knew in her heart that as much as she was drawn to the Landing, she was too much her father's daughter not to be drawn still more to the sea.

She started to walk toward the dock and halted again. A single-mast sloop was skimming the surface of the James like a water spider, her white, triangular sails full and curved as they cupped the air. She was expertly handled, gliding with such perfect ease that she seemed to be racing the wind rather than being guided by it.

The moment Courtney was certain of the sloop's destination she raised her skirt and petticoats and began running for the dock.

Cameron Prescott eased the sloop into its berth and tied it down. He moved with the grace of the sloop he had commanded, silent and deft, with an economy of motion borne of confidence and purpose. He raised his tricorn, touched his forearm to his brow, and adjusted his hat over his dark blond hair. He glanced over his shoulder at the dock, lines fanning out from the corners of his cool blue eyes, as he squinted in Courtney's direction. "Give me a hand, will you, Court? You weren't always so useless."

Courtney laughed. "You beast!" She jumped down beside him, careless of her skirts or her modesty. "Useless, am I?" She began helping him with the sails, her expert handling of the ropes and hoists equal to his own. "If you weren't my best friend, Cam, I'd . . . I'd . . ."

"Yes?" he asked, sidling up behind her.

She turned as his arms went around her waist. Her own encircled his neck and she raised herself on tiptoe, kissing him on each cheek, and finally hugging him hard. "I'd use you for fish bait."

"Fish wouldn't have me."

Stepping back, Courtney looked at him consideringly. He stared right back at her, giving as good as he got, his pale blue eyes amused. She liked Cam's straightforwardness, the way he dealt with her honestly and fairly, as he would any of his friends. She didn't have to watch what she said or did around him, he'd known her too long for decorum or strained politeness to be any part of their relationship. "You're right," she said finally, flashing her single-dimpled smile at him, "the fish wouldn't have you. You're too tall and too skinny." She reached under his navy jacket and tried to pinch him. He managed to elude her. "There! You see? Nothing to grab."

He chuckled. "Lean," he said. "I'm lean, not skinny."

Courtney's snort was more derisive than delicate. She pushed a lock of black hair from where it had fallen across her cheek. "Who told you that? Mavis Hamilton, I'll wager. Or Alice Parks. She's always interested in knowing when you're coming to the Landing. Someone's trying to flatter you, Cam."

He snatched her up, whipping an arm around her waist, and brought her flush to his body. He tweaked her nose with his thumb and forefinger, ignoring her when she yelped and holding her securely when she tried to wiggle out of his embrace. "Then it's a good thing I have you around to set me straight again, isn't it?"

Courtney's smile faded. She shook her head, her eyes darkening. "No, it's a good thing I have you to set me straight."

Cameron frowned and set Courtney away from him. "What is it, Court? What have you done now?"

She looked at him sharply. "Why does it have to be me who's done something? Why couldn't it be Papa or Mama or someone else who's done it to me?"

"Is it Monroe? Has George done something to you?" He cupped Courtney's chin and raised it, searching her face. "If he's hurt you . . ."

She placed her hand over Cameron's wrist and shook her head. "No, it's nothing like that. I'm afraid you were right the first time, Cam. It's me who's done it now. I've cried off again." She looked away too quickly, afraid of the censure in Cameron's eyes, and missed the shutter that had been drawn over his features. When she looked up again his only expression was one of concern. "There's not going to be any wedding tomorrow. I told George last night and I told my family today."

"I see," he said lowly. He touched her cheek, brushing away another lock of hair that slid across it. "Come on, let's get you out of this wind and up to the house where it's warmer. You can tell me all about it there."

Courtney hugged herself again. "No, I don't want to go back to the house. I just came from there. But if you want to go, I won't hold you back. I know you're looking forward to seeing everyone."

He was anxious to see the family. It had been three months since his business for the McClellans had brought him directly to the Landing and, before that,

another three months. On that occasion he'd been
given command of his own ship. It was still a stunning
thing to him that these McClellans trusted and treated
him as one of their own.

It had been Courtney's father who had first brought
him into the fold, hiring him as a cabin boy for the
Clarion when he had yet to reach his tenth year. Later,
at the grand old age of thirteen, he'd proved himself
helpful to Noah and Jessa McClellan when their child
was abducted. They had thought him incredibly brave.
That was ten years ago and Cameron knew now what
he'd only suspected then: He'd been more foolish than
courageous.

No McClellan since then had been interested in
Cam's modest denial of his real contribution in that
intrigue. Abandoned by his own family years before, he
had been happy to make his own way to escape his
father's brutal fist. Without ever knowing quite how it
happened, Cameron became, for all intents and pur-
poses, a McClellan. And Courtney, who had been his
boon companion in the early days, who practically lived
in his pockets when he was on shore, became as much
sister as confidant.

At least from Courtney's perspective. It was a view
Cameron had never shared.

He sighed now. "Of course I want to see everyone,
but it can wait. I'm going to be here until the New Year.
I'd rather hear about you first." He shrugged out of his
jacket and slipped it around Courtney's shoulders. His
white shirt billowed in the wind. He tucked the tails
more securely in his buff breeches, then adjusted the
collar of his jacket around Courtney's ears. "That's
better."

"What about you?"

"I'll be fine. Where do you want to go?"

"The gazebo?"

"All right." He tossed the duffel bag containing his
belongings back into his sleeping quarters in the hold.

"Lead the way." His hand slipped around her waist and he lifted her easily onto the dock. When he would have climbed out himself he saw she had turned and was holding out a hand to him. Clasping it, Cameron pulled himself up. He did not let go as they followed the path halfway to the house, then deviated from it to go to the gazebo.

"What have you been doing these past months?" Courtney asked.

"I thought we were going to talk about you."

She hesitated. "Not just yet. It's so boring to cry on your shoulder all the time."

"They're broad enough."

Courtney glanced sideways. His shoulders were broad. She hadn't really noticed that about him before. It seemed odd to notice now when he'd probably filled out years ago. If she hadn't been so busy crying on them, she might have seen.

"Now what is it?" he asked. Cameron was too aware of Courtney not to see when worry shaded every aspect of her features.

"What? Oh, it's just that I'm always realizing how selfish I am."

"Well, if that's all it is."

She smiled at the dry, indifferent tone he affected. He could always make her laugh. "You're very good for me, Cameron." She squeezed his hand. "Now tell me about you."

"If you're hoping to hear an adventure, you're sorely out of it there," he said. "I've spent most of these last months on the water. Oh, and a few weeks in Calais, then Paris."

"Paris," she said wistfully. "I've been there with Papa and Mama . . . but that was so long ago. Is it still so very beautiful?"

He nodded. "It rained hard one afternoon. I watched it from my room. When it stopped the sun came out and reflected off the rainwashed cobblestones. The street looked as if it were paved with gold. It's a sight I won't easily forget.''

Other people would have told her about the cathedral of Notre Dame or the Royal Palace. They would have described the river traffic along the Seine, the crowded markets, perhaps the Sorbonne. Cameron told her about sun beating off water-glazed streets, and ribbons of gold winding through the city. Courtney rested her head against his shoulder as they walked.

Inside the house Courtney's Aunt Rae motioned to her sister-in-law to come to the window. She drew back the curtain a few more inches as Jessa approached.

''What is it you want me to see, Rae?'' Jessa asked. ''Oh, never mind. I see.'' And just to needle Rae a little she added, ''That boy should have on a coat.''

Rae let the curtain fall. ''This is no time to be practical.'' When she saw Jessa was having fun with her, Rae's own smile turned rueful. ''All right, laugh if you will, but you do see that he's been waylaid by Courtney. She's the only person who could keep him from coming here to see you first.''

It was true, Jessa thought, taking another peek out the window. Cameron was but a decade younger yet Jessa had embraced him as a son. She had tutored him, helped him round off the rough edge to his manners, and encouraged him to attend William and Mary. He only stayed there two years, the sea's call was too strong, but Jessa didn't count it as a failure, not when she saw his cabin on the *Cristobel* was fairly lined with books.

Jessa looked at Rae curiously, a question in her clear gray eyes. ''Did you know Cam was coming? You don't seem very surprised to see him.''

Rae shrugged. ''I know he likes to be here to celebrate Christmas.''

''I know that, too. But that wasn't what I asked. Did you know he was coming?''

"And he would have wanted to be here for Courtney's wedding."

"I'm not so certain that's true."

Tossing a secretive smile over her shoulder, Rae left the dining room in search of Ashley. Courtney's mother would want to know about Cameron's timely arrival.

Sighing, made both amused and anxious by Rae's penchant for scheming, Jessa followed in her wake.

"So then I had to pay their fines," Cameron was saying, "or they would have had to spend another night in the Paris jail and I would have had to find a way to set sail with only half my crew."

Courtney was laughing so hard tears had gathered at the corners of her eyes. She laughed harder when Cam gallantly offered his sleeve. She pushed his arm away and swiped at her luminous eyes with her fingertips. The single dimple at the corner of her mouth deepened. "Oh, Cam, and you say you don't have any adventures. I thought the French were rather blasé about their brothels."

"Not when they're taken over by American seamen and the poor Frenchies can't even get in. I assure you, that was a matter of considerable concern."

She gave him a sidelong glance. "How was it that you weren't arrested?"

"I was at the ship, working out the details of the tobacco sale."

"Really?"

He nodded.

"Would you have gone to the brothel later?"

"What is it you want to know, Court?" He watched her squirm a moment before he took pity on her. "This particular brothel was filled with cabriolet chairs and marble cherubs. Drinks were served from a scarred cherrywood sideboard and the women lounged in their chemises, smoking cigarettes and playing chess."

For all that she was fascinated, she was also suspicious. "You're making this up."

"I'm not. The bedrooms were—"

She held up her hand. "Just how many bedrooms were you in, Cam?"

His smile was enigmatic and a direct answer was not forthcoming. "The bedrooms were papered in lavender and rose. The canopies on the four-posters matched the paper. Above one bed, suspended on chains at each corner, there was a mirror."

"Now I know you're teasing me." When she saw his brows raise a fraction, she became a little less sure. "Aren't you?"

"The women weren't especially pretty, at least not as pretty as you might think," he said. "But they were friendly, even a little curious about us. They don't see all that many Americans."

Courtney snorted lightly in disbelief. "How could you answer their questions? You and your crew don't speak French so that anyone can understand it."

"I said they were curious. I didn't say they asked questions."

"Oh, you mean they—they—" Words failed her.

He nodded. "Their curiosity ran in the direction of making comparisons. It wasn't something any of the men had to talk about." Now Cameron watched a becoming pale rose color flush her face. "I wondered when you were going to blush."

She gave him a playful jab in the side with her elbow, then slipping her fingers out of his, Courtney ran ahead to the gazebo. For a moment Cameron simply stood there, watching her go. His eyes, shaded by thick lashes much darker than his hair, passed over her flyaway ebony hair, her narrow shoulders, and the slim line of her back. The wind lifted the hem of her hunter green gown. He could see her lacy petticoats and the turn of her delicate ankles. Cameron's mouth flattened, his ice-blue eyes were remote, even pained. But when Courtney turned on the steps, waiting for him, she only saw his smile.

The gazebo was a white octagonal structure with latticework framing the lower half of each side. Benches were built along the inside walls. The roof was an ornately carved cupola. A black iron ship was perched at its crest, pointing out the direction of the wind.

"There's a bit of protection against the breeze in here," Courtney said. She sat down on one of the benches and indicated the space beside her.

"It would be warmer in the house," he said, sitting next to her. He leaned back and stretched his long legs, crossing them at the ankles.

"It's more crowded in the house, but you're welcome to go."

He didn't move. "They've all come to the Landing, then?"

She nodded. "There are children underfoot in every room. Grandmother keeps counting heads to make certain none of the little ones have wandered off. There are sixteen of us now. Seventeen, counting you. We'll all eat Christmas dinner in the kitchen, you know, while my grandparents, parents, and all the aunts and uncles eat in the main dining room."

Cameron said gravely, "I suggest a mutiny. We'll take over the dining room and force the first and second generations to feast in the kitchen."

"It's really not very amusing, Cam. You have a ship at your command. No one treats you as a child, at least not until you step foot at the Landing."

Cam said nothing. There was no reason to point out Courtney herself was the most guilty in that regard. He was surprised she mentioned his command. He thought there were times that she still thought of him as a cabin boy, taking orders instead of giving them, avoiding responsibilities instead of shouldering them.

"I can't seem to avoid being treated as if I have no more sense than my littlest cousins."

"Perhaps you should tell me about your broken engagement," he said. "I take it the news was not well-received."

One half of Courtney's full mouth lifted derisively. "Can you doubt it? I've embarrassed everyone. Mama took to the news better than Papa, of course, but I knew she was deeply disappointed." Courtney pulled Cameron's jacket more tightly around her shoulders. "I told everyone at once in the drawing room. It would have gone to a public hearing minutes after telling my parents anyway so I decided to do it myself. It was simply awful, Cam. Once I gave them the news they acted as if I weren't there any longer, or at least as if I were deaf."

Cameron felt the press of the latticework at his back. His arms were folded across his chest and his head was tilted to one side. He looked over at Courtney's bent head and said consideringly, "And after the rousing debate, how did the voters line up? All against you? Or was there some support among the ranks?"

She smiled and her darting look at Cam was appreciative. Trust him to understand how her family had discussed the matter. "It appears to be evenly split. All the men see it one way and the women the other. Even my grandparents are divided over it."

Cam's brows rose a fraction and he whistled softly. "It was a serious discussion then."

Nodding, Courtney slipped one hand under Cam's folded arms and leaned against his shoulder. "I've ruined everyone's Christmas." Her short laugh was humorless. "The thing is, I planned the wedding for Christmas on purpose. I didn't want anyone going to the trouble they had with my first two engagements. There's always a feast here for the holidays so there wouldn't be a lot of extra preparation and Mama decorates the house so beautifully that nothing else is needed."

"How considerate of you."

She lifted her head and studied Cam's profile a moment, uncertain if she should take his words at face value. Finally she lowered her head again and said, "I thought so. I was trying to do the right thing by everyone this time."

"Did it never occur to you, Court, that by making the arrangements you did, you were really planning for just this end?"

Courtney moved away from him quickly, her back stiff. "That's a perfectly horrid thing to say! Of course I wasn't planning to cry off. I had every intention of marrying George Monroe when I became engaged else I would have told him no."

Cameron was not at all perturbed by her prickly anger. "Then why aren't you marrying him tomorrow?" he asked reasonably.

"Because I don't love him!"

"But you did."

"Of course I did!"

He was quiet, thinking it over. "So what happened to change your mind?"

Courtney stood up and went to the other side of the gazebo. Through the trees she could see the mast of Cam's sloop, bobbing and swaying on the James. "Nothing happened," she said quietly. "I woke up yesterday morning and knew absolutely that I didn't love him and that I couldn't marry him for any other reason."

"Then there's nothing wrong with George."

She shook her head. "Not a thing. He's generous, very thoughtful, and gets on well with my family. All of them. You and I both know that's no mean feat. We share a number of the same interests and he's never been put off by the fact that I have my own opinions. In fact, he displayed a remarkable degree of deference."

"A paragon," Cam said dryly. The last thing Courtney needed was someone always giving in to her. "Who was it before George? Tom Broadwater?"

Courtney nodded. "There was nothing wrong with

him either. He was quite handsome, very intelligent, and he played the spinet beautifully. He didn't seem to mind that I couldn't. He accepted me for precisely who I am. It never bothered him that I wasn't nearly as accomplished as he.''

That's because he hadn't appreciated any aspect of Courtney save her beauty, Cameron thought. "I see," Cam said. "And before Tom? It was Peter Davies, wasn't it?"

Courtney turned suddenly. "Oh God, no. I never said I would marry Peter. That was the story he put out. Credit me with some good sense, Cam. Peter and I would have never suited. He didn't enjoy riding or sailing. He toured his plantation in a carriage! Can you imagine? He was much too old for my tastes."

"Too old? He was younger than either Tom or George. They're both in their thirties. Peter can't be more than twenty-eight."

"Well, he seemed older than my grandfather."

Cameron chuckled at that, "So you were never engaged to Peter. That leaves who? John somebody-or-other?"

Courtney was not amused. "You know very well it was John Rourke. I cried on your shoulder often about him."

"You thought he'd never love you."

"I was seventeen. I thought he'd never notice me."

"He did."

"That's because you helped me make him jealous." She sat on the bench opposite Cameron. "Do you ever regret doing that?"

"What? Pretending an interest in you?"

She nodded.

"I am interested in you."

"Oh, you know what I mean."

"Yes," he said after a moment, his pale blue eyes implacable. "I know what you mean, and no, I don't regret it."

"I just thought . . . since things didn't turn out quite as I had planned, well . . . I thought perhaps you were sorry for your part in it."

"I'm not the one who got engaged nor the one who broke it off. What was it you eventually found not to love about John?"

Courtney raised her hands in a helpless gesture, at a loss to explain. "There was nothing about him not to love. I just knew one day that I didn't." She had to raise her chin a notch, not in defiance but as a way of holding back the tears that welled in her eyes. "It's not them, Cameron. It never has been. It's me. There's something about me."

Cameron went to her then, lifting her by the elbows so that she stood in the circle of his loose embrace. Her cheek was warm against his chest and where her tears touched his shirt, he could feel the dampness on his skin.

"What am I going to do?" she asked plaintively.

His voice was gentle. "It's not the end of the world, Court."

It wasn't precisely what she wanted to hear. "I wish it were."

He found a handkerchief in one of his jacket pockets and gave it to her. "Here, wipe your eyes and blow." He smiled when she obeyed without hesitation. "No, I don't want it," he said when she tried to hand him the handkerchief. "Put it back in the pocket. Good. Now tell me why you're so sure it's you and not them."

She shook her head. "I don't want to talk about it."

He didn't press. "All right. Then tell me why you're so bent on avoiding your family right now. Surely the worst is over. You've already told them the news."

"Yes, I've done that," she said a shade reluctantly. Courtney lifted her face and drew back so that she could see Cameron better. "I threatened Papa."

Cameron's eyes narrowed. "What have you done, Court?"

"It wasn't only me," she said defensively. "Papa did his share of rash speaking."

"I'm certain that's true." Because you could cause a saint to bargain with the devil, he thought. "But I care for what you said."

"Oh, very well," she said, pulling away from him. "I told Papa that he needed not worry about another engagement. I fully intend to marry the first man I lay eyes on and have done with it."

"You told your father that?"

"I did."

"And?" he prompted, his voice carefully cool.

"And what? I mean to do it. I've been very careful about my choices in the past and we see the pass I've come to as a result." Her smile was self-mocking. "This time I'm not going to advance cautiously at all. Actually I was trying to think how I might meet some man here at the Landing. It isn't likely we'll have many eligible guests for the holidays, not when word circulates about what I've done to poor George. I'll be a pariah. What about you, Cameron?"

He was silent a moment. His heart thudded loudly in his chest. Could she hear it? "Me?" he asked.

Courtney slipped into his coat. The cuffs touched her fingertips. She began rolling them up. "Yes, do you have any ideas how I might meet some man here?"

She wasn't looking at him and for that Cameron was grateful. He'd come as close to making a fool of himself as he ever had. Except for his slightly indrawn breath, the brief gasp when pain struck his soul, Cameron managed to keep his balance as the very ground seemed to shift beneath his feet. His heavy lashes shaded the frost blue color of his eyes.

"No, Court," he said, his tone neutral. "I don't have the least idea how you'd meet a man here." He thought the pain could only go so deep but the longer he stood there, watching her roll the cuffs on his jacket, indifferent to his hurt, indeed, indifferent to him, the more thoroughly the knife was driven. He stepped away. "If you'll excuse me, I should be going up to the house now."

She paused at her task and looked up. "You're not going to leave me now, are you? I thought you'd help me arrive at some plan."

"Not this time, Court. I think you'd do better to work out of this scrape on your own." He turned and stepped lightly down the gazebo stairs. It was difficult not to run.

Courtney leaned against one of the supports, watching him go, miserably aware that she hadn't even her best friend to stand with her. When he turned toward the river she called out to him. "I thought you were going to the house."

"I have to get my duffel," he called back. Then he disappeared over a rise.

In her bedroom, Ashley's breath misted the window pane. She wiped the spot with her fingertips and glanced at Jessa. "Where do you suppose he's going?"

Jessa's eyes followed Cameron as he walked away from the gazebo. She had hoped he would turn toward the house. "I'm not sure. You don't think he's leaving, do you?"

Rae was peeking over the top of both their heads. "I want to know why Courtney isn't following him. That isn't like her. Do you suppose they've had an argument?"

Nodding, Ashley's eyes sought out her daughter standing on the steps of the gazebo. Courtney's head was bent. She was absently rubbing the sleeve of Cam's jacket with her palm. "Look at her. I've never seen her so alone. She's likely to break my heart."

"This is simply not to be borne," Rae said. "I'm of a mind to go out there and have a talk with both of them."

Jessa and Ashley spoke simultaneously. "Don't you dare!"

Rae blinked at their vehemence. "It was just a thought."

Neither Jessa nor Ashley were entirely convinced by Rae's sheepish defense. Exchanging a glance, they rolled their eyes. Be certain it remains just a thought," Jessa said. "It seems to me you've done quite enough simply getting Cameron here."

"Getting Cameron here?" asked Rae. "What do you mean? If you suspect me of something, Jessa, then you may as well say it outright."

Ashley placed her hand over Jessa's wrist. "Don't bother accusing her of anything. She'll deny it."

Rae smiled. "Would you expect me to admit to something I didn't do?"

Jessa's sigh was cut off as she saw Courtney start running toward the river. "Do you think she's going after him?"

"If she has any sense," Rae said firmly.

Watching Courtney go, Ashley felt the heaviness in her breast ease.

Cam was rising from the hold, the duffel bag slung over his shoulder, when Courtney came running across the dock. He looked up, his features carefully indifferent. "What is it?" he asked.

Courtney came to an abrupt stop and held up one hand as she tried to catch her breath. "Let me take out the sloop," she said.

"No."

She was so startled by Cam's answer that she could only blink stupidly. "No?"

Climbing out of the sloop, Cam stood on the dock. "No," he repeated. He made to walk around her but Courtney grabbed his forearm.

"Why not?" she asked.

"I don't need to give you a reason. It's my sloop. I don't want you taking it out."

Courtney's silver-gray eyes widened. She almost stamped her foot in frustration but held back, knowing what Cam would think of such a childish gesture. "Oh, all right," she said, not quite able to keep the sullenness out of her voice. She looked at the sloop then back at Cameron. "Go to the house if you must."

Releasing himself from her grip on his arm, Cameron took a few steps, stopped, looked back at her and said, "Aren't you coming?"

She shook her head. "Not yet." Courtney moved to the end of the dock and sat down, dangling her legs over the side. She leaned her shoulder against one of the pilings, pointedly avoiding Cameron. She could feel his eyes on her, boring holes in her back, and though she grew uncomfortable, Courtney refused to give in. Waiting him out, she was finally rewarded by the sound of his retreating footsteps.

When she was certain he was out of sight, Courtney's legs stopped their rhythmic, childlike swinging. How many times, she wondered, had she waited for Cameron's return with just that posture? And how often had her enthusiastic greeting left him no doubt he was welcome at the Landing? The memory of the picture they'd both made on those occasions brought a smile to her lips. Years ago she had fairly danced on the dock, whooping and yelling, laughing and jumping, when the ship he was on came into view. He'd lean over the edge of the taffrail, his hair bright yellow in the sunlight, and wave so hard that she feared he would drop overboard.

"If you were here right now I'd push you in," she mumbled to herself. "And it would serve you right. Do you think I can't handle your precious sloop?" She stood, hesitated only a few seconds while she glanced in the direction of the house, then jumped on the sloop's deck. With an efficiency born of long practice, Courtney made ready to set sail.

It was the duffel bag, tossed carelessly at her feet, that stopped her cold. Her posture was defiant, the set of her mouth mutinous, as she looked up at Cam. He was an imposing presence on the edge of the dock, towering over her, his body rigid with anger.

"You needn't have thrown your duffel at me," she said coolly, taking the offensive. "I might have been hurt."

Cameron's pale blue eyes were hard. He ignored her gambit. "What is it that you did not understand? Can you not comprehend the word 'no'?"

"I don't think I like your tone, Cameron."

"At this moment, Court, I don't think I like you." He saw her wince.

Being hit by the duffel would have hurt less. Some of Courtney's reckless bravado faded. Her fingers toyed with the rope they held. "I would not have damaged your precious sloop," she said, unable to look at him now.

He was quiet a moment, staring at her bent head. "I wasn't concerned about the sloop."

She raised her face. "Then why . . ."

Cameron climbed down and took the rope from her hands. His voice was carefully neutral, his chiseled features set impassively, but hard. "There's a storm coming."

Courtney looked to the west. Dark gray clouds had gathered in the distance. "I hadn't noticed."

"I know." He stood there, waiting for her to make some move toward the dock. When she didn't, he said, "Come back to the house with me, Court."

"No. Not yet."

His sigh was barely audible. "Very well," he said. "Then help me take her out. There's time enough before the storm gets here."

Courtney threw herself against him, laughing joyously, and kissed him on both cheeks. She repeated her thanks several times, as eager and grateful as a child. Her eyes shone. "You won't regret this."

He gently disengaged himself from her fierce hold. Turning his back on her he said under his breath, "I already do."

Some of Courtney's pleasure faded when Cameron turned away. She stared at his back. The wind pressed his white linen shirt against his skin. There was tension in every line of his body. "Cameron?" she said softly.

He glanced over his shoulder. His brows were arched in question. "What is it, Court?"

For a moment she didn't answer. Couldn't answer. There was an odd wrenching in the pit of her stomach, a missed beat of her heart. His tricorn rested slightly back on his head. There was a fringe of dark blond hair at his brow. She suddenly had an urge to touch his hair. She envied the breeze that caressed it.

"Court?"

She blinked. "Nothing," she said. "It was nothing." Looking away hurriedly, afraid he might see something in her eyes she did not understand herself, Courtney bent to her task.

Once they had the sloop out Cameron let Courtney take the sail. He sat against the side, his legs stretched out across the deck. His hands were idly busy with a rope, making a series of knots—sheepshank, bowline, figure eight—with no thought at all to what he was doing. His long fingers wove the rope, dismantled it, then wove it again.

Courtney watched his hands as she ran the sloop directly before the wind. Why had she never noticed what beautiful hands he had? His fingers curled around the rope, twisted it. How would they feel sifting through her hair?

Cameron felt her eyes on him and looked up, saw the direction of her gaze, and held up his hands, examining them critically and a little self-consciously. "Not as soft as George Monroe's, are they?"

"More capable though," she said. Her eyes wandered away, uncomfortable and uncertain with the direction of her thoughts. It was difficult to look at his hands and not think of them touching her. The calluses on the pads of his fingers would be pleasantly abrasive. His hands would chase a shiver across her skin, raising heat just below the surface.

"Are you feeling quite the thing?" Cameron asked. "You're flushed. Perhaps I should take the sail."

"No," she said quickly. "No, I'm fine." She concentrated on the sail, letting it all the way out. A sudden shift in wind or course would cause a jibe. The boom would come slamming hard to the other side and knock one of them senseless if they weren't careful. Her dark hair fluttered around her cheeks and shoulder. She pushed it back, tucking it into the raised collar of Cam's jacket. "Do you remember the first time we went sailing together?" she asked.

He grinned. "We had too many captains and not enough mates."

"There were only the two of us."

"My point exactly."

She laughed. "You thought you knew everything."

"I'd been working on your father's ship for three months."

"Yes, but you were the cabin boy, not the captain."

"It seemed all the same to me back then. Besides, you were only a—"

Courtney made a distasteful face, finishing his sentence for him. "A girl." She feigned a shudder. "How awful for you that you were bested by a girl."

"Odd . . . I don't recall being bested. We both took a swim that day. And you went in first."

"You threw me in."

"You disobeyed an order."

"You weren't in command. I was." Her eyes crinkled as her smile widened. The dimple appeared. "I got you in the water, didn't I?"

Cameron's own smile was playfully derisive. "That's because you lied. You said you couldn't swim."

"It was sweet of you to want to save my life."

"I was thinking of my own skin. Salem would have killed me if anything had happened to you."

Courtney's smile vanished. Her eyes were grave. "Is that really the reason you did it?" she asked. "Because of Papa?"

No, he thought. He had loved her even then. What he said was, "We were friends, Court."

She nodded. The sweet, wistful smile shaped her mouth. "We were, weren't we? The very best of friends." Courtney hauled in the sail as she changed course. The wind came abeam now. The leading edge of the sail fluttered. She drew it in a few inches for the perfect rim. The sloop skimmed the surface of the water effortlessly.

"Where are you taking us?"

"Norfolk. That's where your ship's anchored, isn't it?"

"That's where the *Cristobel* is. There was cargo to unload. But we're not going that far." He cut her off before she could question his decision. "I just came from there," he said. "I have no intention of going back. And I am the captain now."

"A despot and a tyrant." His easy smile, not a whit remorseful or apologetic, held Courtney still. The wind beat at the sail. She held it steady, glad Cameron could not know the vibration had started with her, with his smile, and not with the beating breeze. "Oh, very well," she said lightly. "We'll only go as far as Jamestown."

Having averted a mutiny, Cameron settled back. While his fingers worked and reworked the rope he watched Courtney's competent handling of the sloop. Her touch was sure. She raised her face to the wind and it blew color into her cheeks. "You'll have to go back to the Landing sometime," he said.

"But not yet."

"No," he said. "Not yet. Not if you're not ready."

She was silent. Courtney's eyes were the same gray of the clouds as her glance darted between the sky and the shore. There were breaks in the pines and white willows, places where the bare oaks opened up to landscaped gardens grown brown and tangled in the winter, places where graveled paths led to magnificent red-brick plantation homes. The tidal waters of the James lapped at the side of the sloop. Diamond droplets of water cascaded against the bow.

"I never meant to hurt George," she said. Tears were diamond drops in her eyes. "I would have married him if I thought I could."

Cameron's eyes were shaded by his lashes. The corner brim of his hat cut a shadow across his face. "Did you fall out of love?"

"I don't know." She looked at Cam helplessly. "How does one know something like that? I'm not certain I loved him ever. I know I wanted to. I know I should have."

"Should have? What makes you think that?"

"Because I went about it so carefully this time." Her smile was watery as she swiped impatiently at her eyes. "George was a proper age for me. Responsible. Respected. There was nothing about him that one could fail to admire. His proposal made me envied."

"And?"

"And . . . nothing," she said lowly. "I couldn't bear it when he touched me."

Cameron sat up a little straighter. His fingers stilled around the bowline. "Courtney."

She waved aside his concern. "It wasn't always like that. Not in the beginning anyway. I felt uneasy at first but then I told myself I shouldn't enjoy being kissed, not before the marriage, certainly not before the engagement."

"That's absurd."

"Is it? I don't think so. It's happened every time. I like the idea of being in love I think, but I've no interest in what must accompany it. There's no passion in me, Cam. I'm not like the rest of my family."

He snorted. "How do you come by these notions?"

She heard the laughter in his voice and it angered her. Courtney turned away, set her mouth tightly, and refused to respond.

Cameron moved beside her, laying his hand over hers on the rudder. "I didn't mean to laugh, Court, not when it distresses you so. It's simply that, well, it's laughable."

She removed her hand from under his and let him take control of the sloop. "I shouldn't have told you. I'm sorry I did."

"No, Court, I'm sorry. I swear I'm sor—" Cameron saw tears gathering in her eyes again. "Oh, hell . . . it's just that . . . oh, hell." Slipping his free arm around her waist, taking her completely by surprise, Cameron kissed her full on the mouth. Hard. And long. And deep.

The sloop shuddered as the wind came over the port bow. Cameron broke the kiss, steered the sloop into the wind, filling the sail from the other side. "I'm sorry." He said it because he thought he should, not because he meant it. Courtney hadn't been cold in his arms. Quite the contrary. After the first moment her response had been as full and promising as he'd known it would be. "There's passion in you, Court," he said lowly. "I'd be no kind of friend to let you think otherwise."

Slightly dazed, Courtney nodded slowly. Unconsciously her hand was lifted to her lips. Her fingers lightly touched the swollen curve of her mouth. She had been kissed before but no one had ever curled her toes. She told him that.

Cameron concentrated on the sloop, tacking first to starboard, then to port, and pretended not to hear. Overhead the sky was darkening. The sloop raced against the onset of the storm. He glanced upward. Grimaced.

He could still taste her against his mouth. That kiss had been a stupid thing to do. He would never forget the taste of her, the scent of her hair, the color in her cheeks as he drew away, color the wind hadn't put there. He would never forget. The memory would be torture.

Courtney stared down at her hands. "You taught me how to bait a hook. Do you remember? Papa always let me fish with him but you were the one who let me bait the hook. You taught me about bowlines and sheepshanks, how to make a reef knot or splice a line. We have been good friends, haven't we?"

Cameron didn't look at her, not certain he liked where she was heading. "We've been good friends," he said.

"You taught me how to climb into the sails of my father's ship. You taught me how to whittle."

"Jericho taught you that."

"You taught me better."

He shrugged.

"We were up to every trick together. To this day no one knows we're the ones who finished off that keg of beer in the cellar. Remember that woman Uncle Noah was going to marry?"

"I'm not likely to forget Hilary."

"Remember how she flogged Big Billy with her whip for being slow? We cared for him without anyone's help afterwards, and when he begged us not to say anything we didn't."

"He was afraid it would have gone the worse for him."

She nodded. "And we kept the secret. Over the years we've kept a lot of secrets and promises between us, crossed our hearts and spit. I suppose that's the sort of things friends do."

"Sometimes," he said, a cautious note in his voice and in his eyes.

Courtney brushed a strand of hair from her cheek as she turned toward him. In profile his face was hard, the line of his jaw clean and taut. A muscle worked in his cheek. "Teach me about kissing, Cameron."

The muscle ticked faster. "No."

Before she lost her nerve she said, "Teach me how it is between lovers."

His hand tightened on the boom. "NO!"

"It will be our secret. No one has to know."

"No."

"It's not as if you'd have to marry me. I wouldn't expect that."

His eyes rolled upward. "Thank God for small favors."

"That wasn't a very nice thing to say, Cam."

If both his hands hadn't been occupied just then, Cameron Prescott would have throttled her. With a sidelong glance he managed to convey the thought nonetheless. "Stop it, Court. I've said no. There are boundaries to friendship, at least to my way of thinking there are. I shouldn't have kissed you like that. I'm sorry if it put ideas in your head."

She paled. "You didn't like the kiss. I didn't do it right, did I?"

Was she serious? "Don't play the fool. You know perfectly well I—" Then he looked at her, really looked, and saw the anxiousness and uncertainty. He told himself to leave well enough alone, let her believe what she would and be done with her latest cork-brained scheming. Even as he was thinking it he heard himself saying, "I liked the kiss, Court. You did it fine."

"Oh."

"You don't need any lessons. You need the right—"

"Man," she said. "I know. But can't you help me until I find him?"

It only got worse, Cameron thought. Like an expert marksman her aim was always true. Somehow he managed to speak. "I—don't think so." She looked as if she might object. Cameron was thankful for the skies opening up just then. A fat drop of rain splattered on Courtney's shoulder. Another one hit the back of his hand. "Get below."

"I can help."

He shook his head. "I can manage. There's no need

for both of us to get wet. We've almost reached James-town. I'll take her to shore myself.''

Courtney stood and began to slip out of the jacket he'd loaned her. "Take this at least. It will help.''

The rain was already coming harder and faster. "Below, Courtney. Now.''

There was no brooking him when he used that tone. She kept the jacket on and hurried below deck. The sloop's hold was utilitarian. Besides the duffel bag there was nothing in it that belonged to Cameron. In spite of maintaining the sloop as his, he had merely borrowed it from the McClellan armada at Norfolk. The single bunk was unmade. Chipped cups swayed on their hooks above the small Franklin stove. Wood was neatly stacked beside the stove, held securely in a canvas sling. There was a cupboard with clean linens, a washstand with basin and pitcher inside, fresh water in a cask, and another cupboard with a few staples. She found tea and coffee, sugar and salt, raspberry preserves and jerky. In the spring and summer when the sloop was used to make regular pleasure runs between Norfolk and the Landing the larder would be filled. Courtney wished that was the way of it now.

With skillful tacking Cameron reached the dock. The sloop stopped when he headed it directly into the wind. Lashing it to the pilings, he hauled in the sails so the boat wouldn't be battered against the dock. By the time he climbed down the ladder into the hold, his shirt was soaked. When he tipped his head water rushed from the curled corners of his tricorn as if it were a down-spout. He tossed the hat in the direction of Courtney's laughter, spattering her with water.

"That was very bad of you," she said, placing the hat on the stove where it could dry. "I've made some tea. Would you like some?''

"Put a little whiskey in it and I'll accept." He plucked at his wet shirt. It clung to him like skin he needed to shed. "Below the bunk," he told her. "In one of the storage drawers. I think there's a bottle there."

Courtney knelt in front of the bunk. The sheets she'd placed over it were clean but slightly musty. She smoothed a corner before she opened one of the drawers. "Here it is." She held the bottle up and looked over her shoulder for Cameron's approval. Her breath caught in her throat.

He was simply beautiful. Droplets of water glistened on his naked shoulders and clear beads clung to spiky strands of hair at his nape. The muscles in his arms bunched as he rolled up his soaked shirt and tossed it in a corner. The buff breeches molded his thighs, clinging to the long, hard length of his legs. He may as well have not had them on.

She changed her mind about that when Cameron started to take them off. "What are you doing?" she asked. Her voice was pitched a notch too high. She pretended not to notice.

Cameron was not so polite. He laughed out loud. His thumbs hooked in the waistband of his breeches. "I'm going to take off my breeches. I'd be pleased if you'd get out a dry pair from my bag."

Putting down the bottle of whiskey, Courtney rooted through the duffel, found a pair of soft leather hunting breeches, and threw them over her shoulder at Cameron.

"I need a pair of dry drawers," he told her.

Heat flushed her cheeks. Biting back a small groan, Courtney found the drawers and tossed them to Cameron as well. She could hardy understand what was wrong with her. She'd been swimming in the James with Cam since she was eleven. She'd grown up in a home with brothers and uncles, lived on a ship for months at a time in almost the exclusive company of males, had nearly married on three separate occasions, and now with Cameron, she was hot and cold in the same moment, fevered and shivering in the same heartbeat.

She didn't turn around until he reached over her shoulder to get the whiskey.

"What about you?" he asked. "Whiskey in your tea?"

Courtney nodded. Definitely, she thought, whiskey was important right now. The roll of distant thunder brought her to her feet. She found some candles, lit them, and closed the hatch just as lightning seared the sky.

Cameron saw her jerk at the sight of the lightning. He handed her a mug of tea. "Not quite the Christmas Eve you expected, is it?"

Her smile was rueful. "You know I'd forgotten. About it being Christmas Eve, I mean. I haven't the right spirit for the season." She sipped her tea. Over the chipped rim of the cup she found herself staring at Cameron's naked chest. The bent of her thoughts gave her a guilty start. A droplet of tea fell on her chin. Before she could brush it away Cameron's finger was there, touching her gently. The sloop's hold suddenly seemed very, very close quarters.

Cameron saw her shiver. "That jacket's wet. You'd do better to exchange it for a dry blanket. There must be some where you found the sheets." The first thing he'd noticed when he entered the cabin was that she had made up the bunk. He had been trying to rein in his thoughts ever since. He set his tea down. "I have to get a shirt." Turning away, he missed the expression of relief in Courtney's eyes.

Courtney hung the jacket, wrapped herself in a faded quilt, and sat down cross-legged on the bunk. The mug warmed her hands and the tea and whiskey warmed her throat. There was a small ball of heat in her stomach that had no reason to exist save for Cameron. "How long do you think we'll be here?"

He finished tucking in the tails of his dropped shoulder shirt. The button at his throat was left unfastened. "I'm not sure. It doesn't seem the rain's going to let up any time soon."

"I suppose I should have thought of that before I insisted we take out the sloop."

"I'm the one responsible, not you. You could have insisted all you wanted and I could have still said no." He picked up his tea and joined her on the bunk. "The pity is, I don't tell you no often enough."

Courtney thought of their conversation on deck before the storm broke. He'd told her no then. Several times.

He searched her face and plucked the thoughts out of her mind as if they were his own. "Forget about that kiss and everything else you want from me. Your family trusts me to take care of you, Court."

She leaned forward until her mouth was a moment from his. Her breath was sweet, her voice soft. "Then take care of me." Her lips settled over his.

Salem McClellan stamped his feet as he entered the house from the side door. Water dripped from the fringed sleeves of his leather coat. He took off his hat, gave it to Ashley, and spoke to the other family members huddled in the large kitchen. The warm, inviting aroma of freshly baked bread and sugar tarts could not soothe the expectant faces. They waited to hear from Salem.

"The sloop's gone," he told them. "There's no sign of Courtney nor Cameron anywhere. They must have taken it out."

"What could Cam have been thinking?" Jessa asked. "He would have seen the storm coming, wouldn't he?"

Ashley sighed. "I doubt when all's said and done that the blame for this will fall at Cameron's feet. He'll accept more than his share of the responsibility—he always has—but this is Courtney's doing."

Salem was torn between fear for his daughter and guilt that he had forced her to this pass. He sought out Ashley but there was no accusation in her eyes. She helped him out of his sodden coat. "Cameron will take care of her, Salem. He loves her as well as any of us."

"That does not assuage all my fears, wife."

Rae laughed at her brother's dry pronouncement. "I wondered if you knew," she said.

"Knew that Cameron loves my daughter? I'm not so blind as you might think, Rae. The only person at the Landing who doesn't seem to understand is Courtney herself." His eyes darted to the other members of his family. "I suppose everyone here has been thinking Cameron's timely arrival is Rae's doing. If I know my sister, she's been careful not to take the credit but somehow manages to make everyone think it just the same."

Ashley poked her husband in the chest. "You!"

"I'm not certain your surprise flatters me. Cannot a man further the interests of true love, or is that strictly a woman's province?"

One of his brother's laughed. "I think Cupid was a man."

Another sniggered. "Cupid was a baby. It ain't the same."

Ruddy color touched Salem's complexion but Ashley was hugging him hard and he liked having her with him again. He slipped his arms around her and spoke over the crown of her soft ebony hair. "Whatever I might have wished for Courtney and Cameron, this bit of business was not part of it. The weather's right for fog. It won't be long before the entire river's shrouded with it."

Ashley lifted her face. "Then there's nothing we can do."

"Not now. Cameron will know what to do." Salem had to believe that. He couldn't have lived with himself otherwise.

Her lips were soft. They tasted faintly of tea and whiskey. The tips of Cameron's fingers pressed whitely against the mug he held. He did not move. He did not encourage.

Courtney drew back. She searched his face, her own eyes pained. "Why won't you teach me this?"

"I've told you why." The rain beat a steady tattoo against the upper deck. Cameron concentrated on that and not on the unsteady beat of his heart.

"I don't believe those reasons. There is something wrong with me."

"Only that you can't see past your own nose."

"What does that mean?"

"Leave it, Court," he said sharply. He rose from the bed and leaned against the ladder. He wanted to go topside and stand in the cold, driving rain. His jaw ached from clenching it so hard.

"You're angry with me," she said.

"I'm angry with myself."

"Why?"

Cameron bent, picked up the whiskey bottle and poured two fingers worth into what was left of his tea. He swirled the contents before he took a long swallow. "It's nothing you would understand," he said finally. "Nothing I can share."

Courtney sat up straighter. "Stop treating me like a child! I'm a woman!"

"Then act like one! Act as if you know I'm a man!"

For a long time there was only the sound of the rain and the drumming of thunder.

"I'm sorry," he said. "I shouldn't have—"

The blanket slipped from Courtney's shoulders as she shook her head. "No, it's true, isn't it? I've not been seeing things very clearly. That's what you meant about not being able to see past my nose."

He shrugged. "It's not important."

"But it is." Every time she'd noticed something about Cameron today the prickle of heat had been accompanied by a twinge of guilt. She hadn't understood it then.

She did now. He was her best friend and she wanted him in a way that had very little to do with friendship,

Unfortunately he didn't want her in the same way. He'd told her no often enough. He was a man and she had been insensitive to his feelings. She'd called on their friendship to get him to teach her about passion. He'd been right to say no when there was no passion or love in his heart.

"I'm the one who's sorry," she said, unable to meet his gaze directly. "I didn't take your feelings into account. Only my own." Her faint smile was filled with self-mockery. "I told you I was selfish."

Cameron wished he had not given himself away. Loving Courtney was never meant to burden her, yet she seemed to be weighed down by the revelation. Her head was bowed, her shoulders sloped. Her smile had mocked but her eyes were sad. He finished off his whiskey. "It's not as if there's blame to be attached. Neither of us can help the way we feel. Not about this."

She nodded slowly, raising her eyes to him. "Friends?"

"Friends."

There was an uncomfortable silence, then Courtney grinned. "I feel as if I should cross my heart and spit."

He laughed. It had been that sort of solemn vow. Their shared laughter pushed aside the awkward moment. "I have a deck of cards in my duffel. Do you want to play a few hands while we wait out the rain?"

The diversion was a welcome one. They sat on opposite ends of the bed, tossing their cards between them. Cameron was a methodical, thoughtful player. Courtney appeared to pick up and discard on whim but she won two out of every three hands played.

Courtney gathered up the cards to shuffle them. One of them had slipped under Cameron's knee. Her fingers brushed his leg as she reached for it. A frisson of awareness touched her and she glanced at Cam to see if he noticed. His pale blue eyes were distant, his features stoic.

She snapped up the card and started shuffling. Suddenly she was aware of the silence. "Listen!"

Cameron cocked his head to one side and looked at her inquiringly. What he heard was the cards passing through her hands.

"The rain," she said. "It's stopped."

He stared at the ceiling. "So it has." He honestly didn't know whether he felt relief or disappointment. Swinging his legs over the side of the bunk, Cam went to the ladder and climbed topside. In less than a minute he was back. "It's no good, Court," he told her. "We're not going anywhere tonight. The fog's as thick as cotton batting. I can't get the sloop upriver in this. We'll have to wait 'til morning."

"But it's Christmas Eve."

"And tomorrow will be Christmas. There's really nothing I can do about that. You can't spend the holiday with your family *and* run away from them."

"I wasn't running away."

His look was patently skeptical. "Oh no?"

"No. I had every intention of returning tonight."

"With a husband on your arm."

"What? Oh, you mean that threat I made to Papa. I've had time enough to think on it. I've changed my mind. I'm never going to marry."

Cameron blinked. His fingers raked his damp hair. "You're never going to marry," he repeated, shaking his head. "When did you decide this?"

When I realized the first man I met wouldn't have me as a gift. "Does it matter?" she asked. "I've made up my mind."

"You really are a piece of work, Court."

"Courtney," she said. "My name's Courtney. You make me feel all of twelve when you call me Court."

He blinked again, startled by her tone.

She saw his reaction. She could not bring herself to

apologize. She was unaccountably angry with him for reasons she couldn't even name. Courtney dealt the cards. "We may as well play. There's nothing else to do."

"We have to sleep sometime, Courtney," he said gently.

And that was the very thing she was trying to avoid, the thing that had fired her anger. Was she always so transparent to him? "We don't have to sleep now," she said. She picked up her cards and fanned them open. "I'm not the least tired."

Cameron returned to the bed. "Let me know when you are," he said calmly. "You can have the bunk and I'll take the floor."

She chose a three of hearts to discard. "We'll argue later," she said. "It's your turn."

In the end it wasn't much of an argument. They played cards until Courtney could not keep her eyes open. She made a few tired protests about taking the floor in his stead but they were ignored. Cameron helped her with her gown, unfastening the buttons then politely turning his back while she slipped out of it and into the bunk. He hung the gown on a peg and made up a bed on the floor.

Courtney came wide awake the moment his boots thumped to the floor. By the time he snuffed the candles and stripped down to his drawers, she was one exposed nerve.

Cameron listened to her breathing and knew the even cadence was forced. He knew because he was guilty of much the same thing.

"You're not sleeping," he said.

"No." She stared at the darkened ceiling. The sloop rolled in its berth, rocking the bunk like a baby's cradle. "I'm not tired anymore. Are you?"

"No." He hesitated. "Are you afraid I'm going to attack you?"

"Not at all," she said quietly. "I'm afraid you won't."

Cameron sighed. "I thought this was settled. Why are you so nervous?"

"I just told you why." She turned on her side and leaned over the edge of the bunk. "Only you don't believe me."

"What is it you want from me?"

"You," she said. "I want you."

It seemed he'd waited forever to hear those words and now they meant so little. "I'm not tutoring you."

"I don't want you like that. I just want you."

Cameron sat up. His head was level with hers. His voice was husky, resigned. "I don't say no to you nearly enough." He found her mouth in the darkness.

Courtney's lips parted beneath his. She felt his tongue trace the soft inner side of her lip. It was the most exquisite sensation she'd ever known.

Rising to his knees, Cameron cupped her face. He held her steady while his mouth explored hers, nudging and nibbling. Her response was tentative at first, then eager, every movement mirroring his. He kissed her closed lids, her brow, the curve of her cheek. Courtney's hands slipped over his. The feel of his work-roughened hands beneath hers seemed so very right, the touch of his fingertips on her face, adoring.

He raised himself to the edge of the narrow bunk. It was too dark to see her clearly. "I want to light a candle." His thumb brushed her lower lip. He felt her nod her assent but it wasn't enough. "Courtney?"

"All right," she said softly. "Light a candle."

Cameron lit two. Shadows chased light across the bunk and then across Courtney's face as she sat up. Her eyes were wide and luminous, and as Cameron approached she moved to the far side to make room for him.

"You haven't changed your mind?" he asked.

Now she understood about the candles. It wasn't merely about seeing her. It was about giving her a chance to think. "I know what I want, Cameron." She raised the sheet and blanket. "I finally know what I want."

He stared at her upturned face for a long moment. Slipping in beside her, he kissed her. They fell back on the bunk together. His fingers threaded in her hair. He sifted through it, let the soft strands curl around his fingers, cross his palm like the whisper of silk. She touched his shoulder. Stroked his arm. Her darkening eyes never left his face. She raised her hand and brushed his cheek, caressed his temple. She thought she knew him so well, but now, touching him, she knew him differently.

Her mouth parted beneath his. She reveled in the taste of him, the weight of him as he moved over her. The wide straps of her cotton chemise slipped over her shoulders. Cameron traced her collarbone, first with his finger, then with his mouth. The edge of his tongue was warm and damp. There were tiny, tasting kisses on her neck and at the hollow of her throat. He nuzzled her, blowing gently against her skin just below her ear.

"That tickles."

"Hmmm."

The vibration of his voice had the same effect. "That tickles too," she whispered. She turned her face into his neck and kissed him.

"I like it," he said.

"So do I." Her teeth caught his earlobe and tugged.

He kissed her hard. Courtney's chemise was pushed lower. His hands covered her breasts, and when she gasped at the sensation he tasted the sound of pleasure against her lips. His thumbs brushed her nipples. They stiffened at his touch.

Courtney caressed his shoulders, his arms, his back. Her neck arched as his mouth covered her nipple. His lips were gentle but the suck of his mouth was hot. Fire traveled on a taut thread just below the surface of her skin. Heat coiled at the very center of her, resting heavily between her thighs. She twisted under Cameron, arching, reaching, pressing herself against him in a way that relieved the ache. She felt the length of him, hot and hard against her abdomen.

She said the first thing that came to her mind. "Can I touch it?"

Cameron had imagined making love to Courtney any number of times. It was the stuff of daydreams and nighttime fantasies. He had thought he might be tender, loving her slowly, delicately sipping her flesh, making her want him with caresses that were so pleasuring she would cry. He had thought he might love her with urgency, as if there could be no waiting or holding any touch in reserve, needing and desiring so essential that she would cry out.

But this was Courtney McClellan, his best friend, his secret sharer, and he knew now he should have imagined loving her with laughter.

"God, yes," he said, burying his smile against the curve of her throat. "You can touch it."

Courtney's fingers slipped below the edge of his drawers. She felt him suck in his breath; his skin rippled in the wake of her touch. Shyness was simply overwhelmed by curiosity. Her hand closed around him. There was a soft murmur of pleasure that could have belonged to either of them.

Cameron stripped off his drawers. Courtney squirmed out of her chemise. Both items sailed over the side of the bunk. They stared at each other, their eyes as eager as their hands. She caressed his back from shoulder to buttocks. His skin was taut and warm and smooth. The ridge of his spine fascinated her. She traced it with her thumb.

His kisses spiraled around her breast. Her flesh swelled under his attention. There was a small cry at the back of her throat as his tongue flicked across her nipple. Her fingers pressed in his back. She moved restlessly and his legs separated hers. She liked the sense of her body defined by the shape of his. She knew the curve of her breast by the cup of his palm, the indentation of her navel by the exploration of his tongue, the length of her legs by the strength of his.

"Courtney?" Cameron asked for assurance and reassurance.

In response Courtney's hand slipped between their bodies. Her thighs opened as her legs curved around him. She did not tell him she was ready; she showed him.

Caution was abandoned. Cameron pushed himself into her as Courtney rose to meet him. His mouth slanted across hers, swallowing the urgency of her sweet cry. He drew back slightly, his lips barely touching hers. "Have I hurt you?"

"No," she whispered. She held him tightly, her eyes wide and black as she searched his face. "That is . . . not overmuch . . . oh, Cameron . . . it's . . . it's splendid."

He groaned as she shifted under him, moving to accommodate his entry. A grin split his face. "Splendid?"

She nodded. Her own smile was serene. He started to ease out of her and her smile vanished. Courtney's legs tightened around his flanks. Her fingers curled around his arms. "Don't leave me."

Thrusting into her again, he kissed her hard. Loving her, not leaving her, was on his mind.

Pleasure was a pinwheel of heat at the center of their joining. Their bodies rocked in unison. He touched her; she held him. They were eager traders, bartering their kisses for comfort, their passion for pleasure. They shared desiring and selfishly clung to excitement.

Their bodies glistened in the candlelight. The gold threads in his hair mingled with the ebony of hers. When she shuddered in his arms he felt the vibration pass from her into him. His body tensed moments after Courtney's release. He whispered her name and without even realizing it, he whispered something else.

She rested in the curve of his arm as her breathing

calmed. She listened to the sound of his breathing, felt the beat of his heart just beneath her palm, and sensed the passing of tension from every line of his body.

"Did you mean it?" she asked after a moment, her voice soft, hesitant.

"Mean what?"

Courtney's face tilted toward his. She was afraid to hear his answer and afraid not to. "Did you mean it when you said you loved me?"

Ashley patted the space in bed beside her. "Come away from the window, Salem. It's no good watching for her. You said yourself the fog won't lift until morning."

He used the back of his hand to wipe where his breath had misted on the cold pane. Salem padded softly to the bed and slipped under the covers that Ashley held up for him. They both curled on the side, one body curving against the other. His arm slid around Ashley's waist just below her breasts. "I keep thinking I'll catch sight of the sloop returning. God, Ashley, I never meant to send her flying from the Landing."

"She's of an age," Ashley said quietly. "This is her time to use her wings."

Salem's breath fluttered strands of his wife's dark hair. "I wish she had more sense," he said. "How did we raise her not to have more sense?"

In the darkness of the bedroom they had shared for twenty-one years, Ashley smiled, laying her hand over her husband's. "We raised her just fine. Courtney has as much sense as she wants or needs to have right now. We should be very happy that she showed so much courage in breaking her engagements—all three. She wasn't suited to marriage with any of them. She was very wise to know it, even if it only occurs to her at the last moment."

"I'm glad we're not fighting. I didn't know if you'd ever speak to me again."

"You knew I'd speak to you," she said, correcting him. "It's other things you were worried about." Ashley's feet nudged Salem's as she warmed herself against him. "Tell me something. If you had already invited Cameron here, why were you so angry with Court when she cried off with George?"

"I didn't know that Cam would come, or even if he did, that it would mean anything to either of them. We still don't know that. As the wedding approached I thought I'd been wrong about Courtney and George, that perhaps they were suited, and then she suddenly decides poor Monroe is not what she wants after all. I meant what I said today, Ashley, most of it anyway. Courtney cannot keep getting herself engaged and crying off."

"It was good of you to command Cameron back here."

Salem's low chuckle ruffled her hair. He kissed the back of her head. "I was not so demanding as that. I simply made certain he knew the wedding date was set for Christmas and that he might find it in his best interests to share the holiday with us at the Landing."

Ashley was silent a moment. "I know he loves her, Salem, but do you think she loves him?"

"Of course I love you," Cameron said.

Courtney did not care at all for the lightness in his voice, the way he dismissed the question as if it were of no account. She sat up, drawing the sheet to her breasts and stared down at him. "I see," she said softly. He hadn't meant it, not the way she hoped. Nothing had changed and she had been naive to suppose it might. She bent her head and kissed him lightly on the mouth. "Friends?" she asked.

"Friends," he repeated, whispering. He watched her straighten, his heart in his throat, and just as she was turning her head he glimpsed the gathering of tears in her eyes. He reached for her but when his hand touched her shoulder she jerked away. His fingers only grazed her skin. Cameron sat up, taking the quilt as Courtney drew off the sheet and wrapped it around her. She left the narrow bunk and went to the bottle of whiskey sitting on the floor. After pouring a small amount in her mug she stood by the stove, warming herself.

She held up the mug, composed now, her beautiful features shuttered and cool. "Would you like some?"

Cameron shook his head.

Courtney shrugged. "It must be after midnight," she said, glancing toward the hatch. "Christmas Day."

He studied her carefully. Behind her candlelight burnished the slope of her shoulder and bare arm.

"Mama likes to tell the story of her first Christmas Day at the Landing. Have you heard it?"

It wasn't what he wanted to hear now, but he didn't say so. It was almost as if Courtney were in shock, stunned by the enormity of what had occurred between them and needed to put it from her mind. "I don't think I have," he said lowly.

"Mama was only weeks away from bearing me. You can imagine how she looked, so petite and delicate except for an enormous belly." Courtney laughed. "She always looks sideways at my father as she tells it, reminding him her condition had much to do with him."

Cameron blanched a little but Courtney didn't notice.

"It was not long after news of Bunker Hill had reached the Landing. All along the Tidewater people expected the British to invade their homes. My mother didn't know that plantation owners greeted Christmas morning with a cannon salute. When Grandfather's cannonade announced the day, Mama thought the Landing was under siege from the redcoats. She couldn't wake Papa so she determined to save the Landing herself. She found a pistol that wasn't even primed to protect everyone. When Papa finally roused himself he thought she was a most amusing sight.

"Actually he says she was plainly ridiculous, barefooted and wearing his nightshirt, waving a pistol about as if she meant to take on the army alone. He also says it was love for her, not fear, that put his heart in his throat just then." Her smile and her voice softened. "I think I should want someone to love me like that, love me at the moment I look most ridiculous."

Cameron's fingers tightened on the quilt. "What happened then?"

"What? Oh, you mean with Mama. Well, when she realized there was no danger, she took strong exception to my father's laughter. She thought to serve him a lesson and aimed her pistol and fired."

Cameron's brows arched. "Never say . . ."

Courtney nodded. "Mother didn't know it, but the pistol was primed. Papa ducked and the bullet went through the headboard and into the wall. Mama fainted. Aunt Rae was there, watching this last piece of business. She says that she decided then she wasn't suited to marriage."

His smile was faint. "She changed her mind," he said. "What about you, Courtney? Might you change your mind?"

Courtney ignored the question and sipped her whiskey instead. "It must have been quite a Christmas morning," she said wistfully.

"You may still have the adventure you crave, Court. I shouldn't be surprised if there are pistols aimed at both of us on the morrow."

"Why ever would you think that?" For a moment she was genuinely bewildered, then she saw his eyes drift pointedly to the bed and back to her. "Oh, you mean because we . . ." She finished her drink instead of her sentence. "No one's going to do anything, Cameron, because I'm not going to say anything."

"Perhaps not," he said, "but I am."

Courtney set her mug down hard. "I forbid it."

"I don't see that you can do anything about it."

"Why would you want to?" She approached the bunk but did not sit down. "Surely what happened here is no one's concern but our own."

Cameron's voice was quietly earnest. "What happened here, Courtney? No, perhaps that's not the right question. What did you want to happen?" He caught her wrist and pulled her down on the bunk. "No, stay here. Tell me what it is you wished? Or was it only about a lesson in loving for you?"

She could not meet his eyes. Courtney stared at his hand around her wrist instead. "It was a lesson in loving," she said, "but not the one you thought I wanted. You don't really want to hear this, Cam. The knowledge won't ease your mind."

"Let me decide," he said. His hand squeezed her wrist, not threateningly, but encouragingly.

I love you. She meant to say the words aloud but they remained caught in her heart. She lifted her eyes to his. "I love you, Cameron. It's what I knew before I lay with you and what I knew after. I wish I had known it forever, but I didn't. Perhaps I couldn't. Before today I wasn't ready." She saw the change in his features, the tension replaced by something she could only identify as shock. She tried to pull away but he held her fast. "Let me go, Cam. I told you you didn't want to hear. I knew you didn't feel the same for me. It wasn't fair to tell you."

"I want to hear," he said. "You tried to tell me before, didn't you? And I wasn't listening then."

"You aren't listening now. Let me go."

He did, but it was only to take her by the shoulders. "Do you mean it, Courtney? Do you really lo—" He stopped. Courtney wasn't paying him the least attention. Her nose was wrinkled and she was looking around, trying to find the source of the pungent aroma that was only now assailing him.

"Do you smell it?" she asked. "Something's burn—"

He saw it in the same moment as she. His tricorn was smoldering on top of the stove where Courtney had placed it hours ago to dry. "I think it's done," he said.

Courtney leaped from the bed, dragging her sheet and stumbling as she tripped over its ends in her hurried attempt to save his hat. She picked it up between two fingers, juggled it in her hands when it proved too hot, and blew on it. Her last effort only served to fan the smoke and spark the flames at the brim. She dropped it on the floor and tried stamping on it. It skittered out from beneath her feet. She chased it down and tramped on it again, this time with lightning quick steps.

Cameron watched her dance, smashing his hat with heel and toe as if it were a thing to be despised. His heart swelled. She looked plainly ridiculous, holding up her sheet with one arm, the other flung out to give her balance. Her hair swung across her cheek, slipped over her shoulder. Her face was a concentrated grimace. She stopped suddenly, surveyed her handiwork, then looked up at him and solemnly pronounced, "It's only fit for burial, I'm afraid."

He slid off the bed, hitching the quilt around his waist. He stopped when he stood directly in front of her. His eyes grazed every part of her face. Her lips were damp and slightly parted. Her cheeks were flushed. Her dark brows were arched in question and her silver-gray eyes were luminous. "Don't you know, Court? There's never been a time I haven't loved you." Then his arms circled her and over the smoldering, crushed remains of his hat, he kissed her breathless.

They did not make it even the few steps necessary to reach the bunk. The tricorn was kicked aside. The sheet and blanket tangled around them as they knelt on the floor. Their makeshift clothing was discarded as their arms and legs became the tangle. They loved furiously, hungrily, each knowing what had not been known before, that the love they bore was shared and returned measure for measure.

They only noticed the floor was cold and hard beneath them in the quiet aftermath. Holding hands, laughter reminiscent of the childhood conspirators they had been, they returned to the bunk and cuddled for warmth.

"You're going to marry me, aren't you?" she asked.

"I was the first man you laid eyes on."

Courtney's happy smile faded as she remembered the things she had said to him then. "I was horrible to you. You were right. I couldn't see past the nose on my face."

He placed a finger over her lips. "As long as you can now and as long as I'm the only man you see, little else matters."

She kissed the rough pad of his finger, then drew his hand to her heart and held it against her breast. "Why did you come to the Landing, Cameron? Was it because it's Christmas?"

Cameron smiled. "Do you want to hear that it was because of you?"

"Only if it's true."

"It was because of Christmas . . ." He heard her soft, disappointed sigh. "And you."

She punched him lightly and was pinned to the bunk for her efforts. She tried to evade his kisses but in the end she was happy to surrender.

"I came back," he told her, "because your father managed to get a letter to me in Paris. He wrote you had set a date with George Monroe and if I cared anything at all for you I'd be here for the wedding."

"Papa did that?"

"He did."

"What do you suppose he meant?"

"I don't know. Perhaps only that I should come as your friend."

"And perhaps something more."

"Something more is why I came. But you had already

cancelled the wedding and there seemed no need to rescue you from your own folly. In any event, you didn't look on me as anyone who might save you."

"I should have. You've always been the one I measured the others against. George and Tom and John. I wanted to love them, I think. I tried to love them. But none of them were you and I didn't understand that then." She smoothed back a lock of hair across his brow. "I'm glad you waited for me to learn my own heart, Cameron."

He bent his head and kissed the tip of her nose. "And I'm glad you don't accept no for an answer."

A cannonade at McClellan's Landing celebrated the arrival of Christmas morn and the return of Courtney and Cameron. Like prodigal children they were taken back into the fold, surrounded and blessed, their happiness multiplied in the sharing of it.

Courtney eased herself from her father's fierce and loving embrace. "It's Cameron I'm going to marry, Papa. No engagement this time, just the wedding. Will we have your blessing?"

He did not have to ask if she knew her own mind this time. This was his daughter as he had never seen her before, radiant when she looked at Cameron. "It will be everything I could have wished," he said. As Courtney turned to Cam, he felt Ashley's hand slip in his and squeeze it gently.

There was a wedding that day after all and no one seemed to mind that every guest, save the minister and the servants, was a McClellan.

Salem gave his daughter over to the care of a man he admired. Ashley watched her firstborn take flight with a kindred spirit. A handkerchief was surreptitiously passed among the women. Noah's arm slipped around Jessa as they listened to Cameron speak his vows in a clear and steady voice. The entourage of Courtney's brothers and cousins were suitably impressed by the solemn affair, but anxious for it to be ended. There were pies and presents waiting and, being McClellans, they had opinions regarding the priority of events.

"I now pronounce you husband and wife."

The words were said with all the import and gravity the ceremony called for and yet when Courtney looked at Cameron there was a glint of mischief in his eyes. He lifted her veil and bent his head. His voice came soft and deeply to her ear. "What would they do if we crossed our hearts and spit?"

Laughing, Courtney threw her arms around him and raised herself on tiptoe. "Friends?" she whispered against his mouth.

"The best of friends."

ABOUT THE AUTHOR

Jo Goodman lives with her family in Colliers, West Virginia. She is the author of twenty historical romances (all published by Zebra Books) including her beloved Dennehy sisters series: *Wild Sweet Ecstasy* (Mary Michael's story), *Rogue's Mistress* (Rennie's story), *Forever in My Heart* (Maggie's story), *Always in My Dreams* (Skye's story), and *Only in My Arms* (Mary's story), as well as her Thorne Brothers trilogy: *My Steadfast Heart* (Colin's story), *My Reckless Heart* (Decker's story), and *With All My Heart* (Grey's story). She is currently working on her newest Zebra historical romance, the first of a new four book series set during the Regency period (to be published in 2002). Jo loves hearing from readers, and you may write to her c/o Zebra Books. Please include a self-addressed stamped envelope if you would like a response.